## TENDER CARESS

"I don't want to trust you, Trace Cord," she whispered.

"Why . . . why, Jenny, why?"

"You're dangerous."

"Not to you." His voice was a whisper as he drew her so close their bodies touched. "Never to you, Jenny, my love. You are too sweet and special to have doubts."

She was shaken, though she tried to ignore his words and the thunderous explosion of flame that leapt from somewhere in the center of her being and threatened to melt her very bones. This is impossible, she thought wildly. He is lying! He is trying to destroy my will so he can have what he wants.

If Jenny was fighting a battle, it was no more violent than the one Trace was fa̶_____ her. Desire stimulated ev_____ knew he could take he_____ nd fragile and he ached _____ fears. He wanted her to _____ urrender completely. It

# SYLVIE F. SOMMERFIELD

# Moonlit Magic

**ZEBRA BOOKS**
**KENSINGTON PUBLISHING CORP.**

ZEBRA BOOKS

are published by

Kensington Publishing Corp.
475 Park Avenue South
New York, NY 10016

First printing: December 1986

Printed in the United States of America

*To my mother*

# Prologue

*April 12, 1864*

It was over. There would be no escape. The final event occurred in a little town named Appomattox. It was the ultimate defeat, yet it served as an expression of the courage and honor of the Army of the South under the leadership of General Robert E. Lee.

Lee had fewer than thirty thousand soldiers now, and not even half of them were armed or in workable military formation. The rest were worn-out men who were doing their pathetic best to stay with the army though they could not this day be used in battle.

Lee went now to meet General Grant in the bare parlor of a private home in Appomattox and surrender his army. For four long years that army had been unconquerable. Twice it had carried the war north of the Potomac. Time and again it had beaten back the strongest forces the North could send against it. Not many armies in the world's history had done more.

There was no sounding of trumpets, yet the defeat could clearly be seen on the face of one officer who rode at the head of his column. He was riding with heavy spirits and a downcast face. Catching the subtle noise of shifting arms, he looked up. Quickly he understood his men's intentions and wheeled superbly, making himself and his horse one uplifted figure. Then, facing his command, he gave the silent word that straightened their weary shoulders and lit their faces with renewed pride and courage.

Now there was an awed stillness, a holding of breath. Finally the man spoke in a tone that suggested he was used to command. With tears in his eyes, Trace Cord ordered his men to surrender their arms.

The men faced forward and obeyed, as they had obeyed Trace's commands for over three years. They had shared much with him and felt a oneness with him now as they tenderly folded their battle-worn and torn, blood-stained, heartrending colors and laid them down. Then the lines broke and began to melt. Trace had only one final duty to perform and that was to witness the signing of the papers of surrender.

He was weary, bone weary, as he dismounted before the entrance to the house and walked up the three steps to the door. When the signing was over he shook hands with General Lee, a man he admired even more in his defeat than he had in their shared victories.

"What will you do now, Major Cord?" Lee inquired.

"I suppose I shall go home, sir, see my family and decide what we can do to rebuild."

"You are young and strong, Trace," Lee added gently. "You have been a fine officer. Now you must take the same courage you have shown here and do all you can to help us mend our wounds."

"I will do my best, sir."

"I know." Lee smiled. "You always have. Good-bye, son. I wish you the best of luck."

Trace gave General Lee the smartest, sharpest salute he had ever given. He could have wept when Lee returned it, then strode away.

Trace walked out of the house. He felt so alone, so weary of heart. The only thing that seemed tangible enough to cling to was the idea of home. Home—his parents, his brother, Michael, and his sister Allison. He had not seen them for three years.

With hundreds of other exhausted, heartsick men, he began the long journey home. It was a hard, hungry trip. He had little money, yet there would have been very little to buy had he had more. He was weak and tired and he scavenged anything he could. The only thoughts he had were of home . . . home . . . home.

After what seemed to him an eternity, he found himself on Georgia's black soil.

# Chapter 1

The bay horse picked his way slowly, for he was as exhausted as the man who rode him. Trace Cord rolled easily in the saddle like one well accustomed to it. His body was lean, not thin, and ridged with taut muscles. His shoulders were broad and his legs gave evidence of the height he would attain when standing, which was well over six feet.

He took off his hat and wiped his sweaty brow with the crook of his arm as the sun glinted in his ebony hair. It was thick and long, and now curled near his collar and drooped in wet tendrils against his cheek and forehead. His smoky grey eyes missed nothing as he slowly moved along. His mouth was wide and firm and seemed badly in need of smiling, though he now pressed it together tightly, emphasizing his square, solid jaw. The brilliant Georgia sun could add no more color to his already bronzed skin, but it did catch the moisture on thick lashes that flickered beneath close-drawn brows of the same ebony.

He removed a cigar from his breast pocket and clamped it between straight white teeth that seemed to glitter against his dark skin. He snapped the match into flame and lit the cigar. Lord, Trace thought, were the miles so endless? It had not seemed so far a few years ago.

He had observed the destruction about him as he rode and now the anxiety within him could barely be controlled. Was his family all right? Did they think he was dead? Did Fallen Oaks still stand, or was his home like the others he had passed on his way?

He remembered the tall, white-pillared house and fondly recalled the loving care his parents had put into building it. He imagined vast green lawns and rich, planted fields. His memory brought forth the gentle sounds of soft laughter that had seemed to live within the walls of the house. He clung to these pleasant recollections, even as darker thoughts attempted to force their way into his mind. He refused to accept them, summoning more fond memories to keep them at bay.

Now his heart began to thud heavily as he crossed the boundaries of his father's land, knowing it more by sense than by accurate measurements. The land seemed dry and fallow, and his concern grew. He moved slowly, letting the exhausted horse pick his own way. One more mile, one more hill, and then he crested the last hill and looked with weary, disillusioned eyes at the scene before him. What he saw brought a ragged, muffled groan from his lips.

The fields that had been so green and fertile when he had gone were barren now, and looked as if they had been so for some time. There was also a deserted look to the house, and closer examination told him the house was in a disastrous state of disrepair.

There was no sign of life in or about it and that alarmed him. He nudged the horse into motion and rode down the hill, praying silently that the suspicions stirring within him were untrue.

He dismounted and walked up the steps to the door,

certain his horse was much too tired to wander away. Again he was shaken when he found that the door stood slightly ajar. His hand shook as he reached out and pushed the door open. An empty, dirty, completely deserted foyer met his searching gaze.

His boots clicked sharply against a debris-strewn floor. He remembered the immaculate home his mother had kept and knew her hand had not been felt here for a long time.

"Mother!" he shouted and heard his voice echo through the empty house. "Father! . . . Allison! Is anybody here?"

There was no answering call, only the hollow echo of his voice reverberating through a vacant shell of a house.

Now his search became urgent, almost desperate. His speed and intensity grew as he moved from room to room. He found no one, no sign of life.

He strode down the long hall to the back door that led to his mother's garden. It was overgrown with weeds. With sinking heart he faced the reality that it had been a long, long time since a human hand had touched it. His mother had loved her garden with a passion and would not have left it willingly to ruin—not willingly.

At the far end of the garden was a small cottage; Trace knew it had once belonged to the gardener. He started toward it, then suddenly became aware that a fine wisp of smoke was rising from the chimney. He ran toward the cottage, stopping only when he had reached the door. His anxiety had left him insecure. He was almost afraid to open the door.

Finally he pushed it open and stepped inside. The kneeling form in front of the fireplace gasped in surprise, then gave a joyous cry.

"Trace! My God, Trace!" she cried as she leapt to her

feet and ran to throw herself into his open arms.

"Allison!" Trace groaned in relief as he hugged her tightly, closing his eyes to let the pleasure of knowing she lived course through him. "Allison, baby."

"Oh, Trace," she sobbed. "You're alive! You're home. I thought you were gone too."

The words struck him a blow that stunned him completely. He held her away from him and looked into her tear-filled eyes.

"Allison?" he questioned, not really wanting to hear her answer. "What happened?"

"Trace, I'm so glad you're here. I've been so frightened."

"I know, baby, but tell me what happened."

"It was terrible, Trace. When the war got bad, Daddy . . . well, he went to fight . . ."

"Pa? But . . ." Trace shrugged. "I guess at the end we were desperate. I suppose with Pa's ability to lead, they would ask him."

"He . . . Mother got word a few weeks later . . . he . . . oh Trace," she sobbed.

"Where?" Trace said through clenched teeth.

"Some . . . some small town in Pennsylvania called . . . Gettysburg."

"Mother? What happened?"

"I don't know, Trace. Just after she got word about Daddy a man came. He told her Michael had been reported missing. They . . . they said he was most likely dead too. Mother just couldn't seem to stand it. She . . . well, she got funny. She wouldn't eat or sleep and she cried all the time. Then she got sick. It . . . it seemed like she just didn't want to live anymore." Her voice grew strained and quiet. "She just didn't seem to know I was here at all. She kept calling for Daddy and for you. Then . . . she died."

Trace drew Allison back into his arms and rocked

her against him.

"You poor thing," he murmured. "It must have been terrible for you. It's all right, baby. It's all right. We're together now. It's all right, baby." He comforted her as best he could, though his own eyes burned with unshed tears and his heart felt as if it were being torn from his body.

He knew he would have to contain his grief now while he did his best to turn Allison's mind from all she had suffered. "Come and sit down," he said firmly. Allison obeyed and he sat beside her, taking her hands in his. "Have you been staying here alone?"

"No, Marsh and Amanda have been here with me. Marsh . . . he buried Mama . . . He's been so good to me, Trace. He kept saying, 'Don't you worry about Trace. He'll be back here to take care of you.' He and Amanda were so certain you'd be back."

"Well, they were right, kitten. I'm here, so you don't need to be afraid anymore."

He held her hands until her tears ceased and she regained her composure. His eyes missed nothing about her. She was too thin and her face looked tired. There were dark shadows beneath her eyes and the lustrous, thick black hair she had always had was now dull and pulled back carelessly in a long, heavy braid. Her clothes were patched and threadbare, and sadly he mused that in the past his sister had always taken such pride in her personal appearance.

She sniffled and Trace tipped up her chin with a gentle hand. "It's all right, kitten," he said gently. "You've been through hell, but it's over. We're together and we must have faith that Michael will be back too. Mother and Father wouldn't have wanted to see you like this."

"Oh Trace, I'm so glad you're home!" She gulped. "I don't think I could have gone on much longer."

"Where're are Marsh and Amanda now?"

"Marsh is fishing along the creek. He didn't have a gun to hunt with. The damn Yankees took everything—everything Trace. Even Mama's jewelry and clothes and . . . just everything. All our horses and cows and chickens. The pigs . . . they just cleaned us out and left us to starve."

There was a sparkle in her eyes for the first time since Trace had seen her, but it was a spark of hatred and it hurt him to see it in a girl as pretty and as young as Allison.

"I think fish will do just fine. I'm so starved I could eat hay," he told her with a laugh.

"I'm so tired of fish I could scream," she replied, but her lips quirked in a half smile. "But I guess with you here I can celebrate and eat a little more."

He chuckled. "That's my girl. Where's Amanda?"

"She took some wash out back."

"Well, let's go tell her I'm home. Maybe we can get some meat for the table." He grinned. "I've been lugging a gun for four years. I guess it's time I hunted the four-legged animal for awhile."

"Trace," she said softly, her eyes luminous with unshed tears. He looked deeply into the mirror image of his own smoky grey eyes. "It . . . it has been so hard for us, but for you . . . you were always so gentle, so kind. I can't believe . . ."

"The gentle time is a long time gone, kitten. For now, we have to survive. We begin surviving by looking ahead to tomorrow and not back over our shoulders."

"I suppose you're right, Trace. I've been so frightened. I'm so grateful you're here. I guess maybe . . . if I have you, I won't stumble so often."

"You're stronger than you think you are, pet. You wouldn't be here if you weren't. Don't underestimate yourself."

"I haven't even been able to think since everything in my world has been destroyed. I thought I would never see you or Michael again. I thought . . ."

"That I was dead. C'mon, Allison, I'm tougher than that. Besides, I couldn't just leave you. I believe, little sister, that you need chaperoning. You've become a very beautiful young woman since I've been gone."

"To what purpose, Trace?" Allison questioned somewhat bitterly. "All the young men around here are gone, or dead. Besides, who would give me a second look now? I look like the old scarecrow Marsh used to put in the gardens to scare the birds away. Oh, I wish this terrible war had never happened!" She clenched her small fist and pounded her lap.

"So do I, pet, but there's not much we can do about it, and tears and self-pity aren't going to help."

She looked up into his eyes. "Besides"—he grinned—"you're still the prettiest girl in the county, even though your face is dirty."

She giggled softly. "You always have a way of making things better. Even when I was a little girl and fell and skinned my knees, you were always the one to stop the tears."

Trace was pleased to see her smile again, but before he could speak, a voice sounded from the doorway.

"Lord have mercy! Is dat you, Trace?"

Trace spun around at the sound of an old, familiar, and well-loved voice.

The man framed in the doorway was huge. Trace stood two inches over six feet, yet the man before him was at least two inches taller and outweighed Trace's two hundred pounds by a good forty. He was ebony black, with hair as white as crystals of snow, and his obsidian eyes were alert and filled with intelligent good humor.

"Marsh!" Trace shouted as he held out his hand. The two men clasped hands firmly, and both were momentarily speechless as thick constrictions filled their throats and made speech temporarily impossible.

"I sho was afeared y'all was dead, boy," the old man rasped.

"Not me, Marsh." Trace grinned. "You taught me to hunt too well. There isn't a Yankee born that could beat me on my own ground."

"An' they didn't beat yuh, did they boy?" Marsh asked softly, his all-seeing eyes penetrating Trace's.

"No, Marsh . . . they didn't beat me. I think I owe you another debt, Marsh, among all the other debts I owe you. You took care of Allison?"

"Yassah, me and Manda. But you doan owe us nuthin' fo dat. Dat chile is too good and sweet fo us to let somethin' happen to her. 'Sides, she been through enough already."

"I guess it's time to start picking up the pieces, my friend. Are you and Amanda going to stay and help me? I can't do it alone. I know that, just as I know I don't have any right to ask you and Amanda for anything more than you've already given."

"Sho boy." Marsh chuckled. "This here place, it's de only place me and Manda gots. Where y'all thinks we's goin'? I think we kinda needs each other."

"You're right, Marsh"—Trace's eyes sparkled—"but I'll bet you know as well as I that I need you a lot more than you do me."

"Wal . . . let's just take one day at a time. For now, let's get those fish I got fried up. You's probably just as hungry now like you always was when you was a boy."

"You're right, Marsh," Allison announced with a laugh. "He said he was so hungry he could eat hay."

"Well then," another voice came from the doorway, "I 'spects we best feed him."

18

"Hello Amanda." Trace grinned as he went to the woman who had just entered and put an arm about her shoulder, adding, "It's wonderful to see you again."

"It's been well over three years. Marsh and I, we thought you might not come back after the terrible things that we heard."

As large as Marsh was, Amanda was as small. Her height measured a mere five feet and she weighed barely a hundred pounds.

"Amanda," Trace explained with a chuckle, "I remember your cooking, and I'd walk across the state to have a meal you cooked. That fish of Marsh's sounds like it might cook up real good."

"I'll fix it up right fine for you," Amanda answered, responding to Trace's smile with one of her own. "Why don't you wash off some of the travelin' dirt whilst I gets it started?"

"I think," Trace began, looking at Allison, "that there is something much more important that I have to do first."

Allison smiled, took Trace's extended hand, and together they left the cottage. Amanda and Marsh exchanged glances.

"Dat boy," Marsh said, "he smiles fo' his li'l sister, but his eyes is sho full of hurtin'."

"Ah 'spects he done seen too much. Then he has to come home to this."

"Well, they got each other. Dat's more than some has. They kin hope maybe Michael will come home too. They just might make it if they kin hang on to each other."

"Ah just got a feelin'," Amanda whispered, "that there's more trouble still acomin'."

\* \* \*

19

Trace and Allison stood side by side at the grave of Constance Cord. Neither spoke for some time, but Allison clung to Trace's hard-muscled arm as if to draw strength from him.

"Trace, I wish she could have seen you come home. With Daddy gone and Michael . . . well, she would have been so happy to know you were here."

Trace was silent while painful memories ran through his mind. This was the last time he would permit them to control his emotions. It was the last time he could afford it. The future looked too grim for him to allow further intrusions from the past.

"I wish I could have seen her, and Pa too," Trace said gently, "but it's too late. Now I guess it's you and me, Allison."

"And Michael."

"But, I thought . . ."

"They said they *thought* he was dead. But I'll never believe it unless they prove it to me."

Trace grinned. "For the baby of the family, you sure have a lot of faith and determination. You make me a little ashamed of giving up so easily."

"You never gave up, Trace. You're just tired. Let's go back to the house. I'll fix you a nice, hot bath; then we can eat. Maybe later, when you're rested, we can talk about the future."

"You're right. I am really tired. That bath sounds good too."

They turned and walked back toward the cottage. Trace silently noted how Allison clung to him. He was a rock in her otherwise topsy-turvy world. It helped him contain the grief that was roiling within him. He was frightened, even more than he had been when he had had to face an armed enemy. But could he control his own fear and despair over the loss of almost all his loved ones? He felt hot tears sting his eyes, tears he would never shed. His chest felt crushed and heavy with the desire to surrender to the mountainous pain he felt. Mother, Father, and Michael, he thought. The war had very nearly taken all his world, and he wasn't so very sure he could rebuild it.

Amanda had prepared the fish and a short time later they sat together and ate. The mood of the meal was quiet and restrained, for the ghosts of those who were missing lingered. After they had eaten they talked quietly for awhile, then Marsh and Amanda found their way to bed.

Trace knew Allison was exhausted, but he suspected she was afraid that if she went to sleep, she would open her eyes the next morning to find Trace gone. He could read the fear in her tired eyes.

"Allison," he said gently, "why don't you get some sleep? We'll talk tomorrow when we're both not so tired. We have a lot of time to talk."

Allison's lips quivered and her eyes grew moist with tears. She rose and went to Trace and knelt before him, looking up at him with eyes that were almost pleading for reassurance.

"We do, don't we, Trace? You'll be here?"

"I'll be here, kitten." His voice softened and he reached to caress her hair.

"It's just that . . ." she said in a choked voice, "so many times I've needed . . . wanted someone, and he was taken away. You won't leave me, Trace? It would be much easier for you just to be on your own, without having to worry about me."

"Don't talk like that, Allison," he said roughly to hide the emotions that tore through him. "You're my

21

baby sister. We're all the family we've got. The Cords stick together." He laughed shakily. "Where's the old Cord stubbornness?" he chided. "Why kitten, you used to be the stubbornest one of all of us." He tipped up her chin and looked deeply into her eyes. "I love you, kitten, and I won't leave you alone . . . never again. You just reach out and I'll be here. Remember that." With a sob, she threw herself into his arms. He held her close while she wept away her fears, and the dark shadows that had been a part of her life for four years slowly began to fade. "Now you get some sleep, and tomorrow we'll plan our future, all right?"

She nodded. "I'll be all right, Trace, now that you're here. I'll be all right."

She rose and as he watched her disappear into the shadows of her room, he wondered if he had lied to her, if he truly had the strength to make everything all right. It would be a superhuman job to try to rebuild what his parents had created, and he was so exhausted now he wasn't certain he could do it.

Tired as he was, he knew he wouldn't find sleep yet. He rose and walked out onto the porch. From where he stood, he could see the big house. It seemed so desolate and lonely now, and he felt the urge to weep as he thought of his father's strong hands that had built it and his mother's delicate touch that had made the house a home. He conjured up the vision of him and Michael as boys, romping freely over the lush green land.

"Michael," he murmured aloud. Michael was younger than Trace by three years and had always been Trace's shadow. He was a laughing boy, prone to mischievous tricks. But he was also gentle and warm. Trace would not allow himself to believe Michael was dead. It was a thought he would reserve until he was able to handle it. Tonight he was too vulnerable.

22

"What's da matter, boy? You can't sleep?"

The soft question caused Trace to turn around. He could barely make out Marsh's shadowy form in the darkened doorway.

"No . . . I guess I'm finding all this"—he waved his hand to encompass the area about him—"just a little too hard to handle."

Marsh moved forward to stand beside Trace and breathed deeply of the cool night air. "I 'spects it's hard fo' you. But at least you gots this. They's some dat doan have nothin' . . . nothin' at all. Most places been burnt to de groun'."

"I know. I saw a lot on my way home. I guess I'm just feeling a little sorry for myself tonight."

"Dey's nuthin' wrong wit dat," Marsh replied softly, then added, "fo' a while. Long as you doan live with it fo' too long. You gots to pick up the pieces, Trace boy, or you loses everything in you own cryin'. I 'spects you goin' t be all right in a while."

"You so sure of that, Marsh?"

Marsh's white teeth gleamed in the moonlight. "I done helped raise you, boy. I knows you like I knows Manda. Ya 'all needs to get yo wind back. You be all right."

"I can't do it alone, Marsh," Trace admitted softly.

"Me and Manda, we helps you. We all work together and we builds somethin' new. 'Sides, maybe yo brother be comin' home too."

"I hope so." Trace sighed. "I hope they're wrong and Michael is still alive."

"We prays," Marsh stated. "Maybe de good Lawd be listenin'."

"I could sure use a little of His help. I'm only one man, Marsh. I need a little strength from somewhere."

"It be worryin' you dat yo li'l sister seems so broken and afraid?"

"She's only a sixteen-year-old baby, Marsh."

"You should have seen her when things was goin' bad. When yo Pa left, she was strong for yo Ma. When yo Ma got sick, she sat with her and nursed her fo' days. She been strong fo' a long time. Now I guess she needs to have someone hold her and let her cry."

"Lord, Marsh. It must have been hell for her."

"It was. Hopin' you and yo brother would come back was de only thing keepin' her goin'. You have patience, boy. She gonna be all right too."

"Well"—Trace grinned—"I guess you've got us all on the right track."

"Been doin' dat most of yo life," Marsh retorted with a low, rumbling chuckle. "You bes' get some sleep now. Come mornin', we find out jus' how we gonna go on."

"You're right. Good night Marsh."

"Night, boy," Marsh answered, then turned and went back into the house.

Trace stood for a few minutes as he realized his load seemed significantly lighter. Maybe, he mused, with Allison, Marsh, and Amanda, and with the hope that Michael was still alive, they might just be able to make it. He knew he had very little money, but perhaps it would be enough to buy some seed and to get what they would need to mend the house. As far as furniture was concerned, he and Marsh could build what they needed as time went on.

He stretched and yawned, suddenly feeling extremely tired. Tomorrow would be a new beginning, but tonight he needed rest.

He went back inside and sat on the edge of the rough-hewn wood-frame bed. The mattress stuffed with straw would not be comfortable, but lately he had slept on much harder surfaces.

Removing only his boots, Trace lay back on the bed without even undressing. He was asleep almost instantly, but it was a sleep filled with dark shadows and broken dreams. He saw flames as the house he loved was destroyed. Then he heard Allison cry out his name and he felt a great sense of loss. The emotional torment brought him awake in a cold sweat. It was a long time before he again found sleep that night.

## Chapter 2

Trace had been home for just short of a year, and the small amount of money with which he had returned home had slowly been drained until there was very little left. Yankee carpetbaggers were in complete control of everything and even the smallest item of food was exorbitantly overpriced. He had become angry, and once he had even tried to fight back. He had found himself beaten, thrown into an alley, and forced to stagger home later. Never had he felt so defeated, not even during the four years of the war.

The culmination of his frustration occurred later that week. Trace was walking out the cottage door at daybreak with Marsh right behind him.

"You shore you doan want me to go with you, Trace?" Marsh asked.

"For what money I have left, I don't think I'll be needing any help to bring the things back," Trace explained with a grin.

Before Marsh could answer, the attention of both men was drawn to a horse and carriage coming up the long drive.

"Now who could be visiting us?" Trace said.

"Ain't nobody I knows. Sure is a fancy-lookin' gent,

ain't he?" Marsh said with a chuckle.

Trace's eyes narrowed as he watched the elaborate and very expensive carriage with its team of matching horses draw to a stop before him.

"Good morning, sir," the man boomed, smiling a broad, toothy smile as he stepped down from the carriage and extended his hand to Trace. He made a point of studiously ignoring Marsh.

"Good morning," Trace responded, instinctively disliking the man. He noted that the stranger's effusive smile extended only to his lips and did not reach the cold, calculating eyes. "Is there something we can do for you?"

"Well, yes. I'm told Miss Allison Cord, the young lady who owns this plantation, is here. I would like to talk to her about a little proposition I have."

"Miss Cord is still asleep," Trace replied.

"Oh, I see." The man grinned. The lascivious smirk told Trace exactly the path the man's mind was taking as he looked up and down Trace's lean, hard frame. Trace's irritation began to grow into something more formidable.

Marsh, who had known Trace from childhood, could see the Devil's anger touch Trace's grey eyes with yellow flame.

"Maybe you'd better tell me your business with Miss Cord," Trace suggested in a deceptively soft voice.

"Well now," the man replied arrogantly, "you got any claim on the . . . um . . . lady? I expect she can make her own choice about my . . . ah . . . offer. Looks to me like you haven't much to offer."

"And you do?" Trace inquired mildly, his eyes alive with a glowing flame that should have warned the stranger he was treading on dangerous territory.

"I can offer her this plantation back. You see, in a matter of three weeks it will be mine. I'm sure, if she's

28

smart, she'll realize I have a lot more to offer than you. She can have a very comfortable time here if she's smart and listens to reason."

"You know Miss Cord?"

"Seen her quite a few times. Pretty little piece. She's ripe and sweet and I can show her a fine time if she's reasonable. I been lookin' forward to tasting that sweet little thing. Teach her what a man's all about."

"I'm not interested in any offer you have to make," Allison's cold voice told him from the doorway. "You would brighten my day, Mr. Franklin, if you would get out of my sight."

"Still uppity, Miss Cord," Franklin sneered. "Still think you're a little too good for everybody else. You'd best listen to me before you get hasty. You're going to lose this place and I'm the only one who can get it back for you. All you have to do is learn to be a little nicer."

"What do you mean, lose this place?" Allison demanded. Trace listened intently as well. He wanted the answer to his sister's question before he threw Mr. Franklin off the porch or set about rearranging his sneering face.

"Taxes, lady, taxes. They ain't been paid for four years. Come three weeks, the time will be up and this place'll be sold for the taxes. I have a friend who's already gettin' the papers ready for me to sign. Three weeks and it'll be mine, so you'd best be a little nicer or I'll see you thrown off on your fancy little bottom. Beggin' in the streets will bring you around soon enough. You'll be willing by then to be a little sweeter to me."

Allison's face was grey from both anger and fear, and the sight of her expression caused Trace to reach the limit of his endurance. He moved toward Franklin and spoke through clenched teeth. "Get the hell off this property before I break every bone in your slimy little body. What kind of man preys on helpless girls?"

"Who are you?" Franklin squeaked, his eyes registering fear at the fury in Trace's face. "You can just let the lady speak for herself."

"I'll speak for her, you little worm. She's my sister. If you aren't gone at the count of three, I won't be responsible for the condition you'll be in when you get found . . . if you get found."

"Sister . . . but I thought—"

"I know. You thought she was alone and helpless and you'd just move right in. One," Trace began.

"But . . . wait . . . I—"

"Two," Trace said firmly. Franklin could see that Trace meant what he was saying, but he had decided to bluff it out, that is until Trace began to reach for him.

"Three!" Trace roared. Franklin leapt onto the carriage and startled the horses with a slap of the reins. They jumped forward and soon the carriage disappeared in a cloud of dust.

Both Allison and Marsh had broad grins on their faces as Trace turned around to look at them. He chuckled then, too, but his anger was still uppermost in his mind. "I take it Mr. Franklin has annoyed you before this, Allison?"

"He's been a pest, Trace, but I've never taken him seriously."

"Well, he was serious. It's a good thing Marsh and I were here."

"Trace . . . what he said about the taxes . . ."

"I'm going into town. I don't believe anything that snake said, but I'll look into it."

Trace made no comment about the fact that if what Franklin had said were true they would lose all they had, for he had little money left for taxes—irrational and unprecedented taxes the Yankee occupational forces must have placed on his home. He knew the sum

30

would be excessive and wondered where he could possibly obtain enough funds.

Trace saddled his horse and rode off toward town, leaving Marsh and Allison watching him, their eyes filled with questions. They were questions for which he had no answers as yet.


The town of Eatonton bustled with activity. Everywhere one looked, there was a flurry of rebuilding. Reconstruction had begun, and it had begun with opportunists and money from Northern sources. Greedy men took advantage of having the helpless South at their mercy. They grabbed for property, without a care for the families to whom the land had belonged for generations.

Trace was well aware of the stares that followed him as he rode into town. Since his uniform was his only clothing in decent repair, he wore it now, and with a sense of arrogant pride that set the teeth of the Yankee opportunists on edge.

Trace dismounted in front of the courthouse and walked up the three steps to the door. Inside, he found it cool and quiet.

The central hall of the courthouse was small, and several doors opened from it, each labeled with the service provided within. He opened the door that read "Tax Office" and stepped inside. His heart fell when he saw the men seated behind the three desks in the otherwise bare room. Yankees, all three of them. The blue uniforms glared at him and the eyes above them were cold and calculating.

A fourth man, not in uniform, stood by the only window in the room. He turned as Trace entered and watched Trace intently as he walked toward the nearest officer.

"What can I do for you?" the officer asked gruffly. Trace read the name that was on a small plaque on the desk: Lt. James Collins.

"Lieutenant Collins, my name is Trace Cord. I've come down to check on the taxes on Fallen Oaks."

"Check on 'em or pay 'em?" Collins asked. The amusement in his glittering dark eyes told Trace he knew quite well that most of the returning Confederates had no money. The land grab was a well-organized plan, and Collins would make a profit if Trace could not pay the taxes.

"Check on them," Trace replied. He knew he had to control his rage, but it was difficult, for he understood too well the smug look on Collins's face.

"Check on 'em," Collins repeated. With deliberate slowness he opened a drawer and took out a sheaf of papers. "Cord . . . Cord . . . ah, here it is. Fallen Oaks. Taxes due . . . six hundred dollars."

"Six hundred dollars!" Trace repeated in shock. "That's out of the question. It's ridiculous. You must be wrong."

"No sir. It's right here. House is still standing, and the land is good. Taxes are six hundred dollars. And," he added with a grin, "they have to be paid in full in three weeks or the place will be put up for sale."

"And I'll bet you have a buyer already," Trace snarled. "Cut and dried. A whole plantation for six hundred dollars. Somebody else's sweat and tears and you take it for nothing."

"I don't make the laws," Collins retorted. "You Rebs should have thought about this before you got so cocky. Seems to me losers always pay."

Trace was trying to control his fury. He knew that committing the act of violence he had in mind would only get him into trouble, and he knew if he were to be put in jail Allison would be very nearly helpless. Yet he also knew that six hundred dollars might just as well have been a million. He would never be able to get that kind of money in three weeks. He knew it just as he knew that Collins knew it. But he wasn't going to give Collins the satisfaction of begging. He could tell by the look in Collins's eyes that he expected it and instead he said, "Thanks, Collins, for your kindness. I'll be back."

He turned and walked out, leaving Collins staring at him openmouthed. It was not what Collins had thought he would do. He had wanted Trace on his knees so that he could break him.

The man who stood by the window smiled. "Tougher than you thought, Collins?" he asked softly.

Collins glared at him. "He'll come around. Before three weeks are over, he'll be back here on his knees cryin' and beggin' for more time."

"Somehow," the man replied softly, "I just don't believe that will happen."

"Well, he's going to lose his land no matter what he does."

Again the man smiled, then he walked toward the door.

"Where are you going, Colonel? I thought you needed me to scout you up some men?"

"I do, Collins. I'll be back in a little while."

Before Collins could answer again, the door closed behind Colonel Maxwell Starett.


Trace stepped out onto the porch of the courthouse. He forced himself to stand still and breathe deeply in order to control the inflaming anger that coursed through him. He easily could have attacked and murdered Collins, he realized. His hands still trembled with the urge.

"Six hundred dollars," he groaned. In his pockets he

had less than forty. It was like reaching for the moon. What worried him the most was not just losing Fallen Oaks, but where he and Allison could go. Alone he would have been able to find some work and sleep outside if necessary. But he would never think of subjecting Allison to that kind of life. He would have to find a way, but at the moment the future looked very bleak. He sighed deeply, reluctant to return home to bring such news to Allison.

Memories of Fallen Oaks and his growing years flooded his mind. How would they be able to leave it? Wasn't it enough, he raged against fate, to lose his parents and his brother? Must he lose Fallen Oaks as well?

He started down the steps toward his horse but stopped abruptly at the sound of his name being called from behind him.

"Mr. Cord?"

He turned to see the man who had been standing near the window in silence as he had confronted Collins. Trace was irritated now. Had the man come out to gloat a little more? Was he another buyer interested in Fallen Oaks, another scavenger looking for blood? Trace's eyes piercingly conveyed his roiling anger.

"I'm not interested in talking to bloodsuckers who are planning to rob me. You'll excuse me, I'm sure," Trace said coldly, "if I don't waste my time."

"Mr. Cord," Maxwell said mildly, "it would be well worth your while to have a talk with me. I have an offer that might be of interest to you."

"An offer?" Trace asked suspiciously. "What does the conquering Yankee have to offer me? If it's an offer to buy Fallen Oaks, you can go to hell. I'll find a way."

Maxwell chuckled. "It's not an offer to buy Fallen Oaks. If I wanted that, I would need only to wait and be the highest bidder. I'm trying to help you, Mr. Cord."

"With nothing in return?" Trace inquired belligerently.

"I didn't say that. I'm not a fool. I don't give anything away free, but I don't expect anyone to give me anything for free either. Now, can I interest you in a drink and a little conversation?"

Trace shrugged. "What do I have to lose?"

They walked across the street to the nearest saloon. Inside Maxwell chose a table in a corner so they could remain undisturbed and unheard. When the bartender came to their table, Maxwell ordered a bottle of whiskey and two glasses. Trace took this time to evaluate Maxwell. He was a firm-looking man, his jaw square and hard. His skin was tan and unlined, and Trace could not be sure of his age. His eyes were a piercing blue and his hair crystal white. There was no excess fat on his body, which gave Trace the impression he was used to outside activity. The man had planted a question in Trace's mind that now needed an answer. When Maxwell turned back to face Trace, it was Trace who made the first move.

"Who are you, and what's your interest in me?"

"Direct and to the point, Mr. Cord," Maxwell said with a chuckle.

"Suppose you do the same."

"My name is Maxwell Starett."

"Why do I feel you're a military man?"

"I was. It was Colonel Maxwell Starett up to a few weeks ago. Now it's just plain Mister."

"I also get the feeling it's not just plain anything."

Now Maxwell laughed heartily. "Maybe you're right. I would like to think so."

"All right, now that we've named ourselves, suppose you tell me what you want."

"I want to do you a favor."

"In return," Trace concluded, "for a very big favor."

35

"You're right."

"Suppose you tell me what you want."

Maxwell remained silent as the bartender placed the bottle and glasses on the table. After he left, Maxwell poured them both a drink. "Suppose instead I tell you first what I have to offer you."

"All right."

"I'm going to give you back your plantation and offer you a job that will give you enough money to keep it going until you get your feet under you."

"And just who do I have to assassinate to get all that?"

Maxwell laughed again. "No one. In fact, I think you will appreciate the work. I take it the name Starett means nothing to you?"

"It has a familiar ring, but I don't think I know any Staretts."

"You've heard of the Central American Railroad?"

"Of course! Now the name's clear. You're part of the Overland Railroad Association."

"Not any longer. I've decided to strike out on my own. I have a contract, but I've got a very limited amount of time to accomplish my goal."

"Which brings me back to the same question, Mr. Starett. Why me? You could find a lot of men up North. You're a Yankee. Why come down here for help?"

"I'm afraid when I broke my . . . ah . . . relationship with Central I stepped on a few toes. They've made it impossible for me to maneuver. They've decided to have my blood and my railroad, Mr. Cord, and I've no intention of giving them either one. I had a feeling you would understand how it feels to be on the short end. Maybe it's one way you could fight back."

"What is it you want me to do?"

"We're about a hundred miles from here, heading

west. We have a lot of rough terrain to cover and I need some men who are good leaders."

"What makes you think I'd be? You don't know anything about me."

Again Maxwell laughed softly, then he squinted his eyes as if he were reciting a well-rehearsed poem. "You are . . . Trace Cord, oldest son of Richard and Constance Cord. One brother, Michael, and one sister, Allison. Parents are deceased. You're thirty-one, well educated, and served four years as major directly under Lee. Got several medals and a remarkable reputation for both good leadership and good luck. Your men liked you and fought well under you. That's what I need, a man who can lead. I have a whole new kind of war to fight, and I need a man I can depend on. You're broke and about to lose your inheritance. We can help each other a great deal, Mr. Cord."

Trace gazed at him, surprised and just a little annoyed that this stranger knew so much about him and his family. He wondered where all the information had come from. Obviously Starett was a very thorough man who had access to just about anything. Trace would keep this valuable information in mind. For now, he needed questions answered too.

"How long would this take?"

"About a year and a half. But your plantation would be safe and on the road to recovery by the time you got back."

"Sounds like a good offer . . . almost too good."

"I'm not going to lie to you." Maxwell bent closer to Trace, resting both elbows on the table. His eyes were intent and his voice grated with a kind of subdued fury. Trace was very much aware of the latent strength of the man. Here was a man who would fight the Devil himself and with the Devil's own rules, to win what he wanted. The thought flashed through Trace's mind that it was possible Starett would use him as long as he was needed, then discard him. The uncertainty of this prospect shook Trace. "There're some out to stop me. It might get rough in places. But I'm not going to lose my railroad. It means as much to me as your plantation does to you. I don't have all the time in the world, Mr. Cord, and you have only three weeks."

Trace took a sip of his whiskey while he contemplated Maxwell, who now remained silent. It would not have been a hard decision for Trace if he had had only himself to consider. But he wondered what would happen if Allison were left alone again at Fallen Oaks. Marsh and Amanda would not be able to defend her against all possible dangers. And the three of them would not be able to protect themselves or Fallen Oaks.

"Give me a week, Mr. Starett."

"Maxwell."

"Give me a week, Maxwell, and I'll see if I can arrange for someone to help at my place. Allison will need some protection. If I can find someone, I'll go with you."

"And if you can't?"

"I won't leave Allison to face the wolves alone."

"Commendable," Maxwell replied. "Maybe I can help you. Say we meet back here in one week."

"All right," Trace agreed.

Maxwell raised his glass to Trace. "To a long and I hope very rewarding partnership, and to the Starett line. I hope, with your help, both may prosper."

Trace touched his glass to Maxwell's, then drank its contents. He rose then and stood looking down at Maxwell. "You'll pay the taxes if we agree?"

"Yes, and three-fourths of your pay will be sent home to keep the plantation growing. With us you'll get food, a place to sleep, and one-fourth of your pay for . . . ah . . . rest and recreation."

"Just how much is this pay going to be?"

"Three hundred and fifty dollars a month."

Trace whistled. "Big pay."

"You'll earn it. I'll see that two hundred and thirty is sent home. The other hundred and twenty will be in your pocket. Fair?"

"More than fair. It's more money than I've made in the last four years. The place should be able to pick itself up on that."

"Then we agree. Think it over and I'll be here one week from today."

Trace nodded and turned to leave, and Maxwell watched as he walked away. He wanted Trace with him and he had been prepared to offer more. If Trace turned out as he thought he would, he would see that the rewards were comparable. Maxwell tossed off the last of his drink, dropped some money on the table, and left the saloon.


Trace rode slowly. He still could not quite believe the offer he had just been made. He had no doubt that working with the railroad was going to be a lot rougher than Maxwell admitted. There would be hot or rainy weather, Yankees to work with, and an antagonistic railroad association that might be trickier than he imagined.

"Damn," he muttered. "When I get problems, I sure as hell get problems." He reached down to pat Captain's neck. The horse's ears twitched at the sound of his beloved master's voice. "It's all right, Captain. I'll find some way. The thing that really worries me is, if I find a way to go, what's Allison going to say about my leaving her and going away again . . . and for a year and a half, too? She's not going to like it, Captain. No sir, she's not going to like it."

When he approached the front of the cottage, Allison was the first one on the porch to greet him. She was a completely changed individual, no longer the frightened ragamuffin he had first encountered on his return nearly a year ago. He could see that startling difference now in the sparkle of her grey eyes. She had gone back to bathing regularly and washing her clothes frequently. They were worn and ragged, but she looked neat. Without a doubt, he knew that his return had been responsible for the transformation. It only made matters worse.

"Trace? You didn't buy the food?"

Ruefully, he admitted to himself that this was the first time in the past few hours he had even thought of the reason he had gone into town. He watched Allison's smile fade.

"Trace . . . the taxes . . . Franklin?"

Trace dismounted and walked up to put his arm about her shoulder. They walked into the cottage together.

"I'm afraid, Allison, that Franklin was right."

"Right! You mean they've put taxes on our own land? Can we get the money somewhere? How much do they want?"

"Six hundred dollars," he replied grimly.

"Six hundred dollars!" Allison gasped. "That's impossible!"

"I'm afraid not, honey. For the Yankees right now, just about anything is possible. They want six hundred dollars . . . in three weeks." He turned to look into her eyes and watched the tears escape to slide down her cheeks.

"Trace, what will we do? We could never raise that much money."

40

"Well . . . I want to talk to you about that. Where're Marsh and Amanda?"

"Out back."

"Let go out. This concerns them too."

"What? What concerns them? Tell me, Trace. Do you have some plan, something we can do?"

"Let's go out and talk with Marsh and Amanda. Come on." He put his arm about her and they walked outside together.

Marsh immediately sensed that something was drastically wrong. Trace silenced Amanda's questions and all three listened carefully while Trace, in a quiet voice, explained what had just occurred.

Allison's face seemed to become more pale with every word. When he finished, she gazed at him and the look in her eyes was frightening.

"Allison . . ." he began, but the words refused to come.

"Trace, no," she whispered. "Don't leave me here alone, please . . . not alone again. I couldn't bear it. If . . . if you go away again . . . I shall die."

Any plans he might have had withered and died when he looked into Allison's eyes. He knew there was no way he could leave her. She seemed so small and fragile that he felt certain she would break if she had to face loneliness again.

Emitting a resigned sigh he went to her, drew her into his arms, and held her.

"It's all right, baby," he whispered against her hair. "It's all right. I won't leave you alone, not ever again."

She wept and clung to him. He held her until the tears ceased. Over her head he could see the pity in the eyes of Marsh and Amanda.

"Amanda, take Allison inside and get her something to drink . . . something strong."

"No," Allison protested.

41

"Go on, Allison. Marsh and I have to form some kind of plan. Go on. I'll be in in a little while and we'll talk."

It was only with that assurance that Allison let Amanda lead her away.

"Lord, Marsh," Trace whispered, "I didn't realize she was that frightened."

"De po' chile was alone with too much grievin' fo' too long. She's jus' a baby and dis has been jus' too much fo' her."

"I don't know what to do, Marsh. There's no possible way I can keep Fallen Oaks unless I work for Starett . . . and I can't work for Starett and leave Allison alone here."

"Why doan you think 'bout takin' her with you? Changin' places might be good fo' her."

"Take her with me! Marsh, it's bound to be hard."

"Any harder than bein' here alone will be?" Marsh asked softly. "There you can protect her and Fallen Oaks. Here . . . here you cain't even protect yo'self. You best think on it."

"And what about Fallen Oaks? You and I both know, war or no war, you won't be allowed to hold this place. I've got to have someone here."

"Wal, since you tol' me I been thinkin'. You remember the Anderson boy?"

"Reid Anderson?"

"Yes, wal, he came home from de war a few months ago. His wife, she be dead, and his family's all gone. House got burnt. He be a good man, Trace, but he got no roots left. He been drinkin' a lot. Maybe . . . you could save another life by lettin' him gets his feet under him. He could run dis place real good whilst you be gone."

"I remember Reid. He was a good man. He had a good place going before the war."

"It be all gone now."

"You say he's been drinking. Is he reliable anymore, Marsh? I've seen liquor do a lot to a man."

"He ain't all right," Marsh replied bitterly, "but he needs the help and maybe you can do a lot to pick him up and set him on his feet."

"I'd be trusting him with a great deal, Marsh."

"An' I'd be here to help him . . . and to keep an eye on Fallen Oaks. 'Spects I kin handle the money until I gets him sober. He be a good boy, Trace. I doan think yo' trust would be put wrong."

"Well, Marsh"—Trace grinned—"there's nobody I'd trust more than you. If you say Reid would be all right, then I guess he'd be all right. I'll go talk to him tomorrow. For now, I think I'll go and tell Allison that we'll go together. I just wonder . . ."

"Wonder what?"

"What Starett's going to say about it. I don't think he bargained on getting two Cords for the price of one."

"Wal," Marsh replied with a grin, "maybe you oughta tell 'im jus' how lucky he be."

Trace chuckled as they walked inside.


The next day he found Reid Anderson. He was drunk and lying in an alley in town. He took him home and sobered him up.

They talked for a long time, with Reid denying his ability and Marsh and Trace refusing to let him get away with it. After three days Reid finally agreed. His gratitude, though unspoken, was obvious to Trace in the renewed purpose he saw reflected in the young man's eyes.

But in the end it was Starett who protested most strenuously. He put forth every argument he could muster, from the harshness of the traveling conditions

43

to the threat of Indian attack, and then he added the personal concern that his opposition might hurt them in an attempt to stop him. It did no good. Trace stood firm.

Two weeks later the taxes on Fallen Oaks had been paid, Reid Anderson was firmly entrenched with Marsh and Amanda at Fallen Oaks, and Trace and Allison had made their good-byes and were just setting out on their journey.

The brother and sister looked back only for a moment. Then they turned their faces to the challenge of their future. They had to survive. They had to return to Fallen Oaks and redeem it, and both vowed silently to do what they must in order to make that dream become reality.

# Chapter 3

*Colorado Territory . . . Summer, 1866*

The small house was nestled between two green hills. The land rolled beyond it, lush, green land. Surrounding almost the entire house was a porch and, at the moment, the woman who stood on it seemed as inanimate as everything about her. She was small, but her curvaceous figure was extremely feminine. Her hair glistened like red gold in the late afternoon sun as she shaded her unusual turquoise eyes with her hand and remained motionless, watching the long, dusty road that disappeared into the vast distance. After a while her hand dropped and she paced the porch, keeping her eyes on the dirt road.

She was rewarded for her patience soon thereafter when a cloud of dust suddenly appeared on the horizon. It was not too long before she could make out the wagon and the two men who sat in the seat behind the team of horses, but it was the rider on the large chestnut galloping alongside the wagon that brought a murmur of angry protest from her lips.

"Oh Pa," she whispered. "Why, Pa . . . why?"

She waited silently until the wagon drew to a stop

just in front of her. She did not have to look to know her father lay in a drunken stupor in the back of the wagon.

"Buck," Jenny Graham said to her brother, "can you and Stu get him into the house?"

"Sure we can," Buck Graham answered bitterly. "Don't we always manage?"

Buck was older than Jenny's twenty years by a little over a year. His given name was Joseph, but he had been called Buck from childhood. His hair was almost as gold as his sister's and his smile was usually just as quick, with the exception of today. Today neither was smiling.

Jenny was doing her best to ignore, for as long as possible, the third man, who sat on his horse patiently with an amused half smile on his face. She watched her brother and his friend, Stu Benson, lift her father and carry him into the house. It was only then that the third man chose to speak.

"He'll be fine as soon as he sleeps it off, Jenny."

Jenny spun around and anger deepened the turquoise of her eyes until they were nearly purple. "Why do you let this happen, Taylor? If you know it's going to happen, why don't you try to help stop it!"

"Now be reasonable, Jenny. How am I going to stop him? Your father's a grown man who drinks when he wants to."

Jenny put her hands on her hips and glared at him. "What do you want here Taylor—to do some gloating?"

Taylor Jessup dismounted and walked up the steps to stand beside Jenny. He was a very tall man whose Irish ancestors had mixed their bloodlines with the English, giving him expressive eyes that were deep brown and a glowing contrast to his golden hair. He had a full mustache that matched the gold of his hair

46

and grew above a wide, firm mouth that smiled much too easily. Taylor recognized his charm and skill with women quite well. Confidently he stood looking down into Jenny's angry turquoise eyes.

"Now Jenny," he said gently, "why would I want to gloat? What do I have to gain but your anger, and you know I don't want that. Just because my bank has the mortgage on your ranch doesn't mean I'm some villain out to take your home from under you. It's your father you should be angry with, not me."

Jenny turned away to hide the tears that sprung unwelcome into her eyes.

"Jenny, won't you at least invite me in for a cup of coffee? I've some very important news that I'm sure you'll be interested in."

"News? What news?"

"May I come in, or do we have to stand on the porch and talk?"

"I'm sorry. Come in. I've already made some coffee in case Pa . . . I mean . . ."

"I know what you mean. Come on, let's have that coffee. I'll tell you my news. Buck wanted to know before we got here, but I thought it best to tell you together."

They walked into the house just as Buck and Stu came out of the bedroom.

"He's tucked in, Jenny," Buck told her. "I think he'll be sleepin' 'til suppertime."

"Yeah," Stu agreed with a grin, "but I don't think he'll be much interested in supper when he does wake up."

Jenny's glare made Stu want to bite his tongue for forming the thoughtless words. The last thing Stu Benson intended was to say anything that would hurt Jenny in any way. He quickly made the excuse of chores to do out back and left.

Jenny poured three cups of coffee and placed them on the table. Buck and Jenny sat side by side and Taylor sat opposite them.

"Now," Buck said, "come on and tell us this great news you've been holding over my head all the way out here. You've got me real curious now."

"All right." Taylor smiled. "The railroad is coming through Brighton's Point."

Both Jenny and Buck stared at him silently, as if they had expected much more exciting news.

"What in heaven's name does that have to do with us?" Jenny questioned.

"A very great deal. I have a feeling they'll be looking for a right-of-way through this very valley. You two could end up very rich if you play your cards right."

"I still don't understand what you're talking about," Jenny insisted.

"He means," Buck supplied, "we could hold the railroad up for a lot of money to cross our land."

"Sell them our land?" Jenny cried in alarm. "The land Ma and Pa fought Indians and snowstorms and drought for? I'll never sell even a piece—not to the railroad or anyone else. This is Graham land and we're going to keep it!"

"I agree with you, Jenny," Buck added, "but it's not our land yet. Pa and the bank own it."

This frightened Jenny, though she did her best to hide the fact from Taylor Jessup. Could her father, in a drunken condition, be convinced to sell their land to the railroad? She vowed silently that no one representing the railroad or working for it in any way would be allowed near her father, or even on their property.

As for Taylor, his mind was on very nearly the same course. He wanted the Graham land, but he wanted Jenny Graham more. He had wanted her, in fact, from the very first time he had ever seen her. It was the basic idea behind his having agreed to lend Howard Graham money, and it was also the reason he now helped Howard drink away the sorrow of the death of his wife, Martha. Eventually, if he made his moves carefully, he would have both Jenny and the ranch.

Howard had never recovered from the death of Jenny's mother. It was a grief it seemed he could only drown temporarily in a bottle of whiskey. He never noticed that Taylor Jessup was always there to supply the drink.

"It's as much our land as Pa's!" Jenny cried defiantly. "And I'll make the first railroad man sorry he set foot on it. We aren't going to lose this ranch, Buck. It's our home. Ma's buried here."

"I know, sis," Buck replied. "If the railroad sends a man, we'll just say no. They can find another way. You're right, Jenny. This is our land and we can protect it."

Taylor Jessup watched the two astutely, wondering if the day would come when he would have to rid himself of Buck Graham.

"Jenny," Taylor said suddenly, "the Martins are having a party for Caroline's birthday. They've asked me to extend an invitation to you since I was coming out here." He turned to Buck, adding, "The Marshalls will be there too."

"What's that supposed to mean?" Buck asked with a chuckle.

"Just thought I'd let you know Emily Marshall's home from school. She'll be there."

Buck remained silent, but Jenny replied, "Buck and I will both be going."

"I thought you might come with me, Jenny," Taylor suggested hopefully.

"I'll save you a few dances, Taylor, I promise."

"And a walk in the garden? I'd like to talk to you

about something pretty special."

"All right," Jenny agreed.

"Good. Well, I guess I'd best be going," he said regretfully. He smelled the meal Jenny was cooking but waited in vain for an invitation. Reluctantly he left.

"Are you hungry, Buck?"

"Yeah. I'll go out back and get Stu. Pa won't be interested."

"Did you have trouble finding him, Buck?" she asked softly.

"I . . . I found him in the alley in back of the Golden Horse. He must have been there all night. Lord, Jenny, what's happening to him? It's like he just doesn't care anymore, like he doesn't even know we're alive and we need him."

"He loves us, Buck; we both know that. It's just that he loved Ma so much it's hard to face the days and nights knowing she'll never be here. You know how close they were."

"Yeah," Buck replied, "but it's been so hard. Sometimes I'm talkin' to him and he's lookin' out over the ranch and it feels like he's just gone. It scares me sometimes."

"It scares me too, but he needs us now more than he ever did."

"I know you're right. I just hope we're enough for him. God, I wish things could be as happy as they were when Ma was here. It seems Pa was always laughin' then. But then, I guess we were too."

Jenny wanted to cry out her loneliness too, but she knew it was useless to do so anymore. She determined to change the subject before her stinging eyes let loose the tears that hovered close.

"So Emily Marshall has come home. It's been over a year this time." She smiled.

"Yeah . . . a year, three days, seven hours, and I'm

not sure how many minutes"—Buck grinned—"not that I'm keeping track of the time."

"No," Jenny said with a laugh, "I can see you're not."

"It really wouldn't make any difference if I did."

"You don't know that, Buck. Besides," she added defensively, "she certainly couldn't do any better than you."

"You're prejudiced."

"Maybe. But I know a lot of girls who feel the same."

"In old Jacob Marshall's eyes I'm not good enough for Emily. With what they've got, maybe he's right. He wants Emily to marry well, and by that he means someone with as much land and money as he's got. We both know for sure that I could never offer her that. A small rancher is what I'll always be."

"So far," Jenny replied gently, "you've only said what her father wants for her. Have you asked Emily what she wants? Maybe being the wife of a small rancher is exactly what she has in mind."

"Come on, Jenny. You know damn well old Jacob is not going to let that happen."

"Why, brother dear," Jenny said with a mischievous gleam in her eyes, "I've seen you break the stubbornest horse with grim determination and patience. Are you going to let one little thing like Jacob stand in your way?"

Buck flushed, but he smiled. "Listen, you little devil. I'm the oldest in this family and I don't need advice on how to win a lady from my baby sister, who, I might add, has done one great job of dodging every eligible bachelor for a hundred miles around. Take Taylor, for instance; he's practically frothing at the mouth to lead you to the altar. He's tolerably rich and handsome. So, what's holding you up from taking your own advice?"

"Taylor . . ." Jenny mused thoughtfully. "I don't

51

know, Buck. I know he's all the things you say, and he's never been anything but a gentleman with me. But . . ."

"But what?"

"I just don't know, Buck. Sometimes I feel like there's some mystery about him, something I don't know and should. I keep getting the feeling he wants much more than me."

"What else has either one of us got? This ranch gives us just enough to survive on. We'll never be rich, Jenny; that's for sure. We'll just be what we are now, comfortable. That's good enough for me."

"And it's good enough for me. I was always happy here until Ma died. Buck . . . ?"

"What?"

"Do . . . do you think . . . I mean, if Pa were short of money or drunk . . . you don't think he'd sell our land to the railroad, do you?"

"I hope not, but I'm as scared about that as you are. We're between a rock and a hard place. The railroad on one side and a mortgage we're finding harder and harder to pay on the other."

"At least Taylor seems to be a friend of Pa's. He hasn't pushed him about the mortgage and Pa has missed a few payments along the way."

"Jenny, if Pa keeps drinkin' like this, we're not going to be able to make the next one either."

"I know . . . I know," Jenny whispered sadly. "Oh Buck, I wish I knew how to help him. I'm so afraid sometimes. I see everything slipping and I don't know how to stop it."

"Well, Stu and I can keep things going for awhile. Maybe Pa will come out of it. In the meantime, I'm selling those two horses I just broke to the Neilsons. It'll bring us some money, at least enough to stock up on supplies. Maybe I can find a way to scrape together some more by payment time."

"I know this isn't easy on you, Buck." Jenny said, looking at her brother intently. "Buck," she questioned suspiciously, "are you sure Jacob is the only reason you're not courting Emily? Are you sure me and Pa aren't the real reason?"

Buck rose and came to stand close to Jenny. He searched for words to keep Jenny from realizing she had struck the truth. He placed his hands on her shoulders and gave her his most disarming smile.

"Now Jenny, come on. You just told me I was determined and patient. Do you really believe I'm that dumb? Old man Marshall won't let me within a mile of Emily. I'm here because of that and, since I am, I'll help Pa all I can."

Before Jenny could answer, the door opened and Stu entered.

He smiled. "I could smell food clear out in the barn, and I'm starved."

"Come on in, Stu." Jenny laughed. "Sit down, both fo you. Food will be on the table in five minutes."

The two men sat, Stu with a growing appetite and Buck with relief that Stu had come in when he had. He wondered how much longer he could have fooled Jenny. She was much too clever to be taken in for long by anyone or anything, especially him, for they had been close since childhood.

They ate in muted camaraderie, keeping their laughter and conversation under control so that Howard Graham would not be disturbed.

When the meal was over, Stu and Buck prepared to take the horses Buck had sold to their new owners. After they had gone, Jenny began to clean up absently, letting her mind dwell on her suspicions. She felt very nearly certain the only reason Buck had discontinued his efforts to find his own happiness was his concern over her and their father. For the first time in her life, she began to feel anger toward her father. The truth of the sudden, intense emotion startled her. Somehow, some way, she had to do something to make her father return to his old self, to be a responsible father and rancher again.

She was so deep in her thoughts that she did not hear the bedroom door open. Howard Graham stood in the doorway and watched his daughter through bleary, red-rimmed eyes. How pretty she is, he thought, and a strange ache filled him, the same ache that had possessed him since the day of Martha Graham's death. It was Jenny's resemblance to her mother that tore at him now. She was almost a complete image of her mother. Martha's death and Jenny's beauty were barriers Howard was finding it impossible to surmount. He needed a drink, needed it with near desperation. But he knew Jenny and Buck would have made sure there was no whiskey in the house.

"Jenny," he rasped. Jenny spun about. She could have wept at the sight of her father. He was unshaven, and the stubble of his beard shone white against his tan face. His eyes were red and he trembled slightly. Howard might still be considered a handsome man who carried his forty-five years well, but excessive drinking was beginning to take its toll.

"I'm sorry, Jenny girl," he choked out. "I'm sorry."

"Oh Pa," Jenny whispered as she went to him. Her wide turquoise eyes, so like her mother's, brought tears to Howard's eyes. That he could not read condemnation in them was painful to him. If she would only cry out against him, be angry, he thought to himself, maybe that would help ease his guilt. But he saw only gentleness and understanding, and the loneliness he felt was almost unbearable. He needed something to fight, and there was nothing but the cobwebs of loneliness and despair.

"Sit down, Pa. Are you hungry? Can you eat?"

"No . . . no, girl, I don't want to eat. Jenny, how did I—"

"Buck . . . Buck brought you home."

Howard groaned. He sat at the table, rested his elbows on it, and buried his face in his hands. He felt ill.

Jenny moved to stand behind him. She placed her hands on his shoulders and very gently began to knead the taut muscles.

"I'm going to heat some water," she said firmly, "and you'll take a nice hot bath. Then you'll shave and, by that time, you'll be hungry. I've saved you some food and I'll warm it while you shave."

"Lord, Jenny . . . I . . . I can't . . ."

"Yes you can, Pa. You'll be all right."

He turned and looked up at her and she smiled reassuringly at him. "You'll be all right, Pa. You just need time. We love you, Pa," she added in a whisper. "Just remember that. We love you."

Howard rose and put his arms about her and felt her arms slide about him. Then she stepped back and smiled up at him.

"I'll go get the water and heat it."

He tried to smile, but his trembling lips refused to cooperate.

Jenny moved quickly and with assurance. An hour later, bathed and shaven, Howard again sat at the table and obediently ate the food Jenny placed before him. Jenny sat opposite him."

"I got some news, Jenny girl."

"What news, Pa?"

"Met a man in town. He told me the rumors we been hearin' about the railroad comin' through Brighton's Point are true."

"That's what Taylor told us. He came home with Buck."

"Where's Buck now?"

"He sold two of the horses to the Neilsons. He and Stu took them over."

"Sold? I thought Buck was building his herd. I thought he didn't take too well to selling any of his stock."

Jenny tried to make her voice kind and not condemning. "We need the money, Pa."

Howard was silent and the fork stopped between the plate and his mouth. Then gently he laid down the fork.

"It's been hard for you, Jenny girl," he said softly. "It's been hard for Buck too, I guess, tryin' to do the job of two men. I've been a failure to you both. Maybe . . . maybe it would be best either to sell to the railroad or let the bank take it over. We could go back East."

For the first time Jenny let her anger at all that was happening to them center on her father. "Pa!" she cried. "How can you say that? You and Ma struggled so hard to build this place. You fought for it and it belongs to us. How can you even think of turning over to the railroad the land Ma's buried on? Can't you think about what Buck and I might want? Don't you care how we feel?"

He winced under the harshness of her words and her reminder that the wife he had loved more than his own life lay beneath the sheltering trees not far from the house.

Jenny was immediately sorry when she saw the pain in his eyes. She came to her feet, moved around the table, and put her arms about her father.

"I'm sorry, Pa. I didn't mean that. I know you love us. We'll be all right if we just stick together. You, me, and Buck—we're a family, Pa, and we can do anything. We just have to stick together and work together."

He drew her down onto his lap and caressed her hair.

Then he turned her so she faced him.

"You're so like her, Jenny. You're strong and beautiful and full of fight. But me, girl . . . I just don't think I can fight anymore."

"You can, Pa. We have so much. We just can't let those Eastern railroad men dance in here and take what they want. This is Graham land."

"I don't know Jenny . . . I just don't know."

"Well, I do, and Buck does too. We're going to stay here, and no railroad or bank is going to beat us. We're strong, Pa. With Stu to help, Buck and I can do it. Just don't . . ."

"Don't what?"

"Don't let someone come along and soft talk you into selling."

"Soft talk," her father replied bitterly. "You mean, don't let someone take advantage of me when I'm drunk . . . or when I'm playing cards. You mean, don't miss a payment at the bank, payments I don't have any money for."

"We're managing, Pa, and we'll keep on managing. The most important thing to Buck and me is that you get better. Back to the way we were before—"

"Before I lost the only thing that kept me going," he finished. This hurt Jenny and, seeing the tears filling her eyes, he instantly regretted his words.

"Aren't Buck and I enough, Pa? Don't we love you enough?" she whispered, her voice ragged as she held back the tears.

"Oh, baby," Howard groaned. He held his daughter close and rocked her against him. "I love you, my little girl. I love you. You and Buck are the only good part of my life."

It was the sound of an approaching rider that broke the ensuing silence. Jenny rose and went to the door, but before she could reach it, it opened and Buck entered. He smiled a reassuring smile at Jenny, then moved toward the table and his father. He searched inside his shirt and took out a pouch that jingled encouragingly.

"I sold the two horses I just broke, Pa. It's not a whole lot of money, but we can manage on it for awhile. Old man Neilson has made me an offer. If I can break him four more by winter and another three in spring, he'll pay me enough money to cover the payment."

"Oh, Buck!" Jenny was excited. "At least we'll have another month."

Buck smiled, but his eyes held his father's. He needed the reassurance that his father was proud of what he had done. He needed this small thread that would bind them again and help brush away the cobwebs that held uncertainty and fear in their lives.

Howard gazed at the children he had sired and felt the turmoil of conflicting emotions. First there was pride, then shame that they had been forced to carry the burden for him.

"Good job, boy," Howard said kindly. "You've sprouted into some man. Your Ma would have been proud of you. She would have been proud of you both . . . and I'm proud of you too. Maybe . . . we just might make it."

Buck grinned and Jenny reached to touch his arm. "We'll be fine, Pa."

Howard nodded, then turned and walked back into his room, closing the door softly behind him. Inside his room he leaned against his door and allowed tears of guilt to run down his face. "Martha," he whispered softly, unable yet to let go of the painful memories that tied him to the past.

"Jenny," Buck began, "do you think he'll be all right?"

"I don't know, Buck. He has to fight this battle alone, I guess, and we just have to have patience."

"Yeah . . . patience. But I hope we don't lose everything we have while we're having all this patience."

Buck left the house then and Jenny stood in silence for a long time. Her heart grew cold and angry. She vowed silently that she would not lose what they had fought and sacrificed so much to gain. She would find a way, with Buck's help, to keep up the payments on the mortgage. But no matter what else happened, she would do anything she had to do to make sure none of her land went to the railroad.

"Let them come," she muttered. "Let one of them touch my land. I'll kill him . . . I swear I'll kill him!"

## Chapter 4

It was early morning when Trace and Allison accompanied Maxwell to the tracks upon which rode the engine and three cars that would carry them to the end of line and would be their home for a long time. Allison, who had never had an occasion to ride a train, was awed at the large, black, smoke-exuding engine.

The engine, as the engineer told a fascinated Allison, was named the *Tiger*. The stack, firebox, and steam dome were painted black. The rest of the train exhausted the rainbow. The wheels and pilot were not only red, but vermilion red. The boiler rose high, with the railroad's title, "The Starett Line," done in flowing ribbon and surrounded by curlicues of gold. The outside of the cab was exquisite with scrollwork in gold, and underneath the window was a painting in natural colors showing a Bengal tiger obviously stalking some unseen prey in a jungle as green as emeralds. The nameplate, set well forward on the boiler, spelled *Tiger* in great circus-type letters; another jungle painting appeared on the side of the headlight and, as a final effect, the American flag flew from a special pole atop the pilot. Each of the newcomers could see that the engine crew had attempted to maintain anything approaching the original beauty of the engine.

Allison and Trace placed what effects they had brought with them in the car that would be theirs to share. It was large enough for two, and, in fact, looked reasonably comfortable. The narrow, hard-backed seats had been removed and two small but adequate beds provided. The twenty-five feet of length had been divided to provide a six-feet area at one end closed off by a door, in which Allison might dress and complete her toilette.

"Well"—Trace grinned at his sister who was gazing about her—"it's certainly not the luxury we had at Fallen Oaks, but it's better than sleeping in the rain."

"Only a little," Allison replied, chuckling. "This monster scares me a bit, Trace."

"Scares you? Why?"

"I don't know," Allison answered softly. She shivered then, as if a cold breeze had touched her. "I just feel—"

"Feel what?"

Allison shook her head negatively, trying to discard her thoughts; then she turned to smile at Trace. "Don't pay me any mind, Trace. I didn't mean to act like a baby. I should be grateful the railroad and Mr. Maxwell are giving us such an opportunity to rebuild our lives."

"It won't be long, Allison," Trace comforted her. "The two years will pass, and then we'll go home. At least this way we will still have Fallen Oaks to go home to."

Allison looked up into Trace's eyes. "We will go home, won't we, Trace?"

"We'll go home, Allison," Trace replied gently. "Nobody beats the Cords, not as long as we stick together. C'mon, smile. We'll be on our way soon. Let's look at it as an adventure. One day we'll tell our grandkids about it."

Allison smiled obediently, then rose on tiptoe to kiss Trace lightly.

Before she could speak again, the door opened and Maxwell entered.

"Well, are you two comfortable? This car and mine are about the same. It's the best we can provide, and a darn sight better than most of the hired men will have at the end of track."

"This is just fine, Maxwell. Allison and I will be quite comfortable. Will we be staying in the same car all the way?" he asked; and Allison eagerly listened for the answer to Trace's question.

"Yes, you will. We ride to the end of track. As they complete each few miles, we just keep moving ahead. We're something like turtles; we carry our homes right with us."

"How long before we reach this . . . end of track?" Allison asked.

"Thought you might be asking. Come over to the table."

As Maxwell unfolded a map and laid it on the table, Allison and Trace moved to stand close by. The map showed the sparsely settled territory west of the Mississippi River. With his finger, Maxwell traced the markings on the map as he spoke.

"We're at end of track here. It will probably take about ten or twelve days of travel to reach it." He pointed to a black dot on the map labeled "Sedalia." "We're going to extend from there through Abilene, across Kansas and Colorado, through Utah, and on out to Virginia City and then to Sacramento."

"That's traveling at night too?" Allison questioned.

"Yes, day and night. We'll stop for water and food, but that's all."

63

"There doesn't seem to be much between us and Sacramento but empty land," Allison observed.

"Not so empty," Trace replied. "The Homestead Act must have put quite a few farmers and ranchers between us and Sacramento."

"You're right," Maxwell replied as he refolded the map and put it in his pocket. "That, my friend, is part of your work." He grinned amiably. "With your Southern charm, it's your job to get us some rights-of-way across a few of those farms and ranches."

"Shouldn't someone have gone on ahead and done that already?"

Maxwell's eyes grew shuttered. "I tried that. It seems my opposition made it impossible. The men I sent . . . ah . . . all had their minds changed rather drastically."

It was obvious he did not want to say more in front of Allison for fear of frightening her, and Traced did not want him to continue for the same reason. He understood too well what Maxwell was telling him. Allison remained quiet, but despite the men's sudden silence, the truth was obvious to her as well.

"Trace, there's a walkway between our cars. Once we're underway, I want you and Allison to come over and join me. My niece has decided to come with me. Since her mother died, Eileen has been away at school. I invited her to come at least part of the way with me because it's been a long time since we've been together. Besides, I thought Allison would like some feminine company."

"How wonderful!" Allison cried. "It will surely be much more fun to talk to someone about something besides Indians, railroads, and weather."

Trace was only too pleased to see Allison's mind taken from the problems of the trip. "We'll be pleased to join you," Trace answered.

"Good. I'll see you later then." Maxwell turned and left the car. Just minutes after he closed the door, the car gave a violent jerk, shuddered, then jerked again. In a short time, it was in rapid but rattling movement.

"Well, Allison, here we go. We're on our way to California."

"Yes, inch by inch."

"Allison, inch by inch is still better than standing still."

Allison laughed and took hold of Trace's arm. "You aren't going to let me feel sorry for myself, so we'd best join Mr. Starett and his niece."

It was precarious walking for ones unused to such rocking motion, but they made their way safely to Maxwell's door. Trace's knock was answered quickly by Maxwell, who invited them in.

Trace's eyes were caught immediately by the woman who sat on a low couch across the car from them. He had no idea that Eileen Starett's position was a studied pose meant both to startle and impress him.

Eileen presented a striking picture. She was very beautiful, and she knew how to use her beauty well. She sat on a couch covered with a dark material, which was framed against a wall of oak paneling. Against this frame, her pale golden hair and the emerald green gown she wore were magnetic. Her eyes were innocently wide and cornflower blue. Her oval face was dominated by them and the lush, full lips that were invitingly pink and moist. It had been a long time since Trace had been with a woman, and his physical reaction was so strong that it startled him.

Eileen rose and extended her hands, one to Trace and one to Allison, but her warm, inviting look was for Trace alone. Allison's eyes narrowed, for she had seen through Eileen with an understanding only a woman could have of another woman. Her mind whispered

65

softly to her: *This woman is a cat and she has her claws set for Trace.*

"Welcome to the *Tiger,*" Eileen said, her voice throaty and warm. "I must say the trip looks much more inviting now that there will be people my own age along. I think we shall become delightful friends before this trip is over."

"Thank you, Miss Starett," Trace replied. "I hope so. It's nice to know Allison will have another woman to talk to. I was worried that my work would leave her alone too much."

"Well," Eileen declared, "we shall all become very close friends. Come, sit down. Can I get you something to drink?"

"Brandy for both of them," Maxwell said firmly, "and one for me, my dear."

"Of course, Uncle Max." Eileen moved gracefully to the mahogany bar. It was impossible for the three of them not to watch her, though all three watched with entirely different thoughts in mind. What none of the three seemed to realize was that Eileen was well aware of both their eyes and their thoughts.

Eileen had welcomed Trace's arrival with warm pleasure. A dull and boring trip suddenly had been transformed into something exciting. Now she could feel his eyes on her and knew her body was echoing the desire that filled his. She wanted him so, and intended to take full advantage of the situation at the proper time. Until then, her eyes would tell him all she wanted him to know.

Eileen carried glasses to Allison and her uncle, then returned to the bar to bring Trace's and hers. As she handed Trace his glass, she let her hand brush gently against his. Their eyes caught, Eileen's offering and Trace's acknowledging the offer openly. It never occurred to Eileen that Trace would not be an easy conquest.

"Here's to a profitable and successful trip," Maxwell said as he raised his glass. The others raised theirs to touch his. "May we all get what we want from it."

"Yes," Eileen murmured. "May we all get what we want."

They drank and chatted companionably as the train rattled onward down the track.

It was after a surprisingly good dinner that Trace and Allison made their way back to their own car. Once inside, Trace sat on the edge of his bed and removed his boots. Then he lay back on the bed and laced his fingers behind his head.

His eyes caught those of his sister, who stood leaning against the door watching him. He did not doubt, as he chuckled softly and winked at her, that he knew exactly what she was thinking.

"How can you lie there and grin like a cat that has just eaten the canary?" she demanded. "That Yankee is a bitch and she's got her claws out for your hide."

"Allison," Trace chided with an amused gleam in his eyes, "is that a ladylike thing to say? Mother would have been shocked by your wicked thoughts."

"Mother would have slapped me silly if I had acted like that with any boy, and it's not just my thoughts that were wicked. The way you looked at her, you might just as well have undressed her."

"Now, come on," Trace protested guiltily, "that's not true. It's just that she's a very beautiful woman and I am a man who appreciates beauty."

"That isn't all you'd appreciate, but I'd bet she's willing to find out the rest."

"Now, Allison, this has gone far enough. I'm a little too old for my baby sister to be telling me about women. I can take care of myself without your help. Now, why don't you go to bed and get some sleep?

Besides"—he laughed—"we're here and she and her uncle are there. Just what do you think I could do about that?"

"I'm really not too sure," Allison said, grinning in reply, "but from the look in her eyes, I wouldn't put it past her to find a way."

"You are becoming a brat. Now go to bed before I turn you over my knee and straighten out all your twisted thoughts."

Allison entered the smaller cubicle and Trace could hear her moving about as she made her preparations for bed.

He turned his mind from Allison to Eileen with a great deal of pleasure. His mind eagerly sought some way he could accept Eileen's open invitation. She was a beauty and he found it stimulating merely to envision what charms she might offer. A moving train on which her uncle and his sister continuously remained so close certainly presented major obstacles, but he could surely enjoy his thoughts.

When Allison returned, she sat on the edge of his bed. She looked quite childlike with her dark hair in braids on either side of her face. "Trace . . . I'm sorry. I know I've been a brat. But . . . I guess I got scared again. You're all I've got, and I couldn't bear it if you were hurt in any way . . . by anybody."

Trace reached out and took hold of one braid, tugging it gently.

"Stop being so frightened of everything. We started this trip together, as a family, and we'll end it the same way. I'm not going to get hurt. Enjoy the trip and try to forget some of the past. We'll make a whole new future for the Cords, and it won't include the railroad. I'm a planter by profession. It's a profession I choose to remain in. Now, do you think you can get some sleep?"

Allison nodded, bent to kiss him, then went to her

bed. After some time her relaxed breathing told him she slept. He reached into his pocket for a cigar and rose from the bed, intending to smoke it in the small area between cars. It was an enclosed platform, and he knew the smoke would not bother Allison. He left his coat behind and, dressed only in snug, fawn-colored breeches and a white shirt, he opened the door of his car. He froze for a moment in utter surprise as he confronted Eileen, who stood against the closed door of her uncle's car with a half smile on her face. Without a sound, he stepped out and pulled his door shut behind him.

Only moonlight touched them now, just enough so that they could see each other. The robe Eileen wore enhanced her lush figure more than concealed it.

"Can't sleep, Miss Starett?" he asked softly.

She laughed a soft, almost caressing laugh. "You have called me that all evening," she replied in a velvet voice. "Can you not use my name?"

"Eileen . . . very pretty."

"Thank you."

"And you," he added, "are very beautiful."

"Thank you again. Trace Cord, you are a very interesting man."

"Me?" Trace laughed. "How?"

"From your speech I can tell you were Southern born, yet you work for a Yankee far away from your home. You're a mystery, Trace," she added seductively, "and I am intrigued by mysteries . . . I like to solve them."

"There is not much to solve. I was on the losing side, if you remember, and what I came home to left me very few choices. When your uncle made me an offer, I took it, and that's all the mystery there is about me."

Eileen moved close to Trace, close enough that the scent of her perfume touched him. She reached out a hand and laid it lightly against his chest, enjoying the feel of hard, taut muscle against it.

"I doubt that," she whispered softly, "but I am quite interested in finding out for myself."

Trace drew her unresisting body against his, and his entire being suddenly came alive with the feel of her. His arms went about her as her arms came up around his neck. She molded her slim, firm body against his and their lips met. The kiss was ravaging and greedy. It had been a long time since Trace had touched a woman, and the fires within him blazed like those of a furnace.

His heat was answered by the hunger of Eileen's passion, passion that soon grew almost violent. Deliberately, tauntingly, her hands moved to his shoulders, then lower to his waist, then to his muscular thighs.

If he was shocked by her wild abandon, he controlled his reaction enough to keep her from knowing. Trace was no fool. Eileen was a woman who made her choices, then tried to take what she wanted. She was a predator Trace knew well, the predator who devours her prey.

When they moved apart, both were breathing rapidly.

"It is going to be a long and very delightful trip," Eileen said softly. "We will stop now and again for supplies. I hope we will continue this at a much more convenient time." Before Trace could answer, the door opened and Eileen vanished.

When Trace had controlled his wayward body, he put the cigar between his strong white teeth and lit it. Smiling in the dim moonlight, he decided that he agreed with one thing: this was going to be a very intriguing and enlightening trip, and maybe even a little dangerous.

After a while, he threw the stub of the cigar away and went inside to seek his own bed and some very stimulating dreams.

It was not until late the next day that they stopped for the first time. Trace had had ample time to think. He had concluded that this was not the time nor the proper circumstances to become seriously involved with anyone. His innate Southern pride would not allow him even to consider marrying a wealthy woman when he had less than nothing to offer her. It had never occurred to him that if he had truly fallen in love with Eileen no obstacle would have been to great to overcome. He had also considered his responsibility to care for Allison and had concluded that Allison and Eileen would never have been able to live together. They spoke politely, but Eileen considered Allison a child and a nuisance, while Allison considered Eileen a threat to her brother's happiness.

Trace knew that although he desired Eileen he would have to make his position clear to her. There were very surprising results when he tried to do just that.

The train had chugged to a shivering, rattling stop to take on the needed supplies. They would be near the small town of South Bend for the balance of the day and leave just after dinner. How the situation came about Trace was never quite sure, but that it had been well planned by Eileen was obvious when they were left alone in her uncle's car while Maxwell escorted Allison into town for some shopping.

Trace took the drink Eileen offered him, then they sat opposite each other on the couch. Eileen lightly touched her glass to Trace's as she smiled.

"To us."

Trace drank, then set aside his glass. Eileen raised an

inquiring eyebrow.

"I wasn't too sure there really was an us," Trace began.

"How could you doubt it?" Eileen laughed softly. "I was sure the first moment I saw you. I told you, Trace, you're a puzzle and I find solving puzzles quite interesting."

"Eileen," Trace began, "there's something we have to get clear between us."

"Oh?"

"You're a very wealthy lady . . ."

"Very wealthy."

"At this moment I don't have a penny to my name."

"Is that supposed to make a difference?"

Eileen knew her words were wrong the moment she saw the flash of angry pride in Trace's eyes.

"Trace, for heaven's sake, do you think I am suggesting you marry me tomorrow? I know you are the type of man who must find his own destiny. It is one of the things I liked about you at once. I admire strong men with pride. Can we not just take the time on this trip to . . . ah . . . get to know each other better?"

"You make me sound a little foolish." Trace grinned. "I think you're a beautiful woman, but I don't want you to have any misunderstandings about me. I've lost almost everything I have, and I plan to rebuild it. It's going to take some time. Until I do . . . I don't plan on any permanent relationships."

Eileen put her glass aside and turned again to look at Trace. She was intoxicatingly close, and her beauty, combined with the soft scent of her perfume, was playing havoc with Trace, who had been under enforced celibacy too long. He slipped neatly into Eileen's scented trap as she reached out to lay her hand gently on his cheek.

"Trace . . ." she whispered softly, "I understand you.

72

Maybe more than you think. But, while you build your dream, can't I be part of your life . . . just a small part?"

Her movement seemed slight, as did his, but in that moment she was in his arms. Her lips parted beneath his and she returned the heat of his kiss. Tongues searched, then tasted the sweet, heady wines of passion. His arms drew her so tightly against him that she moaned softly. Slowly they slid together to the carpeted floor.

Blindly he tore his mouth from hers, only to brand her soft flesh with the heat of his exploring lips. They were wild with abandoned passion now, and Trace was momentarily lost in the heat of it.

The violence of his passion exhilarated her. This was what Eileen Starett wanted, needed, in a man—a wildness, a possessiveness. Very few men had dominated Eileen from the time she was fifteen and had discovered the pleasure her body could provide.

She had planned this seduction well, but she had not planned Trace's command of her body, nor had she planned the new emotion that sparked to life within her. For the first time, she realized, she wanted a man for longer than just once. She wanted him permanently. By the time they lay still and fulfilled in each other's arms, Eileen was already making plans for the permanent conquest of Trace Cord.


For Trace and Eileen the ten days to Sedalia were vivid and memorable. Maxwell seemed to be interested only in his railroad, and Allison, quite sure that Trace was involved in something more dangerous than he thought but unable to do anything about it, stewed in silent fury. She was surprisingly pleased when Maxwell announced that the next day they would reach the end of track. Allison, knowing Eileen for what she was, was

73

certain she would not stay long in the rough camp of the rail workers. It was her fondest hope that Eileen would soon become bored with the lack of entertainment and go home. In fact, Allison would have liked to have seen Eileen anywhere but where she was.

Trace was awakened on the morning of the eleventh day when the train came to a screeching, bone-rattling halt. He sat up in his bed the same moment Allison sat up in hers wide eyed with fear.

"Trace?"

"We've stopped. I'll go check. Stay in bed." He rose and went to the door. He opened it to find Maxwell just outside and preparing to knock.

"I was just coming for you both. We've arrived at our destination. If you two hurry up and dress, I'd like to introduce you to some of my crew chiefs."

"We'll be ready in a few minutes."

When Trace closed the door, he turned to smile at Allison.

"C'mon, Allison. Let's go see what's going on."

"I'll be dressed in a minute."

True to her word, Allison dressed quickly and rejoined Trace. Together they opened the door and stepped out on the platform, where they were joined by Maxwell and Eileen.

Amid cheers of welcome, Maxwell descended the steps to the ground, then he reached up to help first Eileen then Allison. Trace followed and they stood together until the cheers died down. It was fairly obvious to Trace that the men who worked for Maxwell had only respect and admiration for him. It made Trace feel somewhat better about the job he had undertaken.

Maxwell raised his hands as if to encompass the entire mass of men.

"Thanks for the welcome," he shouted. "We've

completed our staff. Tomorrow . . . we move!"

This news was greeted by cheers and shouts. Trace and Allison smiled at each other, for now both were more comfortable about their future. Eileen smiled also, and about the same future—the future she planned.

## Chapter 5

Jenny brushed her wayward curls into some semblance of control, twisted the shining mass into a knot atop her head, and pinned it securely. Frustrated tears of anger were hovering near and she was doing her best to control them. She finished buttoning her shirt and tucked it into the snug breeches she wore. Then she sat on a chair and drew on her boots.

This time she would have to go after her father herself. He had not been home for two days and Buck had gone with Stu to try to catch more horses to break.

"Damnit, Pa . . . Damnit!" she cursed, and the unaccustomed words bespoke her fear. Rumors had flown that the railroad was near. Had her father been drunk and done something they would all regret? The worry was so strong she could taste the salt of unwanted tears.

She rose quickly and left the house. It took her very little time to saddle her horse. In the light of the early morning sun, she rode toward town.

It was a long, worrisome ride, and it gave her too much time to think. And as she thought, her ever-growing hatred of the railroad and all connected with it swelled within her until she choked on the taste of it.

On the outskirts of town, she drew her horse to a walk and began scanning the alleys between each building.

The town was just coming to life. Businesses were opening their doors, and wood sidewalks were being swept and washed for the day's trade. In front of a dressmaker's shop Jenny dismounted and tied her horse to the rail. She despised the bitterness and the embarrassment she felt, but she had to find her father.

Slowly she walked into each alley and examined it, pleased yet frightened when she found each one empty. Good Lord, she thought, I just can't walk into a saloon to find him. She very nearly panicked and started to go home, then she bit her lip and tilted her chin determinedly. She would find him if she had to walk into Hell to do it.

She stood a few feet from the door of a saloon, gathering her courage.

"Jenny?"

The voice from beside her startled her and she turned to see Joanne Carter standing near. Joanne and her husband had owned a small farm near the Graham ranch, but now Joanne was a widow and worked the land herself. She was also a very good friend of Jenny's, and, suspecting the reason for Jenny's presence in town, she could barely keep the sympathy from her eyes.

"Hello, Joanne."

"I haven't seen you for awhile. Why don't you and Buck come over more often?"

"I'm sorry, Joanne. Buck and I have really been busy with the ranch and all."

"Why don't you come over for dinner tomorrow night?"

Before Jenny could answer, her attention was drawn to the door of the bank. It had opened and Taylor had stepped out, accompanied by two men.

Joanne turned to follow Jenny's stare, and smiled. The young widow's attraction to Taylor was obvious in her eyes, but Jenny's eyes were for the other two men.

"Who are they, Joanne?"

"Who, the two with Taylor?"

"Yes."

"I don't know the younger one, but the older one is with the railroad. He's Maxwell Starett, and he owns it. I expect the good-looking one is with it too."

"Railroad," Jenny murmured as her eyes grew cold and her stare seemed almost to pierce the younger man. He must have sensed the violence of her thoughts, for he turned and looked at her. His startling smoky grey eyes held hers for a long moment, then he was drawn back into the conversation. Jenny was breathless with the sudden feeling that he had actually reached out and touched her.

Jenny tore her gaze from him, annoyed with this feeling she could not understand or explain. He was a complete stranger, and, worse yet, a stranger who was part of the threat that filled her restless nights with nightmares.

Joanne had been watching as Jenny's eyes had held the stranger's. She smiled. Jenny was a very good friend about whom Joanne quite often worried. She knew the problems that plagued the Graham ranch and was of the opinion that a husband for Jenny would help cure many of them. Of course she was aware of Jenny's independent spirit and was even more curious to see the man who could channel that spirit toward a happier course.

"He's so handsome," Joanne said softly. "I wonder who he is?"

Jenny's eyes darted from the conferring men to Joanne.

"I don't care who he is. He's with the railroad. That

makes him unwelcome anywhere near my ranch."

"Goodness, Jenny, I'm sorry. I didn't mean to make you angry."

"I'm sorry I snapped at you," Jenny replied quickly. "I guess I'm just a little on edge today."

"Can I help?"

"No, I . . . I just have a lot to do. You will excuse me, Joanne; I've really got to go."

"Of course . . . Jenny?"

"What?"

"If . . . if you need someone to talk to . . . a friend . . . come over."

"Thanks, Joanne," Jenny replied, giving a light squeeze to Joanne's shoulder. She turned away quickly then to keep the uncertainty and fear in her eyes from Joanne's astute gaze. She walked away and Joanne watched the proud lift of her head and the straight back. She felt again a touch of sympathy. As she turned back, she caught sight of the three men whose presence had sparked Jenny's anger. Joanne smiled again, for she saw that the unknown man was watching Jenny's retreating figure with an intent and admiring gaze.


Slowly, under the watchful eyes of Maxwell and Trace, the rails had been moving forward. Maxwell was well pleased with his wisdom in hiring Trace, for the men seemed to respect him and work well for him. They had increased the daily amount of track laid by over half. Soon the only signs of civilization were found in the small dots of little towns and sparsely scattered ranches.

It was with the owners of these ranches that Maxwell would now have to deal, and he knew he could trust Trace to work with him to negotiate with these ranches and help him acquire the land the railroad would need to continue its progress.

Trace and Maxwell had left the train very early in the morning. They had ridden from dawn to nightfall, stopping only to eat and rest their horses. They had made camp and had gone to sleep early that night, then had repeated the same routine the next day. Again they had made camp.

"If we start early in the morning, we will reach Bentonville by late morning. I want to contact a Mr. Taylor Jessup. From what I understand from my advance surveyor, he has, or will have, access to the land we need to lay track through the Roaring Fork Valley," Maxwell had explained.

"Where do we meet this Jessup?" Trace had inquired.

"He owns the only bank in the town."

"Is that how he got hold of the land we want?"

"I don't know for sure. It was mentioned that he's planning to marry into a big chunk of the land we want. Anyway, we'll talk to him and see what's going on. Once we find out who has all the area we want, I'll go back and get the crews started moving this way. Then it's up to you to do what has to be done to get us what we need."

"What limits do I have on money to offer?"

"I want the right of way through this valley, Trace. If I have to go around, it means a loss of time I can't spare and that will cost me more than money. It might cost me my railroad. I can't go around, Trace. I must go through this valley . . . I must."

"I'll do the best I can, Maxwell."

"Good. Get some sleep. We'll get an early start and talk to Jessup tomorrow. In a matter of a few hours we'll know where we stand and what it's going to take to get what we want."

They had rolled themselves in their blankets near the

fire then and had slept. They had awakened hours later to the warmth of the morning sun.

After a quick breakfast, they had broken camp, mounted, and had continued on their way. They had arrived in the small town of Bentonville and soon had found the bank and Taylor Jessup.

They were ushered into his office immediately. He smiled as he rose from behind his desk and extended his hand to them.

"Mr. Starett, it is a pleasure to finally meet you. I received your last letter and am genuinely overjoyed that you have decided to bring your railroad through our valley."

"Thank you, Mr. Jessup. This is my right arm, Trace Cord."

"Mr. Cord," Taylor replied as he extended his hand to Trace.

All three men sat down, Taylor behind his wide mahogany desk and Trace and Maxwell opposite him.

"So Maxwell," Taylor began with a smile, "just how far away are you?"

"About seventy-five miles from town and a little more from the valley," Maxwell answered quickly. "Now, tell me, Taylor, do I have access to all the land I need?"

"Well . . . just about."

"What do you mean, just about? I can't lay track on land I just about have."

"Let me tell you where we stand."

"Yes, tell me."

"Mrs. Carter—she's a widow who owns one block of land—well, we're close to an agreement. The Marshall place is also pretty close to an agreement. The only one holding out is Howard Graham, and I feel safe in saying I can deliver his place in time."

"I'll be nearing town in another ten days, and we'll be

ready to head for the valley in a little over two weeks, right, Trace?"

"That's right," Trace answered. "About twenty days will find us at the valley mouth."

"What makes you think the Graham land will be ours in that much time?" Maxwell probed.

"Because"—Taylor grinned suggestively—"I am going to marry Howard's daughter, Jenny. I guarantee that strip of land will be yours very soon."

Trace could not explain why Taylor's smug words irritated him and he felt the distinct urge to wipe the grin from the banker's mouth. He began to wonder about Jenny Graham.

"Well, that sounds good to me. We'll go back and keep the boys moving," Maxwell announced.

"Fine. I'll ride out to meet you when you get close to town. You said about ten or twelve days?"

"That's right."

"I'll have your deeds ready for you."

Maxwell and Trace rose, and Taylor followed them from the room. He walked with them, chatting about unimportant things, until they stood together on the front walk of the bank.

As Maxwell and Taylor spoke together, Trace became aware of a strange prickling sensation, as if someone were aiming a gun at his back. He turned slowly. She stood across the street, but he could feel the hate that emanated from her. She was staring at him as if she hated him, yet he had never seen her before in his life. Lord, she was beautiful! he thought. Why in the hell was she looking at him as if she could have murdered him? He considered the idea of walking across the street and talking to her, but her attention was suddenly drawn back to the woman who accompanied her. Trace turned back to the conversation, knowing he would not soon forget the girl with the sunlit hair and light eyes. He found himself wondering if he could find out who she was and just what color her eyes really were, and why she hated him when they had never met.

Trace and Maxwell left Taylor and walked down the sidewalk to the closest saloon, where they shared two drinks.

"Trace, I want you to do something for me."

"What?"

"I want you to ride out to that valley and take a look around. Maybe listen to see if you can tell what's going on there."

"You sound like you don't quite trust your banker friend."

"I'd just like to know the lay of the land for myself."

"You don't want me to talk to any of the families that own the land we want?"

"No, not yet. We'll give Taylor his time. I just want you to know where they're located, and what the feelings might be. You can camp out there a few days, can't you?"

"Sure, that's no problem," Trace agreed, surprised at himself when the first thought that leapt into his head was the possibility of seeing the light-eyed woman again.

"I'll ride back to camp with you and get my things. Then I'll come back to town, stay the night, and ride out tomorrow. I'll keep my ears and eyes open."

Maxwell nodded and they left the saloon. Maxwell announced his intention to purchase a few things at the general store and Trace decided to walk around the small town for the short time it would take him to do so. Still present in the back of his mind was the look in the eyes of the woman who had stood across the street from him, and he did not deny to himself that the chance that he might run across her somewhere in town was the motive for his stroll.

Jenny had continued her search for her father, braving the taunts of the men in the saloons in her search. There were four such establishments, and it was in the last one that she found him.

He was slumped over a table in the farthest corner of the room, and Jenny ran to his side as soon as she spotted him. Her initial efforts to stir him were ineffective, so she gripped his shoulders and shook him gently.

"Pa," she said softly, trying not to draw any more attention than necessary, for she was nervous about the stares she had already attracted.

"Pa, come on. Wake up, please. I have a wagon. Come and let me take you home . . . Pa . . . please, wake up."

Howard stirred and lifted blurred, red-rimmed eyes to a daughter he did not recognize.

"Martha," he mumbled. "I'm tired, Martha."

"Pa, please . . . it's me, Jenny. Let me take you home." She tried again to move him, but Howard was a large man and it was nearly an impossible feat.

"You need some help, little girl?"

Jenny's heart pounded furiously as she gazed up at the man who stood a foot or two away. He was large, but his body appeared soft, dissipated. His face had several days' growth of beard and the unwashed scent of him reached her from where he stood.

"No . . . no, thank you. I don't need any help." She bent over her father again and this time she shook him violently, her fear lending strength to her hands. "Get up, Pa," she whispered in angry desperation as she sensed the large man moving closer.

To her relief, Howard stirred again, sat up, and, with

her help, rose to his feet. She could have wept with relief, but it was short-lived.

"Now, come on, little girl, let the old drunk sleep. Come on upstairs with me. I'll make you forget all about him." He reached out and took hold of Jenny's arm. "It'll shore be worth your while, little girl. I'll show you a good time and you'll forget all about this old drunk."

Jenny had taken all she could bear. A combination of fear, frustration, anger, and desperation destroyed what little control she had left. She shook her arm free and reached out to slap him as hard as she could across the cheek.

He was stunned momentarily and Jenny took that moment to slip her arm about her father's waist and again urge him toward the swinging doors. They had covered half the distance when the big man regained his equilibrium. He started toward Jenny and Howard at the same moment Trace walked through the doors.

Several things happened simultaneously. Trace quickly assessed the situation and reached for the gun that hung low on his hip. The big man saw the movement and stopped in his tracks. Then he raised both hands in a surrendering gesture and backed away. Jenny looked up in time to see the railroad representative looming before her, the man whom she felt was the physical manifestation of the threat that filled her sleepless nights and anxious days.

Many unbidden thoughts touched her mind: that he was extraordinarily handsome; that he seemed to be so strong and substantial; yet he wanted to take from her all she loved and needed. The bitter taste of that possibility choked her and unwanted tears of frustration filled her eyes—tears she would rather die than let him see.

She glared at him, and her reaction took Trace by

86

surprise. She had radiated the same hatred earlier and still he could not fathom why.

He admired her slim, graceful body and the sunny gold of her hair, but what pleased him most was to look into the deep turquoise of her eyes. Then he made a mistake. He slid the gun back into its holster and started toward her. "Let me help you," he began, sensing her need to get the man she was half supporting out of there.

Jenny was embarrassed at his obvious comprehension of her plight.

"Stay away from me!" she cried. "I don't need any help from your kind—not now or ever. Just get out of my way." She moved forward and Trace stopped and looked at her dumbfounded.

"My kind? I think you've made a mistake."

"No, and I don't intend to make one. Please let me pass."

Trace moved aside slightly and Jenny urged her still-dazed father toward the door. She passed very close to Trace, who had to control the sudden urge to put his arm about her and try to ease the distress he saw in her eyes.

As she passed him, she stopped and looked up at him. "Why don't you leave Bentonville? It would be better for all of us if you did. But no matter what else you do, stay away from my family and my land."

She passed him and moved with her father through the doors and was gone. Trace could feel the absence of her beauty the moment the doors swung closed behind her.

He looked at another man who stood near. "Is she always this ungrateful for help?" Trace asked with a puzzled frown.

"Naw . . . Jenny . . . she ain't really like that. She's a damn sweet girl. It's that damn drunk of a father that gives her so much grief. I guess she's just a scared little girl right now. But she's a good woman."

"Jenny?"

"Jenny Graham. Her and her Pa and her brother own a small horse ranch a few miles down the valley. They been makin' out so far, at least before her Ma died. Now it seems the whole thing's fallin' apart on her."

Trace looked at the man closely. He was middle-aged and seemed sympathetic.

"Do you have time for a drink?" Trace asked.

"Sure do."

They walked to a nearby table and Trace ordered a bottle and two glasses. He was completely intrigued by an angry, turquoise-eyed beauty, and he felt he had found a source of information about her. But what he wanted to know most was how much truth there was to Taylor Jessup's boast that he would soon be marrying Jenny Graham and that he would soon have access to her land, land she had been furiously protecting a few minutes before.


The train sat silently at the end of track. It had been three days since their arrival and Allison sat alone in the car she and Trace shared. She did not want to leave it, mostly because she refused to remain in Eileen's company any more than she had to. Trace and Maxwell had ridden ahead to some small town a two-day ride away to make contact with a landowner to negotiate some purchases for rights-of-way. It would be at least a five-or-six-day trip and Allison was more than slightly annoyed to have been left with little to do and unwelcome companions.

It was warm and, despite the possibility of running into Eileen, Allison rose and decided to leave the car.

She stood for a while on the platform watching the workmen in the distance, as they systematically extended the rails that would lead them into the wilderness.

The sky was a deep ocean blue with white clouds brushed in ruffled streaks across it. Allison could not help but admire the raw natural beauty of this rugged land. She even felt she and Trace might both be happy here if it were not for—

"Good morning, Allison," came a sugared voice from close behind her. Allison turned reluctantly, as if she might wish Eileen away.

"Good morning, Eileen. I see you're dressed for riding. Isn't that a little dangerous in this wilderness? How do you know what's out there?"

Eileen laughed softly. "I have company. Besides, only children are afraid to discover something new and interesting."

Allison knew this last barb was aimed at her, but she chose to ignore it.

"Company?"

"Yes, Mr. Wilson, one of the crew bosses, if you remember. He's been very kind the last few days since Uncle Max and Trace have been gone and he's ridden with me . . . for protection."

Allison doubted that protection was Eileen's goal, but again she kept silent. She had seen Poe Wilson, and she suspected the extent of his "company."

Poe was handsome, in a rough and arrogant way. He was tall and very strong. Allison had actually seen him lift one of the huge, rough-cut railroad ties by himself, and she knew its weight to be close to 150 pounds. His eyes were dark and missed nothing that occurred about him. Allison had often felt them upon her and had seen the hungry glow within. It frightened her, and she made sure there was never an occasion to be left alone with him.

Before Allison could speak again, the attention of both women was drawn to Poe, who was striding purposefully toward them leading two saddled horses.

Allison could feel her nerves grow taut. She would admit he was ruggedly handsome, yet she could feel an undercurrent of something malicious and cold. It was as if she had just come upon a coiled snake that was preparing to strike.

"Good mornin', Miss Allison, Miss Eileen." He grinned. "It's a beautiful day for a ride. Miss Allison, would you care to join us? I could rustle up another horse pretty quick."

"No . . . no thank you, Mr. Wilson. I have some paperwork to do for my brother."

If Poe noticed Eileen's displeasure at the invitation, he ignored it. Eileen he had already tasted, but Allison was the one he wanted. His desire for her ran second only to the dislike he felt for her brother, Trace. He was waiting for an opportunity to dispose of both problems to his satisfaction.

Allison watched them mount and ride away, and found herself wishing Trace were already back. Thoughtfully, she turned and walked back to the train.

## Chapter 6

At the same time Jenny and her father were riding home in strained and uncomfortable silence, Trace left the saloon and met Maxwell. He told the older man nothing about his chance meeting with Jenny, nor did he say anything about what he had been told by the stranger in the saloon. He wanted to find out more about the situation before he presented it to Maxwell, and he was determined to learn everything he could about Taylor Jessup's relationship with Jenny. He was no longer convinced that Taylor's words about Jenny had been anywhere near the truth. In fact, he had some deep suspicions about Taylor's real interest in Jenny Graham, for those turquoise eyes, brimming with anger and uncertainty, haunted his thoughts. He had sensed that she was very vulnerable and very afraid, but he could not be quite sure of what. She had lashed out at him in quick defense and he vowed to discover why he should have affected her so.

This brought to mind more subtle thoughts about how she had affected him. He was startled even now as he recalled her, for he had been able to summon a vision of her easily, without taxing his memory. She had, in a very short moment, struck at all his senses at once. He could almost feel the creamy texture of her skin, the soft, vulnerable mouth that seemed to have been made for tasting. He had seen a flame in the depths of her eyes that had ignited some deep need within him, and he was eager to again confront the volatile Miss Graham as soon as possible.

He had learned the location of her property from his saloon acquaintance, and when he and Maxwell had parted company, he turned his horse in that direction.

Jenny was silent, only because she did not want to say the angry words that choked her throat. She could not find the strength to hurt her father any more than he already was.

Howard's guilt was like a burning coal in the pit of his stomach. He was creating a chasm between himself and the daughter he loved, and he seemed to be helpless to do anything about it.

When they reached the ranch house, he climbed down unsteadily from the wagon. He stood and watched Jenny drive the wagon to the barn, then he turned, entered the house, and went directly to his room and closed the door behind him. He stood leaning against it and buried his face in his hands as his large body shook with uncontrollable grief.

Jenny felt only bitterness, but she quelled it. She was going to fight all that was against her, no matter the difficulty. Grimly, she determined to keep her family and her land together if she had to kill to do it.

It was late afternoon, yet she had no desire to return to the house. Instead she saddled her horse and rode off toward a more solitary place where she could be alone for awhile. She had to think. She had to draw together her resources and her strength.

She rode easily, the sun glinting on her hair, and the

peacefulness and beauty of the scene before her slowly relaxed her taut body.

It was then that thoughts of him leapt into her mind and refused to leave. The aura of overpowering strength that had emanated from his hard, lean body had struck a responsive chord within her. She could vividly envision the intense smoke grey eyes that had first seemed warm, then puzzled. His dark bronze skin had made his white smile even whiter, and when he had reached for her she had noticed how large and strong his hands were. The thought of him touching her tingled through her for a moment before she cursed it away. He was the threat! He was the dark shadow that lingered too near to be tolerated.

Her horse followed a well-worn path along the wide river, the waters of which were exceptionally blue and clear. Just past the small town the river forked in two directions, one slow and the other rippling with rapids. Her father had been the first to call the latter the Roaring Fork and the valley had taken its name from that. It had a strong-flowing current, but it eddied into small, tree-covered coves.

Jenny arrived at the place she had called her own from childhood. She could remember all the troubled times that she had sought its comforting refuge. The water was deep, but still. There was a wide, grassy area that slanted down to it, and this was surrounded by low-hanging trees the branches of which nearly touched the ground. Here Jenny always found sanctuary.

It was beneath the branches of one particularly large tree that Jenny now sat. She had hobbled her horse some distance away, unsaddled him, and carried the saddle with her to rest upon.

She sat on the soft, grassy ground and leaned back against her saddle. For a long while she searched for answers, but the peace and contentment of her surroundings finally reached for her and she drifted off into fitful slumber.

Trace reached Graham land as the sun was nearing the horizon. He was giving this undertaking second thoughts. If he arrived after dark he might seem more of a threat than if he arrived by day. As usual, he made his decision quickly. He would make camp and go to the Graham ranch in the morning.

He had been riding very close to the river and decided to make its banks a place to camp. Besides, he was hot and tired, and a good swim would ease his body and relax him. Then he could eat, sleep, and be prepared for the confrontation the next day. With a slight movement of hand and body, he expertly turned his horse toward the river.

The soft ground of the riverbank silenced his horse's approach, and he did not notice the unsaddled horse that contentedly munched the sweet grass just around a slight curve in the river's bank.

He unsaddled his horse and cared for him, then he eyed the cool, inviting water. Quickly he removed his clothes and strode toward it. It was refreshing to the touch, and he sighed gratefully as he dove into it.

His splash awakened Jenny, who sat up abruptly and wondered what sound had roused her. She knew it had to have been something alien to her surroundings to startle her from sleep.

She rose very slowly, then gently, without a sound, she slid her rifle from the saddle and moved very cautiously through the trees toward the source of the noise she now heard. When she reached the edge of the trees, she brushed the low branches aside slightly to see what had created a disturbance in her Eden. The sight that held her eyes forced a startled gasp from her that was almost a moan.

The sun was just barely touching the horizon, glinting across the water and caressing Trace's skin, turning it gold in its light. He was waist deep in the water, but, to her horror, she saw that he was slowly walking toward the shore.

She couldn't move; no muscle seemed willing to respond. She could only gaze at him as he slowly materialized from the water like a god from a forgotten time.

His body gleamed in the light, bronzed and golden, the muscles sleek and exuding a virile strength.

She licked lips that seemed to have become very dry and tried to control the sudden racing of her heart and the pulse of its beat that sent a tingling message to all her senses.

She watched in rapt fascination as he shook his dark hair free of glinting silver drops of water, and she resisted the thought that it would be pleasant to run her fingers through its thick mass. Her startled eyes were aware of every inch of his body, so much so that she felt her breathing deepen and her body grow warm, as if some heated breeze had gently brushed it.

A sudden noise, probably made by one of the horses, caused Trace to lift his head and listen. He stood immobile and the wide-eyed woman who watched him was, for this forbidden moment, mesmerized by has masculine aura. He was man, primitive and wild, and something just as primitive stirred to life within her. It sang along every nerve in her body, drawing forth a touch of fiery desire that shook her to her core. It was only then that a small part of her mind screamed out a warning, a danger signal that caused her to gasp for breath and raise the rifle almost as if to defend herself.

As rapidly and as violently as the other emotions had

claimed her, fury replaced them. What was he doing here? she wondered. This representative of the railroad was trespassing on her land as arrogantly as if he already possessed it! Her fury grew to the point that she raised the rifle to her shoulder and sighted it, and again the same fury made her squeeze the trigger.

Trace was feeling exuberant. The swim had been invigorating, and he felt his blood stirring warmly. He reached for his pants, which lay across a rock just a foot or two from where he stood.

The bullet ricocheted off the rock and startled Trace so violently that he leapt back a step or two, then turned angry eyes toward the bullet's source.

He could not quite believe his eyes when the vision from his memory stepped from the trees, her rifle now aimed at a very vital part of his anatomy. He stood naked and defenseless, and both dilemmas made him as much angry as embarrassed. To be caught in this situation was unbelievable, he mused in annoyance, but . . . did he see the glint of laughter in her eyes? It was just a little too much. He decided to fight fire with fire, or laughter with laughter.

"Well, well," he chuckled gently, "I've really dreamed up a beauty this time. I'm afraid you have me at your mercy."

"Don't be so arrogant," Jenny snapped. "I might take a notion to shoot off something very useful to you."

"Oh, I wouldn't do that if I were you."

"Oh?"

"No . . . you look rather violent, and if you're planning rape"—he paused, then shrugged—"I'll do my best not to fight you too hard."

96

"You! . . . Damn you! How dare you trespass on my land, then talk to me like that?"

"I'm sorry. I just thought"—he grinned with a devilish gleam in his eyes—"that you chose this moment for some purpose. I'd hate to waste your efforts. I'm a very obliging man to a lady as beautiful as you. By the way, just how long have you been there?" The last words were said with the obvious suggestion that she had been watching him for some time.

Jenny could feel her cheeks redden and the warmth of his soft laugh did nothing to help. She was so angry now that her hands shook and she could barely speak.

"Put your pants on before I shoot you!" She fairly yelped in her fury.

"Oh," he said in a deeply disappointed voice, "and I had such hopes . . . I—"

"Shut up! I don't want to hear about your hopes. Get your pants on and get off my land, and don't ever set foot on it again."

Trace shrugged and reached again for his pants. He pulled them on, but, to her distress, his eyes never left hers. He saw her anger; he could read it clearly, but he sensed her awareness also. There was a sensitive woman behind those angry eyes and he was momentarily sorry for his crude words. He started to walk toward her and saw the rifle come up to point at his chest, yet he knew she would not shoot him.

"Stay where you are."

"But you told me to get off your land," he replied as he took a few more steps that brought his chest within inches of the rifle. He stopped and spoke gently. "I don't think you are capable of murdering an unarmed man."

"Don't count on it. You're nothing but trouble for me and my family. It would be better for us all if I just shot you and buried you here."

"Do you really believe that would end all your problems?"

"It's a good start."

"And from today on you'll just kill one man after another? You can't stop some things, Jenny Graham, and progress is one of them. The railroad will eventually go through, with or without me."

She had jerked in surprise at his use of her name.

"How did you know my name?"

"I asked about you. I'm Trace Cord," he said gently. There was enough sympathy in his voice to stir her resistance.

"I see," she said coldly. "And were you informed about my father too? Yes, I can see the answer in your eyes. If I ever catch you near him, I will truly find a way to see you dead. Why don't you find another valley— someone else's life to destroy?"

He could hear her cry of fear and pain as clearly as if she had put it into words, and he was suddenly overwhelmed by a desire to hold her in his arms and soothe away the pain and fear. She seemed like a lost little girl, and only by supreme effort did he control his urge to protect her from whatever frightened her.

"No one wants to destroy you or your family, Jenny. Why don't you at least talk to us, give us a chance to show you we're not the ogres you believe we are."

"What do you know or care about what you destroy? It's only your railroad that's important."

"I know a lot about destruction," he said gently, "maybe more than you do. Let me talk to you, Jenny . . . let me explain."

"Oh, you're so smooth." She laughed harshly. "Is that why they sent you, to sweet talk the ignorant rancher's daughter out of her inheritance?"

"That's not true."

"I don't care. Just go away. Stay off my land, or the next time I won't talk or let you go. I'll kill you."

Trace knew that in her present state there was no more point in arguing. He shrugged and went back for his shirt and boots.

But Jenny was to have the last word. Again a bullet sang so near his hand that he jerked it back. He spun around to look at her.

"Suppose," she smiled evilly, "you just go home without your boots and shirt. Maybe your railroad friends will get my point."

"Come on now!" he exploded angrily. But the next bullet sang too close for him. His anger sparked and he turned back toward her. Her eyes widened when he purposefully strode in her direction as if the rifle were no longer between them. She backed up a step just as his left hand gripped the rifle, tore it from her grasp, and tossed it several feet away.

With the other hand he gripped her arm and jerked her into the iron grip of hard-muscled arms. She found herself suddenly held against a chest that seemed massive. Her hands ineffectually pressed against rippling, taut muscle. His skin was warm and slightly damp to the touch, and she gazed up into angry grey eyes that promised no quarter. She was completely and utterly shaken by the tumultuous response of her own deceitful body.

"You," he said angrily, "need a little lesson in hospitality. Didn't anyone ever tell you that you shouldn't point a rifle at someone unless you intend to use it?"

"I fully intended to use it!" she snarled. "And I'm sorry I didn't."

The fire in her eyes could have burned him to a cinder, but it was her inviting lips that drew his attention—that and the warm curves that molded reluctantly against his body. His first unconscious thought was that she seemed to fit so well against him, as if they were two pieces of a puzzle put together. His anger gave way to another, much stronger, emotion.

"Let go of me!" she demanded.

"After I get an apology," he retorted, grinning irritatingly.

"Apologize! Never. You can go to hell!"

"I expect I will," he said with a laugh, "but I'm perfectly content to stay until you decide to adopt some manners." He tightened his arms about her to emphasize his words.

"You are an arrogant, overbearing, conceited . . ."

The words faded as he held her with one arm and slid his fingers into her hair, gripping it firmly. He drew her head back and her muffled yelp of fury was silenced by the hard mouth that took hers in an unrelenting, demanding kiss.

She struggled violently, but the struggle was as much against herself as it was against him. His lips played on hers like a master musician on a well-tuned instrument, eliciting a song that echoed through her being until she soared with the melody.

For Trace it began as a challenging game and he never realized just when his thoughts and body went astray. Soon he was only concentrating on the taste and the scent of her and the soft, sweet curves that seemed to be melting within him.

For that one shattering moment, both were lost in a magical world where nothing existed but the swelling sensual need that had taken possession of every sense each had. It ended in stillness as he released her and she stepped back from him. Neither could believe, or would believe, the powerful emotions their embrace had elicited.

Jenny's eyes were wide and filled with self-denial as

well as denial of him. This could not be happening! she thought. She could not, would not, allow it.

She struck sharply, leaving the print of her hand against his cheek, then whirled about and ran for the rifle before Trace could react. She grabbed it up and swung around, and at that moment Trace could not be sure she would not use it. For him the game had suddenly changed. Despite her efforts at control, he could see the desperate vulnerability in her eyes.

"Get out of here! Get off my land! I don't ever want to see you on it again, or I swear I'll kill you!" she screamed.

He would have given anything at that moment to have been able to hold her and tell her that he was no threat to her, but he knew she was beyond reasoning with now. He shook his head regretfully and turned to pull on his boots. The shirt he had dropped was wet and muddy. He picked it up gingerly and was startled again by the sharp crack of the rifle as the shirt seemed to leap from his hand.

"I shoot what I aim at," Jenny said coldly. Trace shrugged helplessly before he walked away. In only a few minutes she heard the sound of hoofbeats diminishing slowly.

The rifle slipped from Jenny's trembling hands. Her whole body suddenly seemed to be beyond her control as it remembered the wild need that had stirred her dormant emotions awake.

She wrapped her arms about herself as if they could be some kind of protection against an unseen threat. Her world was in a tremendous upheaval and she seemed to be losing control of everything. The shattering climax had been Trace's breaching of her fragile defenses. Damn him! she thought angrily. Did he think she would tumble into his arms, be seduced out of her land and her life so easily? Well, she wouldn't, she thought grimly. If he wanted a battle, he would have it. Her mind screamed a denial, though her body taunted her with the remembrance of a moment's flame that refused to be ignored. With a soft, anguished sound she returned to her horse, saddled him, and rode slowly home.

Trace rode slowly also, trying to sort out the tangle of emotions for which he had been totally unprepared. Several things stood out clearly in his mind. One was that somehow he had to see Jenny Graham again. The second was that he had to make sure she understood that the railroad meant her no harm, and, last and most important, he had to find out the truth about Jenny's father and Jenny's relationship with Taylor Jessup.

He rode several miles to put some distance between him and the Graham property. Then he made camp, prepared a small meal, and made himself comfortable. For a long time he sat in the silence of his thoughts and recalled a very sweet moment when, despite her battle, he had felt a fleeting instant of surrender, a surrender so consuming that it had left him breathless. It had also left him with a need so strong he could hardly believe it. He had to see her, hold her once again. He was determined to find a way—and soon.

He would go back now and make Maxwell understand that they were most certainly not welcome in the Roaring Fork Valley and that he had developed some very different feelings about Taylor Jessup.

## Chapter 7

Trace could very well understand the emotions that governed the valley. The inhabitants did not look favorably on the arrival of the railroad, and this posed a problem that would have to be handled carefully. He needed to talk to Maxwell so they could form some plan of negotiation, a plan that did not include Taylor Jessup. He was reasonably sure that Taylor was negotiating for himself and not for the valley's occupants.

He found the train crews several miles closer than when he had left, and he was welcomed back very enthusiastically by Allison.

"Oh Trace, I've missed you!" she cried as she ran to greet him at the door of their train car. "The next time you ride out of here you take me with you."

"Camping out is no fun for a lady," Trace told her with a laugh, but he was remembering a turquoise-eyed beauty who seemed quite at home in the wilderness.

"You leave me here again with that she-cat," Allison threatened, "and I certainly won't be a lady. Trace, have you any idea of what she's been up to? She's about as trustworthy as a—"

"Don't say it, Allison." Trace laughed outright now.

"And stop worrying about Eileen Starett."

Allison bounced down on her bed, her enthusiasm renewed by Trace's return. "Tell me what you've been doing. Who did you meet? Are there any social events in the town? Will we get a chance to go to any?"

"One question at a time is all I can handle. It seems like a nice, respectable town. I didn't meet anyone but the local banker. I don't have any idea about social events, but I expect if there is anything going on in the next few weeks you'll find out about it and stir up some way of getting there."

"It's time for a little fun too, Trace. It's so boring here."

"Well, don't look forward to much more entertainment along the way. We're here to do a job and not to have fun."

"Well," Allison pouted, "you and Eileen won't be bored, I'll bet."

"Allison, stop being a brat. I have to go—" Before Trace could continue, there was a knock on the door that sounded slightly frantic.

"Trace," a voice called from outside, "can you come out here? We got trouble."

"Damn," Trace groaned. He was tired from the ride back and had been looking forward to a few hours of rest before he talked to Maxwell. Trace strode to the door and jerked it open quickly. The man who stood outside had been one of the best men in any of Trace's crews. If he was upset, Trace knew there had to be a problem.

"What's the matter, Phillips?"

"We got a little problem. There're some new men signed on while you was gone. It seems their bein' here don't set too well with a few troublemakers."

"Why?"

"Best you come and see Trace. I think this is

something you should handle."

"Let's go."

It was just after dusk and campfire lights had begun to blossom about the length of newly laid rails. Dark, faceless shadows of men moved about them. Around one there seemed to be a much larger gathering, and the sound of angry male voices reached Trace and Phillips as they moved closer. It took Trace very little listening to tell what the disturbance was all about. Several men were involved in a pushing and shoving match, though at this point the argument seemed to be less physical than verbal.

Trace stepped into the area of firelight and raised his voice to be heard above the rumble of men's voices. "What's going on here?" he demanded.

Three men seemed to be the center core and they were surrounded by four or five others. They separated slowly as Trace approached. He could hear mutters and the words "damn rebels" came to him more than once.

The three men in the center appeared a little worse off than the others. With their hats drawn down over their eyes, they stood dejectedly, as if they expected the worst from the arrival of the boss.

"Slater, Maken, Tucker," Trace demanded, "just what's going on?"

"Nothin' much," the man called Slater responded. "Nothin' for Phillips to come runnin' to you for," he added as he glared at Phillips, who glared back.

"Damn you Slater," Phillips cursed. "Why don't you tell the truth? You and your mates have been roughing up these men for the past two days."

"Why, Slater?" Trace interjected. "What are they doing wrong? Are they breaking any of Maxwell's rules?"

"No sir, Trace," Phillips added quickly. "They're

rebels, that's what's got under Slater's skin."

"Damn you, Phillips. Shut your mouth!" Slater snarled. The fact that Trace was a rebel made the situation precarious for Slater and he knew it.

Trace had been aware of anti-rebel sentiments from the moment of his arrival, but he had handled the situation carefully. Now it was explosive again. He looked closely at the three newcomers. "Who are you?" he questioned.

One man had been studying Trace closely. Now he raised his head and spoke in a slow drawl. "Now y'all just have to look close and yuh might remember, if railroading for the Yankees hasn't affected your vision."

Trace leaned closer as the other two men also lifted their heads. It took him only a moment to recognize first the voice, then the faces of men he had known for years.

"Will? Will Bracken?" Trace grinned. A face from home was a more than welcome sight.

"Sure is." Will grinned in response.

"And Jamie Bond, is that you?"

"Yessir, me and Joey Mason."

Trace extended his hand to all three and they responded with relief and strong handshakes. "Lord, it's good to see y'all," Trace said with a laugh. "I never expected to see a face from home out here. You're sure a welcome sight."

"Can't say you're not a welcome sight either," Will said pointedly, his dark eyes swinging toward a glowering Slater. "Looks kinda like the war isn't over yet."

Trace was well aware of the building tension. He needed his crews working at their best, and he valued the friendship of the three childhood companions who stood before him. He turned toward the circle of men.

It took only a moment for him to realize that Slater was the prime force behind this confrontation.

"Slater, we have a job to do here, and there's no room for past problems. There're no Yankees or Rebels here. There're just men who have to work together to get a job done." Trace knew Slater would have to be soothed in some way that wouldn't interfere with his pride; otherwise Trace would have a real problem on his hands. "Your crew has to be on the job at sunrise. Why don't you break this up for now. Besides, I'd like to talk to you about the change in direction for tomorrow's tracks. I've been looking it over and I'd like your opinion before we get started."

Trace was relieved when Slater nodded. It took Slater no time to snap orders that sent the men back to their own fires. Trace turned to Will. "I'd like to talk to you too, Will. Come on over and say hello to Allison before you bed down."

"All right, Trace. Be kind of nice to see her again too."

Trace and Slater walked away some distance and stood talking.

"Trace hasn't changed much." Joey laughed. "He can still give orders and get 'em obeyed with no trouble."

"He's a born leader," Will agreed. "Always was. You two coming over with me?"

"To see Allison's pretty face again?" Jamie grinned. "You bet. This camp isn't the sweetest place to be, and there sure aren't many pretty faces to look at."

The three walked toward Trace's car and many eyes followed. Most were just inquisitive, but a few were filled with the brooding tension that bad memories sometimes retain.

Allison was totally surprised but excited and pleased to see old neighbors and friends.

"Why Will Bracken!" she exclaimed enthusiastically. "And Joey and Jamie! How wonderful to see you. I didn't know you were here. Why didn't you come to see me before this?"

All three men were slightly embarrassed, but Will voiced their thoughts in a soft-spoken drawl.

"We just didn't want to make any problems for you, Allison. We figured we'd wait until Trace got back. That way"—he shrugged—"if he didn't want us hanging around, we wouldn't make any trouble."

Allison's eyes clouded with quick anger. "How can you talk like that! Why, how could you believe Trace would forget friends?"

"Allison," Will said defensively, "we just thought it might be hard on Trace. We're not saying Trace wouldn't welcome us."

At that moment Trace entered the car.

"Of course you're welcome."

"So Allison says." Will grinned.

"Break out a bottle from the cupboard, Allison, and pour some drinks. We need to celebrate. It will be wonderful to talk about home again."

Allison complied quickly and, amid laughter and warm conversation, old memories and old ways were relived. It was several hours later that Allison went to bed and Trace walked a short way with his three friends. Joey and Jamie went on to camp, while Trace and Will stood together for a few last words. It was then that Trace asked the question that had been on his mind all evening. He had been afraid of the answer.

"Will . . . Joey and Jamie . . . I can see why they're here. They're both free. But . . . well, you had a pretty good farm when you left . . . and . . . Kathleen and your son . . . ?"

"They're dead, Trace," Will answered softly.

"Dead . . . Yankees?"

"No . . . funny, isn't it?" Will laughed harshly. "It was renegades . . . our own who came to prey when everyone was helpless. They . . . they killed Kathy and the boy and burned the house. I couldn't rebuild and I just couldn't stay there. I had to get away. The memories hurt too much."

"I'm sorry, Will."

"So am I, Trace, for the whole damn war. But it's over, and I've got to make a new start somewhere. I'm just glad to find a friend from home. It makes it a little easier."

"So you'll go with the railroad to Sacramento. What then? Will you stay with it?"

"No, I don't think so. I think I'll plant myself in California and see what I can do."

"You were a damn good farmer, Will."

"Yeah . . . well, I guess for awhile I have to be something else. I'm saving my pay. Maybe I'll find a piece of land out there. Trace, are you staying with the railroad?"

"No." Trace went on to explain his agreement with Maxwell. "When I get enough money to get Fallen Oaks on its feet, I'll go home."

"What about Michael? Is he staying there to keep things going? If he is, you should have left Allison with him. This is a dangerous place for a girl like her."

"Michael . . ." Trace repeated softly. Will felt the sudden touch of pain and regretted his question.

"I'm sorry, Trace."

"I don't believe he's dead, Will. Neither does Allison. He was reported missing and presumed dead. Until they're sure—until I'm sure—I'll never believe it. I keep expecting him to show up one day as if nothing ever happened."

"Be like him to do that. Well, morning comes early. I guess I better get some sleep. Thanks, Trace."

"For what?"

"Oh, I guess just for being a friend. They're hard for a Rebel to find in these parts."

Trace laughed with him. "Good night, Will."

"'Night."

Will walked away, vanishing into the dark, and Trace stood with unseeing eyes, remembering a time that was forever dead. Then he returned to the train for a restless night of sleep.

Dawn found him awake and at Maxwell's door. It was Maxwell who let him in. Trace had not expected to see Eileen, for it was her usual habit to sleep late into the day.

Maxwell was already dressed and eating his breakfast, which was being served by a small-statured Oriental named Lee Chu.

"Sit down and eat, Trace," Maxwell said.

"I've already eaten. I'll take some coffee though."

"Lee Chu!"

Lee Chu's head appeared in the doorway and Maxwell laughed at the pleasant little man's questioning eyes, then requested that he bring Trace coffee.

"Yes, Mista Maxwell, I bling Mista Tlace flesh coffee pletty quick."

"Good. Sit down, Trace. Tell me what you found in Roaring Fork Valley. How is the situation out there?"

"Well, I can tell you there's going to be a problem."

"Why?"

"The town wants the railroad because it will bring business, but the ranchers in the valley don't want it crossing their land. I think they're going to fight you every inch of the way and I don't think they'll be afraid to pick up guns if they have to."

"But Taylor told me—"

"Taylor Jessup is another thing. I've got a hunch he's not working to help you but to help Taylor Jessup. I have a feeling he intends to make a big profit out of this somehow, and I don't think he cares which side he makes it from."

"How can he expect to make a profit other than interest for the bank? He doesn't own any of the land himself."

"Not yet, he doesn't."

"Do you think if these ranchers don't want the railroad, they'd be foolish enough to sell to the banker who's so friendly to us?"

"That's what worries me—just how he's going to do it and if the railroad is going to end up paying the price, both in money and in hatred."

"Well, Trace, what are you suggesting?"

"Let me go talk to the ranchers."

"If they don't want the railroad, you sure won't be welcome."

"It's better that I try and we find out for sure rather than let Jessup handle it and make us the villains. We might as well try to carry a little good favor rather than hand everything to Jessup."

"Maybe you're right," Maxwell mused. He remained in silent thought while Lee Chu served Trace his coffee. Maxwell's eyes glittered with humor as he turned to Lee Chu.

"What do you think, Lee Chu? You always have your ear to the ground and you seem to know what's going on all the time and everywhere."

Maxwell's tone carried more than amusement. He respected both Lee Chu's talent for knowing what was going on about him and his innate ability to use common sense to find the answers.

"Mista Maxwell, you send Tlace pletty quick. No tlust Mista Jessup. He make for him. He no make for

111

you. Mista Tlace, he tell tluth. If you fight, railroad lose, then evlibody hurt. If you don't fight, just talk, evlibody win. You send Mista Tlace."

He said it so firmly that both men laughed.

"All right, Trace, I guess you go. But walk easy. I don't want to antagonize anyone. Just keep this in mind, Trace: I've got to have this valley."

Before Trace could answer, Eileen's voice came from the doorway of her small room. "Why don't you simply offer them more money, Uncle Max?"

"There're times, Eileen," Trace answered, "that it isn't the money that makes the difference. These people love their land."

"Oh pooh, Trace." She laughed softly. "Everybody has a price. All you have to do is find out what it is. There's no one alive who can't be bought if the offer is right."

Trace suspected the possibility that Eileen included him in this mercenary way of thinking. He wondered if Eileen might feel she had already bought and paid for him. The idea irritated him and, as he watched Eileen approach, he noticed for the first time that there was a cold and calculating look about her. Mentally he found himself comparing her with the turquoise-eyed beauty he had held so briefly. There had been a gentleness, a vulnerability about Jenny, even though she had fought him with such bitter anger. He had to admit the truth to himself—that it was the thought of seeing her again that had prompted his suggestion to Maxwell.

"I don't think that's true, Eileen. I think there are some things that just can't be bought, just as there are some people who don't have a price attached to their honor."

"You're going to find out you're wrong, Trace," Eileen said coolly, "and you're going to find that the best thing to do when you want something is to go out

112

and take it."

"It isn't always that easy. Besides, we just can't come in here and take what we want."

"Well now"—she laughed softly—"I think Uncle Max will tell you different."

"Maxwell?" Trace questioned.

"Now don't get excited, Trace. I don't intend to make any trouble. I want to do this the easy way. But there's a law that will give us the right-of-way we need. Some of the bigger railroads are amassing large amounts of land that way."

"There will be one hell of a war out here if you try that. These people have put a lot into their land. They've fought for it. I know how hard it would be if they lost it. We have other choices."

Trace could remember well the fear and anguish he had felt at the thought that he might lose Fallen Oaks. He sincerely felt if he could talk to the ranchers he would be able to negotiate a fair bargain for both sides. Subconsciously, he was looking forward to negotiating with Jenny Graham. Once she understood that they meant to take nothing from her and she became more reasonable, he could begin negotiations on a much more important level—for himself.

"Maxwell, let me talk to them. We can find some neutral ground to agree on."

Maxwell's eyes narrowed shrewdly and he smiled. "Trace, you sure sound certain to me. Kind of like you might have run across one or two of them already. Is that what gives you the idea you could make some headway dealing with them?"

"I . . . ah . . . had a little run-in with one," he admitted reluctantly.

"A run-in?"

It was with obvious annoyance at himself for even bringing up the matter that Trace reluctantly explained his confrontation with Jenny Graham, though he did not include the detail of his state of undress.

"So . . . this Jenny Graham, she owns some of the land we want?"

Trace was unaware that Eileen was listening closely.

"Her father does. I asked a few questions about her . . . them. It seems there's just the three of them. They raise horses and seem to be doing all right."

Eileen decided immediately that Jenny Graham would bear some looking into. She had plans for her future and they included Trace. She was not about to let them be jeopardized by some ignorant horse rancher's daughter.

"Well," Maxwell said thoughtfully, "maybe it would be best if you tried your hand, Trace. You can go talk to Taylor first. See if you can feel out just what he's doing. Then go on out and talk to the Grahams and the others. Maybe you're right. Maybe we can make a deal of our own that will keep everybody happy."

Trace was quite pleased and the look in his eyes made Eileen wonder if it was the challenge of the job he had to do or the thought of seeing Jenny Graham again that seemed to make him so happy.

"I'm going today," Trace announced as he rose to leave. "Slater can keep the crews moving until I get back."

"Fine," Maxwell replied. "Make me a good deal, Trace. Get me a right-of-way through that valley and there's a bonus in it for you."

"I'll do the best I can."

"I'm sure you will."

As Trace turned to leave, Eileen spoke his name softly. He turned questioning eyes to her. It had been some time since they had been together and Eileen wanted to renew the hold she felt she had on him. What she did not know yet was that Trace's whole train of

114

thought was tied to a turquoise-eyed beauty and his main goal was to find a way to Jenny. Eileen had no idea that the tentative hold she had had on Trace had totally disintegrated and that he had not even thought of her for days.

He raised a quizzical eyebrow now and she answered in a soft, purring voice, "I'll walk out with you, Trace. I'd like to talk to you."

He shrugged slightly and held the door open for her to precede him, but his mind no longer focused on the seductive sway of her hips or the way she brushed against him as she passed him.

Once outside, they walked side by side. Eileen linked her arm in Trace's and pressed against him. "Trace, why is it necessary for you to go to see these people? Uncle Max has Mr. Jessup to do this kind of thing." She looked up at him, warm invitation in her eyes. "Besides, you are needed more around here . . . by everyone. Why don't you just stay here and let someone else do these . . . these dirty little jobs."

"Dirty little jobs?"

"Well, really Trace, how important are they? There's no doubt we will get the right-of-way, no matter what they think. Why go to the bother of trying to pacify these ignorant horse ranchers and farmers?"

"What you're saying is we should just go in and take what we want, no matter how they feel about it?"

"After all, it's to their benefit in the long run."

"I wonder," Trace mused, "if that's what Sherman said when he started into Georgia."

"What?"

"Nothing. I was just thinking of how much you had in common with a Major General I knew of during the war. You seem to have the same attitude about getting what you want."

She laughed softly, unaware that what he had said

115

was much more an insult than the compliment she had thought it to be.

"Trace?"

"What?"

"This Jenny Graham . . . is she pretty?"

Although Trace kept his face impassive, Eileen could see the tensing of his muscles and noted the slight hesitation before he answered.

"Yes, I guess you'd say she was pretty. But that's not important, is it? It's a right-of-way we're after, not a social contact."

"It's not important to me," she said with a forced laugh, "as long as it's not important to you."

"What's important to me is getting this railroad on its way so that I can go home and get on with my life at Fallen Oaks."

Trace said a quick good-bye to Eileen, mounted his horse, and rode away, unaware that Eileen's darkening blue eyes watched his retreating figure until it vanished from sight.

"We shall soon see just who and what this Jenny Graham is . . . and just how much it will take to get her out of my way. Maybe . . . she just needs to be convinced . . . firmly."

Eileen turned back to camp to search out Poe Wilson and send him on his way with instructions to seek out the information she wanted.

Trace rode slowly, a new excitement beginning to grow within him. No matter how difficult a battle it might be, he intended to see Jenny Graham again. The thought of it brought remembrance of a sweet moment, a moment he had felt surrender and a moment he intended to relive, no matter the cost.

## Chapter 8

Taylor Jessup rode relaxed and easy. He was usually a self-assured man and felt even more so today. The railroad—his first step toward immense wealth and power—was near. Now he was beginning to put all his well-laid plans into motion.

He smiled to himself, satisfied with the developments that had already taken place. He was about to move another pawn in his game, and the excitement and challenge filled him with a now familiar pleasure. The game of wealth and power was indeed a heady one, and he was thoroughly intoxicated by it.

He chuckled softly at the thought of the lives and land he would soon be holding in his hand. He had no sympathy for those with whom he dealt, nor did he feel one pang of guilt that he was about to rob them. The world and its possessions were destined to go to the strong, and ones who could take what they wanted and hold it. And he was one of these, without the scruples of the weak, who did not deserve what they were too timid to fight for.

He drew his horse to a halt and looked at the small ranch house that sat nestled against the foot of a large, tree-covered hill. It belonged to Joanne Carter. A fine wisp of grey-white smoke rose from the chimney to tell him that Joanne was busy in her kitchen, probably preparing food for her daughter, Georgina. He despised Georgina. She was a nuisance to him and a constant interference in his attempts to win her mother's trust. Again he smiled to himself, for of course he had not always allowed her presence to inhibit his deft seduction of Joanne.

Joanne Carter had been lonely and afraid after her husband had been killed. Taylor had had no compunction about moving into the void before Joanne could gather herself together. Now, he thought with satisfaction, her faith in him was complete and she would do whatever he told her. He patted the sheaf of folded papers in his breast pocket, sure that within a few days he would have what he had set out to get and be done with Joanne and her troublesome brat.

He urged his horse forward and rode down to the house. After dismounting and tying his horse to the rail in front of the dwelling, he walked up the four steps to the door and knocked.

The door was opened by Georgina, whose smile faded when she saw who stood on the porch. Taylor gladly would have slapped the closed look from her face.

"Good morning, Mr. Jessup," she said, but he knew quite well that it was good manners and not her pleasure at seeing him that put a welcoming tone in the phrase.

She was small for her age, which was just under ten, and her body was as slim as a reed. Her eyes were wide and dark blue, fringed by thick, dark lashes. Her raven-dark hair was parted in the center and hung in two wrist-thick braids.

"Good morning, Georgina," he returned with a tight smile, trying to hide his dislike. But Georgina, with an instinctive sense of which only children seem capable, was aware of something about this man that was dark and frightening, though she was still too young to put words to what she felt deep within.

"I'd like to talk to your mother," he said firmly.

"Come in. Mama's baking bread." She stood aside and let him enter.

"How domestic," he muttered to himself.

Joanne turned from her oven, where she had just placed loaves of bread. Her face was flushed with the heat and she smiled at Taylor.

Joanne was still a very pretty woman. Her body, slim from hard work, had retained its softly rounded curves. Her dark hair had been coiled atop her head to keep it out of her way, but Taylor had felt the soft weight of it in his hand and knew its sweet scent and texture. Her blue eyes were warm and glowing with trust as she walked toward him.

"Good morning, Taylor. What brings you out here so early?"

"I'd like to talk to you for a minute, Joanne. It's business . . . I'd like to do it in private if you don't mind."

Joanne turned to Georgina, whose eyes had never left Taylor. She stood quietly, but Taylor could feel her distrust. It annoyed him that he had been so successful with Joanne, but had not been able to reach past the barriers Georgina had raised.

"Georgina," Joanne said softly, "go finish the beds and the lessons for today. After lunch we'll go for a ride, all right?"

"Yes, Mama," Georgina replied. Even she could not understand why she felt her mother was in some kind of danger from this tall, too handsome, too smiling man. Reluctantly she left the room, closing the door to the bedroom quietly behind her.

119

Taylor immediately reached for Joanne, drawing her firmly into his arms and kissing her with a rough and demanding kiss that left her weak and clinging to him.

Joanne had been deeply in love with her husband, Jim, and he had loved her completely. His death had left her with such an aching emptiness that she had fallen easy prey to Taylor's expert lovemaking. If, at times, it had left her unfulfilled and incomplete, and if, at times, it had been more violence than love, she had tried to make herself believe that the perfect love she and Jim had shared had been a once-in-a-lifetime thing and could never happen again. She would have to settle for less. But at least, she thought, marriage to Taylor would secure her future and, most important, Georgina's.

Joanne was aware that Georgina did not really care much for Taylor, but she felt, in time, when their lives were easier and safer, Georgina would relent. She kept to herself the quiet desperation and blackness that sometimes threatened to overcome her, and with it the thought that if Taylor married her she would be able to keep the darkness away from the child she loved so much.

Taylor's hands caressed her warm curves with ardent familiarity. He was silently wishing Georgina were not in the next room so he could rid himself of the barriers of clothing and possess her slim body as he had only a few nights before.

"I've missed you," he whispered raggedly against the soft flesh of her throat. She moaned softly under his explosive attack upon her senses, then moved away from him slightly before abandoning her wits completely.

Taylor was quite satisfied. He had her exactly where he wanted her. Now was the time to achieve what he had been working for from the first time he had come

120

to see her several months earlier. He had seduced her coldly and deliberately, understanding full well her vulnerability and her loneliness.

He sat down at the table and smiled at her as if he were somewhat hurt that she had moved out of his arms and felt bereft without her. Joanne's gentle heart interpreted his look as warm and loving, and she barred entrance to the thought that he would have taken her, even with her child in the next room, if he had had the chance.

"Joanne, I have to talk to you," he said as he slid the papers from his pocket and laid them on the table.

"Of course, Taylor. Do you want some coffee?"

"Yes, please."

He watched her as she lifted the pot from the fireplace and poured a cup. Her body was brushed lightly by the glow of the fire and he felt his loins tighten. He silently vowed he would return that night. He had been too long without her and was anxious to taste her warm and willing love again.

"Come and sit down, my dear," he ordered gently. Obediently Joanne sat across from him. "Joanne," he began, "you know I will always work in your interest." She nodded and he reached to take her hand, noting with distaste the calluses from the hard work of running the ranch. "The railroad wants the right-of-way across your land. They will most likely send a lot of glib-tongued lawyers to confuse you and try to take your property with very little profit for you."

"But I can't sell my land! It's all I have. It's all Jim could leave Georgina and me."

"I know that, my love, and I want to protect both of you. You trust me, don't you?"

"Taylor, you have been very kind to Georgina and me. Just giving me all this time to pay the bank what Jim owed has shown me your patience and understanding. What must I do?"

He could have shouted with joy. By the time she had fully realized that she had given him the land, the profit would be his.

"You must sign these papers. It will look to the railroad as if you have sold your land to me, but in truth I will just hold it so I can negotiate with them and get you their best offer. After that, I will return it and you and Georgina will be comfortable enough so that the ranch will be safe and Georgina can get a good education, as Jim wanted." He squeezed her hand reassuringly and smiled warmly. "I want to do all I can for you, my sweet. I can bargain with the best of them. . . . Be assured I will give you all I feel you deserve," he added smoothly, allowing her all the misunderstanding he saw in her eyes.

Now he moved smoothly to ease any thoughts of resistance she might have. "I will leave the papers here and you can sign at your convenience." He drew her hand to his lips and kissed the palm lightly, then her wrist. "May I come back later tonight to get the papers . . . and to thank you for your love and your trust?" he added in a seductive whisper.

She was caught in his spell and her eyes warmed as she smiled and nodded. Taylor stood and drew her into his arms. His lips claimed hers in a passionate kiss that wiped all reason from her mind and left her trembling in the heat of his sensual attack.


Georgina stood just inside her bedroom door. Her wide blue eyes were moist with angry and frustrated tears. Her little heart held all the hatred it could bear. The smooth and smiling man in the next room seemed to her a black force that stood between her and her mother. She could never put into words her reason for distrusting and disliking Taylor Jessup. She only knew that when he was near, her mother was different and she could feel the frightening loss. Georgina had worshiped her father. When he had been alive, it had been warm and happy in their house. She could remember his laughter and the bear hugs and the way he had tossed her giggling into the air, only to catch her to him and kiss her. She remembered the way he had made her feel, as if she were a vital part of him and her mother. He had always included her in everything. Now this cold man came and always forced her away and locked her out of the moments he shared with her mother. Georgina did not understand him; she only knew he was a threat and that she hated him more every time he came.

Now she listened to their whispered words and her mother's soft, trusting laugh, and she could not bear it.

She went to the chest of drawers and drew out her riding pants. After dressing quickly, she ran to her window, pushed it open, and climbed out. It was an escape she had made often, whenever she had wanted to be alone. She ran to the barn and saddled her pony. Then she mounted and rode away, trying to outrun the strange feeling of fear and impending disaster that pursued her.

She rode until both she and her pony were tired. Then she stopped by the side of a small clump of trees hovering near a shallow creek. Sitting by the creek, she summoned memories of her father until tears stung her eyes and she was overcome with what was to her a nameless agony. Throwing herself down onto her stomach, she buried her face in her folded arms and wept. She cried until no more tears would come, until her body was racked by dry sobs. It was then that a gentle voice spoke.

"What's the matter, little one? Little girls shouldn't

have anything to cry so hard over. Do you need some help?"

Georgina jerked her head up and through her tears she looked into the kindest and gentlest eyes she had ever seen.

Taylor left the Carter ranch as soon as he could and headed in the direction of the Graham holdings. His first step having been accomplished, he would now begin to maneuver the second.

It was quite a distance between the two ranches, and Taylor was unaware that he was slowly riding a trail parallel to Trace Cord's, who was headed toward the same destination, though with a completely different intent.

Taylor arrived less than an hour before Trace and was quite pleased to find Jenny, not only alone, but seated on the front steps of the porch watching the slow descent of the late afternoon sun.

He knew she had spotted his approach at some distance, and he was slightly annoyed that she gave no indication that she was pleased by his arrival. Taylor had found the hearts and the beds of many of the women in the area, but the one he truly wanted, the one he would have made his wife and given all she could want, remained resistant to his advances. He knew he had one overwhelming advantage, the fact of her father's very large debt to him. He wanted her willing in his bed, but if he were forced he would use this leverage, for he was determined to have her as his wife no matter how he had to do it. After they were married, he would find the time and patience to teach her to be obedient to his will. In fact, he rather savored the thought of teaching her to bend to his desire.

He rode up to the porch, dismounted, and walked up

the steps to sit beside her. "Good afternoon, Jenny. It's a beautiful day, isn't it?"

"Yes, it is."

"Where is everyone?" he asked, hoping they were well away from the ranch. He was quite pleased with her answer.

"They're out with the horses Buck and Stu have caught. Pa wanted to look them over."

Taylor tried to look disappointed, but within his heart leapt. There was no way the men would be home before morning. Somewhere inside an insistent voice whispered to him that if he played his cards right he just might share Jenny's bed this night. All thoughts of returning to Joanne were forgotten.

He was stricken by a violent surge of raw desire so intense that for a moment he could not speak. He felt the heat of her in his blood and his hands had to be clenched to keep from reaching for her.

"That's too bad. I wanted to talk some business with your father."

"Is it important? We could ride out to the holding pens."

"No, no, there's no need for that. I can talk to him tomorrow. It's about the railroad." He added the last words deliberately to observe her reaction and was quite satisfied when he saw her cheeks flush with anger, her mouth grow thin, and her lips firmly press together.

"They have a lot of smooth-tongued experts coming in to work on the ranchers."

"It will take much more than that," Jenny said grimly. "We're not foolish little children to give up our land and lives so easily."

"Jenny . . . don't misunderstand what I'm about to say. I know you won't want to sell or give up what you have here . . . but . . . what about your father?"

Jenny suddenly became very still, then she lifted her

125

turquoise eyes to Taylor and he could see the insecurity in them.

"My father," she said, trying to keep her voice even and deliberate. "My father loves this land as much as Buck and I do."

"Of course he does . . . but is he always aware of what he's doing?"

"Taylor . . . I . . ."

"I know, Jenny," he said gently. He reached out and took her hand, holding it gently between the two of his. "Jenny, I want to help you. You are too sweet and good to have to put up with all this. Jenny, together we could handle anything or anyone the railroad might throw at us. I could protect you, Jenny. I—"

"Taylor . . ." Jenny tried to draw her hand from his, but he pulled her to him. She pressed her hands against his chest. But this time he meant to kiss her. He wanted to taste the sweet, quivering lips so very near his. Slowly he bent his head, but before their lips could touch, the sound of an approaching horse interrupted. Both turned to look at the lone rider. It only took a moment for each to recognize Trace Cord. Both were startled, then both reacted. At first Taylor was too angry at the interruption to realize that Jenny was trembling like a leaf in a hurricane and that her wide turquoise eyes were frozen on the tall man who drew his horse to a stop before them.

"Good afternoon." Trace grinned. His eyes lit with humor. He was quite pleased to have interrupted what had looked like a cozy scene. "I'm not interrupting anything . . . important, am I?"

Jenny quickly moved away from Taylor, her cheeks aflame at Trace's innuendo, and anger lit her eyes with a glow that held Trace's rapt attention. He felt he had never seen any woman quite so beautiful. It also conjured up a devil within him that urged him to rid

126

himself of Taylor as soon as possible. He could see Taylor's obvious irritation and wondered just how far he could push him. He grinned again, a smile that set Taylor's teeth on edge.

"Jenny, this is one of the railroad men I've been telling you about," Taylor said coldly.

"Oh, is that what you were doing?" he asked innocently. Jenny uttered a muffled though angry protest at his insulting implication. "But"—Trace chuckled evilly—"you don't have to introduce Jenny and me. We've already met. It was a very pleasant meeting, for me at least. By the way, Jenny," Trace asked, his smoky grey eyes again alive with mischief, "do you have that shirt I left down by the river when I was with you the other day? I'm afraid I was so . . . involved . . . I forgot it."

Jenny gasped at the obvious assumption that leapt into Taylor's eyes as he turned toward her. Now her anger at both men had reached a boiling point, Trace for his evil suggestion and Taylor for obviously believing it.

Her rage was cold and so were her words. "Taylor, please leave. I'll do my own negotiating with the railroad." She turned her frosty gaze to Trace, who smiled in innocent warmth that raised her fury another notch.

"I've no intention of leaving you with this man," Taylor protested. "You know why he is here. I can deal with him better—"

He had no opportunity to finish. A furious Jenny turned her anger on him.

"I don't need your arrogance or your interference to take care of me! I can take care of myself! Be so kind as to let me handle my own affairs. Leave my property right now, Taylor. I assure you I am not in any danger from Mr. Cord. I can tell you that Mr. Cord will also be leaving, just as soon as I convince him that neither he nor his railroad are welcome in this valley, or in this house. I," she said in a cold, clipped tone, "can handle Mr. Cord and his arrogant, conceited attitude."

There was nothing more that Taylor could do without jeopardizing all that he wanted. He would tend to Trace Cord later, and he would be sure to make Jenny pay for her attitude one day soon, when she was his and knew it.

Taylor mounted his horse and his cold stare could have killed Trace had it been a weapon. He rode slowly away.

Now Jenny turned her eyes to Trace, who calmly dismounted and walked to her side. He looked in the direction Taylor had taken, then back to Jenny, his grey eyes filled with innocence.

"I do hope I haven't interrupted anything . . . important."

"You are the most insufferable, arrogant bastard!" Jenny raged.

"Jenny"—Trace chuckled—"I thought I gave you a lesson in manners before. Didn't anyone ever teach you it's not nice for a lady to talk like that?"

"How dare you make him think . . ."

"Think what?" he asked. "Is the man evil minded? I only said I forgot my shirt."

"Damn you! He thought we were . . ."

"Were what?" he said gently, his eyes holding hers. The realization came to her that he was a danger that was intoxicatingly close, along with the fact that in her anger she had sent Taylor away and now found herself alone with the one person with whom she should not be alone, the only man who had ever breached her defenses and had found the vulnerable woman within.

"What are you doing here?" she demanded. "I

128

thought I warned you about trespassing on our land again."

"I've come out to talk to your father. Jenny, the railroad is not here to rob you. I just want to talk to you and your family."

"It's impossible. There's nothing to discuss."

"Don't you think you're being a little unfair? Doesn't your father have anything to say about it?"

"Leave my father alone. Go away!" she cried, and very suddenly Trace could see beyond the defiance and anger and again he realized that she was afraid of something, only now he was not sure what. At the river she had seemed quite capable of handling anything or anyone. But now, now he could see she was trembling and that her cheeks were heated. Her eyes were wary and insecure. To him, she suddenly seemed like a bereft child desperately in need of strength and support.

"Jenny, I'm sorry," he said gently. "We got started on the wrong foot. I never wanted to cause you any problems. Can I stay just for a few minutes? We can talk about anything you want"—he raised one devilish brow and grinned boyishly—"even your late friend, Mr. Jessup, although there are a lot more interesting things I'd rather talk about. But maybe you need to talk about Mr. Jessup. There are several thoughts I have on that subject that might interest you."

"I don't care to discuss Taylor with you, and I'm quite sure your remarks would be less than the truth. Taylor was the first to warn us of your coming here and your attempt to grab our land."

"I'll bet he was," Trace replied grimly, "but I'm not too sure of his motives. Maybe you ought to look into them yourself."

"Judging everyone's motives by your own, Mr. Cord?" Jenny replied.

"I'm not judging anybody. But you are. You tried and convicted me before I even had an opportunity to defend myself. Do you think that's fair . . . or honest? Why can't we have a cup of coffee and talk? Maybe we can gain a better understanding . . . of both sides. It's been a long ride, Jenny," he coaxed. "I'm a man who's dying of thirst. Now tell me, do you have the heart to throw me out into the wilderness when I'm in that condition? Don't you have any sympathy at all?"

Despite her wariness and anger, Jenny was forced to respond to his pleading smile. Something within her stirred to life and, despite her efforts to stifle it, it urged her to listen to him. She was not sure why, but something in his laughing grey eyes held her captive and she found herself agreeing to the few minutes he wanted.

"I don't think I can trust you, Mr. Cord."

"You might begin by calling me Trace and letting us call a truce for a few minutes. I promise not to cause you any problems."

"Just your being here is a problem."

"You're jumping to conclusions like you did at the river. You're seeing a danger in me that isn't there." Again he grinned. "I haven't eaten since this morning. If you have a little something to go with the coffee, I swear I'll be as gentle as a lamb."

"All right," she agreed. "Some food and some coffee . . . and then you leave."

"If that's what you want."

"That's what I want. I agree to listen, and you agree to listen. Then you'll understand why the idea of your right-of-way is impossible."

She moved ahead of him to the door and he followed, enjoying the enticing sway of her hips, his mind much more involved in being with her than in anything she might have to say. He knew for certain

130

that Jenny was the most exciting woman he had ever known and he had no intention of leaving until he found some way to breach her defenses and touch the real, sensitive Jenny he knew existed beneath her deceptively cool surface.

He could still taste the softness of her lips and feel her vibrant, soft body in his arms. He knew he would never forget the moment they had touched. In fact, he had to control the memory, but it lingered just below the surface of his thoughts, waiting, hoping, for its repetition.

## Chapter 9

Trace could feel the comfort and warmth of the house as soon as he closed the door behind him. It brushed against his memory with unseen fingers and brought pictures to his mind that he had carefully stored away. He remembered childhood hours in vivid scenes and flashes of pictures of warm summer days at Fallen Oaks when his mother had supervised the large dinners that he could still taste.

The room he had entered was obviously the center of family life, for it had a comfortable, lived-in look. It was large, dominated by a rough stone fireplace with a huge stone slab for a mantel piece upon which sat several photographs and other memorabilia. The pieces of furniture were large, comfortable looking, and obviously handmade. The room was rough and rugged but it looked as if it were well used. It consisted of two large couches in front of the fireplace, a large desk and chair in one corner, and two rough-hewn but inviting-looking rocking chairs. From this room he could see into the kitchen, which was bright and clean and from which came the inviting scent of food being cooked.

Two closed doors at the far end of the room and

another on the opposite side suggested bedrooms. He pushed their close proximity from his mind, for this brought thoughts of him and Jenny of which he was sure she would not approve.

Jenny was already entering the kitchen, so he crossed the room and joined her.

"Dinner will be ready in a few minutes," she told him. "If you'd care to wash up, there's water in the pitcher." She pointed to a small mirrored stand in the corner that held a pitcher and bowl. "There's a towel on the shelf." With grim determination Jenny kept her voice cool and reserved, and Trace never knew that her pulses beat a rapid tattoo and that she felt a strange, magnetic pull that left her shaken, though she vowed to battle its effect on her senses.

Trace moved to the far end of the room. He washed his face and hands, then turned back to look at Jenny, who seemed to be inordinately busy. What was it about this slim beauty that excited him so deeply? He had had many women that he could say were more beautiful, yet he had never felt such emotion stir him alive as when he looked into her turquoise eyes.

From the first moment he had seen her, he had felt this special, nameless something. Now it seemed to be growing past anything he had known. Her fragility, or seeming fragility, called out to the protective instincts within him, instincts he was quite certain she would resent.

For the first time in his life Trace felt a strange confusion. To suddenly tell her how he felt would be a mistake. He knew she would never believe him, yet he wanted to tell her. He wanted to hold her, to take that soft, pouting mouth with his own, to entwine his fingers in the soft strands of her hair, and, most of all, to feel the soft flesh of her body pressed close to his. His body's reaction was most unwelcome and he walked back to the table, concentrating on its control.

He took a seat at the table where, after a few minutes, Jenny placed a steaming plate before him. She prepared another for herself, then sat down opposite him. There was no penetrating her calm exterior, and there was nothing he could do but make casual conversation.

"Smells good," he began hopefully.

"Thank you," she replied in a quiet voice filled with cool reserve. Trace was quite sure the balance of his visit was going to be difficult unless he could reach her somehow.

Jenny had lit the oil lamps while Trace was washing, because the setting sun was slowly leaving the room in darkness. In the mellow glow of the lamps, Jenny's gold beauty was enhanced. At this moment he could not imagine spending the balance of his days without her. She seemed to fill every void he had ever felt and the hollow ache of his losses was diminished just by her presence. He watched, fascinated as the pale light formed a halo about her hair and brought soft gold flecks to her eyes. It was then he realized she was watching him just as intently.

"This good kitchen smell reminds me of home," Trace explained with a smile.

Jenny looked at him, curiosity in her eyes. "Home? Where is home?" she asked. For a moment he was caught in harsh memories and Jenny watched them flicker painfully across his face. It startled her for a moment, for she began to suspect that Trace Cord had lost something also.

"Eatonton, Georgia," Trace answered.

"Georgia," Jenny said gently. "You're a long way from home." She placed a cup of hot coffee before him.

"Yes, I am," Trace replied quietly.

"Why?"

"Why what?"

"Mr. Cord—"

"Trace," he interrupted with a quick smile.

"Trace," she acknowledged. "Why are you so far from home? You're from Georgia, so obviously you were involved in the war, and when I hear that drawl of yours, I get the feeling you weren't always a railroad man."

"Well, I'm glad about one thing." Trace chuckled.

"What?"

"You're finally getting a feeling about me besides anger and distrust."

"I said nothing about trusting you. I was just surprised that you would choose to go with the railroad."

"Why does it surprise you?"

"I see you as master of the plantation, a grower of crops, owner of slaves, maybe even a little more military, but . . ."

"But not as a pioneer of sorts?" he questioned with one rakishly raised eyebrow. "Maybe you're right. But sometimes a man can be forced to be a lot of things if it's a matter of survival."

"Survival? Force?" She smiled. "Funny, I can't see anyone forcing you to do something you don't want to do. Especially if that something is leaving your home and family." She was unprepared for the shadow of pain that flickered across his face before it was forced away.

"My sister is traveling with me. My brother, Michael"—he was silent for a moment as old memories crowded into his mind—"was reported missing . . . presumed dead. My parents . . . they both died." His mouth grew momentarily firm and hard, and Jenny had to contain, by force, the urge to go to him and touch those bitterly hurt lips with her own. "I guess," he continued gently, "you might say they were casualties of war." He went on to explain not only how his parents had died, but the bargain he had made with the Starett line to try to preserve his family's heritage. "So there were not many choices left, either for my sister or me. It was go with the railroad or lose everything we had left, which I assure you wasn't much when the Union Army finished with it."

"And so," Jenny added in a soft challenge, "you, of all people, should understand why I feel as I do. You are fighting to preserve what is yours and yet you would deny me the right to fight to preserve what is mine. Does that sound quite fair to you?"

"You can hardly put our situations on the same level, Jenny. The railroad only wants to cross your land, not destroy it. You will still have your home and most of your land. I would have had nothing left . . . nothing at all. It would have been impossible for me to have rebuilt under the circumstances. We," he added softly, "were on the losing side. I don't think you have any idea what that means. The force that occupied our city would have made it hell."

"I'm sorry. I guess it's none of my business," she said quickly.

She could feel the heat in her cheeks, and her hands, to her annoyance, trembled. She had eaten very little but could not seem to swallow another bite. Trace, with his usual appetite, had finished most of his food.

"The meal was excellent. You're a good cook. I imagine your father and brother appreciate that. They're lucky . . . very lucky," he added softly.

"Thank you," she replied to the compliment, annoyed that he had such a confusing effect on her.

She lifted both plates and carried them to the sink. She had to resist the strange magnetism and control the unexplainable emotions she felt. She heard no sound from behind her and resisted the urge to turn and look into those all-seeing grey eyes. She was startled when she felt his touch on her arm and spun about to find him standing within inches of her. Before she could speak, he reached out and took hold of her shoulders. His eyes seemed to be penetrating all the barriers she had put before the world and seeing the loneliness and the unhappiness she had endured for so long.

"I came here because I want to answer your questions. I want you to know and to understand both me and why I'm here. I don't like to see distrust when you look at me."

"How can you expect trust when you come here for the purpose of taking something others have worked so hard for?"

"You have decided to believe that from what others with motives of their own have told you. You have passed judgment on me and I'm not even allowed to defend myself. I will swear one thing, Jenny." He softened his voice to a gentleness she found difficult to ignore. "What I truly want more than anything else is to be able to talk freely with you and have you listen without the barriers you built before you even saw me."

"I don't want to trust you, Trace Cord," she whispered.

"Why . . . why Jenny, why?"

"You're dangerous."

"Not to you." His voice was a whisper as he drew her so close their bodies touched. "Never to you, Jenny. You are too sweet and special. Please don't doubt me."

She was shaken, though she tried to ignore his words and the thunderous explosion of flame that leapt from somewhere in the center of her being and threatened to melt her very bones. This was impossible, she thought wildly. He is lying! He is trying to destroy my will, to seduce me so he can have what he wants.

She pressed her hands flat against the breadth of his chest. She could feel the ripple of hard muscles beneath her fingers as she tried to keep some distance between them. Her greatest difficulty was in suppressing the desire to slide her arms up around his neck, rest her body against his, and surrender to the comfort of his strength.

If she fought a battle, it was no more violent than the one Trace fought. He wanted her. Desire stimulated every nerve in his body. And he knew he could take her if he chose. She was small and fragile in his arms and he ached to hold her, to kiss away her fears and feel her surrender to him. And yet he fought this urge, for he knew that forcing her would never satisfy him. He wanted her, true, but he wanted her to want him, to be willing, to surrender completely. It was the only way.

Anger was her only defense. She stood on the brink of trembling surrender as he drew her to him and his lips hovered much too close. She pushed against his chest ineffectively and almost groaned her resistance.

"Is this why you have come here?" she cried. "Did you think it would be so easy? I don't give up my land for a kiss, Mr. Cord, or is it more you had in mind? Bed me and I'll sign your papers, is that it?"

Trace knew he had made a drastic mistake, but the knowledge did not stop the desire. He had to taste the soft, trembling mouth below his. He had to, once.

He heard her muffled sound of denial as he bound her to him and took her mouth in what he meant to be a moment's gentle possession. Thundering, heated emotion swirled about them, engulfing them roughly, overwhelmingly. His mouth closed over hers and his tongue plunged between her soft, moist lips, savoring the sweetness as if it were heady wine. Jenny gasped both in outrage and with a desire she had no strength to fight.

The sensations were wild and so unexpected and new that she could not raise her defenses. She had tasted nothing as intoxicating as this inexplicable emotion that caused her world to tremble in its throes, then disintegrate about her.

Her traitorous body was moving at its will, and against the screaming demand of her mind it molded itself to his lean frame. She felt as if she were melting as his hands caressed and touched as no man's had ever done before.

His lips moved from her mouth to the soft flesh of her throat, where the pulse drummed in wild passion. He teased her skin with his tongue and teeth until she was nearly powerless.

Over and over he kissed her as if he would never stop. His lips seared hers until she was weak and clung to him, all resistance drained away, rendering her helpless. Her mind was devoid of all thoughts except the wild, hungry passion he was awakening within her. She felt as if she were an empty, hollow shell waiting to be filled with the touch of something magical and something she had never before experienced.

He held her so tight she could hardly breathe, but even then he was kissing away what little breath she had. Her surrender was almost total, almost complete. Her eyes were closed and she was on the very brink of being lost. It was only then that she felt the warmth of his hand as he deftly loosened buttons and caressed the soft globe of passion-hardened breast. He bent his head to caress and tease with his tongue until he elicited a ragged groan of unbridled need from her.

She felt as if every nerve in her body was aflame and she was being devoured by the conflagration. Yet her body felt more alive at this moment than ever before.

How had she allowed him to reduce her to such blind passion? How had she allowed him past all her defenses and let him use her like an innocent school girl? With sudden violence, she jerked from his arms, thrusting him away with an angry sob.

"Damn you! Get out of here!"

"Jenny . . . I . . ."

"Go back to your railroad! Tell them it was not so easy to bed me and get what you wanted! I should have shot you the first time I saw you!"

"Damnit, Jenny! I'm sorry. I never meant for this to happen. I'm not even sure how it got out of hand. It's just . . . you're so damn sweet and beautiful."

"And gullible?" She laughed bitterly.

"If you think that's what I came here for, you're crazy," he said. "I don't think you're gullible or stupid. You want everyone else to understand how you feel, but you won't give an inch. I don't have many choices about what we're doing. I have a job to do and I intend to do it. But I don't intend to take. I'm trying to bargain. I'm trying to make it fair on both sides. Everybody has to make concessions, to make bargains in their lifetimes. Do you think I wanted all I had ever known destroyed? I didn't. It's changed me . . . I've learned there has to be a lot of give and take in life. You have to bend sometimes, Jenny, or you'll break. I . . . I don't want to be responsible for hurting you, or anyone else in this valley for that matter. I want to help you," he added gently.

"Is bedding me how far you will go to get what you came after?" she asked in feigned amazement.

Now Trace's anger was also beginning to grow. "Sorry, Jenny," he said firmly, "but I don't make it a habit of lying to anyone, and not about something as important as that. I wanted to help you when I came here."

"Of course you did. Help me out of my land and my clothes at the same time!"

"You're wrong!" he said, his temper rising. "For your damn land I'd negotiate; for you I don't make terms. I know what I want."

"What you want! Oh, you conceited ass! Did it ever occur to you what I want?" Tears, which she brushed angrily away, continued to course down her cheeks. "This is Graham land! Graham land!" she cried as she pressed her closed fist against her breasts. Now she seemed unaware of the loosened buttons that were exposing soft curves, though she made a picture Trace would never be able to forget. She was wild, untamed beauty, like the land for which she fought.

"My parents fought Indians, drought, and sickness to get it and to hold it. My mother is buried beneath those trees. Do you believe I will ever give it up? It is all we have; it is our life." She was openly crying now and he wanted desperately to take her in his arms. "I will never give it up, never. So go away, Trace; leave me alone. Play your little games somewhere else on someone who might appreciate your . . . offers."

Trace knew he had lost a battle, but grimly he reminded himself that losing one battle was a far cry from losing the war.

# Chapter 10

Trace took a step toward her, trying to close the gap of misunderstanding that stretched between them, but he only succeeded in making Jenny's defenses grow stronger. He watched the glow of defiance light her eyes and bring a flush to her cheeks. He saw the stubborn lift of her chin. He wondered if all the emotions his embrace had let loose were not more a barrier than her anger at the railroad. Perhaps if he could break through the wall she had built around her, he would be able to talk to her and make her understand that all her fears were unfounded.

"You shout about this being Graham land and how you want to defend it, yet you'd give control of it to a man whose motives you don't really see or understand," he declared angrily.

She was silenced for a moment as the impact of his words registered through her rage.

"What?"

"You heard me. You'd fight the ones who don't want to hurt you and hand over everything to one who does."

"I don't understand what you're talking about."

"I'm talking about your friend, Mr. Jessup."

143

"What does Taylor have to do with this?"

"He's trying to negotiate with Maxwell for your land."

"I'm sure he's doing his best to make sure we're not cheated. He's been my father's friend for some time."

"Friend?" Trace laughed derisively. "His negotiations with Maxwell are real clear. He says he's going to marry into the Graham land and, when he does, the right-of-way will be ours. He says it as if he's quite sure there will be no problems . . . with any of the Grahams."

"I don't believe you!" Jenny gasped, but her voice carried much less conviction than she meant it to.

"You're sure about that, Jenny?" Trace said gently. "Or are you just hiding from the truth?"

She turned her back to him to escape the sincerity she saw in his eyes and to attempt to regain her composure.

But Trace was not about to let her rebuild the shell he had penetrated. He gripped her shoulders and turned her to face him.

"Damnit, Jenny, your stubbornness is leading you to trust the one who would betray you and to distrust those who would help you."

Jenny was confused and uncertain, and vulnerable. The fears that had filled her nights with nightmares and her days with worry all seemed to be crowding in on her now, and Trace could read the concern in her eyes.

"Jenny," he said as he drew her closer to him, his voice now very nearly a caress, "don't you think I understand how you feel? I want you to believe I would never take from you what you love so much. I remember too well the hurt that losing what you love can bring. I want you to believe I would never hurt you. I want . . ." His voice died as her eyes lifted to his.

Their sudden awareness of each other was a time-stopping phenomenon, for truly it seemed as if everything came to a breathless halt. They stared at each other for a moment of suspended time, then slowly, almost fearfully, Trace lowered his mouth to cover hers.

The shock was so severe that it startled them both. Then suddenly his mouth lost its hesitancy and blazed with raw, hungering need. Trace lifted his head and gazed into her turquoise orbs. Trace's grey eyes had deepened in color with the heat of passion that was gnawing at his heart. Anger had melted into desire, rage had turned to hunger. All battles were held at bay by the white heat of their mutual need. The bittersweet ache of yearning could not be denied by either of them and they dissolved all differences for a forbidden moment.

The murmur of her name was the only intelligible word Trace muttered as again he took her soft, responding mouth with his. This time he was relentless in his mastery. This time he could not stop and, for this one overpowering moment, Jenny did not want him to.

One hand caught the back of her head and held her while the other stroked the roundness of her buttocks and thighs, molding her to his lean frame. He wanted to press her to him until his body knew every line and curve of hers.

A flame of brilliant pleasure swept Jenny away and she was lost in the intensity of the wildfire. Wave after wave engulfed her as his mouth forced her to respond with a hunger that matched his. They were in the universe alone, it seemed, as his mouth again grew gentle to savor the sweet taste of hers and their tongues met and played upon each other's.

Trace brushed her open dress from her shoulder and leisurely caressed the soft flesh of her breasts. She shivered in ecstatic delight and called out his name without hearing. But Trace heard—heard and was filled with her.

With closed eyes, Jenny felt the tensing of his muscles as he bent slightly and lifted her from the floor. Her head rested on his shoulder and her slim ivory arms wove about his neck. She kept her eyes closed, for it seemed they were weighted, yet her senses were alive as they had never been before. Her breathing was shallow and rapid as she inhaled the heady masculine scent of him.

Beside her bed he let her feet drop gently to the floor. In the semidarkness, with only her senses free to feel, she savored the gentle touch of his lean fingers as they removed the rest of her clothes.

Then suddenly there seemed only a blank, empty moment as he rapidly divested himself of his clothes. She was bereft, lost as if she were without a vital part of herself. Then again he was drawing her body close to his and she gasped as they touched and the hot strength of him seemed to melt her against him. Her pulses leapt frantically and from somewhere in her depths came a soft, moaning call that echoed within him. It was the predestined cry of a mate calling to her mate.

His hands were stroking her body in gentle caresses. Without warning he was shaken to the very core by the tenative touch of her cool hands as they hesitantly began an exploration of their own. Her hands seemed to have their own will as they slid from the breadth of his shoulders to his broad, fur-matted chest. Her mouth cautiously tasted his flesh as his had done and found the reward stimulating as she felt his iron-hard arms bind her gently but firmly against him.

The shaft of his passion throbbed hard against her belly, and her hands continued to trace a path toward it, drawn by desire as old as time itself, the desire to know and to feel the sweet pleasure of total possession.

146

His body seemed to become molten fire as her seeking hands discovered his maleness. A low, sensual groan escaped his lips as her hands moved upon his hard, muscle-corded body.

He contained the desire to be within her now to ease the aching need his tormented body demanded be assuaged. He closed his eyes for a moment to bring the conflagration under iron control. Then again hard, sinewed arms lifted her and she felt the power of his possession and was inflamed and completely intoxicated by it. She closed her eyes again as he lifted her against him. Her body seemed to be afire. She had never felt so alive and so sensitive to touch, for each caress of his hands, each touch of his warm lips, made her want to shriek in rapturous agony, yet she could only murmur soft, unremembered pleas for this remarkable awakening to continue.

In moments she felt the soft bed beneath her and the iron-hard, muscled body above her. Her breathing was rapid and uncontrolled as again he fed the growing passion that was destroying any restraint she might have harbored.

Their bodies came together in a blending that made her cry out in blinding ecstasy. It was torture, but exquisitely beautiful torture. It was pleasure beyond anything she had ever known. She opened to him with a striving as strong as his own and was filled as his fiery shaft plunged to the depths of her again and again.

Sweat glistened on their bodies and each strained to give more fully and capture more completely. It was gentleness enclosing hardness. It was sensitive, wondrous need turning to sheer, overpowering rapture. It was a complete merging of two into one. Something unique and forever unforgettable was formed as waves of pure, ecstatic pleasure washed through her, and somewhere within them both was embedded the knowledge that this joy, this belonging, this rightness could only happen between them. It was two souls reaching to unite and succeeding in a total and absolute consummation.

They lay very still for some time, Trace burying his face in her soft, scented hair and holding her still-trembling body close to him. Their breathing slowed as the primitive force that had captured them and transported them beyond reality subsided.

Emotions and thoughts plunged from the heights and intruded on their interlude. Trace lay very still, holding Jenny close, wondering if there were a way he could retain what they had found beyond the first words and thoughts Jenny might have.

A shaft of soft gold light from the room beyond them lay half across the bed and was joined by pale moonlight that had found its way through the curtains.

Trace rose on one elbow and looked down into Jenny's eyes, almost afraid of what he might see. Would she reject this rare, sweet passion they had found? Would she call it something else?

Again their eyes held, hers moist with the tears of newly tasted passion, and his with unanswered questions, questions only she could resolve.

He lay his hand against her cheek and bent his head to brush her lips in a feather touch.

"Jenny," he murmured. "Sweet Jenny, can't you see that what we shared cannot be a lie? You must believe what we feel is the only truth we need to know. I want to hear you say it. Say that you can feel the same sweet thing I do—love, Jenny."

"I'm afraid, Trace," she whispered. "I'm afraid if I let go . . . if I find all this is not true . . . I won't be able to bear it."

"Christ, Jenny," he groaned as he took her in his arms and rocked her against him. "I could not stand the thought of you being afraid of me or of being afraid to love me. This is the truth, Jenny, the real truth and the only truth. Love me," he whispered softly.

His voice faded as her arms crept about him, and he felt an indescribable pleasure as he realized she was surrendering. She was coming halfway and trying to eliminate all the barriers she had set before her. He knew hers was a tentative and very sensitive trust that could be shattered easily, and he meant to preserve it, to build it into complete trust.

"We have to talk about a lot of things," Jenny began.

But Trace's attention was centered more on the soft feminine form in his arms than on words he felt could wait until later—much later.

"This"—he chuckled softly as he nuzzled the sensitive flesh of her throat—"is no time to talk. We can always talk tomorrow."

"Trace . . ." she began to protest, but his lips stopped hers in a most effective way, taking her mind and her senses from all else but him.

"Tomorrow, love," he whispered as his arms bound her close to him. "Tomorrow we'll talk about anything you want. Tonight there is only one language we need to speak to each other." The kiss blossomed into a roaring blaze of passion that swept Jenny into a world of unbelievable pleasure and, for those miraculous hours, also swept away the thoughts and barriers that had stood between them.

Waking in someone's arms was a strange and pleasant experience for Jenny. She lay very still in the curve of Trace's arms, pressed close to him as if he were holding her protectively. She could hear the steady beat of his heart and she smiled at the sense of security and rightness she had found in the arms of this man she

149

had promised to hate.

She gently caressed the hard, fur-matted chest, then let her hand drift slowly downward. When her hand lay quivering and uncertain on his taut belly, she could feel the heat of remembered passion from the past night. Her breath grew short as she recalled her wanton behavior, but when she started to withdraw her hand, Trace lifted his hand and placed it over hers.

"Your hands are cool, and I have never awakened in a more delightful way."

Jenny looked up, a flush of embarrassment staining her cheeks. Grey eyes, warm with love, smiled into hers. Gently he lifted her hand and brought it to his lips, placing a kiss on the sensitive palm.

"Do you know you're more beautiful now than you were last night, and that is a remarkable feat! And do you know that I love you, woman?" he added in a softened voice.

"Trace . . . It's so . . ."

"I know, so unbelievable. It is for me too. I don't think I've ever met a woman quite like you. You're something extremely special."

"You make me feel that way. This is all so . . . over-whelming. I've never felt this way about anyone."

"Because this is something very special. Jenny, few people have ever had the good fortune to share what we have. Some people go through their whole lives and never experience the sweet taste of loving that we've found. It's as if we have always belonged together. I don't intend to let you go, Jenny." His voice was soft but carried warning. He meant exactly what he said. "Not ever . . . no matter what happens."

For a moment Jenny was held by the fierce, possessive light in Trace's eyes. She felt a sudden chill, knowing she was still half lover, half enemy of this strong man. She had to have some time to think—free of his arms, where she was so weak.

"Trace, I want you to come somewhere with me."

"I am right where I'd like to be with you," he said with a laugh as he tightened his arms until she was breathless.

"Trace, please. It's important to me that you see and understand—that you know why I feel what I do."

"Is it that important to you?"

"Yes, it is."

"Then we'd best get out of this bed, because my resistance is extremely low. A few more minutes and I'm afraid I won't have the strength to let you go."

Jenny laughed and wriggled from his arms. She left the bed and for a few brief moments Trace was treated to the view of her slim, golden body as she dressed. Then, reluctantly, he followed.

An hour later they stood by a lone grave beneath the trees while Jenny told of her mother's untimely death. He held her as she wept over her father's inability to cope and his retreat into the bottle.

"I'm sorry, Jenny. But once this is settled, maybe I could help a little."

"I think he just needs time, Trace. Time and those of us who love him . . . and our land. Come with me now, Trace. There's something else I want you to see."

They saddled their horses and within minutes they were riding away from the ranch. They rode for some time in silence. Trace admired the beauty of the valley. Rolling hills and flat meadows made it a perfect place to raise horses—or anything else for that matter, he thought to himself.

After a while he noticed that they seemed to be following the course of the river that appeared to nearly cut the valley in half. Eventually their trail crossed the river at a narrow, somewhat shallow point. After they had crossed, Trace saw the ground rose on a steady grade. When they crested the hill, Jenny drew her horse to a halt and Trace stopped beside her.

"Look," Jenny said as she stood in the stirrups and pointed. Trace followed her gesture.

Ahead of him lay another green meadow. Across it, in a diagonal cut, ran the river they had just crossed. In his mind he followed the meanderings of the river. It obviously fed her property here, in this meadow.

"That," she said, "is the piece of land the railroad wants to buy." She watched his features and knew the moment the realization struck him. "Yes," she explained, "they want that land . . . they want the river . . . and they want control of the water that makes my valley live."

Trace realized her words were the truth. The valley could be jeopardized if someone were to tamper with the river. A nagging thought in the back of his mind annoyed him but refused to become clear. There was something wrong with this whole thing, yet he could not seem to put his finger on what it was.

"Now you know why we will never surrender a right-of-way across this land. If the railroad damages the water, or even if its digging changes the flow of the river, all that my family has worked for all these years would come to ruin. I just can't let that happen."

"I can see your point," he said. "Jenny"—he turned in his saddle to look at her intently—"let me go back and talk to Maxwell. It could be that he doesn't understand what is going on here."

"Taylor has already done that."

"What?"

"Taylor, he spoke to Mr. Starett. He was told that it is impossible for the railroad to cross anywhere else. Mr. Starett refuses to listen, so we have no choice. He cannot have the right to cross our land. Not now . . . not ever."

"Taylor Jessup," Trace said meditatively.

"Taylor has been a good friend to my father, Trace."

"I'll bet he has," Trace replied with irritating coolness.

"The people in this valley needed someone to protect them from the railroad's destruction. He has gone to a great deal of trouble to help us. Why, most of the surveying was done at his expense because most of us couldn't afford it ourselves."

"Well," Trace said decisively, "the people in this valley do need some help, all right, but I'm not too sure they're getting it."

"Are you still trying to tell me—"

"I'm not trying to tell you anything, Jenny. All I'm asking is that you give me some time to talk to Maxwell. I have a feeling some of our problems can be worked out." His eyes held hers. "Don't make a judgment about us until all the cards are on the table. You might get a surprise."

He nudged his horse closer to her and reached out to lay his hand over hers on the saddle horn; he could feel it trembling beneath his.

"Jenny," he whispered softly. She seemed stilled by some mesmerizing emotion as he bent forward and lightly brushed her lips with his. "Don't judge me too soon either. Give me some time, Jenny, a little time. I need your trust for now. I want much more . . . much more. But at least we could begin to understand each other." He waited for several minutes as she remained completely silent. Then he questioned, "Jenny?"

"All right, Trace. I won't do anything now. Have your time . . . but don't deceive me, Trace, or, before God, if you come here again, I will see you dead before I surrender one inch of what is mine."

"We have a bargain?" he asked hopefully.

"For now," she replied.

"I'll change that in time, Jenny. You'll soon find out the railroad means you no harm. What we want we'll bargain for . . . at least what the railroad wants. For me, as I told you, I won't bargain. I want you, and I don't want you on a temporary basis."

"Do you always get what you want, Trace Cord?" Jenny questioned with a haughty smile.

"Always," he said arrogantly. "So stop fighting me, woman. It wastes too much time that could be spent in a much better way."

Jenny had to laugh at his forceful attitude. But Trace was well aware that his words were all show. He understood the fragility of their relationship and that he was going to have to guard it carefully, for once broken, it might never be mended.

"Let's go back, Jenny. I want to get back to Maxwell. It's time some serious talking was done."

They rode slowly and the sun was high when they came in view of the house. Both were startled to see a wagon and two men. As they drew closer, Jenny could identify Stu.

When they had dismounted, Jenny walked quickly to Stu's side. He eyed Trace speculatively. "You're not one of the ranchers from around here—I know them all—so you have to be from the railroad."

"I'm Trace Cord, Maxwell's foreman."

"I kinda thought so. You're the one responsible for the shooting."

"Stu? What shooting?" Jenny asked fearfully. "Is it my father?"

"No, Jenny. . . . It's Buck. He's been shot."

"Shot! Who . . . When?"

"I'll tell you when," Stu said coldly. "We found him just an hour ago. And I'll tell you who's responsible," he ground out between clenched teeth. "Buck talked before he passed out, Mr. Cord. You didn't expect that, did you? He overheard the name of the man who tried to kill him. He talked and he told us who was to blame, who had given orders to kill Buck Graham—Trace Cord and his friends from the railroad."

Jenny grew pale and directed hurt, disbelieving eyes toward Trace, who watched in dismay as they slowly turned to turquoise ice.

# Chapter 11

Buck Graham had watched his father ride away from their camp. He had felt so utterly defeated, sure that his father was not going back to the ranch as he had said, but into town and the nearest saloon. Again, as he had for some time, he wondered where and how his father had found enough money to buy whiskey. He had tried many times to discover the source but had always run into a stone wall.

He and Stu could not leave the camp yet. They had worked all the day before in moving a small herd of eight wild horses from a temporary camp to a more permanent one. Now they would have to be broken. It would be some days before he could go home again, with the exception of the night to come, when he had a rendezvous to keep. He sighed as he watched his father's retreating figure. If the promised money had not been so necessary to keep his family together and to protect the ranch, he would have followed his father and forced him to go home with him. Keeping Jenny and the ranch out of trouble weighed heavily against a loss of his own that was eating at his heart and bringing him closer to feelings of despair, feelings that were becoming harder and harder to fight.

It was nearing dusk, and Stu and Buck had just closed the makeshift gate on the small herd. The camp would remain until the horses were broken. It had been used for this purpose since Buck had begun to build his herd. Because of such periodic sojourns, he and Stu had built a small, one-room shack in which they ate and slept.

Stu walked up beside him now, his eyes following Buck's. He felt sympathy for Buck's obvious distress, but he was too much a friend to say anything.

"You hungry, Buck?" he asked to break the heavy silence. Buck did not answer and Stu was sure he had not even heard him.

"Buck?"

"Huh! What?" Buck stammered as he looked at Stu, almost surprised to find him there.

"I said, are you hungry? I could eat one of those horses—uncooked."

"Yeah, I'm hungry."

The two men walked back to the shack, where they prepared a quick meal of bacon and flapjacks. Once the meal was over, Stu began preparations for bed, for their day would commence long before sunup. Buck too made preparations, but not for sleeping. He waited what to him was an interminable time for Stu to be completely asleep, then he slipped from his blankets, donned his boots, and silently left the cabin. What he did not realize was that Stu was not sleeping, but merely pretending slumber so that Buck could leave.

He had known about Buck's nocturnal rendezvous for some time and usually remained awake just to make sure Buck returned all right, which he usually did two or three hours later. Stu even knew it was Emily Marshall whom Buck was meeting. He wished Buck and Emily could work out their problems and marry as they both wanted to do. It seemed to him that Buck Graham had loved Emily since they had been children. He folded his hands behind his head and, while he waited for Buck's return, tried to figure ways that he could help Jenny and Buck.

Buck rode slowly and with ease, for he was accustomed to riding without concentrating. He was the master, and his horse obeyed his unconscious commands completely, leaving Buck time to think.

He traveled for a little less than an hour before he came to a solitary stand of trees that formed an island in the center of a grass meadow. Even though he could see no one, he knew that Emily waited for him there. His horse nickered softly and was immediately answered by the unseen horse that stood in the shadows of the trees.

He rode swiftly now and soon entered the darker area of the trees. Only shafts of pale moonlight streaked the ground, casting just enough light so that he could see the shadowed form that detached itself from the deeper shadows and, with a soft call of his name, ran toward him. He dismounted quickly and opened his arms, catching Emily in his embrace and binding her to him. Her arms went about his neck and they clung to each other for a long, heart-stopping moment. He kissed her feverishly, hungrily, until she was gasping for breath and clinging weakly to him. Only then did he capture her face between his hands and attempt to read her eyes.

"Em . . . Em, I've missed you so much. It's been hell. Like the very best part of me has been missing."

"I know, I know," she murmured. "Oh, Buck, I'll never go away again. It's been so long. I thought I would die being away from you. I wish . . . Buck, what are we going to do? I can't stand these terrible separations."

"I don't know, Emily," Buck replied in total frustration. "Between your father and mine, I don't know if we stand a chance."

"Buck . . . you know I would go with you wherever you wanted. I know Jenny likes me. We could be sisters. I know she'd welcome me . . . I love you, Buck. There's nothing in the world worth more than you."

"Sure," he said bitterly. "I'll just take you from a place where you have everything money can buy to a place I don't even know if we will own next year."

"Buck, please . . . I love you."

"I know, Em, but don't you see? It's just because of that that I can't do it. I love you too," he added as he kissed her again, a gentle, pleading kiss. "Em," he whispered, "don't be angry with me . . . don't leave me. Life is hard, but I know I can work things out if you just stay with me. I'm not sure if I'd make it if I didn't know you were here to hold . . . to love."

"I'm here, Buck. You know I'll always be here. There has never been anyone else in my life but you for as long as I can remember."

Buck tried to laugh off his subtle fears, but Emily read him well, even before the words were uttered.

"You mean with all those rich, handsome suitors your father has been bringing around?"

"I'd never marry anyone but you."

"Your father hates me, Em," Buck said with conviction.

"No Buck, he doesn't hate you. He's just blinded by money. Once he knows for certain that I will never marry any of his choices, he'll come around. I'll convince him how wonderful and good you really are . . . and how much I want you."

Buck kissed her again, a kiss filled with need she understood, for it echoed the need she had carried all the months she had been away. Emily slid her arms about his waist and pressed her body close to his. Her love for Buck was an overpowering emotion that needed no words to convey it to Buck. His arms encircled her and her mouth parted under the intensity of his kiss. Their tongues played upon each other's, elicited a soft sigh of contentment from Emily.

The kiss ended reluctantly, slowly, and they gazed at each other, knowing a single kiss would never be enough to quell the flame of desire that consumed them.

"I should go," Buck whispered. "Your family will miss you." But the yearning tone of his voice held Emily within his arms.

"Don't send me home ... not without loving me, Buck. I've dreamed of being with you for endless weeks. I want to be in your arms, Buck. I need you."

"God ... Emily," Buck groaned as his arms tightened about her and again their lips met. Both knew that there would be no further talk of separation this night.

Their horses were tied close by and Buck moved to unfasten the blankets that were rolled behind his saddle while Emily waited beneath the sheltering branches of a large tree. In the soft moonlight, she seemed a ghostlike apparition.

Buck spread the blanket on the ground, then turned to face Emily. For a moment they only looked at each other. Then, with a half smile, Emily reached to unbutton the blouse she wore.

"Don't," Buck said softly. Her hands hesitated. He went to her. "I've been dreaming of doing that for a lot of long, lonely nights."

Emily reached up to lay her hand against his cheek as his trembling hands slowly unbuttoned her blouse.

There had always been a special magic in their lovemaking and Emily yearned to recapture that specialness now. Slowly she began to feel the familiar enchantment take hold of her and she gloried in it. She could not tear her eyes away from him until his soft touch on her quivering flesh created such havoc with her body that she closed them to allow herself to feel more deeply.

His palms, hardened and callused from hard work, were gentle as they cupped her breasts and squeezed them gently. Skillfully, his thumbs circled the now-hardening nipples. "You're so very beautiful," he murmured, "just as my memories have told me."

Emily's hands worked open the buttons of his shirt and slipped beneath to caress his lean frame.

Slowly, in fascinated wonder, they leisurely undressed each other, savoring each moment, each touch, each kiss. Buck lowered himself to the blanket, drawing Emily with him and, encircling her in a strong embrace, he kissed her again, deeply, lingeringly. His hands slid down her body to find and caress the moist, sensitive core of her womanhood. Emily felt as if the world were dissolving into the bliss his teasing hands bestowed. She arched against him, seeking more of this pleasure that made her weak with pulsing desire.

Buck was thrilled with her response and her soft, murmured, purrs of contentment. He lowered his head to taste the hardened crest of her breast. His mouth enclosed it and his tongue swirled about it, taunting and creating tingling sensations throughout her body. She ran her fingers through his hair, urging him to deeper possession. He sucked roughly for a moment, then moved to the other to repeat the wild sensation. Savagely he sought her sweet flesh, his mouth roaming across her skin in a hot, fierce flame.

He had been without her a long time and now he

needed the immediate possession. It was the same for Emily.

His hands slid down now to cup her buttocks and lift her to meet him. Then he filled her, driving to the depths of her again and again until she was breathless and totally lost.

Her legs twined about him and her body arched upward to meet each thrust. At the same erotic instant explosive sensations rippled through them both. Buck gave a soft, sighing shudder and collapsed in her arms, which held him willingly.

"Buck . . . Buck," Emily murmured brokenly. "I love you so much."

Buck scooped her body into his arms and turned to keep his weight from her. He wanted to remain this way forever, within her, holding her close, never letting her go away from him to leave his days and nights as lonely as they had been during the past few months.

They were satiated, content to remain still for awhile. He caressed her gently, knowing this sweet moment would be all too short.

"I wish we could run away somewhere," Emily said quietly. "Somewhere where we could be together forever."

"No one can truly run away from his obligations, Emily. You're not the kind to do that . . . and I hope I'm not either. I don't really believe you'd go on loving me if I did."

Emily curled closer to him and kissed his cheek. "I should love you, Buck Graham, no matter what you did—even if you were to kill or steal or anything else. I would always love you."

Buck chuckled and squeezed her until she protested. "I have no idea what I've ever done to deserve you, Em, but I'm sure glad the powers that be decided to reward me for it."

"What are we really going to do, Buck?"

"I've been thinking, Em. I know Jenny is going to be angry, but I'm going to talk to this Trace Cord, the one from the railroad. Maybe I can work out something, something that might satisfy Pa and Jenny so I can start thinking of a way to get around your father."

"Do you know this Trace Cord very well?"

"No, but a lot of people have been talking about him. I've got to find out for myself. Em, I need you. Not for a day or a night, but for always. I've got to find a way."

"When are you going to talk to him?"

"Tomorrow if I can."

"Buck?"

"What?"

"Will I see you tomorrow night?"

She had asked the question softly, her face buried in the curve of his shoulder. He turned slightly and lifted her chin so their eyes met. He bent to brush her lips with his.

"I love you, Em. Don't ever doubt me. I couldn't have gotten by much longer without seeing you. Now that you're here, I can only count the hours until we're together again."

In the pale glow of the moon he saw tears glistening in her eyes. Again he kissed her and slowly the embers of passion were again fanned to blazing life. This time their loving was slow and agonizingly sweet.

Later Buck helped her dress, then rode with her as far as was safely possible. Then he turned his horse toward camp.

With thoughts of Emily on his mind as well as concerns about the railroad and his father, he rode without full awareness of his surroundings.

He was oblivious to the fact that other eyes watched him as he approached the cabin. He was about a quarter of a mile from the dwelling when a shot broke the night silence. He felt the blow and was thrown from his saddle.

He lay still for a moment, the pain in his shoulder burning like fire. But he realized that the attackers might still be near and he wanted them to think their shot had killed him. He was rewarded in a short while by hearing someone approach stealthily. He closed his eyes and remained still, breathing as shallowly as possible.

Someone stood near—no, two, he noted silently, for they were whispering as they approached. He strained to hear.

"You killed him, all right."

"Good. Trace said he'd keep the girl busy while we got rid of her brother. He'll be happy to know there's one less Graham to get in the railroad's way."

"We take care of the old man later and Trace will have the girl where he wants her. By the time he's finished, she'll give him anything he wants."

"You might say the railroad is already across Graham land."

"Yeah, let's get back."

They left and Buck lay still for some time before he tried to move and make his way slowly and painfully to his horse. He had no way of knowing that the two who had attacked him had done so with a purpose far different from the one they had voiced.


A mile or so away they slowed their horses. "You only winged him," one said curiously to the would-be assassin.

"I shoot what I aim at."

"We played that just right. I don't think the Grahams are going to listen to anything Trace Cord and the railroad has to say."

"Jessup sure is smart."

"He's smart, all right. He's going to be a big man in this part of the country, and, besides, he pays well. When that kid gets home with the story we planted, none of the ranchers are going to listen to anything the railroad offers. That land is as good as Jessup's."

"Well, let's go and tell Jessup everything."

They rode off, and the night swallowed them up.

Buck struggled to his feet, grateful that his horse had not strayed too far away. Still it took him some time and a lot of pain to remount. By the time he got to the cabin, he was gritting his teeth with sheer determination. He could not dismount; he simply fell from his horse. It took all his concentrated effort to crawl as far as the cabin door.

Stu had immediately told Jenny that her brother was out of danger and that the doctor was still in the house with him.

Jenny's eyes were filled with something Trace could not bear to see, and he knew there was no defense she would believe. He took a step toward her, but her chilled voice brought him to a halt.

"Stu," she said in cold anger, "if this man is still on my property after ten minutes . . . shoot him."

"Jenny," Trace said quickly, "this is crazy. I had nothing to do with your brother's being shot."

"Buck ain't no liar, Mr. Cord," Stu said. "If he said he heard those men name you, then he heard them."

"Jenny, talk to me," Trace pleaded, ignoring Stu's words. His only thought now was that he had to make Jenny believe him.

"Talk to you?" Jenny inquired scathingly. "Why,

Trace? You've made a fool of me once; that should be enough for you. How ignorant do you think I am? I suppose you didn't expect my brother to live and name you. Well, he did. Now get off my property and don't ever come back, or I will truly kill you."

He heard her cold, controlled words, but the pain he saw in her eyes was much more destructive. He took another step toward her and Stu pulled his gun from its holster and leveled it at Trace.

"And you wanted me to trust you," Jenny said bitterly. "Trust . . . while you kill my brother! Trust while you intend to get rid of my father. Trust! Do you know what the word means? You intended to use me!"

"No! Jenny, that isn't so!"

"Use me! Damn you!" she cried. "Like a naïve little girl, I believed you. I should have known that neither you or your precious railroad has any rules. You'll do what you want, take what you want, and use anybody you have to in order to get your way. Well, this time you failed. Go back and tell them to find another way. I told you once, this is Graham land, and"—she glared at him with hatred mingling with the tears in her eyes— "you or no one else is going to get an inch of it. Get out, Trace . . . before I have Stu shoot you just for your deceitful, lying mouth."

Trace was quite sure Stu had every intention of shooting him, and the bitter disillusionment he read on Jenny's face was enough to make him realize this was not the time for more explanations. But he silently vowed he would be back when Stu and his gun were not so handy, and perhaps by then he would have a few more answers.

"All right, Jenny, I'll go. But I swear to you I had nothing to do with shooting your brother, and I'll prove it. I wouldn't have hurt you. Whether you believe that or not, it's the truth. I'll be back, Jenny." His eyes glittered with grim determination as he repeated. "I'll be back."

He turned and mounted his horse, and Jenny watched him ride away. Angry tears blurred her eyes, and she shook with an emotion she refused to admit. She brushed the tears away with a gesture of disgust and turned to walk back into the house with Stu.

When they entered, the doctor was coming out of Buck's room. Jenny went to him at once.

"Dr. Williams, how is Buck?"

"Now Jenny, don't get too excited. Buck's been hurt worse just being thrown from one of those wild horses he breaks. He'll be fine. He was shot high in the shoulder. The bullet broke no bones and passed clean through. He'll be up and around in no time."

"Thank you, Dr. Williams. I'll come in and take care of your bill next week."

"Fine, fine. Don't worry, Jenny," he said sympathetically. The doctor had long been aware that Jenny always did most of the worrying.

He left and Stu followed him to ride out to the horses and see to their care for the day. He would have to do his work and Buck's too.

Jenny went into Buck's room to find him sitting on the edge of his bed buttoning his shirt.

"Buck! You should be in bed!"

"Come on, Jenny. I'm fine."

She went to him and sat beside him. "Buck . . . what you said about Trace Cord and the railroad being responsible for this . . . was it true?"

"I guess they must have thought I was dead, Jenny. Good thing for me they didn't look any closer."

"But . . . what they said about . . ."

"I heard it clear and true." Buck went on to repeat the words the would-be killers had meant him to hear. He saw the light in Jenny's eyes turn to a darker emotion he found painful to observe, and he began to wonder why Trace Cord and his attack on him had affected Jenny so violently.

But Jenny knew her brother well, and she did not want to answer the questions he would soon be asking.

"I'll go and get you something to eat," she said quickly as she rose to her feet.

"Jenny . . ." Buck began, but Jenny was already closing the door behind her. Buck looked at the closed door in total surprise. He and Jenny had always been able to talk. Now she was shutting him away from something that hurt her. He was going to have to find out why.

Outside his door, Jenny leaned back against it, suddenly feeling the strength flow from her. Tears she had controlled until now fell hot against her cheeks.

"Damn you, Trace," she whispered. "How could you be so deceitful? I was an idiot . . . oh, God, I hate you . . . I hate you! Next time, I will not be such a fool. Next time, I will surely kill you. Damn you! Damn you!"

## Chapter 12

Eileen Starett had coaxed her uncle into the trip to town. She had wanted to shop, she had said, and to see if there were any amusements the town might offer. Maxwell had agreed, mostly because his mind was more on his own problems.

Eileen had made herself comfortable in the best room the small hotel could provide. After she had bathed and dressed carefully, she had left the hotel and had stood for a moment surveying the small but bustling town. Then she had opened her parasol, tilted it over her shoulder, and had walked slowly down the street toward the bank.

Once inside the bank she had smiled sweetly at the tall young man behind the counter. "If you would be so kind, Mister . . . ?"

"Johnson, Ma'am, Ralph Johnson," he had gulped.

"Well, Ralph," Eileen had said in a soft voice, "would you tell Mr. Jessup that Miss Starett is here and would like to see him for a few moments if he could spare the time from his busy schedule?"

"Of course, Miss Starett. It would be a pleasure."

He had very nearly run to Taylor's office and had been gone only moments before he reappeared,

171

accompanied by Taylor.

"Good morning, Miss Starett," Taylor said now.

"Mr. Jessup. Could you spare me a few minutes of your time? I know you are a very busy man."

"It would be my pleasure," Taylor replied as he motioned toward his office door. Eileen preceded him and he turned to Ralph, saying, "I don't want to be disturbed by anything, Mr. Johnson—nothing at all."

"Yes sir."

Taylor entered and closed his office door behind him. Then he turned to Eileen and smiled. "I suppose this is the first chance you've had to get here, Eileen, but you could have sent some word. I've got a lot of things to talk over with you."

"Why, Taylor"—Eileen laughed a deep, throaty laugh—"is that any way to greet an old and dear friend?"

Taylor went to Eileen and put his arms about her, drawing her roughly into an embrace and kissing her with fierce passion.

"Oh Taylor, that is so much better. After all, it's been almost a year since you've seen me. I thought maybe you had forgotten."

"Christ," Taylor remarked with a chuckle, "a man would have to be dead to forget you."

"You got my letters?"

"Every one. It looks as if our well-laid plans are going to work. We are going to have the world in the palm of our hands within weeks."

"Very good. It has taken a long time to put all these plans into motion. We must do nothing to spoil them now."

"I've been following all your instructions since the first moment you hatched this little idea."

"Taylor," Eileen said gently, "what connection do you have to this Jenny Graham?"

Taylor was surprised at the question but did his best to hide it. Eileen was clever and might soon discover he had betrayal in mind if he were not careful. He was playing a game that, with a woman as dangerous as Eileen, could prove fatal.

"Jenny Graham?" he questioned. "She and her brother and father own some property we want."

"And that's all?"

"What else could there be?"

"I want to meet her. Can it be arranged somehow?"

"Quite easily. There's a party to be held by some mutual friends. Jenny's invited. If you like, I could arrange for you and your uncle to be invited also. Maxwell would enjoy making friends with the conflicting forces, I'd imagine."

"Excellent. When will it be?"

"In a few days."

Eileen nodded. "Taylor, you are still certain there is no one to link us together?" She waited for his nod. "It must remain that way. My uncle must not know of our alliance—ever. If we hope to gain all we've worked for, our relationship must be kept a carefully guarded secret."

"Don't worry, Eileen. I'm sure no one around here will think there could possibly be a connection between us. What reason would anyone have to think so?"

"I don't know. It's just that we have to be very careful."

"We will. By the way, what about Trace Cord? He seems to be prying into things with a fervor that goes beyond his position. I don't want him asking the ranchers questions. Can you control him?"

"Of course I can handle him," Eileen began, then she cast a suspicious look at Taylor. "What has Trace been doing?"

"Playing up to Jenny Graham. He's been asking a lot

173

of questions. The last time I saw them, they were together at her ranch. She was alone and they seemed pretty cozy."

"What do you mean, cozy?"

Taylor told Eileen all that had passed between Trace, Jenny, and himself at her ranch the night before. He was still angry and therefore took little notice of Eileen's cold fury.

"So . . . you think they are . . . too close?"

"Too close for our comfort, or for our safety."

"Well," Eileen said softly, "we must see what can be done about this. How is everything else going?"

"Exactly on schedule. By tomorrow or the day after I will have the Carter land tied up. I'm working on the Marshall place and, if you keep Trace Cord out of the way, I'll get Jenny Graham and her family too."

"Don't worry. I'll see to Trace."

"For now, Eileen, you had better get out of here. I don't want Ralph to be inspired to gossip."

"You're right." Eileen turned to leave.

"Eileen." She swung back to face Taylor. They smiled simultaneously. "I do hope you planned on staying in town for awhile?"

"My room number is thirty-three." She laughed. "Come up the back stairs and make sure no one sees you."

"I'll be careful."

Taylor watched the door close behind Eileen, then breathed a sigh of relief. He had wondered if Eileen would ask him what he had been doing alone with Jenny Graham when Trace had come. He was supposed to be working on Jenny's father. He was pleased she had said nothing about it, but still it nagged at him that she might think of it. He did not want her to discover the plan he had put into motion just after he had left Jenny and Trace together.

He had wondered then what would happen if he killed two birds with one stone. He had decided he would set about eliminating the problem of Buck Graham by getting rid of Buck and putting the blame on Trace and the railroad. Then he had thought to himself, better yet, an attempt at first, with the blame placed on Trace. After that, if Buck were to be killed, everyone would look toward Trace and the railroad.

He had to remember to be more careful in the future with Eileen though. He could not underestimate her—never. The old axiom, "Hell hath no fury . . . ," would most certainly be applicable to Eileen.


Trace arrived to find the tracks several miles closer than they had been when he had left. He also realized that the closer the railroad came to town the less time he would have to solve his two problems, the first between the railroad and the ranchers, and the second between him and Jenny Graham.

He went straight to Maxwell and tried to explain some of his thoughts.

"They're really determined that we can't come through the valley," Maxwell said half in anger. "Damnit, they haven't even gotten together with us to talk."

"Take it easy, Maxwell. With a little common sense and some patience, we can handle all this without trouble."

"I'm running low on time, Trace. We're getting close to town. We have everything ready there, but once we get through town, we have to head for the valley."

"Let me use what little time there is to keep the peace."

"I don't want a fight, Trace; you know that. But hell, man, I can take a right-of-way if I want to, and more land than I'm asking them to give me."

"Maxwell, you have the surveyor's maps that your banker friend got you?"

"Sure."

"Can I see them?"

Maxwell rose, went to his desk, and searched through a mass of papers until he found the maps. He handed them to Trace, who unfolded them, laid them on the table, and, bracing one hand on each side to support his weight, bent over the table.

"*My* banker friend?" Maxwell questioned.

"Well," Trace murmured, "he's not mine, and I'm not too sure he's anybody's . . . except his own."

Before Maxwell could question him any further, he saw that Trace seemed to have found what he wanted, for he smiled and rapped the table sharply with the knuckles of one hand. Then he refolded the map and handed it back to Maxwell.

"Now what?" Maxwell questioned.

"Now I have to go into town. Afterward, I'd like to go out and see this Mrs. Carter and the Marshalls. I have an idea somebody's been playing with both the ranchers and us."

"What's going on, Trace?"

"I don't really know yet, and I don't have any proof of anything. When I do, you'll be the first to know."

"Fair enough. You need some help?"

"Maybe . . . maybe I'll take Will with me."

"Can't. He isn't here."

"Where is he?"

"I sent him out to check the area for a supply of wood. We need it for ties and firewood. Once he finds a good stand, he can see who owns it and see if he can strike a bargain to buy it."

"Maybe it would be better if I checked a few things for myself first."

"Good. Maybe you can bring Eileen back with you when you come. She went into town the day before yesterday. I suppose she'll be ready to come home by now. She does get bored easily."

"If she wants to leave, I'll ride home with her," Trace agreed.

Again he left the railroad camp and headed into the town. He wanted to talk to Taylor Jessup and a few other people. Then he was going to convince Jenny that she was wrong about him—one way or another.

Howard Graham rode with the same feeling of inadequacy that always gripped him when he allowed himself to think of the loss of Martha and the struggle his children were undergoing for him. But that was the problem. His children fought because he could not, and each battle they won made him weaker. He yearned for his wife with an agonizing despair that drove him to the bottle. With it, he coped with her absence in the only way he could, by seeking oblivion.

They had struggled together for so long to carve their meager holdings from the wilderness. Together they had watched the small town grow from two or three shacks to two complete main streets that crossed each other and a community that now enjoyed the advantages of a church and a small school.

Wood plank sidewalks had been built to make an area safe for walking, for the streets had become a sea of mud when it rained and almost impassable. The town boasted two general stores, one of which held a small post office in one corner, one millinery shop and several dress shops, two hotels and several boarding-houses, the bank, a stable, three saloons, and a theater that was opened only when traveling actors chanced to pass through the area.

His mind seemed lately to dwell on Martha's unselfish commitment to him and their children. They had always been side by side in all things, both the good and the bad. Now she was gone and had left within him an aching void that made the days bleak and long, and completely unbearable. He had tried, but his weakness, magnified by his children's strength, had made him incapable of facing life at all.

He found the saloon very nearly empty. Going to his usual spot, he beckoned to the bartender from a table in the far corner. The man brought a bottle with him, set it before Howard, and walked away. He did not expect Howard to pay him, and Howard made no effort to do so. Instead he poured a drink and tossed it down.

There was an inexhaustible supply of whiskey for Howard, and he knew it. He no longer cared. Taylor had been sympathetic, telling Howard he understood his need and would take care of the expenses until Howard could pay him back. Howard had no idea just how much money he owed Taylor and that the signed notes now added up to more money than he would see after years of hard work.

But there were other subtle invasions of Howard's ability to control himself, and these were the card players Taylor had hired to make sure Howard's indebtedness grew. He lost to them slowly, small amounts at a time, for Taylor saw to it that the fleecing was done carefully. But Taylor was quite satisfied. Howard owed him more than he would ever be able to repay.

Now Howard sat and drank slowly, methodically, knowing it would end in the peacefulness of oblivion.

Trace rode slowly, trying to put into perspective the

events that had just occurred. Someone believed he was getting too close to finding answers. And the logical person that would be behind the shooting of Buck was Taylor Jessup, he decided.

Trace did his best to figure out exactly what Taylor Jessup might have to gain, or, in fact, just what he was actually doing. Despite his suspicions, Trace could not determine what the plan could be. Dealing with the railroad, even if he owned all the land the railroad wanted, was not going to make Taylor exceptionally wealthy. There had to be something Trace could not see. He wanted to talk to Taylor, hoping that something might slip or that he might be able to discover whether or not Taylor had some scheme by which he could profit. He smiled to himself, knowing he was seeking the information more for Jenny than for the railroad. If Taylor had set some devious plan in motion that had been created to bring him Jenny's land—or Jenny herself—Trace wanted to find out about it.

He was not going to give up Jenny. Despite any forces against them—even her present distrust and anger—he intended to do battle to win her. Jenny had belonged to him for that brief moment, and he vowed to recapture what had been temporarily lost. Whoever or whatever was against him, including Jenny herself, would find out soon that Trace Cord was not a man to be pushed.

When he arrived in town it was late in the day. He went directly to the bank to see if he could talk to Taylor, only to find the clerk closing for the day. He was locking the door when Trace came up behind him.

"Mr. Johnson?"

Ralph Johnson leapt as if something had stung him. "Oh, Mr. Cord. I'm sorry, but if you have any business with the bank, it will have to be tomorrow."

179

"I just wanted to talk to Mr. Jessup."

"I'm afraid Mr. Jessup left a little early today. He said he had some business to transact before tomorrow."

"I see. Do you have any idea where I can find him?"

"No sir, not really. He lives in the last house at the end of the street. But I really don't know if he's there."

"Thank you. I'll try."

Ralph nodded, slipped the bank key into his pocket, smiled, and turned to walk down the street toward his own home.

Trace rode up to Taylor's house. The girl that answered the door was a buxom young woman who told Trace she was the housekeeper. She explained that Taylor was not there and that she did not expect him until late that night.

Her relationship to Taylor was immediately obvious to Trace, but he only smiled politely and left. Taylor's living arrangements did not interest him in the least. What he needed to learn were Taylor's ultimate goals in reference to Jenny, her land, and the railroad.

He had no idea where to find Taylor now, so he rode back to the saloon and tied his horse in front. He was dry and hungry.

Coming in from the light, he found the saloon dim, and it took a moment for him to adjust. When his eyes became accustomed to the gloom, he saw that the saloon was fairly empty except for two men at the bar and a group of men near the rear of the room who were in the midst of a card game. It was only after several moments that he recognized a man he had seen only once before—Howard Graham, Jenny's father.

He had no reason to approach him yet, so he walked to the bar and ordered a drink. The bartender quickly placed the bottle and glass in front of him.

"Is there any chance of getting a good meal?" he

questioned the bartender.

"Sure is. We got some good steaks."

"Fine. I'll have one, rare, and all the fixings that go with it."

"Yes sir."

Trace took the bottle and glass and moved to a table where he could keep one eye on the card game. Soon it became obvious to him that Howard Graham was very nearly drunk and playing recklessly.

He watched while he ate the meal that was brought to him and in less than half an hour he had realized another important thing: Howard Graham was being slowly and methodically cheated by a couple of slick-fingered experts who appeared, to Trace's astute eyes, to be working together.

He thought of Jenny and her desperate defense of her family and her land, and a cold anger formed a knot in his stomach, an anger directed at Howard Graham and his careless disregard for the two who loved and had sacrificed for him.

He was also reasonably sure that Howard was deliberately being set up for one special loss, most likely the ranch someone wanted. All kinds of questions formed in Trace's mind, the first of which was, Who was behind it? He would have bet his life on Taylor. But he was only half sure that this conclusion was the actual truth and not just his wish that it were so.

He saw Howard's frustration grow and watched him consume more whiskey. By that time he knew what was happening and who was cheating. He rose from his chair, picked up his bottle and glass, and walked slowly to the game table.

There were five players including Howard. All looked up when Trace approached.

"Evening, gentlemen." Trace grinned. "Is this a private game or can I sit in?"

"'Course you can sit in," Howard replied to the obvious but silent disagreement of two of the others. "This is a friendly game, isn't it boys?" Howard asked with a laugh.

"Of course it is," a sullen man sitting opposite Howard replied. He was one of the men whom Trace had seen cheating.

Trace set the bottle and glass on the table, then slowly dragged up a chair from the next table. He had a smile on his lips and a look of challenge in his eyes that the others could not ignore.

"What's the game, and what stakes?" he inquired casually as he sat down.

"Five-card draw, no limit," the sullen one said gratingly. "Jacks or better to open and three-card draw only."

"Kind of rich, isn't it?" Trace chuckled.

"If it's too much for you, friend," the second cheat replied with a grim smile, "then why don't you find another table to drink at."

"I don't think so . . . *friend,*" Trace insisted. This time his voice had a knifelike edge. "This game interests me."

As Trace slowly sat down, he withdrew his gun from the holster and set it on the table. "I'm a careful man," Trace explained with a grin. "I get upset if any rules are broken. If I get upset, I tend to use old Bess here." He patted the gun and smiled, but his eyes remained cold.

"You've got a familiar face," Howard said. "Have I met you before?"

"No . . ." Trace replied honestly. "We've never been introduced." The only time Howard had seen Trace had been for the few moments during which he had confronted Jenny and Howard in this same saloon.

Howard still gazed at him as if he were trying to remember. Then he gave a slight wave to the men about him.

"This is Rodger Dulin." The man sitting next to Trace, to whom he had mentally referred to as the first cheat, nodded to him. "The man next to him is Brad Marlin, then Steve Dixon, and next to me is Jake Monroe." The last was the man Trace believed to be the second cheat.

"Please to meet you, gentlemen," Trace said.

"Let's get this game going," Rodger said. He picked up the cards and began to shuffle them.

Trace played carefully, watchfully, and for the first three hands he won fairly good-sized pots. Then he lost two and won another three. By this time he had a sizable amount of money before him, while Howard's pile had dwindled.

Suspecting they were being watched, Rodger and Jake made no overt moves. But Howard's money was low and Trace knew they soon would.

Trace was sure the next hand would be the final one, for Howard had less than five hundred dollars before him. Again it was Rodger's deal. He shuffled and began to flip the cards toward each player. Trace kept his eyes carefully trained on Rodger's hands.

Trace picked up his cards and fanned them slowly. He had three deuces, a queen, and a ten, and the desire to see how far Rodger and Jake intended to push Howard.

Brad tossed some chips into the pot. "I open for two hundred."

"I'm in," Steve announced, tossing in his chips.

"Me too," Jake said.

Howard threw in his chips, Trace followed, then Rodger laid his cards down and lifted the remainder of the deck after he had tossed in his chips.

Brad, who had two jacks, asked for three cards and received a six, a four, and a nine.

Steve, who had three queens, called for two cards and drew a six and an eight.

Jake, who was to remain in the game only to set up Howard for Rodger, held three sevens. He drew two cards and received a nine and a four.

Now it was Howard's turn. He held three kings and, in his liquor euphoria, felt he had the winning hand. He drew two cards and received an eight and a five.

Now Rodger looked at Trace. Trace smiled and placed his free hand gently on his gun. The movement did not go unnoticed by Rodger, who began to sweat.

"I'll take two," Trace said softly. Rodger flipped the cards to him. When he looked at them, Trace found he had drawn another deuce. He now held four deuces.

Rodger gave himself two cards and laid the deck aside. He now held a full house, three aces and two nines.

Again the bet was Brad's. He threw in his chips, saying, "A hundred."

Steve added his chips to the pot and was followed by Jake, who raised two hundred. Howard, sure of his position, threw in his three hundred, as did Trace. Rodger promptly pushed three hundred toward the pot, then added five hundred more with a smile. "I see your three and raise five."

By now Brad knew he wasn't strong enough and folded. Steve pushed in his five and was followed by Jake.

Howard gazed at the huge pot forming on the table. He only had two hundred in front of him. But he still felt he had the winning hand. "It appears"—he laughed shakily—"that I'm a little short."

"Then it looks like you have to fold," Jake answered quickly.

"Look," Howard said desperately, "I'll put my note in the pot."

"Forget it, Howard," Rodger replied. "Cash or fold. We don't want any IOU's."

"No . . . no, not an IOU. I have the deed to my ranch. Will you put your money against that?"

Trace knew very well that this was what Rodger and Jake had wanted. He watched as all at the table agreed. Howard laid the deed before him, confident that it would not leave his possession. With a smile, he placed his cards on the table after Trace and Rodger had agreed to remain in.

"Three kings, gentlemen." Howard laughed. Steve folded and was followed by Jake, who still had a smug look on his face.

Rodger chuckled confidently. "Too bad, Howard. I'm afraid I've got your three beat." He laid down his hand and reached for the pot.

"I'm afraid," Trace interrupted softly, "you shouldn't be so hasty."

Roger looked at him in surprise. Then Trace laid down his cards. "I do believe four deuces beats your full house."

# Chapter 13

Rodger stared at Trace in absolute shock. He had been so sure when he had slipped himself the full house; he had believed he was unbeatable. His surprise turned to rage, a rage so intense that his hands actually quivered. How was he going to explain to Taylor Jessup that he had let Howard Graham's ranch slip through his fingers. He wanted desperately to reach for the gun he had concealed beneath his coat, but Trace's hand was still resting gently on the gun before him. The glow of contempt and challenge lit his grey eyes with the taunting suggestion that he would like nothing better than to see Rodger reach for a weapon.

Rodger's face was lard grey, and there was a knot in the pit of his stomach. He was looking into the eyes of unrelenting death. One false move and the gun before Trace would speak; its destructive voice would end Rodger's life in the blink of an eye. He knew Trace would not hesitate. Slowly he sat back in his chair, trying to regain his composure, while Trace slowly pulled his winnings toward him.

Howard sat in stunned silence. He felt now as if his life were an empty void. He had lost all he had, all that Jenny and Buck had. He wanted to die. He reached a trembling hand for the bottle Trace had set before him, but Trace was angry enough at him for the way he had hurt Jenny. He reached out and took the bottle.

Trace's voice was cold. "The whiskey belongs to me too," he said, then he turned his wintry smile on the others. "I believe the game is over, gentlemen."

There was no argument. In fact, Rodger and Jake were quite willing to leave before there were any more problems. Within a few minutes, Trace and Howard were sitting at the table alone.

Howard looked as if he were about to weep. His face was grey and his now-sober mind was beginning to register what he had just done.

"Who . . . who are you?"

"My name's Trace Cord. I'm with the railroad," Trace said brutally, watching Howard wince under the final blow. He had lost Jenny and Buck's inheritance to the railroad. Now they need not even pay for it. The Grahams were nearly destitute.

"Oh God . . . my God. . . ." Howard groaned as he buried his head in his folded arms on the table.

Trace was still angry, but he felt Howard needed such a severe shock to force him to make changes. Howard had no way of knowing that Trace had no plans to keep the ranch. Trace laughed a little to himself. If Jenny had wanted to kill him because she believed he had had her brother shot, what would she do if she knew Trace had taken the ranch she loved so dearly and had worked so hard to keep? Certainly she would want to see him dead; in fact, she would probably do it herself, he mused.

Trace was going to try to accomplish two difficult tasks at the same time, tasks he was not sure he could accomplish, though for Jenny's sake he intended to try.

"Sit up, man," he snapped. "Don't you have any courage at all?"

Howard jerked as if he had been struck. He was not yet totally lost, Trace thought. He remembered what Jenny had told him about the death of her mother. He wanted to help pick Howard up, just because he knew it would make Jenny happy.

Slowly Howard sat erect. From some long forgotten source he gathered the courage he had lost. He looked at Trace.

"I'm sorry. You are right. You won my ranch . . . all I have. I want the chance to get it back somehow."

"Why should I do that? Since you were so careless with it, maybe you don't deserve it."

"You might be right about that, Mr. Cord, but my children do."

"You should have thought of them a long time ago. I've heard about you, Mr. Graham. You spend so much time feeling sorry for yourself and hiding in a bottle that you never think about what you're doing to others."

Howard took the blows and, to Trace's satisfaction, began to show some angry resistance.

"Have you ever lost someone you love, Mr. Cord?" he asked angrily.

"Yes, Mr. Graham, I have. But you have to remember the others too. I lost my parents and my brother. Does that give me the right to forget my sister, who is not to blame for any of it? It does not! Just as you have no right to make your children pay for a loss that is not only yours but theirs too. You're a fool if you drink away the love of your children," he added softly.

Howard sat in silence for a moment as the full realization of what he had done to Jenny and Buck finally hit him and he saw it as the act of cruelty it had been. For the first time since his wife had died, he felt true compassion, and fear—fear that now what he had lost would destroy his children's faith in him once and for all.

"Mr. Cord . . ." he began in a gentle voice.

"My name is Trace," Trace said with a smile.

"Trace . . . I need to get that ranch back from you . . . please," he added with quiet, renewed pride.

"I'll make you a bargain."

"Bargain . . . what kind of bargain?"

"For now your deed stays in my possession. It will be kept a secret between us. You will be the judge of when I return it to you."

"I don't understand."

"If you stay away from town, quit drinking, and work to rebuild your family and your life for, say, a month, and if you stop talking to or negotiating with Taylor Jessup for that long, then I will turn the deed over to Jenny and Buck and you will sign if over to them. From then on they will be safe."

Howard stared at Trace for several minutes; then he said softly, "Jenny? Buck? You know my children?"

"Yes," Trace replied, annoyed at his slip. "I'm afraid they aren't too fond of me right now."

"Then I shall tell them I—"

"You'll tell them nothing! That is part of our bargain too."

"But if they knew—"

"If you want your ranch to end up in their hands, you will tell them nothing. They must believe you have changed yourself."

Howard sighed. He did not understand, but he could see the resolution in Trace's eyes.

"I agree."

"Good. Then maybe you had best go home," Trace said.

Howard nodded. He stretched out his hand to Trace, who looked at it for a moment. Then he spoke gently but firmly. "I'll shake hands with you a month from now, if you've kept your bargain."

Howard nodded, turned, and slowly left the bar.

Trace sat down and poured himself a drink. He gulped it down hastily then poured another. At the moment he did not even understand himself. He could have made friends, negotiated, brought everything out in the open. He could have had Jenny's gratitude . . . gratitude? No, he realized. He wanted many emotions from Jenny, but gratitude was not one of them.

Suddenly he felt tired. He had promised Maxwell he would ride home with Eileen, so he decided to go to the hotel, get a room, and get some rest. Then, in the morning, he could find Eileen to tell her. He rose, gulped down the last drink, and left the bar, which was slowly filling with nighttime revelers.

Once outside, he walked across the street, then down the plank sidewalk to the hotel.

It took the clerk only a few minutes to provide him with a key to a room on the third floor.

"Miss Eileen Maxwell," Trace said. "What room is she in?"

"Room thirty-three, Mr. Cord."

"Thank you," Trace replied. He walked up the three flights of wooden steps to the third floor. It was only a few doors down to his room. He unlocked the door and stepped inside. His door was half closed when he heard another door open and a very familiar voice speak softly. He held his door open a small crack and was totally surprised by the conversation he overheard and the two conversing. It was Taylor Jessup and Eileen Starett.

Taylor had left the bank early, having decided that his rendezvous with Eileen was as much business as pleasure. He remembered well his first meeting with

191

Eileen Starett. It had been almost two years before. Her plans had begun then and he had been more than pleased to add his help when he found out what her long-range goals were. Together they would be a power—a power bigger than Maxwell Starett had ever imagined.

He walked across the street, then slipped into an alley between buildings. Then he made his way to the back stairs that were used as a safety exit from the hotel. At the top he entered the building, walked down the hall to room thirty-three, and knocked discreetly.

Eileen opened the door. The blue negligee she wore enhanced her blue eyes. She was a picture of sensual beauty that would intrigue any man. She laughed throatily.

"Taylor. It's about time. I had given you up and was about to go to bed."

Taylor's chuckle answered the glitter of seductive invitation in her eyes. He stepped inside, closed the door behind him, and took Eileen in his arms. His mouth plundered hers with a savagery that was answered in kind by hers.

Theirs was a wild and nearly violent passion as they feverishly removed their clothes and fell to the bed, entwining themselves in each other's arms. It was no mating meant to give each partner the comfort and gentleness of love. Instead it was the mating of two human animals for the sake of lust and lust alone.

Eileen's body was smooth silk and exuded the exotic fragrance of very expensive perfume, but for Taylor it was merely a means of relieving the fire that burned within him.

For Eileen it was the same, for she constantly carried an insatiable need and would seek relief from her body's demand wherever she found herself and with whomever she chose.

Afterward they lay contented, like two well-fed cats, and discussed a bargain they had made long ago, the details of which were beginning to work out just as they had planned.

"You are certain this Joanne Carter's land is yours?" Eileen asked.

"All I have to do is ride out to her ranch in a few days to pick up the papers I left for her to sign."

"I take it the foolish lady thinks she is in love with you."

"She is a lonely widow, Eileen," Taylor said in mock pity. "Have you no sympathy for the lady's lonely state?"

"Hardly," Eileen said sweetly. "What will you do when she realizes what has happened?"

"Make it impossible for her to stay here. I have some friends who will see that she and her stupid brat are gone quickly. Believe me, she will run when she finds her child's life is in danger."

"The Marshalls, Taylor?"

"They are quite willing to negotiate. Old man Marshall is quite impressed with money. I think he feels it's going to make him a big wheel in this town. Don't worry about him. A little gold coin and he's ours."

"Then we don't have any worries."

"Not that I can see."

"I shall be glad to see the end of this godforsaken town," Eileen said disgustedly.

"We will have enough power and wealth to travel anywhere in the world we choose."

"Yes," Eileen said softly. She was happy that Taylor could not read her thoughts at the moment, for it was Trace Cord she envisioned beside her, not Taylor.

"What about your dear uncle?" Taylor asked.

"My dear uncle will understand when it's too late. He

shouldn't have been so stingy with my father's money."

"Why did your father leave his money in his brother's control? Why didn't he just will it to you?"

"My dear uncle's influence. He convinced my father that I would squander it. He said, 'Put it in trust, Paul. I'll be the executor. That way our dear little Eileen will have her future secure.' Damn them both! My uncle controls my fortune and I get a trifling sum to spend while he builds his stupid little railroad. Well, I shall have my revenge. I'll have it all—my father's money, my uncle's . . . and his railroad."

"What are his competitors paying you, Eileen?"

"A tidy sum, Taylor, a tidy sum."

"Well, one day soon this will be over and we'll celebrate. Tell me, shall it be France, Spain, Italy?"

"Let's spend our fortune after we get it. For now, we have to be careful. You had best go. You have to keep your reputation intact, at least for a while longer."

Taylor's arms slid around Eileen's slim, delicious curves. His lips teased hers in a deep kiss, nibbling and tasting with luxurious slowness.

"Must I go just now?" he murmured.

"Well," Eileen replied in a ragged whisper of growing excitement, "maybe you can stay a while longer."

Taylor laughed as his hands caressed the length of her, then found the sensitive, hidden place that drew a groan of sheer animal pleasure from Eileen as she twined about him and surrendered to the heat of renewed passion.

It was much later when Eileen, her hair tangled from their lusty lovemaking, her lips slightly swollen, and her eyes languid from satisfied passion, walked to the door to kiss Taylor one more time as he left.

Unbeknown to them, Trace was watching as they kissed. He recognized Eileen's condition for what it was, the condition of a woman who had spent long hours making love.

He felt a moment of disgust, then another emotion filled him as he began to wonder when and how they had met and if passion were the only link binding Taylor and Eileen.

His suspicions began to grow, but he knew he would need proof. He closed his door, removed his boots, and lay down to think.

Trace rose and dressed early the next morning after having had a nearly sleepless night. He just could not seem to be able to put together all the pieces of this puzzle yet, but he intended to, for he was certain Jenny was somewhere in the center.

He walked to Eileen's room and rapped on her door. When she opened it she smiled brightly at Trace. She was as beautiful as always, and the deep rose dress she wore was tailored perfectly to enhance her exquisite form. Her gold hair was coiled at the nape of her neck in a style that seemed to widen her eyes and give her a cool, delicate look. But Trace was no longer enthralled by her beauty, for he knew some form of treachery lurked behind it.

"Good morning, Trace. What are you doing here so early in the morning?"

"I've been here all night," he said steadily. For a moment a touch of alarm lit her blue eyes, then it was gone and her mask was again in place. But Trace had already seen something that had finally destroyed any trust or affection he might have harbored for Eileen. She was involved with something dark and he felt a touch of sympathy for Maxwell. But that emotion was contained quickly. He was certain that Taylor and Eileen had planned some disaster that would soon befall Jenny and her family and the other ranchers in the valley, and any feelings he might have had for Eileen had been drowned by the stronger emotion he felt for Jenny. He had to protect Jenny; he just did not know from what. That was what he had to find out.

"All night?" she purred questioningly. "Why didn't you let me know you were here?"

"It was late when I got here and I was really tired. Besides, I thought you might have gone to bed early."

He watched her eyes as he spoke and saw the flicker of guilt, and her curiosity as to how much he really knew.

"You could have joined me," she said seductively.

"If I hadn't been so tired I might have surprised you, but I was really weary. Your uncle asked me to ride home with you. It's a rough, wild area around here and he felt you might need some protection. I don't understand how he let you ride in alone."

"He didn't . . . Poe rode with me."

"Poe?"

Eileen realized she had made a mistake by using Poe's first name so casually.

"Poe Wilson. My uncle said I could trust him." Her eyes widened innocently. "Do you think he was mistaken?"

"Poe isn't exactly the best he could have chosen. Is he still in town?"

"No, I told him to go on back. I'm sure my uncle needed him more there."

"How were you planning to go back? Alone?"

"Why . . . no . . . I . . . I just assumed my uncle would send someone for me. I'm glad it was you, Trace. We haven't been alone for much too long."

Her look was inviting, and she was disappointed when Trace ignored it. At that moment Trace was irritated with himself for ever having touched Eileen in the first place. He should have been a little smarter, for he had met many women like her.

"Well, we have to hurry, so I'm afraid it's not going to be a pleasure trip. I've got to get back."

Eileen was obviously disappointed by Trace's lack of interest, but she kept quiet and nodded.

They left the room and went downstairs. After leaving their keys with the desk clerk, they went to the stable, where Trace requested that a buggy be made ready. He tied his horse to the back and they used Eileen's horse to pull the buggy. Soon they were on their way back.

Howard Graham needed to think. He needed to form some structure upon which to rebuild his life and find some way to make up for the damage he had done to his children. He needed a drink desperately, but Trace's angry words came back to him. If he were to seek his release in a bottle again, he would lose his children's inheritance forever. If only he could walk a sober path for a month, he would have his land back.

Then came the memory of something else Trace had added to the bargain. He was not to talk to or negotiate with Taylor Jessup again until the bargain had been concluded. Why? he wondered. He had thought of Taylor as a friend. Hadn't Taylor been responsible for him finding solace after Martha had died? Had he not personally lent him money to keep him going? Hadn't he tried to give as much help as he could in negotiating with the railroad? He had made the surveys and laid out all the maps at his own expense.

Howard cringed inwardly at the amount of money he owed Taylor. His mind swirled miserably with unanswerable questions. How could he explain any of this to Jenny and Buck if he couldn't tell them about his bargain with Trace? He had never been more confused in his life, but confusion began to melt into determination. He had injured Jenny and Buck; now he had to try to do something about it, one step at a time.

He arrived home in the wee hours of the morning and was surprised to find light still glowing from the window. When he opened the door he found Jenny and Buck seated at the kitchen table. They turned in surprise when he came in, and it was painful to see their surprise grow as they discovered he was sober.

"Pa?" Jenny questioned in a whisper.

"Morning, Jenny girl," he said gently. It was then that he noticed Buck's pallor and the fact that his arm was in a sling. "Buck, what happened? One of your horses throw you again?" He smiled as he spoke and for a moment Buck could only stare at the resurrection of the father they had had all their lives.

"Uh . . . Pa . . . no . . . no, I didn't get thrown. I'm afraid . . . I got shot."

"Shot!" Howard replied in a combination of fear and shock. "How . . . Who?" he demanded.

"Sit down, Pa," Jenny suggested when she had recovered her voice. "I'll get you some coffee, and we'll explain."

When she placed the coffee before him, Howard sipped its warmth while he listened to Buck's explanation. It was only when the two siblings unanimously placed the blame on Trace Cord and the railroad that Howard became truly alarmed.

"Why do you think Trace Cord is responsible?"

Buck went on to tell him how the men had stood near him and talked.

Howard was in a terrible position. He knew that Trace had been in a card game with him most of the night. He doubted Trace's guilt and began to form questions in his mind. Why would Trace protect Jenny

198

and Buck if he wanted Buck dead? Why didn't he just turn the deed over to the railroad? And, most important, why had he forced the terms concerning Taylor Jessup? Howard vowed that when he had stabilized his relationship and credibility with his children he intended to ask Trace Cord a lot of questions.

# *Chapter 14*

A tearful Georgina blinked several times before she could clearly focus on the man who squatted near her. He was smiling and making no effort to come any closer. Her mother had warned her often about her tendency to be friendly to everyone, but this man with the kind eyes and open smile created a sense of warmth in Georgina.

"Who are you?" Georgina sniffled through her tears.

"My name is Will Bracken, and I work with the railroad," Will offered to help ease any fears she might have. "What's your name?"

"Georgina Carter." Now Georgina brushed the tears from her face and sat erect. She had heard many secondhand stories about the threat of the railroad and the monsters who ran it. But the man before her did not seem like a monster; in fact, she felt a sudden rush of warmth and friendliness.

"So, little Georgina," Will said gently, "what has upset you so much? A little girl as pretty as you should have nothing to cry about."

Georgina certainly had no intention of saying anything that would condemn the mother she loved so much, though it seemed to her that his question did not probe as deeply as his eyes.

"I hate your old railroad!" she lashed out. "If it wasn't for you, he wouldn't be coming around."

Will was quick to note the offending "he" and the child's obvious fear.

"Hate is a pretty strong word for a little girl," he replied. "What do you know about the railroad?"

"Mr. Jessup says the railroad is going to take our ranch away, and it makes Mama cry."

"Mr. Jessup," Will mused softly. "Maybe, Georgina, you'd like to come and see the railroad for yourself. Maybe you should know that the railroad doesn't mean to hurt people. It's there for your good."

"But Mr. Jessup told Mama . . ."

"What?" Will prompted.

"Nothin'." Georgina was confused. Will's kindness and her dislike of Taylor left her uncertain. "Mama says I'm not supposed to talk to strangers," she mumbled defensively.

"Well," Will suggested with a grin, "suppose I ride home with you and talk to your mother and father. Then I won't be a stranger, will I?"

"There's just Mama and me. Daddy died a long time ago, when I was a little girl."

Will stood erect and controlled his laughter at her insistence that she was far from being a little girl. "Come now, suppose we go home. On the way I'll tell you about our railroad. Maybe your mother would like to see it. She could talk to Mr. Starett. You both might get different ideas about us. You are the first person I've met from around here." His eyes sparkled with warmth to which Georgina could not help but respond. "I'd like to make friends."

"Don't you have any railroad friends?" Georgina inquired innocently.

"Sure." Will laughed. "But you never have enough

friends. We're going to be in this valley for awhile. Don't you think it would be nice if we could be friends while we're here?" He watched her interest and curiosity spark as he added, "Maybe you'd even like to take a ride on a train?"

Her eyes grew wide and her mouth round with awe. "Could I really do that?"

"If your mother agreed, I'm sure you both could. Why don't we go to your home and see?"

Georgina nodded. The whole day had taken a new turn. She mounted her pony and Will mounted his horse. They rode side by side and very slowly. Will was again amused as Georgina exploded with a million questions. He answered them as best he could while his mind dwelt on the relationship between Taylor Jessup and Georgina's mother. He knew a good deal about Trace's problems with the surrounding ranchers and wondered just what Taylor's place really was in all of it. He would have to inform Trace of anything he found out.

"Why do you want to come all this way out here?" Georgina questioned.

"Well, I guess for the same reasons men build bridges over rivers. To go to the other side. It kinda brings our country a little closer together."

"Oh," Georgina responded thoughtfully. "If you want to bring people closer together, why do you take their homes away?"

"We don't want to take your home away."

"But Mama says—"

"Your mother doesn't really understand what we want."

"Yes, she does," Georgina argued. "Mr. Jessup told her."

"Well . . . maybe Mr. Jessup doesn't really understand either," Will said thoughtfully.

Georgina's astute gaze remained on Will for some time. "I don't like Mr. Jessup," she finally declared.

Will did not want to push her. He knew he was in very sensitive territory and one false move might destroy any possibility of a relationship developing with her or her mother. He was amused that a little girl's opinion suddenly seemed so very important. Another thing surprised him. He had begun to wonder about her mother, and what existed between her and Taylor Jessup.

"Oh?" he responded casually, as if the answer were not of too much importance to him.

"He's not ever going to be my father! Not ever!" she exclaimed angrily.

"Your mother is going to marry Mr. Jessup?" he questioned in surprise.

"Well . . . Mama didn't say so . . . but Mr. Jessup acts like she is."

He saw a lonely little girl hungry for a father's love, and he felt a pang of sympathy. He had loved his son and his wife so much and even now experienced the pain of loss.

"Well, little one," he replied gently, "maybe your mother doesn't intend to. Don't you think you ought to wait until she says it's so before you get upset about it?"

"I . . . I guess so."

"Is your ranch far from here?"

"No, just a little further."

Again they rode in silence, which was not broken until the house came into view. The dwelling was small and sat low against the dark green of a stand of trees that grew behind it.

"That's where I live," Georgina informed him, pointing.

Will had once owned a productive farm. He had built it from nothing and had taken great pride in it. He could instantly see that the Carter ranch had once been very well cared for but was now slowly deteriorating.

He frowned, knowing how difficult it was even for a man to run such a place. His curiosity was stirred again as he speculated about the woman who had the courage and strength to try it alone. Maybe selling to the railroad would be better for her.

He saw Georgina's mother walk out on the porch and gaze in their direction. He could tell by the still stiffness of her body that she was alarmed when she saw two riders approaching. She knew one was her daughter, but she could not recognize the second rider.

When they halted in front of the porch, Joanne was the first to speak, her voice barely able to contain the strain and worry she felt.

"Georgina, where in heaven's name have you been? I've been worried to death about you. How many times have I told you not to go riding away like that without telling me where you are going?"

"I'm sorry, Mama," Georgina said contritely. "I forgot. I just rode down to the creek."

"I see," Joanne replied, but her eyes had gone to Will, who still remained silent, not wanting to interfere in a family affair.

"Mama, this is Mister Will Bracken. I met him down by the creek. He was lookin' for wood."

Will laughed softly. "Not exactly just looking for wood, little one," he said. "Miz Carter, I'm sorry, but it seems I was trespassing on your property. I work for the Starett Line."

"The railroad?" Joanne questioned suspiciously.

"Yes, ma'am. I guess that must be a very dangerous thing to say around this valley. But if you'll just let me step down, I'll explain what I'm doing here."

Joanne watched him thoughtfully for a moment. He seemed sincere, and certainly not a threat either to her or Georgina, for he had made sure the child had been brought home safely.

"I have hot coffee on the stove and biscuits in the oven, Mr. Bracken. It's the least I can do for the safe return of my daughter. Would you like some?"

"Fresh homemade biscuits, ma'am?" Will said wonderingly. "I'd walk across the whole Indian nation to have some. I haven't tasted them since . . . for a long time. I'd be mighty grateful to you."

"Come in, Mr. Bracken."

Will stepped down from his horse, a pleased grin on his face. "I'd consider it a real pleasure, ma'am, if you'd call me Will. Mr. Bracken seems kinda odd to me."

"All right . . . Will. Come in and eat."

Will followed Joanne and a very excited Georgina into the house.

The biscuits were exceptional and Will ate until he couldn't manage another bite. Finally he sat back in his chair and sighed contentedly.

"Ma'am, I have to say that's the best meal I've had in a long, long time."

"Where are you from, Will?"

"Georgia."

"That's quite a distance from here."

"Yes, ma'am."

His reticence made her aware that he did not want to talk about himself. It made her even more curious.

Will reminded her so much of her husband. Not his features, she mused, for his face was older . . . no . . . more mature, as if something had aged a young man too soon. There was something else about him that brought the memories to the surface. Then she suddenly realized what it was—his hands.

They were large hands, callused and sturdy. They were a farmer's hands, those of a man like her husband, who had labored to tame the land they were on.

Will was aware of her scrutiny, but he had protected his injured spirit too long. He wanted no one to pierce the shield he wore between himself and the memories he had stored away.

"Well ma'am," Will said, rising from his chair, "I better be gettin' on. I have a job needs doin' and I don't want to lose it. By the way, you have a lot of timber on your land we sure could use. It wouldn't do much harm to thin out that stand of trees a little."

"I . . . I'm sorry, Will. I can't do that."

"Why not?"

"You must know your railroad isn't too welcome in this valley."

"I've heard rumors"—Will smiled—"but I sure can't figure out why. I would think the railroad would be a blessing out here."

"Far from a blessing," Joanne replied quietly. "We . . . my husband and I, put all we had into this land; all our sweat and tears are here. It took Jim years merely to clear it to farm and build this cabin. I can't just give it away for a few dollars. It would be betraying all Jim wanted for me and Georgina."

"I get the feelin' y'all don't know much about what the railroad really wants. My daddy always told me not to go into a fight until I knew what both sides was fightin' over. You ought to take a look and a listen to what they want. It can't do too much harm to listen to the other side of the story."

"I know more than you think."

"How's that, ma'am, way out here, not talkin' to anyone from our side?"

"That old Mr. Jessup told us," Georgina said.

"Georgina!" Joanne was mildly angry at Georgina's interruption.

"Well, he did," Georgina said defensively.

"Georgina, I think you'd best clear the table."

"Yes, Mama," Georgina replied. She slid from her chair and began to obey her mother's calm request, but Will could have laughed, for, despite her obedience, he could see the glow of determination in her eyes. She could not voice her anger, but she had not changed her opinion for a moment. She was very little like Joanne and Will began to wonder about her father, and even more about the always-present shadow of Taylor Jessup. His first thought was that if Jessup were so interested in these two people, why didn't he find some way to get her a little help for all the hard work that needed to be done? One such thought gave birth to another. Somehow he wanted to do something for her, and he knew the reason—her daughter's wide and distrustful eyes.

"Despite what you might think, Will," Joanne said firmly, "I have no intention of selling any of my land to the railroad."

"Ma'am"—Will grinned—"you sure are all-fired determined not to trust people you haven't even taken the time to talk to. For the benefit of the doubt, why don't you come down and see. Talk to 'em. I think you'll find there's not as big a problem as you think. I kinda promised the little one she could have a short ride on the train . . . if you don't mind."

"Well . . ."

"Ma'am, I'd hate to disappoint her. It's nothin' but a little ride. What could you lose?"

Joanne smiled as she looked into Will's warm eyes. "You have a way about you, Will. I don't suppose it would hurt to let Georgina see it."

"That's just fine." Will smiled broadly. "And I'll tell you what, ma'am. In return for that little favor, I'll be back tomorrow and give you a hand with that corral fence. It needs some mending."

"Now Will"—Joanne looked more closely at the

twinkle of humor in Will's eyes—"I do believe you are trying to put me in your debt."

"No, ma'am," Will protested. "That meal and the chance to make that pretty little one smile at me again kinda puts me in your debt."

"Will, I don't want any favors from the railroad, because I don't intend to sell land to them," Joanne insisted, trying to be firm.

"Ma'am, this has nothin' to do with the railroad. It's kinda from me to you and the girl."

"Why?"

"Why? . . . Well, I guess it's a lot of things. I hate to see a nice place like this needin' work. I used to farm a piece like this one. Maybe I just. . . ." He paused, then smiled. "I just want to convince you none of us are here to steal anything from you. Shall I come for you tomorrow?"

"All right, Will." Joanne laughed. "You win. Georgina can have her ride on a train and I'll take a look at it myself."

"Good. On my first day free I'll come do some of the repairs. But you have to promise me a couple of more meals like this one."

"It's a promise."

"Thank you, ma'am. I'll be here just after sunsup."

"Fine. Will?"

"Yes ma'am?"

"Do me a favor."

"Yes ma'am."

"Stop calling me ma'am." Joanne laughed. "You make me feel like an old lady."

"Yes ma'am," Will began, and they both laughed.

"Sorry," Will added as his eyes grew serious. "You're sure too pretty to feel old."

Before she could respond, Will rose to his feet, picked up his hat, and walked to the door. He turned and smiled at a surprised Joanne and a very delighted Georgina. Then he was gone and in a few minutes they could hear the sound of a departing horse.

"Mama?" Georgina interrupted Joanne's thoughtful stare at the closed door.

"Yes, honey?"

"I like Will."

"You don't know anything about him," Joanne said positively. "You are entirely too trusting, Georgina, and I've warned you again and again about taking up with strangers."

"Well . . . I like Will anyway."

"You like everyone, my girl."

"No, I don't. I don't like—"

"Georgina, let's take care of the stock. It will soon be time for you to be in bed."

Georgina smiled. "You liked Will too."

"Now Georgina, I'm beginning to lose patience with you."

"Are we really going to see the train, Mama? Can I really ride in it?"

"I suppose." Joanne smiled. "It might be interesting, but for tonight we have work to do."

Georgina trotted after her mother and before the sun set they were both tired but finished with the chores.

After Joanne had tucked a still-chattering Georgina into bed, she returned to the kitchen to sit in front of the slowly dying fire. She looked for a moment at her hands that lay in her lap and found them red and work worn. For a moment she stared at them, remembering how Jim had held them when he had proposed to her. Had it been so long? She drew upon images of Jim and their life together, then became truly shaken when her usually ready visions of her husband became vague and blurred and in his place she saw another, a man who was hard and lean and had the same rough yet gentle hands. No matter how she tried to hold it at bay, the aching loneliness overcame her and she buried her face in her hands and cried.


The sun had barely touched the horizon when Georgina bounced on her mother's bed.

"Mama . . . Mama, are you awake?"

"I am now," Joanne groaned. "For heaven's sake, Georgina, it's not even daylight yet."

"But Mama, if we hurry with the chores we can be ready when Will comes."

"I've never seen you so anxious to do chores before." Joanne laughed.

"Mama," Georgina complained.

"All right, all right. I'm getting up."

Georgina was so excited she could barely eat her breakfast and she pushed Joanne to complete her work until Joanne was totally exasperated. She was about to snap at Georgina when there was a knock on the door.

"It's Will!" Georgina cried as she ran to the door and flung it open. The smile died as she looked up at Taylor Jessup.

"Good morning, Georgina," Taylor said pleasantly.

"Good morning, Mr. Jessup," Georgina replied unhappily. Joanne came to stand behind Georgina.

"Good morning, Taylor."

"Joanne." Taylor smiled. "May I come in?"

"Oh . . . of course," Joanne replied as she stepped back and drew Georgina with her.

"We're goin' out," Georgina said stiffly.

"Oh?"

"Georgina, that's not polite," Joanne admonished.

"You're going somewhere, Joanne?"

"Well . . . yes, Taylor, we are."

"Where?"

Before Joanne could reply, they heard the sound of an approaching horse. All three moved out onto the porch to watch Will as he rode up.

"Mornin'," he called with a grin.

"Good morning, Will," Georgina cried excitedly.

"Y'all ready to go, little one?"

"Sure am."

"Will," Joanne said, "this is Taylor Jessup. Taylor, this is Will Bracken."

"Good morning, Mr. Jessup," Will said, his eyes growing wary.

"Will Bracken," Taylor said. "You're not from around here. Are you new in the territory?"

"I'm with the railroad, Mr. Jessup."

"Really. What business do you have on Carter land then? You are trespassing."

"Taylor . . . no . . ." Joanne began. Taylor turned from Will to Joanne with anger lighting his eyes.

"You know this man, Joanne?" he asked arrogantly. Will was watching Georgina and fighting the urge to feel the jut of Taylor's jaw against his fist.

"Yes, Taylor. I know him."

"He's taking us down to see the train," Georgina bubbled.

"The railroad," Taylor said as if to himself. Suddenly he snapped, "Joanne, can we talk alone?"

"Of course. Come in. Georgina, wait out here with Mr. Bracken."

Once inside, Taylor closed the door and turned to face Joanne.

"Joanne, what is this? What's this railroad man doing here?"

Joanne had finally reached the end of her tolerance. "Really, Taylor, this is my house. I believe I can invite anyone into it that I choose."

Taylor knew he had made a mistake and tried to

212

rectify it quickly. But it had been enough to stir a vague touch of suspicion within Joanne, that she had not felt before.

"Joanne . . . my sweet," Taylor said as he tried to draw her into his arms, "I'm sorry. I guess I'm just a little bit jealous of anyone who comes near you."

"You needn't be, Taylor," Joanne said, but she moved out of his embrace and Taylor's annoyance was heightened.

"Joanne," he began gently, "did you sign those papers for me? It looks like the railroad is moving in on you already. It's a good thing we were prepared for this. I'll just take the papers with me."

"No . . . I haven't signed them yet."

"Well"—Taylor smiled—"we can remedy that. Just get them and sign them and everything will be all right."

"I haven't given it much thought yet, Taylor."

"Don't you trust me enough not to worry about giving it all that much thought?"

"Of course I trust you, Taylor. But I'd really like to have more time to think about it. I'll sign them tomorrow."

"Tomorrow," Taylor repeated. He could have struck her, but instead he smiled. He promised himself to look into Will Bracken and find a way to get him out of Joanne's life as soon as possible.

"I just feel that I have to consider it before I sign. You really don't mind, do you, Taylor? As far as the railroad is concerned, Will just promised Georgina she could ride on a train. It's just a lark for her and I don't want to spoil it. She hasn't had much in the way of excitement since her father died. It's just a day of fun, Taylor."

"Of course. Go and enjoy yourself. But be very careful, my dear. They are a devious lot and they're here to destroy all that Jim built. Just keep that in mind if they try to convince you to sell your land. Remember, I'm here to look out for you."

"I'll remember."

Again Taylor reached for her and ignored the stiffness of her body as he kissed her. Then they walked back out onto the porch.

As Taylor rode away, his mind was centered on one thought: no matter what Joanne had said, she had referred to the railroad man as Will.

# Chapter 15

When Taylor returned to his office, he was in a state of cold rage. He became even angrier when there was a light, almost imperceptible, knock on the door of his office that led outside to a back alley. He knew who was there. He rose and opened the door to admit the two men who had played cards with Howard Graham.

"Well," he said quickly, "I hope you got what I sent you for. The drunken sot should have been easy pickings for you."

"Mr. Jessup . . . we . . . well, it just didn't work out the way you planned."

"What do you mean?"

"Well. . . ah . . . there was this reb who—"

"Reb!" Without a doubt Taylor knew that Trace Cord had intruded on his plans again. "Tell me what happened."

"He won."

"Won . . . money?"

"No, the Graham ranch and every dime you gave us."

"You two stupid jackasses! How did you let that happen?"

"You don't think we planned it that way, do you?"

one man protested. "He just got lucky."

"Lucky . . . damn!" Taylor grated. For several minutes, to the discomfort of the two who watched him intently, he stood lost in thought. Then he smiled.

"Well, well, well, what an opportune situation." He chuckled.

The two men exchanged glances, wondering at the sudden change in Taylor.

"You think we ought to kill this jayhawk?"

"No, no, my friend. He has just made a very stupid mistake. Go on out to the railroad site and keep an eye on what's going on."

"What are you going to do about the ranch?"

"Well, I'm going to take a little ride to the Graham place. When I get there, I'm going to inform Jenny, and her brother if he's there, that our railroad sharp has just taken their ranch from them . . . by cheating their father at cards. I'm quite sure this will put things in just the place I want them."

"Want us to do anything to stop the tracks from being laid?"

"Not yet. I'll send you word if that's necessary."

"All right. We'd better get going."

Taylor let them out the back door, locked it securely, then crossed the room and left his office.

"Mr. Johnson, I have to go out on business. I will probably not be back today."

"All right, Mr. Jessup."

Taylor was quite pleased as he left the bank, despite Joanne's temporary resistance. With a few words he was going to destroy any contact Jenny Graham would have with Trace Cord and the railroad.


The trip back to the railroad site was a silent one for Eileen. There was something that seemed to be weighing heavily on Trace's mind, and she could not penetrate his thoughts. It annoyed her, for she felt that somehow Trace was slipping from her control. When they stopped to rest the horses and eat, she began to seek answers.

Trace knelt by the fire, slowly feeding it pieces of tree branches he had gathered from the ground. Eileen watched him through narrowed eyes. He was so handsome, she thought. His lean body bending close to the fire grew taut, and she could see the hard muscle of his back as the shirt stretched tight. In her mind she could still feel the strength of that body when they had last been together. She wanted him with an almost fierce possessive need.

He had made no move to touch her since the first time they had been together, and since they had started home he had been strangely quiet.

Trace's thoughts were on Jenny; in fact they had been ever since their last moment together. He could still see the anger in her eyes and the renewed distrust that had destroyed what had been only tenuous at best. He wanted her and was forming and discarding plan after plan to be able to reach her again. One thing he knew for certain—he had to try to discover why and by whom her brother had been shot. And the last thing he wanted was for Jenny to find out he now owned her ranch. He hoped at least that the next thirty days would see a change in Howard Graham and give Jenny some peace of mind.

"Trace?" Eileen said softly. His mind was so involved with Jenny that Trace never heard. "Trace!" she repeated with a tinge of annoyance.

"What?" he replied, startled from his concentration.

"Will we camp early?" she said seductively, hoping he would agree and they could share a long, exciting night together.

"No, we're going to eat, rest the horses, then go on. It will be late, but we can make it back to camp tonight."

"Tonight?" Eileen queried blankly. "Are we in that much of a hurry?"

"I've got work to do, Eileen, and I have a lot of things to discuss with Maxwell. At this point we're very nearly standing still. I'm sure Maxwell is nervous."

"I really don't think I can make it that fast, Trace," Eileen pouted obstinately. "I can't really see what one night could do. Don't you want to stay with me?" She lowered her voice and leaned toward him, offering herself blatantly and openly.

"It's just the wrong timing, Eileen," Trace said firmly as he rose to his feet. "You wouldn't want to do Maxwell any harm, would you?" He walked from the fire toward the horses, where he proceeded to see to their comfort. He wanted them both in good shape because, no matter the time, he fully intended to reach camp tonight. He had a lot of unanswered questions in his mind, and his suspicion about Taylor and Eileen being involved in some sort of conspiracy was uppermost. Despite Eileen's beauty, he found he was not drawn to her any longer. He did not have it in him to insult a man like Maxwell, who had given him so much, and the vision of Jenny constantly in his mind was an even more effective preventative.

Eileen gazed at Trace's retreating form with a look that bordered on hatred. She had never been thwarted in anything she had ever wanted. No man had ever turned his back on her. For a moment she was tempted to leap to her feet and scream her anger at him. Then, with determined effort, she controlled herself. She knew that Trace was a man tied to a set of values, and she would deal with those values when the time was right. She narrowed her eyes as she began to wonder if Jenny Graham were in any way connected to Trace' determination to go on. She kept her thoughts to herself, but the idea of Jenny loomed as strongly in her mind as in Trace's, though with totally different resolves.

They ate hastily prepared food and before long were remounted and again on their way.

When they arrived at camp, it was quiet and the night fires had burned low. There was a glow of light emanating from Maxwell's car as well as Allison's. Trace was sure his sister was still awake and grinned to himself as he speculated on the reason.

Leaving a silent and half-angry Eileen at her door, he walked swiftly to his car and entered. He had expected to see Allison awake, but he was surprised to find Will with her.

"Will, is something wrong?"

"I'm sorry for keepin' Allison up so late, Trace, but I wanted to talk to you before morning."

"The last time I saw Maxwell, he said you were off scouting some timber for us."

"Yeah, I was. But I ran across something a hell— sorry Allison—a lot more interesting."

"What did you run across?"

"Well"—Will laughed—"what I ran across was a little girl cryin' her eyes out."

Trace looked at Will blankly for a moment.

"What's that got to do with anything?"

"A lot. You see, the kid was the daughter of the lady who owns the Carter place."

"And?"

"And when I took her home, I talked with her mother for a while. It seems we all have a mutual friend—Taylor Jessup."

"Well, well," Trace said softly. "Sit down, Will. I'll get you a drink and we can talk about this."

"I'll pour the drinks," Allison said.

"Aren't you up late, Allison?" Trace smiled. "I'm sure you must be tired."

"If you think, Trace Cord, that I'm going to go to bed like a good little six-year-old and miss out on all the gossip, you're crazy. You and Will sit and talk. I," she said firmly, "will pour the drinks."

Both men laughed. Trace was tired, but his interest was too deep to ignore what Will had to say. He sat and propped his feet on the small table, sagging wearily in the chair.

"Okay, Will, tell me what's going on."

"I don't know if there's anything going on. I just got a little suspicious when Georgina said she wasn't too fond of Jessup." Will went on to explain to Trace just about everything that had occurred—everything except his attraction to Joanne and Georgina and his deep urge to lay his hands on their neglected ranch and see it grow.

"So you think the same thing I do," Trace admitted. "I have a feeling Jessup is mixed up in entirely too much in the valley. In fact," Trace added, eyeing Allison as he spoke, "I think Jessup and Eileen Starett are in this together somehow."

"I knew it!" Allison asserted smugly. "I just knew that little witch was mixed up in something."

"But I'm not sure of what, Allison," Trace said. He continued on, recounting how he had seen Taylor and Eileen together.

"Well, what are you going to do about it?" Allison demanded.

"Just what do you expect me to do about it?" Trace retorted.

"Tell Maxwell," Allison said decisively.

"Tell him what? That I think his niece is having an affair? That's a little petty, isn't it? I don't have one grain of evidence that the two of them are doing anything."

"Trace," Will interjected before Allison could put into words her disgust, "I asked Joanne . . . Mrs. Carter . . . and Georgina to come down here in the morning. I kinda promised the kid a ride on the train. I could see to that and get you, Maxwell, and Mrs. Carter together to talk. I think she only knows one side of things."

"Sounds familiar," Trace grated. "This Jessup has been filling the Grahams and all the others full of tales about us and the railroad that aren't true. The only problem is, I can't see what he's got to gain. A few dollars from selling a small amount of land just doesn't seem worth all this."

"There must be something we don't see," Allison offered.

"Yeah, but what?" Will replied.

"We'll have to watch and wait," Trace said. "They have to play their cards sometime."

"Well, anyway," Will said as he rose from his seat, "I'll be going out first thing in the morning and bringing Mrs. Carter and her girl in."

"Good idea," Trace said. He followed Will to the door and closed and locked it after him. He turned to see the sparkle of laughter in Allison's eyes.

"Now what kind of mischief is in your mind?"

"You don't listen too well, Trace."

"Listen to what?"

"Will has got a real interest in this lady."

"Now how do you know that?"

"When he slipped and called her Joanne, he got all red and shaken up. I really hope so. Will is a wonderful man and he's a fine farmer. I bet he'd be much happier settling down."

"You been reading those dime novels again, Allison?" Trace laughed. "You're always matchmaking."

"I like Will, Trace," Allison said seriously. "He's been hurt bad enough by the war and all, losing all he did. I'd just like to see him happy."

"I know, Allison. I guess I feel the same. But that's up to Will, and don't you get involved. Why don't we both go to bed? I'm tired and I have a lot to do tomorrow."

Allison nodded, but her mind dwelt on the shadows she saw in her brother's eyes and, as she drifted off to sleep, she wondered if their lives would ever be settled and happy as they had been before the war had ended it all.

Trace lay awake long after Allison slept. He allowed himself the luxury of drawing on his memory of Jenny. He could still see the anger and the hurt in her eyes after she had been told he had been responsible for her brother's injury. Trace knew quite well that Howard could redeem him, but it would mean revealing that he had won their ranch in a game of cards and that would only make Jenny hate him more than she did now.

Stronger and more poignant visions came to him and he grasped them and savored them, yearning for the day he would possess Jenny again. As he envisioned her soft body in the glow of candlelight, his body reacted with a vengeance. Trace refused to believe, even in the smallest part of his logical mind, that Jenny would not be his again. He made his decision. He would go and watch, and when Jenny was alone he would find a way to convince her that he was not guilty of the attack. He smiled to himself, knowing it was the thought of seeing her again that urged him on. He wanted her and he was determined enough not to let anything stand in his way. The last thought in his mind when he went to sleep was the soft touch of Jenny's lips and the sweet wonder of his love for her. He had tasted Jenny's surrender once and he would move Heaven and Hell to hold her again in his arms.

\*　　　\*　　　\*

222

Will had gone long before Trace woke up. It was much later than he had planned to rise, so he washed, shaved, and dressed quickly. He skipped food and walked to Maxwell's car, only to find it empty.

He strode to where the tents were set up and found Maxwell bending over a map.

"Morning, Maxwell."

"Trace." Maxwell laughed. "I thought you were going to sleep all day, boy. Thanks for bringing Eileen home."

"She still asleep?"

"Yep. I guess all that shopping got her tired out."

"Yeah," Trace said quietly, "I guess so. Maxwell, Eileen's your brother's daughter?"

"Yes, why?"

"Just curious. Is she the only relative you have left?"

"The only one, Trace. When my brother died, he made me the executor of his estate so I could make sure Eileen was well taken care of and safe the rest of her life. When I die, she'll get all of her inheritance from my brother and mine as well. By then I hope she'll be happily married and ready to handle all that money."

Again Trace was puzzled. If Eileen was to inherit everything, why would she want to help stop the railroad? Why should she be involved with Taylor Jessup? He grew helplessly angry. What the hell motive did she have? he wondered, And what motive did Taylor have? Most important, how were they linked together?

"I never asked you how you came to do business with Jessup. I suppose he traveled east and you and Eileen met him there."

"No, he never came east. We did all of our business by mail. It was a mutual friend of ours who suggested Taylor, a Martin Rosner. Neither Eileen nor I had ever met Taylor until I met him with you in town."

Trace was totally confused. Taylor had never met the Staretts before, yet the conversation and embrace he had witnessed had suggested a long-term relationship. A lot of people were lying and he needed to find out why.

Trace was about to question Maxwell more closely when Joey Mason stuck his head in the tent.

"Mr. Starett, Trace, Will's here with Mrs. Carter and her little girl. He said y'all might want to be talkin' to them."

"Yes Joey," Maxwell said. "Tell them we'll be right there."

"Sure will," Joey replied and withdrew his head.

"C'mon Trace. I've been anxious to talk to some of the people from around here. This is a good opportunity."

Trace was curious too, so he rose quickly and walked out with Maxwell to where Will was lifting Georgina down from her horse.

Will introduced Joanne and Georgina to Maxwell and Trace quickly, for Georgina seemed galvanized into perpetual motion by her excitement.

"Mrs. Carter," Maxwell said, "if you'd care to come to my car and have some tea, I'm sure Georgina's interest can be satisfied by Will. I'd like to talk to you for a few minutes."

"I'd be delighted by some tea, Mr. Maxwell. It was a long ride."

"Good."

"Georgina," Joanne admonished, "you behave yourself. Will"—Joanne laughed—"if you have any problems, bring her back to me immediately. She can exhaust the strongest of constitutions."

"Won't be no need for that, Joanne." Will looked down at Georgina's happy face. "I like children. I get along with them pretty well. We'll be back in a short while."

"Thank you, Will. I'm sure Georgina will never forget this."

"It's okay . . . it's my pleasure," Will replied quietly.

Though Maxwell seemed unaware of the subtle current of emotion between Will and Joanne, Trace was not. He smiled to himself, giving credit to Allison, for it appeared she had a nose for a romantic situation.

Joanne walked to Maxwell's railroad car between the older man and Trace while Will and Georgina moved in the opposite direction.

"Will?"

"What, Georgina?"

"My daddy always used to call me Georgie."

Will remained silent for a few minutes, remembering another child who had walked hand in hand with him so long ago. He knew Georgina was offering him a very special gift and he wasn't sure he had the courage to accept it. It would mean giving a part of himself he wasn't sure existed anymore.

"Georgie." He chuckled. "Sounds like you two were pretty close."

"We used to do everything. He used to take me fishing . . . do you like fishing, Will?"

"Sure, I like fishing . . . and lots of other things. Right now I like railroadin'," he replied to change the subject of her open invitation. "Here we are."

Georgina's eyes widened as they stopped by the large engine. Never had she seen anything so huge and formidable.

There were at least five miles between the engine and the end of track, where large clusters of men could be seen working.

"Come on, Georgina, climb aboard." Will laughed as he swung Georgina up inside the cab of the engine.

"Mackie!" he called to a man who stood some

distance away. The man walked toward him.

He was a man close to sixty, white whiskered and bushy browed. He was also quite large and for a moment Georgina was unsure. Then he grinned up at her and asked, "Ridin' my engine without me, little girl?"

"Oh, no sir. I can't do that," Georgina gasped.

Will laughed. "Don't let old Mackie scare you, little one. He's going to ride us to the end of the tracks and back, aren't you, Mackie? This little girl needs a lot of questions answered and you're just the man to do it."

Georgina's smile returned as Mackie grinned, nodded, and he and Will climbed up beside her.

"First," Mackie cautioned, "we have to build up a head of steam. Will, you toss some wood in that burner. In a few minutes, we'll be hot and ready to roll."

It was so. In less than twenty minutes the engine shuddered as Mackie released the throttle and Georgina squealed with delight as it slowly began to chug forward.

Her enthusiasm grew as Will lifted her and let her draw the cord that sounded a shrill whistle that echoed down the valley and drew the attention of the workers.

When the engine drew to a loud, rattling halt, Will lifted her down and they began to move among the men, who, when Will had told them about Georgina's interest, began to explain each individual job to her.

Georgina was fascinated by the small, hard-working Chinese men who seemed to swarm about the rails. She had never seen a man of Oriental origin before and it amused Will when, though they could barely speak to each other, Georgina and the Chinese workers found the universal way of breaching such a gap, by using sign language and laughter combined with a genuine desire to communicate.

Will introduced her next to a man named Brady,

whose size a wide-eyed Georgina could barely believe. He was the head of the group of men who saw to the base of the rail bed and the laying of the heavy wooden beams on which the sections of rails would be mounted.

She squealed with utter delight when they demonstrated for her and Brady lifted and placed the huge beams alone. His demonstration of such strength was totally wondrous to Georgina, who weighed a hundred pounds less than the beams. When Brady lifted and tossed her into the air to catch her, each participant in the game became totally captivated with the other.

She was taken next to Tucker McDoud, a burly, red-headed Scot whose job it was to join the rails. "Ya see, lassie," he explained, "the rails have got to be even or else it'll throw the train from the tracks. Let me show you."

He gave orders for a section of rail to be added to a recently placed one. Then he took up a huge mound of hook-headed spikes made of iron. They were each six inches long and nearly an inch in width, with a weight of about fourteen ounces. They were placed and pounded deep into the wood beams by teams of two men to a spike who swung in alternate movements. It took only moments for the spike to be pounded home and there was a lot of laughing challenges as to whose spike would receive the last blow first.

"Ya should see the spike Mr. Maxwell is keepin' for the last," Tucker told Georgina. "It's ribbed in iron, clad in silver, and crowned in gold, and if we get this strip to the coast on time, we're gonna have some names carved into it."

"Whose names?"

"I suppose Mr. Maxwell's and the ones he thinks contributed most to the layin'."

"You, Mr. McDoud?"

"I'm workin' on it, little girl." McDoud laughed. "I'm workin' on it. Maybe, if you was to give me a pretty smile, I might just find a place to carve in 'Georgina.'"

Georgina's smile could not have been broader or warmer. Her next words amused Will.

"I'd like that, Mr. McDoud . . . but I think Will's name ought to be there."

"Why?"

"'Cause . . . if he didn't get your wood for your rails, you wouldn't have any place to nail your spikes."

McDoud chuckled and his eyes twinkled in amusement at Will's pleasure. "I guess you're right about that." He and Will exchanged soundless laughter.

"I really didn't realize ye was so valuable to this line, Will. But I'll keep it in mind."

"You do that, Tuck," Will returned with a grin, "or I'll bring Georgina back to have a firm word or two with you."

A shrill toot on the whistle drew their attention back to Mackie, who motioned to them.

"I guess we'd better get going. Mackie has to back the engine up."

Georgina waved good-bye and ran ahead of Will to be lifted up into the engine by Mackie.

Her chattering questions seemed endless to both men as they slowly backed the engine toward the main camp.

## Chapter 16

Trace recognized Joanne immediately as the woman who had been in conversation with Jenny the first time he had ever seen her on the street. He had a multitude of questions about Jenny he could have asked, but he knew the time was wrong, though there was so much he yearned to know about Jenny.

Maxwell had Lee Chu bring tea to a totally amazed Joanne, who looked about her in awe of the comfort of Maxwell's car.

"My goodness, I had no idea these . . ."

"Cars," Maxwell supplied.

". . . Cars were so . . . elaborate."

"Well, they aren't usually. This is my private car and since my niece is traveling with me, I had it furnished to accommodate her comfortably."

"I see."

"Mrs. Carter. . . ."

"Please, call me Joanne."

"Thank you. I have wanted to come out to your ranch and talk to you for some time."

"I suppose we in the valley haven't appeared exactly hospitable to you, Mr. Starett."

"Maxwell, please."

"You must understand our position, Maxwell. Giving up our hard-earned land for the benefit of people on the other side of the country seems a rather unreasonable request."

"You say giving up your land. What is it that you think we are really asking for?"

Trace listened intently for Joanne's answer, for he was quite sure that the information she had been given was pretty much the same as what Jenny had been told, just as he had a reasonably good idea who had been dispensing all this information.

"Land on which to build your railroad," Joanne said matter-of-factly. "My land, and the land of my friends."

"Of course we need some land. But we're not asking for all of your land."

"I . . . I don't want to give up any of my land."

"Let me show you on the map just what we're talking about here," Maxwell said. He rose and went to his desk, took out the map, and unfolded it, laying it half across his lap and half across Joanne's.

"Here"—he used his finger to trace boundaries—"here is your property. This small track across the bottom near the bend of the river is all we want. You can see it would hardly interfere with your ranch at all."

Joanne looked at the map for a long time, and Trace, who stood just behind her, did the same. Again he was nagged by the thought that a railroad right-of-way was not the real problem here. He just wished he knew what the real problem was.

Joanne was confused. She wanted to believe Taylor, for he had done so much to ease her problems. But she found it difficult not to believe Maxwell and his maps.

"Maxwell, I must have time to think about this."

"I'd like to say, 'Take all the time you need,' but we are on a schedule that forbids wasting more time than we already have."

"I'll give you an answer soon, Maxwell, I promise. But I must think about it before I decide. This decision will affect my life and Georgina's for a long time."

"Of course. I hope you make the right decision."

Before Joanne could answer again, they heard the shrill sound of the train whistle over and over and the screech and rumble of the engine.

"I take it from all that racket that my daughter is back." Joanne laughed.

"I believe she is," Maxwell concurred with a chuckle.

It took the combined efforts of Joanne and Will to get Georgina out of the train, and it was only with the promise that she would get an even longer ride next time and that next time would be soon.

"I'll take Mrs. Carter and Georgina home," Will said to Trace as Maxwell and Joanne were saying good-bye.

"They're a nice family, Will," Trace said. "What happened to Mr. Carter?"

"Died a few years back . . . Trace . . . ah . . . I was kinda thinkin'."

"You were?"

"Yeah. About those trees on Mrs. Carter's property. I really ought to go back out and get 'em marked if she agrees to give 'em to us."

"I imagine they'll need marking," Trace agreed with a grin.

"Might just take me two, maybe three days," Will added.

Trace looked at Will's sober countenance. "Well, Will, if it takes you two or three days, I guess the progress the railroad could make with the Carter property might just be worth it."

"Trace?"

"Yeah?"

"I won't try to talk her out of her property, and if I

231

have any free time I'm going to give her a hand. She needs it."

"Well, we're at a temporary standstill right now, so you might as well take what time you need to . . . ah . . . mark some trees."

"Thanks, Trace. If anything breaks and you need me, send Joey out after me."

"I will. Get going, Will, before Georgina asks Maxwell one more question. I don't think he can handle another one."

It was a pleased Will, a confused and thoughtful Joanne, and a tremendously excited Georgina who mounted their horses and headed back to the ranch.

They had not ridden too far when Will hesitantly questioned Joanne.

"Joanne . . . some of the men were telling me there's going to be a dance in town next week. I'd sure be proud if you would consent to go with me."

"I haven't been to a dance since . . . for a long time, Will. I'd love to go."

"Fine!" Will exclaimed happily.

"Me too! Can I go too?" Georgina urged excitedly.

"Well, I'd be right pleased, Georgina, to escort the two prettiest girls in the territory to a dance. But you got to promise to dance with me."

"I will, I promise," Georgina said seriously.

The three rode on amid animated conversation and contented laughter.


Trace and Maxwell watched them ride away.

"Trace, why do I get the feeling something is very wrong in this valley?"

"Because something is, and the something is Taylor Jessup. I don't think Joanne is the only person Jessup has been feeding lies to."

232

"Don't you think it's about time we did something about it?"

"I'd like to go out and talk to the Grahams," Trace replied. Trace was grateful that Maxwell had no way of knowing he already owned all the Graham property.

"Well, you do that, and I'll go out and talk to the Marshalls."

"Your Mr. Jessup is not going to be too happy with us."

"If the bastard's been double-dealing me and these people, he's going to be a lot unhappier. Besides, I'm tired of sitting and doing nothing."

"The only thing that bothers me is that I can't put my finger on any kind of logical motive. What does he have to gain?"

Maxwell thought about this for awhile.

"If he gets the land to sell us, the most profit he can see is a few thousand dollars. I just don't believe he'd do all this for something that small," Trace explained.

"You think we're missing something?"

"We sure are and it scares me."

"Well, let's head him off. Let's make a deal with these people on our own and forget Jessup. The sooner we start talking, the sooner we'll bring this to a head."

"Sounds good to me."

They had started to walk to the small corral where their horses were kept when the sound of a rapidly ridden horse caused them both to turn around.

Maxwell watched with a questioning frown on his face, but Trace recognized the rider immediately. It was Jenny, and she was riding toward them at a fierce gallop. Her horse skittered to a stop in front of them and Trace looked up into the angriest turquoise eyes he had ever seen.

*     *     *

233

Jenny had sat meditating on the drastic and complete transformation in her father. He had completely changed directions in his life. He had not had a drop to drink and had begun to work with Buck. It was such an abrupt change that neither she nor Buck could understand it, but both were so grateful that they did not question it. It was enough for them that they had their father back the way he used to be.

Her thoughts had drifted then from her father to Trace Cord. She had believed his gentleness. If she closed her eyes, she could still feel his touch, though she was reluctant to let such recollections enter her mind, for they were hard to exorcise. She did not welcome the sudden tingling warmth that invaded her body, nor the breathlessness when her memory refused her attempt at control.

She had found herself unable to cope with the confines of the cabin and the memories it held. Trace was alive in her house and so tangible she could almost see him. She had felt she had to get away for awhile, so she had made the decision to ride to Joanne's and talk with her.

She had taken her horse from the corral and had been in the process of saddling it when she spied a lone rider headed in her direction. She had watched for a few minutes before recognizing Taylor.

Grabbing her horse's reins, she had walked from the corral to the porch, leading him. She had waited, wondering why Taylor was paying a visit.

Taylor had been more than pleased to make another trip to Jenny's home. This time he would make an end to the problems. This time he would make certain the Grahams would never again talk to the railroad people.

He saw her slim form as she led her horse to the

porch and stood waiting for him. At that moment he hated Trace Cord and his interfering railroad. He wanted Jenny. He knew she was alone and for a few minutes he found it hard to choose between attempting to get Jenny into his arms and telling her about her father and Trace. Greed temporarily won. He wanted Jenny to hate Trace Cord. There would be time to seduce her when the railroad was no longer a threat.

He stopped beside her and looked down into her beautiful, curiosity-filled eyes. "Hello, Jenny."

"Hello, Taylor. What brings you out here today?"

He dismounted and walked to her, standing close. "Seeing you is enough to draw me out here anytime, Jenny," he said softly.

"Thank you, Taylor, but I'm sure you must have had a reason besides me."

"I came to see your father."

"Pa's not here."

"Is he in town?" Taylor suggested softly, wanting to stimulate her anger.

"I'm afraid not, Taylor. He's out with Buck. They've been working since sunup. I'm afraid they won't be home for a couple of days. I was just about to ride over to Joanne's."

"Oh . . . that's too bad. I had hoped to talk to him."

"Is it important?"

"Well, yes. I . . . I thought he might need some more money."

"What do you mean . . . some more money?"

"Well, I'm afraid, Jenny, I've personally lent your father a great deal of money."

Jenny's face paled, but she held his gaze. "I'm sure he'll pay everything back," she said quietly.

"Jenny, Jenny," Taylor said, laughing softly, "the money doesn't really worry me. I'm sure we can make . . . some arrangement. It's your railroad friends

235

I'm worried about. I thought your father would need some money to get the ranch back." If possible, Jenny's face grew paler, but she did not speak. She only continued to look at him through wide, surprised eyes. He pressed the blade of shock more deeply. "Did he say how much he might need?"

"I . . . I don't understand," Jenny gasped, but the truth was beginning to hit her.

"I really hoped I would be in time. I thought if your father could get the money he lost in the card game, then that Rebel, Trace Cord, would have to sell him back the ranch."

"I don't believe you!" Jenny cried. "I don't believe you!"

"Oh God, Jenny," Taylor said in mock surprise. "You mean your father didn't tell you?"

Jenny licked lips suddenly gone dry. She clenched her hands at her sides and rasped in a ragged voice, "Tell me."

"It was a card game. Your father was drunk. I guess this Trace Cord challenged him and your father was duped into believing the game was fair. From what evidence I can gather, I think Cord cheated. But I'm willing to lend your father enough money to buy it back . . . if Trace Cord will sell it."

Jenny wanted to scream out her anguish, but she remained silent. She wanted a weapon with which to kill, but all she had was her fury. She stood paralyzed by the tragedy that seemed to be sucking the strength from her.

It was Taylor's next words that snapped her control. "Of course," he said suggestively, "maybe Trace Cord is hoping to deal with you. I've heard he's said many times that he'd like to have you at a disadvantage . . . He said bargaining with you when he held all the cards would be a pleasure."

"Bargain," she whispered. "Bargain with me for what is mine. I told him once. . . ." She ran up the steps and into the house. In seconds she was back out and carrying her rifle.

"Jenny! What are you going to do?"

Jenny went to her horse and leapt into the saddle. "I'm going to make Mr. Cord wish he had never seen this valley. And I'm going to make him understand that if he tries to set one foot on my land—*my* land!—I will see him dead."

She wheeled her horse and rode away, and Taylor watched her go with a smile of utter satisfaction on his face. Now, he thought, I shall go to Joanne, and this time she will sign the papers. It won't be long now, Mr. Starett. It won't be long now.

Will did not say anything about the fact that he intended to stay around the ranch for awhile, but when they arrived home, Joanne insisted she would cook for Will.

"I shore would appreciate it." He grinned. "I don't want to say too much about the camp cook, but he shore can't hold a candle to you."

"Thank you." Joanne laughed. "For that compliment I'll throw in some of those biscuits you like so well."

"My mouth's waterin' already. I'll take care of the horses."

"I'll help you, Will," Georgina offered quickly.

"Okay Georgie, let's get busy."

Georgina was delighted with the use of her pet name and they walked toward the barn together leading the horses. Joanne watched, thinking that Georgina was happier than she had seen her in a long time, but Joanne was wary nevertheless. Will was still very secretive about himself, and he was, no matter how unsuited, a representative of the railroad, which had a great deal to gain by the establishment of a relationship with her. She had to be very careful, and she had to be sure Will's friendship was not just a way to get what the railroad wanted.

In the barn Georgina chattered happily as they unsaddled and rubbed down the horses, then fed and watered them.

"Will, are you going to stay here for awhile?"

"Couple of days. I have to mark some trees, if your mother agrees to sell us some."

"Mark them?"

"Yeah, take a knife and chip the bark so the men can see which ones to cut and which to leave standing."

"Oh . . . Will?"

"What?"

"Can I show you the kittens Maggie had?"

"I'd sure like to see 'em."

Georgina led Will to a far corner of the barn where six kittens tumbled together in a pile of hay. Will bent to examine them.

"Real pretty," he said seriously.

"You can have one," Georgina offered hopefully.

"Well, little one, I ain't got no place to keep a kitten. 'Sides, they can't leave their mama yet."

"But I could take care of it for you."

Will sensed immediately what Georgina was doing. She was trying to form a tangible link that would keep Will close. Will understood her loneliness as only another lonely person could. He smiled at her.

"Well, suppose you do that. Suppose you pick out the prettiest one of the litter and I'll claim it. Then you can help me decide on a name."

"Okay," Georgina said excitedly. She bent to examine the kittens closely, then she pointed to one.

238

"That one. She's the prettiest."

"Good enough. Now we'll think on it a couple of days and come up with a good name, all right?"

Georgina nodded enthusiastically.

"Now let's go eat. I'm hungry. How about you?"

"Me too."

"Let's don't keep your mother waiting."

They walked from the barn and Will said nothing as Georgina slipped her small hand into his larger one and walked close to him.

They washed their hands and faces in a basin on the porch, then walked into a warm and fragrant kitchen, which stimulated their already ravenous appetites.

When they had sat down to eat, Will was the first to speak.

"Joanne, if you're willing to sell a few of those trees, I'd like to mark 'em so's the men could come and cut 'em."

"I don't see any reason why I shouldn't sell you some trees."

"Good." Will grinned. "I'll start marking 'em tomorrow. Looks like," he added quietly, "it will take me two or three days. In the meantime, I'd kinda like to repay you for the food. I see a lot of repairs need doin'. If you don't mind, I'll get to 'em." Joanne looked at him closely, unsure as to whether the trees were an excuse or not. Will's face remained unreadable. "I'll just get my blankets and bed down in the barn."

"That's unnecessary, Will," Joanne said firmly. "You can sleep here in front of the fire."

"No Ma'am," Will said firmly. "I don't want to put you to any trouble. Besides, if you get any company from town, I don't want them to have anything to say. Y'all are a right nice woman and you got a nice little girl."

"Thanks Will," Joanne said quietly. "But they don't

bother me. I make my own decisions and I run my own life. Their judgments aren't important. You will sleep where it's warm and you'll eat well. If you are going to work here, then you need to be comfortable."

"I just don't want to cause you any trouble."

"I never considered help to be trouble."

"Then I thank you."

Georgina's eyes moved from one to the other. Her little heart beat rapidly. Wouldn't it be wonderful if Will decided to stay for good, she rhapsodized silently. He could work on the ranch and they could be friends. Her one hand rested on her lap and she quickly closed her eyes and crossed her fingers to bring luck to her wish.

The unexpected sound of an arriving horse was a surprise to all three. In a few minutes, without knocking, Taylor opened the door and stepped inside. His smile faded to an angry scowl as he saw Will seated at the table.

"What the hell are you doing here?" he demanded arrogantly. "Get off this property!"

"Taylor!" Joanne cried as she leapt to her feet, her eyes angry and her face flushed. Will rose too, and before Joanne could speak again, he chuckled warmly.

"I didn't hear y'all knock," he said mildly.

"Why you . . . !"

"Taylor, stop this!" Joanne said angrily. "Will was invited to supper with us."

Taylor controlled his anger with an obvious effort. He found it hard to believe that Joanne could slip through his fingers. He had to get the deed signed.

"I'm sorry, Joanne," he said. "I just found it hard to believe a railroad man could be welcome in your house."

"I've chosen to sell them some of my timber. It will give me enough money to clear all my debts and to

240

supply us for the winter."

"That sounds fine, Joanne," Taylor said with a smile. But Will was much more adept than Joanne at spotting subterfuge. He was quite certain he was shaking Taylor's confidence somehow and he was mildly surprised to find he was enjoying the idea. He did not know the connection there was between these two, but he was glad to be where he was at the moment. A quick glimpse of Georgina's upset face told him she was not too pleased by Taylor's appearance either.

"Joanne . . . I'd really like to talk to you for a moment," Taylor insisted.

Joanne had been thinking about Taylor's offer from the moment he had made it. It seemed to her now that she had suddenly become stronger, less dependent on Taylor, but she refused to allow the thought that Will's presence had somehow made a difference.

Joanne walked to the fireplace and took the packet of papers from the rough wood mantel. She handed them to Taylor.

"I've decided to stand on my own feet. I'm very grateful for your offer and for all you have done for me. But . . . I feel I have to find my own way. I do want you to know how very grateful I am, Taylor. You have been good to me."

Taylor smiled again and took the unsigned papers. It was rage that kept him silent. He vowed to count Will among those who would pay the price for interfering with his well-laid plans.

# Chapter 17

Jenny's horse skittered to a stop less than three feet from Trace. There could be no doubt that she was wild with anger, but it was secondary in Trace's mind to how extremely beautiful she was.

She had absolute control over her prancing horse as she held the reins in one hand. In the other she held the rifle. With a quick and deliberate action she fired three shots, which splattered into the dirt within inches of Trace's feet. Trace did not move. He refused to give way to her fury before he discovered the reason for it.

"Trace Cord, you liar! You cheat! You thief!"

"Kind of hard words when I don't know what you're talking about," he replied in a puzzled voice.

"Damn you! How can you stand there so smug and self-righteous and lie like that? You have something that belongs to me and I want it."

"I have nothing that belongs to you," Trace stated firmly.

Jenny wanted to shriek at him, but she sucked in her breath deeply, struggling for control. "You think you've won what you wanted, don't you?" she said evenly, her voice now brittle and cold. "But I warn you, set one foot on my land . . . and I will kill you."

"Jenny, don't—"

"I don't want to talk to you; I just want to warn you."

"I don't take too well to threats made at the point of a gun. I think I told you that once before. If you want to talk it over, get down, put the gun away, and talk to me."

"Oh, how arrogant you are when you think you have won. Well, the war has just begun."

"A war takes two sides to fight. I'm not at war with you. But I'm damn sick of being misjudged."

"Misjudged!" Now she laughed harshly. "I don't have the imagination to judge you as low and contemptible as you truly are. There will be no negotiating between the Grahams and the railroad. Stay away from my land! *My* land!" she cried. "Or you will be buried in this territory!"

Before Trace could put action to the anger that had been slowly building in him, Jenny wheeled her horse and was gone.

For several minutes both Trace and Maxwell were silent, for both were still unsure of what had just happened.

"What the hell brought that on?" Maxwell finally said in an awed whisper. "That was one very angry woman."

"That's putting it mildly."

"You know what brought that on?"

"Yes, I know, and I'm pretty damn sure who's behind it."

"You going to tell me?"

"Not right now. I've got to get some answers first," Trace replied as he mounted.

"Where are you going?"

"To talk to the lady."

"Are you crazy? Didn't you just hear her say she'd shoot you? She came mighty close this time. The next time she might not miss. Why don't you let her cool down first?"

"No, I'm going after her right now. There's something that has to be straightened out, and I intend to do it."

"Rifle or not?"

"Yep, rifle or not. I don't believe the lady will shoot me. She's not the kind."

"You could be wrong."

"Yeah, I could be," Trace said quietly, "but I don't think I am. Maxwell, we are in a fight with someone who is playing both ends against the middle. I don't know for sure why, but I intend to find out."

"Trace, let someone go with you."

"No, I can handle this myself. Besides"—he grinned—"if she does decide to shoot, better one than two."

He kicked his horse into motion before Maxwell could protest any further.


Jenny bent low over her horse's neck as she raced at breakneck speed. She was almost blinded by the tears that had finally overtaken her. Her father had lost the one thing she valued the most to the last man in the world she could trust. He had slipped so easily into her world, had reached out to touch her in a way no one ever had before, and now he had deceived her and cheated her. She had wanted to kill him, had even gone there with the intention of doing just that. Half her anger was at herself for not being able to finish it. But she would protect what was hers now with the only method she had left. She would stand on her land and the first trespasser would taste her determination in the form of a bullet.

She rode until her lathered horse faltered, then she

allowed him to walk until he cooled. When he had regained his strength, she again kicked him into a run. She wanted to be home. She wanted the solid walls of her house around her before she gave way to the uncertainty and grief that filled her. Let him come, she thought; let him try to force them out. No matter what he tried, the next time she would make sure her aim was steady and her shot was deadly.

Trace rode at a slow, even pace. He knew Jenny had headed for home. His face was grim with determination. He was reasonably certain it had not been her father who had told her about the card game, just as he was reasonably certain it had been Taylor who had.

Jenny had gotten quite a head start on him and the speed with which she rode made the distance even greater. She reached the house before he had covered half the distance to it.

She put her horse in the barn and went inside, bolting the door after her.

Taylor's path back to town crossed a corner of Graham property. He crested a ridge and looked down into the meadow that ran close to the house. Exhibiting a satisfied smile, he wondered just how violent the confrontation between Jenny and Trace would be. He did not intend to stop at the house, for he did not believe Jenny was there. He was about to go on when he saw a lone rider enter the meadow and head toward the house. He recognized the rider at once—Trace Cord.

At that moment he gave thought to the idea that if

Trace Cord were to die one of the Grahams might be blamed for it. He would see to it that either Buck or Howard was named, since no one was in the house to say different.

He slid his rifle from the boot of his saddle and took careful aim. Slowly he squeezed the trigger. The rifle cracked and the sound of the shot echoed down the valley.

Trace had entered the meadow at a slow trot. In his mind he was sorting out what he might be able to say to Jenny to convince her he never meant to cheat her. "If I get that close," he mused aloud with a grim smile. Jenny had no reason to expect him to follow so rapidly, so he hoped to get close before she knew he was there.

"She won't shoot me," he said half aloud.

It was his last thought before hearing the sharp crack of the gun and feeling the searing pain. He called out Jenny's name as blackness crowded his mind and he slid from his horse to land with a solid thud on the grassy meadow. He lay deathly still as a stream of his blood seeped slowly into the earth.

Jenny, who had been pacing the floor in frustration, stopped abruptly as the echo of the shot came to her. She ran to the door and stepped out onto the porch. It was then that Taylor, who was about to ride down and see that the job was finished, saw her and remained in the shelter of the trees.

Jenny looked out across the meadow in time to see Trace's riderless horse run a short distance, then slow to a walk and finally stop and begin grazing.

She searched, but in the grass and at such a distance she could see no one.

She left the porch and ran toward the horse, slowing to a walk as she neared him to keep him from being frightened.

"Whoa boy . . . easy . . . easy," she murmured softly as she approached. Once the reins were in her hands she patted his arched neck and steadied him. Then she recognized the beautiful stallion that belonged to Trace and suddenly, sickeningly, she recalled the sound of the rifle shot. A surge of panic struck her and she looked around, but there was still no sign of anyone.

With one fluid movement she was on the horse's back. She urged him forward slowly as her eyes searched frantically and her heart beat a fierce tattoo within her chest. She prayed silently that he was not dead. The idea that someone had tried to murder him on her land and its implications had not yet entered her mind. She was only filled with the desire to find him alive. That she herself had threatened to do the same deed was forgotten in her urgency.

Then she saw the inert form and his name passed her lips in a ragged whisper.

"Trace . . . please don't be . . ." She could not finish.

She rode quickly to his side and was sliding from the saddle even before the horse came to a stop. She ran to him and knelt beside him. Gently she turned him over, for he had been lying face down.

She laid her head against his chest and was rewarded by the firm, steady beat of his heart. She sighed in utter relief. He was alive.

She examined him closely. The bullet had been meant for his heart, but the killer's aim had been off. It had struck the left side of his rib cage. There was so much blood that Jenny could not determine how much damage had been done. Her concern now was to get him into the house. There was no one to help her and he was more than twice her size. There was no way she could move him alone.

Trace groaned and his eyes fluttered open. In a hazy mist he saw her face bending over him. He could not seem to focus on her, for she wavered like a dream.

"Jenny," he muttered, "did you come to finish the job?"

Jenny gasped, realizing he believed she was the one who had shot him. It was no time to deny it, and in any case she was not too sure he would hear or understand what she said. Despite the wound, she had to get him on his horse so she could get him to the house.

"Trace . . . Trace, don't pass out on me again. I need help. Please . . . Trace, you've got to help me." There was a sob in her voice that reached Trace's foggy mind.

". . . Help you . . ."

"Trace, get up! You have to or you'll die out here."

She gripped his shoulders and tried to draw him into a sitting position. He groaned again with the pain. "Help me, Trace. . . . God, please help me," she cried. Her relief was almost a pain as he struggled to react to her cry for help. Her pants and shirt and both hands were covered with blood, but still she clung to him, continuing to call to him and urge him on.

Slowly, one pain-filled minute after another, they struggled together. Finally he stood beside the horse, clinging to the saddle. She despaired of ever getting him up and into it. Frustration and fear made her want to scream, but again she shook him.

"Get on your horse, Trace! Get on! Damnit, help me!"

She lifted his foot and put it in the stirrup and with a groan of sheer agony from him she pushed, feeling his large body finally lift itself and settle in the saddle. he lay forward over the horse's neck and she could not determine if he had totally lost consciousness again. She was panting and frightened and knew the next big step would be to get him from the horse to her bed.

Jenny took the reins and drew the horse along behind her. Tears stung her eyes, and she had to swallow the lump in her throat.

"Don't die," she whispered over and over again. It was sheer misery to know he believed she had shot him. Despite the threats she had made just a short time before, she realized now she could never kill him. She held at bay any other thoughts except the determination to see that he did not die.

She walked the horse slowly to the house and tied him, then she looked up at Trace. His eyes were closed, but he was breathing.

"Trace," she commanded sharply as she reached up and gripped his belt and tugged on it. "Trace, come on. Get down."

Again his eyes slitted open. She was sure he had no idea where he was or who she was.

"Trace, you have to help me get you inside. I can't do it alone. Oh damn! Why did you have to be so big?" she cried.

"Jenny . . . Jenny . . . why . . ." he began, but she tugged again on his belt and slowly he began to ease from the saddle. When his feet hit the ground he groaned and sagged to his knees.

"No! No! Get up, Trace. It's only a little further . . . come on, just a little further. You can make it! You've got to make it!"

He staggered to his feet and she gripped his arm, drawing it over her shoulders. She slid her arm about his waist and almost stumbled under his weight. Slowly, very slowly, she maneuvered him into the house and to her bedroom. She stopped by the bed and helped him to a sitting position. Then he collapsed on the bed unconscious.

Jenny stood over him for a moment, then she bent to

lift his legs and swing him completely onto the bed. She ran to put a kettle of water on the fire. On her way back to the room, she grabbed up her sewing scissors. She knew she could never lift him to remove his clothes. They were bloodstained and filthy, so she quickly decided to cut them off. Too much time had been wasted already, and she knew he must be weakening from the loss of so much blood.

She raced back to his side. He was breathing shallowly, and a fine film of perspiration beaded his brow. Quickly she cut away the shirt, casting the pieces aside. She examined the wound closely and saw that it was only the angle of the bullet's entry that had saved his life. If the assassin had been firing from a more direct angle, the bullet would have gone squarely into Trace's body, but as it was, the bullet had entered at an angle along his ribs, cut a deep furrow, and had more than likely ricocheted off the rib and exited. The wound was deep, but Jenny was convinced that it would not be fatal.

She pushed all thoughts aside as she brought in the steaming water and washed the wound clean. She cut several of her cotton petticoats into strips, then padded the wound and, with all the strength she had, she bound him, reaching beneath his body to draw the binding about him. Then she set about cutting away his dirty, bloodstained pants with shaking fingers.

Trace was still deep in an unconscious state, but some intangible thing reached out to touch her; perhaps it was his absolute helplessness or the soft groan of pain torn from the depths of oblivion.

She finished cutting away the soiled clothes, then she bathed him and covered him to the waist with the blanket. As she pressed her cool hand against his brow, she found to her distress that it was warm—too warm.

His lips moved and she bent closer in an attempt to

251

hear. It brought tears to her eyes when he uttered a softly murmured, "Jenny . . . Jenny."

She sat down on the edge of the bed and sponged his face, then cleaned up the discarded bloody clothing. After this, she sat in the interminable silence and waited.

The sun touched the horizon, then disappeared. She rose only to light candles. In the pale light she could see he was drenched with perspiration. Again she brought water and gently bathed him.

In the wee hours of the morning, he began to moan softly, then to mumble soft, unintelligible words. His skin felt hot and dry, like parchment.

She wanted to soothe away whatever stormy dreams he was imagining, for his body had begun thrashing about on the bed. Quickly she bent over him to hold him still, fearing he might open his wound.

Suddenly he gripped her arm in a hold that brought a cry of pain from her. His eyes were open but glassy with fever.

"I'll find out why," he snarled like a tormented beast. "Jenny, don't go . . . don't believe lies . . . Jenny, don't go . . . don't go!"

His grip became fierce and hot pain shot up her arm. "I won't go," she crooned. She pressed her other hand against his hot cheek and caressed it gently. "I won't go, Trace. I'll listen . . . I won't go. I'm here."

Her words seemed to ease him for the moment and he loosened his hold on her. She rubbed her arm where his rough grasp had bruised her skin and then she brushed away the tears in her eyes. After a few moments Trace began to mumble again.

"It's the two of them . . . Eileen . . . Taylor . . . it's the two of them . . . but why . . . why?"

Jenny listened as the hours wore on. He rambled on and on about Taylor, railroads, Eileen, and others

252

whose names sometimes were not clear to her except for his occasional mention of Michael, and someone named Allison. She wondered just who Allison was. She was becoming exhausted and drew a chair close so she could rest and still watch.

Now he lay very still and the mumbling ceased. She touched him again. If anything, the fever was higher. Then he began to shiver as if a tremendous wind had engulfed him. She did not know what to do to ease his misery, but she bent closer to give him the comfort of her presence.

"Trace . . . Trace."

Again his eyes opened, but they were as blind with fever as before.

"Cold . . ." he muttered. "So cold . . . Jenny . . . Jenny."

The shivering grew intense and in desperation Jenny climbed onto the bed beside him. His arms went about her and drew her close against his side. This seemed in some way to soothe him. She drew the blankets over them both and pressed her body as close as she could to warm him.


Deep in a black chasm of pain, Trace felt lost. He was cold and desperately alone. His mind wandered, and he called out to Jenny. In the mist he could see her and tried to reach out to grasp her, but she eluded him with a taunting smile.

The cold grew worse and he could barely move, yet he sensed one touch from Jenny's outstretched hand would release him from the dark anguish. Again and again he called her name.

Suddenly the mist seemed to fade and she stood before him, extending her arms to him. Then he was in her arms and she was welcoming him, holding him.

Their lips met and he felt the darkness recede. She touched him with hands that were gentle and soft, yet he could feel the warmth of them spreading through his entire body.

Her body was a misty warmth that seemed first to swirl about him and mold against him until he felt as if they were becoming one entity.

He bent to kiss her softly, with lingering tenderness that was more a promise, and he felt his breath quicken in anticipation.

He nibbled around her lips, then his mouth brushed hers with a caress so elusive she reached out, mutely asking for more.

Suddenly he captured her mouth in a deep, intense kiss that fanned the smoldering fire deep within him to a new and brilliant blaze.

He experienced a sensation of triumphant pleasure when he heard her impassioned gasps and felt her hands reach to hold him closer. Featherlike they skimmed across his shoulders to caress the muscles of his back.

Now they kissed fervently until the hot flood of desire left them too weak to stand. They fell to the ground like autumn leaves before the first touch of fall, gently gliding downward, clinging to each other.

Jenny bent over him, her hair falling like a shimmering golden veil about him, and he reached up to twine his hands in the thick silken tresses and draw her lips to his.

Her lips found his flesh and moved in seductive slowness to taste it. She nibbled and ran the tip of her tongue across each nipple's crest. Then she moved to seek more. She wanted to give him all the joy and pleasure she possessed and without words he knew this.

He could summon no control as the heat of her seeking lips found him, enclosed him, and stimulated every sense he had to a point that he could not speak an articulate word, only groan his need.

"Please . . . Jenny," he whispered, knowing he could bear no more. He wanted to hold this moment, but he could not. He was powerless.

She became a golden blur above him, swirling and singing about him until the urge to restrain himself was struck away as if with a bolt of lightning.

Her body was a caress and a command. She moved across him and his murmur was a groan of pleasure as she taunted and teased his passion to a white heat.

Her lips moved across his flesh, leaving a path of embers, and her hands urged his response until he found it impossible to control. She commanded the need, drew it from him with soul-shattering urgency.

Her lips swiveled across his and in a blinding moment he was sheathed deeply in the golden mist of her body.

He could not prevent his gasp of pure ecstasy any more than he could prevent the exquisite waves of fire burning higher with each move she made.

His body undulated beneath her while his hands, spanning her narrow waist, urged her to deeper, stronger movements.

She shuddered as hot desire spilled over them like a molten blanket. They were caught in a tempest and could no longer control the impulses that elevated their senses. It whipped them onward, higher and higher until the full force of their combined passion erupted and leapt every barrier reality could present.

She was a brilliant golden flame, swirling, dancing, enticing him beyond the gates of fulfillment, and he surrendered to her power as she overwhelmed his senses and they surged to the highest pinnacle, tossing all control and caution to the wind.


Slowly he opened his eyes to a bright, sunlit room.

He was alone in a large bedroom that looked vaguely familiar. Then suddenly everything returned. He was in Jenny's bedroom, only he could not remember how he had gotten there. He tried to move, which sent a jab of hot pain to his side. He felt his body, and became aware of two things. He was bandaged, and he was totally naked.

With grim determination he concentrated on remembering. It came to him slowly, the confrontation with Jenny, following her, the shot, then blackness interrupted by flashes of what were vague apparitions: a cool hand against his brow and, more sweet, the feel of Jenny in his arms. Had it been real or had it been a dream? He could not remember.

As he regained more and more control over his thoughts, he found that one question had no answer. If Jenny had shot him, why would she drag him into the house and care for him? Why not just leave him to die?

"Damn," he muttered hoarsely, for no matter what amount of effort he put forth, he could not seem to move without pain.

He wondered how long he had been in this condition, and he wondered who had done most of the nursing. It seemed, if he concentrated really hard, he could remember a gentle touch, a softness in his arms.

He turned his head to the side and a smile touched his lips. There was an indentation in the pillow beside his. She had been there. It had not just been his fervent wish that had brought such an idea. He had to have some answers. He could not move too much, so he did the next best thing. He called out. "Jenny!"

He heard a noise as if something had fallen in the next room, then the sound of feet moving rapidly across the floor. The door swung open and Jenny stood framed in the doorway.

Her brow was furrowed in a deep frown, for she

A **FREE** ZEBRA
HISTORICAL
ROMANCE
WORTH

**$3.95**

# BUSINESS REPLY MAIL
FIRST CLASS      PERMIT NO. 276      CLIFTON, NJ

POSTAGE WILL BE PAID BY ADDRESSEE

**ZEBRA HOME SUBSCRIPTION SERVICE**
**P.O. Box 5214**
**120 Brighton Road**
**Clifton, New Jersey 07015**

did not know if he was rational or again calling out in delirium. Slowly she walked to the side of the bed. Tentatively her hand extended to rest against his forehead.

"No fever," she said with a sigh of relief.

"You sound like that pleases you."

"It does. You had a very bad night."

"Jenny . . . tell me how I got here. Or, better yet, tell me why you choose to shoot me in one minute and nurse me the next."

"Shoot you! I didn't shoot you!"

"Who did?"

"I . . . I don't know," she whispered, knowing how it must look to him. Even though she never would have believed such a denial from Trace, Trace did believe her.

He smiled. "The bed felt warm last night. Was I dreaming or were you really here?"

Her face became flushed and she jerked her hand from him as he tried to capture and hold it.

"Getting shot certainly didn't take any of the arrogance out of you. I wouldn't be caught dead in bed with you."

"Then why am I in your bed?" He grinned.

"You're here," she said through gritted teeth, "because I wouldn't leave a dog outside to die. I'll get you something to eat."

She whirled away from the bed to hide the emotions his deep, penetrating gaze had stirred in her.

He watched her walk away and wondered just how long this wound was going to restrict his movements, for he had other movements in mind.

# Chapter 18

In the light of the same dawn a lone rider entered the town and rode slowly down the still-deserted street.

The few merchants that were up early could not help but stare as he rode by. He was tall and lean and rode as if he and the horse were one.

He wore a dark shirt and grey pants that bespoke his Rebel affiliations. His hat hung low over piercing blue eyes, one of which was covered by a black patch. A short beard covered the lower part of his face, masking a strong chin.

He drew his horse to a halt in front of the saloon and dismounted slowly, wearily. As he walked up the saloon steps and across the board sidewalk, he limped perceptibly.

He brushed the swinging doors open and stepped into the dim light of a nearly empty saloon, for there were not many patrons at this time of day. He walked to the bar and leaned both arms on it. The bartender came to him.

"Can I help you?"

"Yes. I need a meal and a bottle." The voice was crisp and firm, as if its owner were well used to command. He was not the sort of patron the bartender would choose to argue with.

"We got some steaks and some eggs," he offered.

"Bring me a steak and six eggs over easy and a bottle of your best."

"Yessir."

The man nodded tiredly and walked to a table in a distant corner. The bartender observed that he sat with his back to the wall and placed an immediate label on him. "Gunfighter," he whispered to himself. He went back into the kitchen to make sure the order was filled quickly.

There ensued a silence that the three other patrons did not care to break; no one wanted to ask this stranger any questions.

When the food was brought, the man ate slowly, pouring himself a drink after every few mouthfuls of food. By the time the food was finished so was half the bottle.

The bartender approached once more to take away the dirty dishes, then he made a point of leaving the stranger alone.

The day wore on, men came and went, but the stranger still sat, the half-empty bottle before him. He listened intently to all conversations but said nothing to anyone.

In the early afternoon he rose and left the saloon. No one followed; no one watched as he stopped occasionally to speak to someone, usually asking a question or two. He wandered about the town, stopping at the livery stable to send a boy for his horse and to ask more questions.

His final stop was at the hotel to rent a room.

"Yessir?" The clerk smiled, but the smile died when his query remained unanswered. "Rooms for two dollars a night."

"Give me one facing the street."

"Yessir. How long are you planning on staying?"

"Until my business is finished."

"Yessir." The young man gulped. He handed the man a key and watched him climb the stairs favoring his leg.

Once inside the room, the man locked the door behind him, threw the key on the dresser, and walked to the window. He held the curtain aside and studied the street for a few minutes. Then he hung his hat and gun belt over a chair, took off his boots, and lay on the bed. Within a few minutes he was asleep.

When he woke, the day was almost gone. He rose and walked to the water pitcher and poured some of the cool liquid into the basin. An hour later he walked out the hotel door and into the street.

He returned to the saloon, where the same bartender greeted him.

"Evenin'."

"Evenin'. Got another one of those steaks?"

"Yessir."

"Fix me one."

"You want the rest of that bottle?"

"Yeah."

The bartender handed him the same half-filled bottle and it was carried to the same table.

The bartender had finally gathered enough courage to talk, and when he brought the food he asked, "You . . . you wouldn't be lookin' for someone in particular, would you?"

"Might be. Why?"

"Well, if you was, I guess I know everyone in this territory."

The man smiled for the first time and, for a moment, his face seemed young. "So you know everybody in this territory?"

"A bartender gets all the news at one time or another."

"Sit down, Mister . . . ?"

"Riggs, Thomas Riggs. Most call me just Tom."

"Well, just Tom, suppose you talk to me for a spell and tell me what's going on in this town. People seem to be upset over something."

Tom could not wait to explain the atmosphere in the town and its reasons.

"So there's kind of another war brewing around these parts?"

"Yeah, I guess you'd say that."

"Looks like the big man around here is Taylor Jessup."

"Yessir, he wants to see this town grow. I guess that's why he's doin' the talkin' for most of the people here about with the railroad."

"Most?"

"Railroad's going to have some trouble with a few of the families out in the valley. From what I hear, Mr. Jessup is kinda a negotiator for both sides."

"Who's speaking for the railroad?"

"A fella by the name of Trace Cord." The bartender laughed. "I don't think he's been doin' so well. Looks like the valley will bring 'em to a stop."

The stranger remained silent for some time, then he spoke softly. "Seems to me if the railroad is going to do so much good, the people ought to help it along."

"What can we do? The railroad wants their land and they ain't about to give it up."

"Well Tom, suppose you tell me where I can find Mr. Jessup?"

"Mr. Jessup?"

"Yes, I'd like to talk to him."

"Well, he lives down at the end of Murdock Street. I don't know if he's there. If you wait awhile, he comes in here sometimes, late in the evenin'."

"Good. I'll enjoy this bottle, and you point him out to me if he comes in."

A gold coin spun on the table brought a smile to Tom's lips. He grabbed it up.

"Yessir, I'll do that."

It was well over three hours later that Taylor made an appearance, and the bartender could not help but be impressed with the consummate patience of the man who sat in the corner and slowly sipped the balance of his bottle.

When Taylor came in he stopped at the bar, ordered a drink, then walked to a table and sat down. When the bartender had placed the drink in front of Taylor, he turned and motioned to the stranger, who rose, lifted the rest of his bottle and his glass, and crossed the room to Taylor's table.

Taylor looked up in surprise when the stranger sank into the chair opposite him.

"Who are you?"

"I think . . . a friend."

"Really . . . friend, why should that impress me?"

"Because I can be of help to you."

"Oh? Really?" Taylor laughed. "What makes you think I need any help?"

"I've been travelin' with this gun on my hip for a couple of years. I know trouble when I see it, and I know how to handle it."

"And," Taylor said quietly, "you have a price on that gun, I take it?"

"Mr. Jessup," he chided, "there is a price on everything in life."

"What is yours?"

"Depends."

"Depends on what?"

"On how much you intend to make."

"Now really, Mister . . ." He waited, but no name was offered. "I'm trying my best to help both the town and the people in the valley from being cheated by the

263

railroad. There is no profit in it for me."

Now the laugh was soft and derisive. "No profit. Then it seems I'm in the wrong company. Maybe I ought to talk to Mr. Cord."

He rose and reached out to take his bottle.

"Wait," Taylor said. There was a moment of silence while they contemplated each other.

"Sit down," Taylor said quietly. "Who are you and where do you come from?"

"Who I am and where I came from has nothing to do with profit. I'm a man who likes profit."

"Maybe . . . just maybe I can use you."

"Use me?" he questioned softly, his eyes darkening dangerously. "No one uses me. Tell me what you have in mind and I'll tell you what I will do."

"I'll think about it. Where can I find you?"

"I'll be around."

He walked away from the table, knowing Taylor's eyes burned into his back. He crossed the dirt street and entered the hotel. Once in his room, he again locked the door. He hung up his hat and gun and removed his boots. Then he lay on the bed and folded his hands behind his head. After a few minutes the soft sound of pleased laughter filled the room.


Trace remained still most of the day only because any sudden movements were painful. He was left very nearly alone by a still-angry Jenny who silently came into the room only to bring him food. This was the source of their first confrontation since he had awakened.

She entered the room with a tray of food she fully intended to give to him, then allow him to fend for himself. Trace knew this, but he wanted her to stay.

She placed the tray on the table beside his bed and

turned without a word to leave, but his quiet voice stopped her.

"Jenny?"

She stopped but did not turn around. "What?"

"I'm afraid I need a little help."

She turned to look at him, suspicion filling her eyes. "Help? Why?"

"Surely if you shoot a man, then have enough guilt to save him, you ought to make sure he can eat to get his strength back."

He had sparked her anger just as he had hoped to do. She spun about to face him, her cheeks pink and her eyes like chips of turquoise ice.

"I said before, you arrogant Rebel, that I didn't shoot you. But I should have, and whoever did the job needs to be whipped for missing!"

"Jenny, you're a damn stubborn female. All you can seem to understand is one side of the story—yours. Do you think I had a whole lot of choices about what I'm doing? I lost a hell of a lot more than anybody in this valley will. I've lost more than anyone is asking you to give. I have a job, Jenny. I have obligations to a man who helped me when I was down. I have no intention of hurting you . . . but I damn well intend to do the job I was brought out here to do."

"No matter who pays the price?" she sneered.

"Why don't you ask what the price is before you scream robbery? You're all fired up about well-planted rumors you heard that you never even took the time to find out the truth about. You go around screaming unfair when you don't have any idea what unfair is. What would you have done in my place, let the carpetbaggers take everything you had? Let them wipe out all your family ever worked for? I took the best way, a way that would hurt nobody—nobody," he repeated firmly. "And I'll do the job I came here to do."

265

He was silent for a moment while she digested what he had said. Then his voice grew softer.

"Come over here, Jenny."

"I'm not that much of a fool."

"You're afraid of me." He laughed.

"Hardly," she retorted.

"Then come over here. I want to talk to you."

She lifted her chin stubbornly, but her pride would not tolerate his insistence that she was afraid of him. She took the few steps that separated them and stood close to the bed.

"Jenny, sit down," he suggested gently. She sat on the edge of the bed. "I want to give you something to think about. You tell me I've taken something from you; I say you shot me. Do you see what we are doing?"

"I don't understand what you're talking about."

"We're doing what someone else wants us to do. We're fighting and clouding up the waters so no one can see what's really going on."

He had reached out and taken her hand. She tried to pull it away, but he held it firmly. With his other hand he lightly caressed her arm with gentle fingertips.

"I came out here to talk to you. You were too angry to even tell me what set you off."

"Don't take me for a complete fool," Jenny snapped as she jerked her arm from his grasp. The gentle touch of his hands had been entirely too disturbing.

"You and I both know I have every right to be angry. You couldn't get what you wanted one way so you got it another. You're a sneak and a pirate, Trace Cord. You've stolen everything from me and now you expect me to fall for your sweet talk. Well, it won't work, not this time."

"You've taken to calling me a lot of undeserved names, Jenny."

"Undeserved! What would you call a man who was

trying to take everything you owned?"

"Undeserved when you're naming the wrong man."

"Of course," she said bitterly. "You're going to tell me now that you cheated my father at cards and stole our ranch because of Taylor. Really Trace, what kind of ignorant, backwoods people do you think we are? I should have left you lying out there to bleed to death."

"If you still claim you didn't shoot me—"

"I didn't!"

"Then aren't you the least bit curious about who did . . . and why . . . and more, why on your land?"

"No!" she lied angrily. "Someone with as good a reason as I have. Possbily some angry husband or father. I don't suppose you've been too particular where you've shared your favors and one of them just caught up with you."

"You sound jealous." He grinned irritatingly.

"Jealous!" she nearly shrieked. "Good God, you are arrogant! As soon as you're able to move, I want you out of here, and take my warning with you. Here we are and here we stay, and if you try to cross my land, we will fight you. There are a lot of us in the valley who would like to see the railroad gone from here. Make no mistake. We will fight."

"You can think that if you want to, Jenny," Trace said gently. "But I don't want to fight with you over anything . . . except maybe"—he chuckled as he reached out and grasped her arm in a much firmer grip than she expected—"how big a family you'd like to have."

She sucked in her breath with renewed fury and tried to pull away. But despite the wound, Trace was much stronger than she. Slowly he drew her down beside him. Their eyes held in determined and silent warfare. He raised his other hand and gripped her hair, slowly pulling her toward him. She pulled against his grip and

267

pressed her free hand against his chest, but despite this resistance, she seemed to be uncontrollably melting. Her mind raged against his strange magnetic pull, but her body betrayed her, urging her to share the too-well-remembered passion that had awakened it.

Their lips were a breath apart, and still their eyes held. Her self-control seemed to be shattering, crumbling away like a sandy wall facing the force of the ocean. No one had ever set her nerves trembling or shaken her control so deeply. He was a threat to every sense she had. His eyes glowed behind thick lashes with a look that sent tremors through her.

"Let me go," she grated in a voice that fell far short of the demanding force she sought.

"I'd be a damn fool to do that," he said softly as his lips drew closer to hers. "I find myself dreaming dreams, remembering how intoxicating your mouth was, and how warm and soft you felt."

Their lips brushed gently and she closed her eyes as sensations exploded within her. He could feel her tremble and reveled in the surge of desire flowing hot through his body. He marveled again that one touch, one moment in her arms, could awaken such a hunger.

She wanted to free herself from his embrace but found herself drawing closer. She wanted to resist the hunger of his kiss, but found her mouth parting to accept his.

She made a soft, inarticulate sound as he drew her down against him and his mouth began to seek a deeper taste. Her reason numbed by his sensual assault, she momentarily surrendered to the wild and unexplainable emotions that tore at all her senses until she was lost in their depths. He held her head between his hands and traced kisses across her cheeks, touching her lips again and again until she could no longer control the desire to have him seek deeper and deeper pleasure.

It was only the soft whisper of her name and the sudden knowledge that his hands were seeking softer places that enabled her to regain a semblance of control. She jerked upright as though she had been struck. She had been giving herself to him as easily as if she had been a harlot.

Before Trace could grab her, she nearly leapt to her feet. Her turquoise eyes blazed and her cheeks were pink with anger, anger directed as much at herself as at him.

Trace knew he could not summon the strength to rise and take advantage of her emotional state. He was helpless to change what he saw lighting her eyes.

"Jenny," he groaned. "Listen with your heart for a change, not with your mind. Admit for one minute that you love me."

"How you would love that, wouldn't you?" she sneered, her anger forcing her breath to come in uneven gasps. "Aren't you satisfied yet? Is it possible you believed I would be so easy the second time? I may be forced to surrender my ranch to you, Trace," she declared in a ragged whisper, "but I will never be forced to surrender myself."

Before he could deny her words, she spun about and left the room, slamming the door firmly behind her.

He cursed his inability to follow her and lay back to contemplate just how he was going to get beyond her stubborn determination and force her to see the truth.

Jenny stood outside the closed door, realizing there was more than a wooden barrier separating them. Tears blurred her vision and ran unheeded down her cheeks. Yet she had to use all her control to keep from reaching for the door handle, flinging open the door, and running back to his arms. She wanted to be there, wanted to feel the heat of his branding lips on hers, wanted the touch of hard, seeking hands rediscovering her willing body.

He had betrayed her, had taken all that she loved, and she hated herself for wanting him.

She would be alone in this small house with him for at least another two days while he slowly regained his strength. She clenched her fists at her sides, vowing that never again would she let him breach her defenses. She did not dare.

As soon as he was well enough to ride, she would make him leave. She gave a thought to the fact that she could ride back to the railroad and have someone come and take him away, but she decided that such a move might cause the wound to open and would probably bring him a great deal of pain. She dismissed the idea without allowing her true feelings to disturb her logic. When he was well he could go. Until then, she would care for him, but she would keep as much distance between them as she could.

Jenny went about her daily chores then, occasionally glancing at the closed door. By the time she lit the lamps against the oncoming night, her nerves were as taut as bow strings. Despite all her efforts, she was more aware of him than ever.

She had prepared a meal and now she placed food on the tray she intended to carry to him.

Slowly she lifted the tray and walked toward the closed door. She stood outside for several minutes, commanding both her body and her mind to obey her will. When she felt she was prepared, she opened the door and entered. Her cold look of self-containment turned to surprise when she found Trace, with a blanket wrapped about him, standing before the open window and gazing out at the newly risen moon.

He turned when she entered.

"What in heaven's name are you doing out of bed?" she demanded.

His face was pale and his deliberate grin was unsteady, but he spoke firmly. "I had it in mind that you would want me out of here as soon as possible. I guess now is as good a time as any to start trying to get going. If"—he chuckled—"you could arrange for some clothes, I expect in a day or so I could make my way back."

She frowned and remained silent, but Trace smiled to himself. Perhaps his new strategy just might work.

# Chapter 19

Jenny was very much aware of Trace's half-naked state. The blanket, wrapped around his hips, accentuated the breadth of his shoulders and chest. He was a heavily muscled man and the candlelight glinting against his flesh created the effect of latent strength rippling beneath bronzed skin. She was also aware of the lean body beneath the blanket. It annoyed her that the thought stirred her.

"Yes, I'll get you some clothes. Buck will have something. You are a little bigger than he is, and his clothes might be a little tight."

Trace grinned and walked toward her. She wanted to strike him for the erotic effect he had on her. Her breath caught as she realized the blanket might fall away at any moment.

"Tight or not, I think I need something a little better than this." He tugged at the blanket.

"Don't do that!" she snapped angrily. He stood close to her now, entirely too close.

"Sorry," he said quietly. "I didn't mean to upset you."

Despite his quiet words, she could see the laughter in his eyes and did not miss the accompanying glow of challenge.

"You certainly don't upset me. I just don't think you should be moving around at all."

Again she bit back angrier words as she saw the smile tug at the corners of his mouth.

"The sooner I move about, the better for me. I need some activity and that bed just isn't going to offer any. Besides, it's empty and cold."

She gritted her teeth and glared at him. "Sit down and eat. I'll go see what I can find in the way of clothes."

"Why don't you sit and eat with me first? The clothes can wait. I hate to eat alone."

"I've had my supper," she said firmly. "No matter what you hate, you have to eat. I'll find some clothes."

She set down the tray with a solid thud and was rewarded by muffled laughter. She spun about and glared at him, then left the room without flinging the angry words at him that she had meant to speak.

Jenny went to her brother's room and took the first pair of pants and shirt she came across. When she returned, Trace was seated before the tray of food and making good work of devouring it. He looked so vital and damnably handsome. If circumstances were different . . . , she began to muse silently, then caught herself. She could not afford to relax her guard with this very dangerous man.

She walked to him and held out the pants and shirt. He took them and stood up, pushing aside the table with the finished tray of food.

For a moment she watched him, then he casually reached for the knotted corner of the blanket. She suddenly gasped and spun about, turning her back to him, for she realized he fully intended to drop the blanket to dress.

She was suspicious of the soft sound she heard that seemed to be barely controlled mirth.

She waited until all sound of movement had ceased, but she told herself he just might be devil enough to wait until she turned again to dress.

"I'm decent." He chuckled.

Tentatively she turned. Her first reaction was surprise, but it rapidly turned to amusement.

He stood before her in clothes that were, to say the least, two sizes too small. The shirt could only be buttoned on the bottom button and left a broad expanse of bare chest. The pants strained about his waist and ended several inches above his ankles.

She stood in silence for several moments, then the humor of the situation became more than she could contain. Her mouth quivered into a smile, then she uttered a muffled laugh that soon grew out of control. She laughed heartily until tears came.

Trace pretended to scowl in embarrassment, but the sound of her laughter was a pleasure to hear. It certainly was much better than the suspicion and anger he had seen in her eyes until this moment.

"I don't think I'm going to be able to sit down without some severe disaster occurring," he said. "In fact, I'm not too sure I can continue breathing."

"Oh Trace, you really do look so . . . uncomfortable. Maybe a pair of my father's pants would be better. He has some worn ones that are softer and he is just a bit bigger than Buck."

"That sounds better. Suppose you fetch them so I can get out of these before my manhood is severely threatened."

With effort, Jenny gulped back the laughter that again threatened her control. She went to her father's room and rummaged through his clothing for his pants. When she returned, Trace accepted them gratefully.

Jenny snatched up the tray and left the room, quite

275

sure that Trace would not hesitate to try to shatter her control again by changing.

As she washed the dishes, she heard Trace enter the kitchen. She turned to look at him and was suddenly stilled by his presence. The pants were snug, fitting his muscular thighs as though he had been poured into them. His masculinity was more than obvious and very disconcerting to Jenny, who was trying to control the effect he seemed to have on her whenever he was near.

He eased himself into a chair, favoring his side with a protective hand to guard it from bumping into the table. He grimaced as he did this and Jenny was sure the effort caused him more pain than he would admit.

"Would you care for more coffee?"

"No . . . I'll tell you what I'd like though."

"What?"

"For you to come over here and sit down and talk to me."

"Trace, we really haven't anything to talk about."

"Nothing you'll admit to," he stated firmly.

"You think I'm running away from something?"

"Aren't you?" he questioned quietly.

"No, I just don't see what point there is in our talking about a situation neither of us is willing to change. The truth is still the truth. You have chosen to take what was refused you and you chose a deceitful way of doing it. Do you blame me for doubting your sincerity now?"

"I don't blame you for anything, Jenny, especially for what you think is true. The only rub is, what you think is true isn't. And if you think about it, you'll find your opinion of us was influenced a long time ago by someone who has interests we don't even know about yet. I know it was Taylor Jessup who found a way to tell you about our little card game. Did he, by any chance, tell you how he happened to know about it? He certainly wasn't there. Your father will back me on that. So tell me, Jenny, how did he know?"

"I . . . he . . . he didn't say . . ."

"Of course he didn't. But I'll tell you how he knew. There were two sharps in that game ready to skin your father, sharps put there by someone else who wanted your ranch. I took it to keep them from doing the same."

"And to kill two birds with one stone and get what you wanted."

"Damn, you're a stubborn woman! I took it because I didn't want a man who was too drunk to know what he was doing to lose what you valued so much. Do I get condemned for that too?"

Jenny realized this could quite possibly be true. "I—"

"Of course I do," Trace said angrily, misunderstanding her long silence. "Why look at the truth when you don't want to believe it? Why not just stick the blame on me? It's so much easier to believe what you heard about the railroad than to believe me. I'll bet you've gotten all your misinformation from the same source." Trace rose slowly and went to her. "Jenny, I've taken nothing from you," he said gently, "nothing that I know you didn't want to give. And if it's truth you want, why don't you recognize it when you see it?"

He stood intoxicatingly close and the masculine scent of him and his overpowering presence forced her to look up into his intense gaze.

"You talk so well, so cleverly, but you still own my ranch . . . and I still say there will be no negotiations between us. Go back and tell them to go around my land."

"What frightens you, Jenny?" he asked softly. He reached out to touch her. "Is it the railroad . . . or are you more afraid of your own self?"

"That's ridiculous," she replied too quickly. He took

another step closer so that they were nearly touching.

"Is it?" he whispered. Her eyes widened as he bent his head. Slowly, gently, like the touch of a soft breeze, his mouth touched hers. Tentatively they tasted, nibbled, caressed. He caught her lips between his and sucked gently, then explored their softness with his tongue. It was an erotic act, and created an overwhelming storm of sensation within her.

She reached out blindly to prevent any further possession and her hand came in contact with a hard, fur-matted chest. Hands that had meant to push him away brushed across his flesh and found themselves rising to reach for him. He drew her into his arms very slowly and with supreme gentleness. He didn't want to do anything that might end this moment of moonlit magic. Silently he cursed the heavily bound wound that gave him a startling jab of pain to remind him that any more severe activity was going to be rewarded by much stronger sensations. He was caught in a dilemma. His body raged with a frantic desire to possess her completely. His logical mind told him not to hurry this moment or it would be lost forever. Again he realized he stood on the edge of a precipice. One move would put an end to something he wanted with near desperation.

Her eyes opened and he looked into twin pools of turquoise. They looked at each other in profound silence, both aware that some vibrant thing was alive between them.

"Jenny, don't deny this," he whispered. "Whatever else stands between us is small . . . is nothing compared to this."

He saw glistening tears in her eyes as she turned her head away and moved out of his arms. Again he cursed the consistent jab of pain that forbade sudden movement.

278

"I can't, Trace. I can't believe. I can't betray everyone in the valley. You're right. I am afraid. I'm afraid of betrayal too. I . . . I have to think . . . I . . . good night," she murmured.

Before he could prevent it she was gone. The door of her bedroom closed softly between them.

The moon rose high in a star-studded sky. A breeze brushed the curtains and entered the room. Trace had been unable to sleep. He had remained in the large parlor of the cabin and now watched the fire he had made earlier begin to die.

He rose from the seat before the red embers and stood erect. Feeling the heavy binding around his body, he realized he had not experienced pain in a while. He unbound the wound to see how much damage had been done. The wound was ragged but showed every sign that it was beginning to heal. He repadded and rebound his body, after which he felt much more comfortable.

He stretched to see the extent he could go and was satisfied to find he could move reasonably well. Still he knew he would not be able to sleep. His mind played tricks on him, conjuring up visions of Jenny, warm and seductive, though he knew she was probably asleep and dreaming of the day he would be gone.

He was mistaken. Jenny lay awake. Her room was aglow with moonlight. Her mind had fought her senses from every direction, but no matter how it tried it could not extinguish the desire that tore at her. Her own truthful nature forced her to see and understand that, despite anything else, she wanted Trace.

Trace was becoming uncomfortable in his tight, binding clothing so he went to the bedroom and removed the clothes. He wrapped a blanket about him

279

and returned to the warmth of the fire.

He sat in meditative silence. In a day or two he would have to leave, and he was no closer to reaching Jenny than he had been when she had fired those angry shots at him.

Trace sighed deeply and stretched again to ease his cramped muscles. It was then he heard the soft click of the door. He turned and had to control the urge to leap to his feet and run to her.

She stood in a beam of moonlight that formed an aura about her. He absorbed her beauty like a starving man at a feast, yet he was afraid to move. He was afraid she was a figment of his dreams that would disappear as quickly as it had come.

Jenny walked toward him slowly. She had loosened her hair, and the soft white gown she wore was like a mist about her.

She stopped by his side and he rose to his feet to stand close to her.

Jenny reached to touch him, sliding her hands across his shoulders and down to rest on his chest. She had a shy, inviting smile on her lips that turned to a murmur of satisfaction as he drew her into his arms. Their lips blended in the sweetest of all kisses—one of total and mutual surrender.

Trace had no desire to question what was occurring. It was a glorious gift and he had no intention of refusing it, despite his condition, for he was quite sure his self-denial would be much more painful than anything else.

Jenny gently touched the bandage. "Your side . . ." she said softly.

"I'll manage," he replied as he reached to loosen the buttons on the front of her gown, then let it drop in a pile about her ankles. He was pleased when with sure, unhesitating hands she loosened the knot of the blanket and let it drop to lay beside her gown.

When he started to reach for her again, he was surprised when she stopped him.

"Jenny?"

"I want you, Trace. I can no longer deny it. But it does not change all the lies between us. We will have this night no matter what else happens. If we must say good bye forever tomorrow, we will still have this to hold. It is my night, and for tonight . . . you must give yourself to me."

"I don't believe any other man has had to face such a welcome miracle as this. Give myself to you," he murmured. "I did that quite some time ago, but it's my pleasure to repeat it. But I warn you, Jenny, are you sure one night will be enough for either of us?"

"And I warn you that tomorrow I will fight for my rights with the same devotion that I fight for your love tonight—completely." She walked to the heavy bear rug that lay in front of the fire and sat upon it, then she extended her hand to him. In moments he joined her.

She was quick to hear his sharp intake of breath as he moved too abruptly and felt a hot stab of pain. She put both hands on his shoulders and he looked at her questioningly. "Let me love you," she whispered.

She pressed him back upon the fur and caressed him lightly as her lips sought his. Her mouth was hot and moist against his and his open mouth accepted hers with a joyous groan of sheerest pleasure. Their tongues explored with explosive abandon and his senses reeled as her hands possessively explored his heated form. Where his body touched hers it burned. He moved against her, his body responding violently to her touch. He tried to join her in this mystifying seduction, but she gently pushed his hands away.

With the knowledge given women from the beginning of time, Jenny knew he was completely hers, a slave to her will. It gave her an exultant feeling of power to know she possessed him. Her hands and lips played across his skin, teasing and tasting the flesh. Her lips paused over each nipple, sucking and nipping until a ragged groan was drawn from him. Still she sought to lift him higher. She followed a path down his lean, hard body with hands and lips until he gasped in ecstasy. But these sensations were mild compared to those that raged through him when her hands found his pulsing manhood and stroked it gently. Like a shattering tornado, broiling heat coursed through him.

But still she sought more. Her lips found him, surrounded him, and tasted deeply. The sweet agony was almost beyond what he could bear. Always he had been the dominant one; always he had been the possessor. Now he was being possessed in a way he had never known. Before he could come to trembling release, her mouth ceased its torment only to again trace patterns of moist kisses along his flesh.

She was above him now and she drew her leg across his body. Now both were lost in total abandon as he felt her body sheath him, drawing him deep within. She laughed exultantly as she felt his body lift powerfully beneath her. He was totally hers, just as she was totally his. They rode the crest of wild passion to a shattering climax. Only when she lay exhausted beside him did he draw her close and hold her in silence.

For a short while they slept. But both were too bound up in this mystical night to sleep for long.

She awakened to his gentle touch. Gazing up at him, half in shadow, half in moonlight, she saw the gleam of his smile. Now the possession would be his. Now she could surrender, knowing she had had the desire to do so and the courage to match his will.

His hands captured soft, full breasts moments before his lips followed, and she caught her breath as licks of flame began to shoot through her. Hot, sweet kisses covered her naked flesh, letting no spot go untasted. His eyes devoured her, touching her everywhere, enjoying to the fullest the sight of her slim body touched with golden moonlight.

She was surprised at the renewed heat of her desire as she came to him again. His hands were beneath her hips, lifting her to him, and again their union was total and fulfilling.

Only now could they sigh in mutual exhaustion. Only now could they cling to each other and drift into relaxed sleep. Only now would they be able to share so much, for in the morning, at the touch of the sun and the beginning of a new day, she was determined that he would go.

*Chapter 20*

When Trace had ridden after Jenny, Maxwell had turned around to walk back to his railroad car. He turned in time to see Allison walking toward him.

"Good morning, Allison. My, you look pretty this morning."

"Thank you. I believe I just saw Trace riding away. Has he gone to town without me again? I did so want to do some shopping."

"Well, you certainly can't go alone, and I'm afraid that was Trace you saw leaving. But he wasn't going into town."

"Oh? Where was he going?"

"Why, out to negotiate with one of the ranchers again," Maxwell said blandly.

"I know Will took that nice Mrs. Carter and her little girl home, so Trace must have gone to see the Marshalls or the Grahams?"

"Yes . . . one of them . . ."

For some unaccountable reason, Allison was getting the impression there was a great deal Maxwell was not telling her. She began to wonder if Trace had been keeping a lot of secrets as well. Her mind, always alert, began to spin its own web. She decided that she would attempt to find some answers on her own. The provocative thought stirred within her, and she realized she would need a place to begin digging. Perhaps, she thought, if she could go into town, she might overhear some gossip that would provide her with the information she sought. Her only problem was she was sure Trace would be quite angry if she were to try to go into town alone. At that very moment the answer to her dilemma presented itself in the form of Eileen Maxwell, and Allison smiled smugly.

Allison was less than fond of Eileen and for the past few days had been elated over Trace's avoidance of Eileen. She had no idea what could have happened between them, but, whatever it was, she was pleased that Trace now seemed to be caught up in something that left no room for Eileen.

She watched as Eileen walked toward them. How beautiful she is, Allison mused, though this thought was accompanied by the warning knowledge that the beauty was as cold as ice and as dangerous as it was cold.

"Good morning, my dear," Maxwell greeted his niece. "You're dressed for riding. I hope you aren't thinking of going alone again?"

"Now uncle, I know how you worry. Poe has consented to take me into town again. Since we're getting much closer, it's less than a day's ride. I really could do it alone, but I bow to your command and am taking an escort. There's a dance to be held there soon and I thought I might stay a few days and get the dressmaker to make me a gown. We will be attending, won't we?"

"Yes. I think it's a perfect opportunity to make some friends for the railroad."

"Eileen?" Allison questioned sweetly. "Would you mind very much if I rode with you? I'd like a new gown

286

too, and Trace is busy. I could get a room and do some shopping. I might be a little help to Trace by volunteering to assist some of the ladies in making preparations for the dance. We could show them just how much we want to be friends."

"I really don't mind your riding along, Allison," Eileen said with her best smile. Inside she smothered her anger at Allison's intruding on the pleasant interlude she had planned to enjoy with Poe before they arrived in town. She knew she would have to be careful with her meetings with Taylor also. Allison was a very clever girl. One slip and it would all be over.

"As for volunteering," Eileen added, "I really am in no mood to putter with decorations and cooking. I've a great deal more interesting things to do. You can volunteer if you like."

Allison was quite tempted to ask Eileen just what she had to do that was so much more interesting, but she bit back the words. She wanted to separate herself from Eileen as soon as she possibly could. She also had a great many suspicions about Eileen and Poe, but no evidence on which to base them.

"I'll go and change and we can leave right away if you like."

"Good. Do hurry, Allison. Poe doesn't like to be kept waiting." Eileen linked her arm in her uncle's. "He worries that Uncle Max might have something more important for him to do and he'll be off escorting me somewhere."

Again Allison was tempted to utter a few epithets that would have told Eileen what Allison really thought of her. But she left the two and returned to her car to change quickly. Grabbing up a few extra items of clothing, she stuffed them into a small portmanteau and went to find Eileen.

Before too long the two women and a seething Poe

were on their way to town. Poe had expected to share the afternoon with Eileen, which amused her immensely. She was sure that if he were disappointed now, his ardor would be much stronger later, and she looked forward to it with great anticipation.

Taylor happened to be in the front of the bank when he looked out the window and saw the three riders arrive in town.

He watched the two women enter the hotel and Poe walk across the street to the saloon.

He made a quick excuse to a customer with whom he had been chatting and left the bank. He was quite sure Eileen would get a separate room and for many reasons he was quite anxious to speak to her alone.

Taylor was completely unaware that another pair of very interested eyes had watched the three arrive. They registered no surprise when they saw Taylor enter the side alley. It took only one quick guess to determine just where his newly acquired employer was going. An amused smile quirked his lips and he spoke softly to himself.

"How very interesting. I must meet this lady that has so much attraction for you, Mr. Jessup . . . and soon. But . . . first things first."

When Poe entered the saloon it was dimly lit and cool. He paid no attention to the man who sat at a corner table and walked immediately to the bar for a drink to ease his frustration.

He tossed down the first drink and asked for a second, which the bartender immediately poured. It was only as he nursed his second drink that Poe gazed in the mirror above the bar and saw that he was being watched. When he saw that Poe was looking at him, the stranger rose and walked to where Poe was standing.

He sat his half-empty bottle between them on the bar.

"Mornin'. Buy you a drink?"

Poe's eyes narrowed. There was something eerily familiar about this man, but Poe could not put a name to him or to the sense of dangerous power that exuded from him.

"I know you?"

"Not yet, but I think you and I have a lot in common."

"Yeah, just what's that?"

"Suppose I buy you one drink and we sit over at my table and talk. You might be surprised."

"You a stranger in town? I haven't seen you here before?"

"Could be."

"You look familiar," Poe urged. He wanted a name to attach to this man.

"Been here for a short spell."

"Lookin' for work? The railroad might be able to use a few more men."

Poe found himself shaken by the intent blue gaze; then he heard the man laugh softly.

"Do I look like a railroader to you?"

Poe observed the low-hung gun and the way it was tied to his leg, as if he might have to draw it rapidly and wanted no mistakes.

"No, you look like a man who's handy with a gun. Ever use that . . . ?"

"I've shot a few men," the man replied coldly.

Poe could feel the chill of his voice and had no desire to question that statement any further.

"You said we have something in common. Just what might that be?"

"Let's sit and have a drink. I don't like to talk where I can be overheard."

Poe nodded and accompanied the man to a table.

The stranger sat down, putting the bottle between them. Then the man placed his folded arms on the table and smiled.

Taylor and Eileen spoke quietly so their voices would not be overheard in the next room. Eileen had quickly warned Taylor that Allison Cord was too close to be ignored.

"It's time we slowed down the tracks," Taylor said. "They're getting close to town. Once they cross town, they'll be headed out to the valley. Time is getting short."

"What have you accomplished? Do you have your hands on that land? One of these days these citizens are going to get wind of what's happening; then you won't stand a chance."

"No," Taylor replied reluctantly. "But I'm close. I'd be safe in saying in a couple of days the Graham land will be ours. As for the Carter place, well, Joanne seems a little reluctant, so I'm going to send Stace out one night to give a little . . . push in the right direction."

"Stace?"

"Yeah. By the time Stace is finished with her and that brat of hers, she'll crawl away from here and be happy to go. We'll have her land real soon, and the railroad will look guilty."

"What about Trace?" Eileen asked nonchalantly, unaware that Taylor had more than a suspicion of the extent of her interest.

"Don't worry about Trace Cord. We'll make sure he doesn't interfere. Before long it won't matter."

"So why did you send me a message that you wanted to talk to me?"

He went to her and drew her roughly into his arms. His kiss was flame upon her mouth.

"Do I have to have any other reason than this?" he asked in a ragged whisper. "It's been a long time."

"I know you too well, Taylor." Eileen smiled as she put her arms around his neck and looked up at him. Her warm curves pressed close. "You have something else in mind too."

He laughed. "I've hired a man."

"So? Why should that interest me? You've hired a lot of men for this project."

"Well, he isn't one of that type. This one is clever, dangerous, and too smart to be foxed. I'd suggest you meet him. He wants to meet the boss. I have a feeling we'll have to offer him a lot more than the others, but I think he will do a better job."

"Who is he?"

"A man who won't share a minute of his past or even his name until he finds out what the offer is. A man who carries a gun and knows how to use it."

"Sounds intriguing," Eileen murmured. "When do I meet this . . . dangerous man?" She laughed in a teasing manner.

"You won't think it's so funny when you meet him. He's a tough gentleman."

"All right. If you think you can trust him with the boss's identity, then bring him up here tonight."

"Good. I think it's a damn good idea to have him on our side before he decides to go see if someone else wants to hire his gun."

"What makes you think he won't go to them anyway and play both ends?"

"He's too smart. We have a lot more to offer. Besides—" he laughed—"one look at you might just make up his mind for him. I'll bring him up tonight."

"Good."

"But for now," he said huskily as he bound her more tightly to him, "I think we have something much more exciting to do."

Her soft laugh was her only reply.

Poe left the saloon and went to have his horse cared for before he found a place to have supper and bed down for the night.

The stranger stood gazing out of the saloon window, watching him cross the street. At the same moment, the door of the dressmaker's shop opened and he saw Allison step out onto the wood-planked sidewalk. He stiffened and moved closer to the window. Then a soft smile played across his mouth as he watched her walk down the sidewalk and into the hotel.

"Pretty little thing, isn't she?" came the bartender's voice from beside him.

"That she is. A damn beautiful woman."

"She's Trace Cord's little sister, so I'd give her a wide berth. He's no one to fool with, and if you was to take a shine to her, you might find it would be Trace you'd have to face. Gun or no, I think he'd be a handful."

"I'm not too worried about Trace Cord," the man replied. "I certainly am not going to let him spoil any plans I might make."

"He's a dangerous man, and he's tough."

"So I hear . . . so I hear." He turned to the bartender. "I'll keep your warning in mind." He smiled a smile that the bartender could not interpret, then he walked back to the same corner table and sat down to wait.

Almost three hours went by before Taylor entered the saloon and walked to the table where the stranger patiently sat.

"If you'll walk across the street with me, I'd like to introduce you to someone."

"Who?"

"Someone who just might want to buy that gun of yours."

"So, I finally get to meet the real boss behind this?"

Taylor flushed at the obvious suggestion that he was only second in command, but the thought of calling the man on it never entered his mind. Taylor might have had no compunctions about shooting Trace as he had, but he was not fool enough to go up against a man who was facing him and had the obvious ability to kill him if he chose.

"She wants to meet you."

"She?"

"Yes, she, and that's all the information you get. Are you coming?" Taylor asked angrily.

"Of course," the man replied with an irritating grin. "Let's go."

As they walked through the saloon doors, Taylor noted that the man looked cautiously up and down the main street before proceeding.

"Any problems?" he questioned.

"No," the man answered. "Just careful. Some people want to be certain that not everyone sees what they're doing. Do you know that the sister of your Trace Cord is in town?"

"Yes, I know, but . . . how did you know? In fact, how did you know who she was?"

"I make it a point to know who everyone is who comes and goes. It's a way of staying alive."

Taylor was satisfied and asked no more questions as they made their way across to the hotel. He was completely unaware that the man's thoughts and his answers had been worlds apart.

They climbed the steps and knocked quietly on Eileen's door. When Eileen opened it, she stood for a moment gazing in surprise at the man who stood before her. She was not too sure what she had expected, but this handsome male was certainly not it.

Her eyes glowed with deep interest as she viewed the attractive, mystery-shrouded man. She noted that he had missed nothing about her either, and he smiled a slow, knowing smile that intrigued her and sent a sudden warmth rushing through her.

"Come in," she said in a deep, sultry tone.

They entered and she closed the door quickly and locked it. Then she turned to face both men.

"You told me the boss was a woman. You didn't say she was so beautiful. Working for you will be a pleasure." The voice was warm and very nearly a caress. Eileen could literally feel his gaze stroke her body and she gloried in the liquid heat spreading within her as his voice suggested that the "work" might be more than just the use of his gun.

Taylor reacted with angry jealousy. He had a lot to lose if Eileen were to abandon him now, and he did not intend to let a strange gunfighter upset any of his plans, no matter how much he might want to use him.

"You'll be working for both of us," he grated. "Maybe you ought to hear what we want you to do."

The man's gaze never left Eileen.

"So," he said softly, "tell me what it is you want. But remember one thing. I get all of the story—I mean *all*— or I want no part of any of it."

"You use that gun well?" Eileen questioned. He grinned devilishly.

"Whatever I aim at . . . I hit," he said with smooth assurance.

"You sound very sure of yourself."

"One's own self is all anyone can ever be sure of," he said, "so I've made it a point not to offer anything I can't give. But . . ." he added softly, "what I promise, I deliver, no matter what it is."

"Really?" Eileen laughed throatily. "You have a name, Mister . . . ?"

"Do I have to be named? I thought it was my gun you were hiring. If it needs a name, you could call it Lucifer."

"Lucifer," Eileen murmured. "The name fits both the gun and the man. I shall call you Lucifer."

"If you put the name to me," he said, chuckling, "remember that once Lucifer touches your soul and gives you something . . . he expects full payment."

"I'll keep that in mind . . . when payment is due."

"Let's get this over with," Taylor interjected.

"Sit down, Lucifer," Eileen suggested, "and I'll tell you what we're after . . . and just what I want you to do."

The three sat together and talked for well over an hour. When Taylor finally closed the door behind Lucifer's broad back, he was filled with conflicting emotions. He was quite sure this man could handle exactly what they needed. He was also aware of a physical attraction between Lucifer and Eileen that could easily burst into flame and consume him. He turned to Eileen, who was wearing a very puzzled frown.

"Something wrong?"

"No, not exactly. It's just that . . . Lucifer is so . . . familiar. It's as if I've seen him somewhere before. I've tried to think, but I can't recall anyone who looks quite like that. Yet . . . there's something about him that . . . I might just have to question him a little more closely. I could swear I have seen him somewhere before."

"Are you sure it's not just that you're interested?"

"Why Taylor"—she laughed—"are you by any chance jealous? Could you really see me taking up with a gunfighter?"

He went to her and gripped her shoulders with a ferocity that made her eyes widen in surprise.

"Don't think it, Eileen, with him or any other man. We're in this thing too deep and we're in it together. Don't get any ideas."

His eyes were deadly cold and, for the first time in their relationship, Eileen was touched by something that frightened her. It was then she decided just where Lucifer's gun might come in handy.

"Taylor, for heaven's sake, don't you think I know what we've got at stake? I'm not planning on making any mistakes. If all goes well," she added as she slid her arms about his waist, "in a few short years we will be sitting pretty. I'm not going to let anything jeopardize that, Taylor—nothing. Now stop worrying. We'll hire him and bring an end to all this worry. The land will be ours, but better still, it will lead to all we've ever wanted."

"Then you want me to get this Lucifer started?"

"Yes, get him started, but see if you can find out something about him. With a little time, I'll remember where I've seen him. Until then, I think he's worth the chance."

"All right. I'll go talk to him now."

"How do you know where to find him?"

"He sits in the saloon—same corner all the time—and nurses a bottle."

"Does he have a room in the hotel?"

"I suppose."

"Do you know what name it's under?"

"He refused to give a name. Just paid and got a key."

"You're going to talk to him now?"

"Yes. The sooner he gets on the job and out of this town, the better I'll feel. People make connections too fast. I want the town to think he went as fast as he came and just as permanently."

"Then no one will suspect when things begin to happen?"

"No one," he stated confidently.

"All right then, I guess we put him to work."

Taylor kissed her and she responded in a way that

she knew would please him. Then he left.

She waited several minutes, then opened the door and left the room. She walked down the stairs and went to the desk.

"Yes, Miss Starett, can I help you?"

"Oh my . . . I'm . . . I'm a little upset. I heard there's a terrible man, a gunfighter, in the room right across from me." She widened her eyes innocently. "Do you think it's really safe?"

"Oh Miss Starett, don't be alarmed. He's way down at the end of the hall by himself in room seventeen. He's quiet and he don't want to have any problems. You'll be quite safe Ma'am. If you have any problems, just call on me. But I assure you he's a safe distance away from everyone."

"Thank you so much. I'm so relieved." She gave him a melting smile. "I do feel much safer now."

He watched in admiration as she went up the stairs, unaware of the satisfied smile on her face.

# *Chapter 21*

Dawn was weaving pale gold threads through the black cover of night when Trace woke. Everything about him was still and quiet. Night sounds echoed from outside and the pale light filtering into the room barely enabled Trace to see.

Jenny lay curled close to him and he did not dare move. To awaken her would mean the end of the few short hours she had let him share with her. He did not want it to end, not ever, but he still could not seem to find the right words to stop her. Oh, she would be in the same house, talking to him, eating with him, . . . but some part of her would push him away and he searched for a means of preventing it.

She stirred, made a soft, murmuring sound and reached for him. He was pleased when her slender arms went about him and her body moved more comfortably into his arms. She sighed again and fell back into deep sleep.

Very gently he held her, wishing the hours before the day would last a long time. His hands tentatively touched the warmth of her skin and he closed his eyes and buried his face in her tangled, sweet-scented hair.

What had she said to him? "I want you, but it

changes nothing . . . tomorrow will be the same battle"? He groaned to himself, for it was a battle he wanted no part of and he was sure she didn't either. One night of such exotic pleasure could never be enough for him. He knew that as surely as he knew the day would come.

Despite all his fervent wishes, the rising sun continued to light the room. He held her closer as time ticked slowly by, then he finally sensed that she was no longer sleeping. Very slowly he lifted his head to look into eyes that were filled with questions and a slight touch of fear.

"Jenny," he breathed softly, "don't leave me yet. Don't end it yet. Not like this."

Tears formed on her lashes and she closed her eyes, feeling the heat of the liquid as it escaped to course down her cheeks.

"Let me go, Trace. Don't make it any harder on me than it already is. Last night was a magical dream, but a dream that can't last. We are too far apart."

"It doesn't have to be this way," he protested.

"Why do you always refuse to understand? You come in here and sweep me up in this crazy emotion I can't fight. Then you put a price on my surrender. I just can't be sure of you, Trace . . . and I can't give up everything my family has worked so hard for. Not for the railroad . . . not even for you, even if . . ."

"Even if you wanted to?" he finished hopefully.

"Don't, Trace . . . don't," she moaned. She rolled away from him and stood up before he could stop her.

The morning sun glazed her slim, golden form and Trace was spellbound for a moment as it enclosed her like a misty web. Then she grabbed up her clothes and ran from the room.

He rose reluctantly. He had hoped this one night had changed her mind, had made her realize that what they

300

had shared could never be enough for either of them. For himself this was surely so, but it seemed she still harbored doubts about his sincerity.

He realized that his voracious appetite for her love had barely been touched and he wondered if it could ever be appeased. He doubted it.

He grabbed up a blanket and again wrapped it about him, wishing he had some clothes that fit. When he entered the kitchen, Jenny was preparing some food.

He came up behind her and slid his arms about her waist, drawing her firmly back against him. She was afraid both to struggle and not struggle. If she fought, she might hurt him physically, but if she didn't fight him she was certain that the ensuing hurt would be much more damaging to her.

He bent to kiss the side of her throat and nibble gently on her ear. She closed her eyes, fighting the tremors that shook her body and her control. They had shared a wild and beautiful night, she thought angrily. Why couldn't she stop this need? Why did she want him again? And worse, would she ever be able to stop the passion this man could arouse in her?

"Stop it, Trace!" she said fiercely.

"Can't," he murmured. "With you in my arms I've no more control over wanting you than I have over the sun's decision to rise."

"Then let me go. I don't want to be a temptation for you," she said warily.

"Don't worry about tempting me too much," he murmured with a soft laugh. "I can cope with any bit of temptation you throw my way."

She spun about in his arms and ineffectually pressed both hands against his chest. "I," she stated firmly, "have no intention of putting any more temptation before you. In fact, it's time you were forced to learn a little self-control."

"I'd have to be dead to be able to control my desire for you when you're in my arms."

"Then let me go and go sit down at the table. I'll get you some food."

"I'm hungry, but not for food," he replied as again he tried to draw her into his arms.

She twisted from his grasp and moved away from him.

"This is no game, Trace."

"Who's playing a game? I'm very serious."

"So am I," she replied firmly. "My father and my brother will be home tomorrow. I'll see to it that you're cared for—not like that!" she added quickly when she saw his lips quirk in a quick smile. "And when they get back, they can travel back to the railroad with you. After that . . . I think it's best that we don't see each other again. We're on different sides of a war, and I"— she lowered her voice to a cool whisper—"have no intention of surrendering again to a passion that has no future."

"So"—he chuckled—"you will finally admit there is something very special here?"

"Of course I'll admit that," she snapped. "Do you think I would have shared last night with you like that if there wasn't? But I also know just how dangerous it is, and I have no intention of falling into a trap that will hurt me. Go back to your future, Trace, and let me go."

She choked back a startled gasp as she was suddenly bound in arms that boasted strength for which she was no match.

"Let me tell you something, Jenny Graham," he said. His eyes glowed with an intensity that shook her. "Come Heaven or Hell or any other barrier you might decide to throw between us, one day I'll make you see that you're wrong. You've got the common sense to see

302

the truth, and if you weren't so damn stubborn you'd admit it."

"I'll never give you the satisfaction of deceiving me again!" she protested angrily.

"What was last night, a game?" he retorted coldly. "Some sort of test?"

"No!" she half shouted. "I don't play such games. But I won't pay the price you put on love. You want it all, don't you?"

"Yes," he shouted. "Yes, damnit! I want it all. I want you and all the love I know you have. I want there to be no false barriers you keep building. I want you, Jenny . . . and I'll fight to get you."

He reached for her again and she knew with deep certainty that if he held her in his arms again, if he kissed her and roused the mystic spell he could weave about her, she would be lost. She would surrender again, and this time there would be no returning. She uttered a muffled sob, pushed away from him, and grabbed up her jacket, which had been hanging on a chair near the door. She was gone before Trace could stop her and the door slammed firmly behind her. He heard her boots as she half ran across the porch. He closed his eyes and leaned for a moment against the sink, sorry that he had lost control and forced her to run from him. After a short while he heard the sound of her horse and knew she would be gone for some time.

Jenny rode only a short distance away before she drew her horse to a halt. She sat beneath the trees and tried to sort out her emotions. She balled her fist and pounded the pommel of her saddle.

"Damn you! Damn you! How can I let you make me run? What kind of coward am I to let one man cloud my thinking and destroy my control! I won't let it happen—never again, Trace Cord," she muttered. "Never again will I ever run from you. We will just see who will run."

She turned the horse so abruptly that it reared, pawing the air. Once again under control, she urged it forward, back to the house and, with grim determination, back to prove to Trace Cord that he could never reach within her defenses again—never.

Trace had listened to the sounds made by the retreating horse and had cursed himself. There was no way he could follow her when he was still half naked, and he had no way of knowing where she would run or if she would come back.

It took him by surprise to hear a horse approaching. He assumed it was her father and brother and wondered what reaction he would get when they found him alone, bandaged, and naked in their house. He was more than surprised when the door opened and Jenny again stood on the threshold. His smile of pleasure faded when he read the cold look of finality in her eyes.

"I'm glad you didn't go," he said softly.

"It was a stupid thing to do," she responded.

"Running away from anything is stupid."

"I know that now." He started to move toward her and she continued. "Don't, Trace, for this will lead us nowhere. You would have to take anything you wanted by force and I don't think you would want it to be that way."

When her eyes defiantly met his, there was no longer any doubt in his mind that she meant what she said. At that moment he wanted her so fiercely that his desire created a ragged pain within him. He wanted her, but not by force. He knew he could make her body respond to him, but he was nearly terrified by the thought that he would not be able to reach the Jenny he loved by doing so.

Jenny closed the door behind her and walked toward him. She had to prove to herself that she could control the rush of desire within her. She had to know for her own peace of mind that she could withstand the magnetic force that drew her to him.

They stood close, but the chasm between them was much too wide for either of them to cross.

"I need to change that bandage," she stated.

"Jenny . . ."

"Sit down, Trace. I'll go get clean bandages."

He sighed and sat down. She had placed a frigid wall between them and his arguments were only going to make it worse. It was not the time to fight and take the chance of driving her out of his life forever. It was a time to move carefully. He was just as determined as she was that he was not going to lose her, in spite of what she thought.

Jenny tore another petticoat into strips. She brought fresh water, then knelt down beside him.

The touch of her hands was cool against his flesh as she unbound the old bandage. He could feel her hands tremble and knew she was denying the awareness that leapt between them.

Her eyes had long since fled from his, and she caught her lower lip between her teeth as she concentrated on what she was doing and not the whisper of desire that seemed to grate over her every nerve.

"Jenny?"

"Umm?" she replied as she reached around him to rebind the wound. She was so close he could smell the sweet, inviting scent of her hair.

"Look at me," he said gently, trying to keep her nervous anger at bay. He did not want to drive her any further from him.

She raised her eyes to his and her hands stilled for a moment. Their eyes held and he had to use supreme control not to take her into his arms and force her to surrender to him.

"You're stuck with me for awhile," he told her with a smile. "Why don't we at least call a truce until we stand on more even ground? We can't just spend the next day or so alone and snarling at each other like a couple of wild cougars."

Her eyes grew wary. She could not be certain he would not hesitate to use any ruse to get her off guard. "A truce?" she questioned tentatively.

"A truce," he affirmed. "I swear, Jenny," he added softly, "I'm not asking any more of you than to talk to me, to relax and be at ease with me. I can't stand the look of anger in your eyes. I want to see you smile."

"I've had very little to smile about since word of the railroad came to our valley."

"Then why don't we forget the railroad even exists for the next day or so? I want to be friends with you, Jenny. I want to be able to talk to you and not see distrust on your face. How about that truce?"

"If you want a truce, Trace, why don't you begin it by giving me back the deed to our land?"

"I can't do that just yet," Trace answered. He did not want to tell her that his holding the deed was all that kept her father steady.

"Then what do we have left to say?" she asked coldly.

"A truce leaves all our problems temporarily at bay. If you agree to a truce now, when your father comes home and I get a chance to talk to him . . . then I'll give the deed to you."

Again her eyes snapped up to meet his. She searched, trying to see the deception in his words. She could not find it. Maybe, she thought, maybe there is a chance to get my land back. She wondered what he could have to say to her father that would make that much difference. He answered before the question left her eyes and formed on her lips.

"What's between your father and me has nothing to do with the railroad. It's important that I talk to him first. Will you agree to a truce until then?"

He waited in nearly breathless anticipation until finally her head nodded.

"All right, until my father gets home and you talk. We have a truce, and in the end you'll give me back my land and go away."

"If," he stipulated gently, "you still want me to go, I'll go."

"Then I agree," she replied quickly. She gave no thought to the verbal trap into which he had just enticed her.

"Good." He grinned and she developed a deeper concentration on finishing the last of the rebandaging, for his grin had caused a wicked reaction in a wayward body she was trying to control.

"There," she said triumphantly. "That should hold you for awhile. The wound is clean and looks like it will heal completely soon."

He stood and flexed his stiff muscles to see just how well he had them under control. There was very little pain and he smiled in satisfaction.

Again Jenny was aware of the latent strength of his bronzed body and irritatingly enticing blanket tied about his waist and the memories it brought did very little for her control. She rose quickly, and tearing her eyes from him took more effort than she would care to disclose.

"I'll finish making us something to eat."

"I'll help," he offered.

"You?" She laughed. "You have a lot of hidden qualities."

"That I do, madam." He chuckled. "You might just be surprised at how good a cook I am. Out on the battlefield a man has to learn quickly to fend for himself."

"Well," she challenged, "why don't you cook breakfast for me? I've cooked enough meals for you. I'm beginning to think you could develop into a lazy loafer who likes to be waited on."

"Tragically that is so." He laughed, pleased at the unguarded amusement in her eyes. "But," he admonished, "I don't take lightly to challenges. You want breakfast, madam, you get breakfast. Suppose you sit down at the table and let an expert go to work."

"Expert," she scoffed. "I'm afraid you'll have to prove that."

"I fully intend to."

He talked as he moved about gathering what he needed to prepare a meal. Jenny bit back a laughing retort about the picture he made half clad in a blanket and preparing a meal.

She began to relax and listen as he recounted stories of his childhood and the often wicked fun in which he had indulged.

"You came from a large family?"

"No, not really. There was only Michael, me, and my sister, Allison."

"Allison," Jenny repeated, ignoring the relief she felt in discovering that the woman about whom he had mumbled in his delirium was his sister. "You've spoken of her before."

"Oh? I don't remember."

"No, you wouldn't. It was when you were unconscious."

He narrowed his eyes and looked closely at her. "What else did I say?"

"Oh, not much I could hear really. You just rambled."

"I'm sorry I caused you so much trouble, and I'm grateful for what you've done for me."

"I'm glad I was there."

"Are you?" he questioned softly.

"I thought we had a truce?" she replied.

"Sorry," he said quickly. But his eyes had not missed the throbbing pulse at her throat that spoke much more eloquently than any words she could have uttered.

True to his word Trace prepared a breakfast Jenny found surprisingly good. Against all Jenny's defenses Trace had seemed to retreat and now they began a tentative search for common ground. They found it in laughter.

The breakfast ended with both realizing that they had a full day ahead of them and the very dangerous area encompassing the small house in which to spend it.

Trace again was forced to clothe himself in Howard's too-tight breeches. His boots hugging his calves and the skintight pants made him a sight that stirred Jenny's senses.

Jenny took Trace to the closer corrals her brother had built to show him the choice horses Buck had broken and trained. She was pleased to observe his affinity for the horses. He offered them sweet clover from his hand and coaxed and soothed them with a gentle voice and hand until they allowed him near enough to stroke them.

"You have beautiful horses," he said as he ran his hand across the broad flank of one.

"My brother is the best with horses in this whole territory," she said proudly.

"You like to ride?"

"Yes, I love it."

"Then let's go for a ride. I'd like to see more of your valley." At her look of concern, he added, "I think my side will hold up if we take it slow and easy."

She agreed quickly, relieved they would not have to return to the house that seemed to her to be getting smaller by the moment.

In the sunlight of the early day they rode across the valley's low, rolling hills. Jenny loved and was proud of her ranch and she took a great deal of pleasure in showing it to Trace.

Bit by bit Trace could see Jenny relax. Her eyes began to glow with her pride. Her cheeks pinkened with the pleasure of riding and the caress of soft breezes that kissed her skin and captured her hair to swirl it about her. In the sunlight her beauty caught Trace's total attention. In fact, he found it growing more and more difficult to keep his eyes off her. He would have found the deepest pleasure in making love to her on the soft green grass and in seeing her slim golden beauty surrendered to him in the light of the sun.

Soon it was early afternoon and hunger drove them back to the house. Again Jenny's smile faded and her nerves grew taut. Again they would be enclosed in the cabin and she felt the subtle urges of her senses demanding a repetition of the new and exciting pleasures they had tasted earlier.

They were silent as they approached the house, but as soon as they drew close enough to see it Jenny breathed a sigh of relief. She did not noticed Trace's scowl of displeasure.

There were obvious signs that someone was there.

"Buck and Pa are home," she announced happily.

She kicked her horse into motion and rode off ahead of him. She missed his wry smile and muttered words.

"Great," he said aloud. "Good timing. Couldn't you

310

both have managed one more night?"

Jenny was already dismounting and running up the steps when Trace reined in his horse and dismounted.

Howard and Buck were surprised to see him, and even more startled to see him dressed in assorted pieces of their clothing. Quickly Jenny explained the situation. Howard's eyes missed nothing about his daughter, including her well-controlled excitement and her attraction to the man who had stirred and changed their lives so drastically.

"It looks to me like you need a bigger shirt," Buck observed with a smile. "You know you're wearing my Sunday best."

"Sorry." Trace grinned. He found himself liking Buck immediately, partly because of his close resemblance to Jenny.

"Sit down, son," Howard said, "and tell us what you think happened out there. Maybe it's past time that we talked."

"That is what I've been telling your very stubborn daughter. First I thought it was one of her well-placed shots that put me here. But"—Trace laughed—"after witnessing Jenny's abilities and her independence, I've come to the conclusion that if she had shot me she wouldn't have missed."

"You're right, she probably wouldn't have," Buck agreed.

"You two can stop your tormenting. Wash up and I'll fix some supper, unless"—Jenny grinned teasingly at Trace—"you want to do the cooking."

"No thanks." Trace chuckled at Buck's and Howard's questioning looks, but he didn't explain any further. He was enjoying the teasing laughter in Jenny's eyes too much.

They made light conversation while Jenny prepared supper, mostly about horses. Howard smoked his pipe and listened, observing astutely that Buck was talking about his beloved horses with great enthusiasm, while Trace listened with only half his attention. Most of Trace's thoughts were on Jenny as she moved about. Howard kept his own council concerning the reasons for Trace's mysterious bargain with him.

## Chapter 22

After the meal was finished, Trace accompanied Howard and Buck when they went to care for the horses. It was now important to him that he talk to Howard alone.

Howard sensed this and drew Trace aside.

"I'm sure there are a few things we have to talk about," Howard said.

"That we do."

"I also believe my daughter carries some heavy suspicions and some rather new thoughts."

"That is also very true. She was told that I cheated you at cards and stole your ranch for the benefit of the railroad."

"Damn!" Howard said in a shocked voice. "Who told her that?"

"Taylor Jessup."

"There's a whole lot going on around here I don't understand."

"I'll tell you what I think," Trace began. He explained the position he thought Taylor was in and the matter of the two men in the card game who had been placed there to cheat him. "He wants your land and he wants the railroad blamed for its loss."

"But why? What does he really have to gain? I and several others owe him money. If he wanted our land, he could just pressure us to sell."

"There's something we don't know. I have to find out what it is. I have a feeling I know one person who can tell me a lot."

"Taylor Jessup?"

"No, somebody close."

"I shall have to tell Jenny the truth," Howard said, "or at least as much of it as I know."

"I would appreciate it if you would. I have your deed in my saddlebag. It looks to me like you're ready to take your ranch back."

"Ready to take it back, work it, and protect it," Howard said. He held out his hand to Trace. "Thanks to you. Will you take my hand now?"

"It's my pleasure." Trace smiled as he clasped Howard's hand.

"Mr Graham, I . . . I have to give Jenny time to think and to decide about . . . well about me and this whole situation. I want to know how you and Buck feel about meeting with the railroad and discussing our problems. If we can make a deal, a lot of problems are going to be settled—maybe most . . . except for Jenny's reconciliation to the idea."

"I can only tell her the truth. Jenny is a very strong young lady. I stopped deciding for her a long, long time ago. She makes her own decisions. As far as Buck and I . . . well, I'll talk to the railroad, and I'll ask Buck how he feels about it."

"That's all I can ask."

"Trace?"

"Yes?"

"You're in love with my daughter." It was much more a statement than a question.

"I think I've been in love with her from the first

minute I saw her. It's going to take some time. Right now she still half believes Taylor and she's still afraid of the changes the railroad is going to bring. How do you feel about it?"

"I think you're a good man. Maybe the truth will change her feelings."

"Maybe. But it would be better if I found out all of the truth."

"You think Jenny won't believe it?"

"Oh, she'll believe you—at least about the card game—when she has the land back. But it's going to be hard to get her to resign herself to the railroad and to me. It might be best if I go in the morning. If you don't mind, I think I'll bed down out here. It's not so . . . close."

Howard understood completely. He was about to speak again when Buck joined them.

"I'm going to bed," he proclaimed. "I'm too tired to do any more. This was a long haul, Pa, but we've got six new beauties to show for it."

"You've got some mighty fine horseflesh," Trace said. "I haven't seen much better anywhere."

"You won't either," Buck stated with assurance. "This group I've been breeding has turned out even better than I expected. Well, I'm turning in. Night, Trace. You comin', Pa?"

"Night, Buck," Trace replied.

"I'm coming," Howard said. He turned back to Trace. "I'll tell her the truth. She's a lot like her ma—smart."

"Jenny and I have a lot of mending to do. I don't have too much hope that it will be easy."

"Maybe Buck and I can be of some help."

"I'd just as soon you two didn't interfere. If Jenny makes a decision . . . well, I want it to be something more than gratitude or some other influence. I want it

315

to be because she wants me and trusts me and for no other reasons. For her to say she trusts me is the most important thing right now."

Buck had stood watching in silence. He knew he would have felt the same if it had been Emily. His father and he had had their first open talk with each other while they had been working together. He now had a totally different attitude toward Taylor and negotiating with the railroad. He planned on having a quiet talk with Jenny at the first opportunity.

"All right, son," Howard was saying. "I'll not give her any pushes, but I will tell her a little more about that game and some of my own suspicions. At least she ought to know you were an honorable man. You could have told the railroad you owned my land and that would have been the end of it all."

"I'd much rather you and Maxwell talk it out. What do you say to riding back with me tomorrow?"

"I'll do that. Least I can do is listen to what you want and see how the land lays. Who knows, maybe we can make a bargain."

"That's about all we can expect," Trace replied.

"You sure you don't want to come back to the house and talk this over."

"No. I'm leaving at dawn. Jenny might not be disposed to apologizing. She's been a little . . . put out with me. If she needs time to think, then it's best I give it to her."

"I think you're making a mistake. Jenny's a girl who gives herself completely to anything she chooses. She'd be one to fight for this land if she thought I was losing it. She'd also be one to admit she's wrong if she finds out it's so."

"Maybe so," Trace replied, "but I've pushed her a couple of times and I won't push her again. Maybe if you come in, she'll come with you. Maybe then we can talk."

"Looks to me"—Buck grinned—"that you're just about as stubborn as she is."

Trace smiled but didn't reply.

"Come on, son," Howard said to Buck. "Let's call it a night. We've got a lot of things to do tomorrow. You'll be all right, Trace?"

"I'll be fine. It's not the first barn I've slept in."

"Good night, Trace."

"Good night."

He watched as Buck and Howard walked toward the house.

He was restless, and even the barn felt confining. He went outside and closed the barn door behind him. He walked slowly toward the surrounding trees.

The moon had just risen over the horizon and was casting lengthy shadows. He could see just well enough to walk without falling. He walked slowly, allowing Jenny full possession of his thoughts. It was a possession for which he would not have to account.

He walked for some time before he heard the sound of swiftly running water. It was a small creek, bubbling with life. He sat beside it on a tree stump and tried to piece together the fragments of his puzzle. It seemed to come down to a few questions. One, where did Taylor and Eileen fit into this? Two, what did they really have to gain? And the most important of all, would he be able to salvage the spark of something unique he and Jenny had shared, or would the magic he had tasted so briefly be lost forever?

Howard and Buck walked into the house and began to remove their jackets. Jenny, who had just finished lighting the lamps, gazed at both of them. Buck and Howard exchanged glances.

317

"I'm going to bed," Buck said quickly.

Jenny looked at him in surprise. It had always been she and Buck who had sat before the fire and talked for hours.

"Where is Trace?" she questioned quickly.

"He's . . . he's out in the barn. Jenny," Howard said, "let's sit by the fire. I've got to talk to you about something important."

"All right, Pa," she replied. They walked to the fire and sat together. "Pa, if it's about having Trace here like this . . . well, I just couldn't let him lie out there and die after someone tried to kill him."

"Now, Jenny girl, I wouldn't have expected you to have done any less. I want us to talk about me."

"Pa, don't worry about anything."

"Stop consoling me, child," Howard said gently.

Jenny's face flushed. "Pa . . . I—"

"I know, girl, you been doing it so long it's become a habit. But it's time we changed things around here. It's time I took hold again." Jenny's eyes widened in surprise. She tried to read her father's face. "It's time I got myself together and took some of the load off the backs of my children."

Jenny could hardly believe this miracle. She threw herself into her father's arms and was nearly speechless from the tears that choked her. It was then she remembered that the ranch that could hold them together now belonged to the one who was their enemy.

She moved out of his arms, but before she could speak Howard interrupted.

"Jenny girl, now you listen to me. I think there's something you should know. I was in the saloon some time ago, and I found myself caught in a card game."

"Pa—"

"Before you ask, yes, I was drinking. In fact I was

pretty drunk. I was so drunk that I allowed myself to be maneuvered by card sharps, who, at any other time, I would have spotted a mile away."

"I know, Pa," Jenny whispered miserably.

"What is it you think you know, Jenny girl?"

"That Trace Cord and his railroad friends cheated you out of our land. I know they own it now."

"Well you're right about some things, but you're sure way wrong about some others."

"I don't understand."

"The card sharps. There were two of them, neither of which was Trace Cord. He sat in and took my land just to protect me."

"So he says."

"He's an honest man, Jenny," Howard said gently. "He took my land and made me a bargain. If I straightened up my life he'd return it to me. I had to stop drinking and start working."

"You believe that, Pa?"

"Jenny . . . Trace Cord gave me back my land tonight."

She was stunned. She gazed at him in disbelief.

"Jenny?"

"I . . . I don't believe it."

"But it's true."

"Why . . . why didn't he tell me?"

"Maybe he was thinking of my pride. Maybe he wanted me to get my daughter back. Maybe, too, he wanted to help me get back on my feet."

"He could have just . . ."

"That's right, he could have. But he didn't. He kept his word. He told me when I got hold of everything he'd return it. He just did that. I have a feeling maybe his word means a lot to him."

Jenny shivered as though a rough wind had touched her. Then she buried her face in her hands and wept.

Howard drew her into his arms and held her.

It was several minutes before she regained control.

"So Jenny, you don't have to worry anymore. It's been hard on you and Buck, but I intend to make up for that."

Jenny brushed the tears from her eyes and tried to smile but failed.

"There's more bothering you than that, isn't there, girl?"

She nodded. "Why is everything so hard?"

"Being hard sometimes makes what you get more precious."

"It's too late for anything, Pa," she whispered.

"It's never too late, Jenny."

"He . . . Trace . . . he thinks I shot him."

"Are you sure of that?" Howard tipped Jenny's chin up to look deep into her troubled eyes.

"Jenny, you think on this. Maybe things aren't as dark as they look."

He rose and left Jenny sitting thoughtfully by the fire. She sat immobile for some time. Then she rose and walked to the door.


Trace rose from the tree stump and stretched his tight muscles. His mind was in a turmoil, and the battle he had fought with his emotions had been no easier.

The moon had risen high and now washed through the trees in misty rays that cast pale light across the rippling water.

He had been thinking of Jenny, conjuring visions of her beside him now, bathed in moonlight. He could see the glow of it in her hair and reflecting in her turquoise eyes. He would have given anything to have shared the night with her.

He wondered if he would ever be able to build a

bridge over the gulf between them.

Reluctantly he turned to walk back to the barn, certain he would find no rest. He had taken only a step or two when he saw the slim form walking toward him through the evening mist. His breath caught and held as he wondered if it was his imagination and desire or actually Jenny. Was she here, or had he dreamed her because he wanted her so desperately?

They stood now, less than a few strides apart.

He remained immobile, unsure of her purpose or what to expect. Then she moved from the trees and walked toward him. when she was close enough to reach out and touch him, she stopped.

"Trace?" she questioned softly.

He moved closer until the depths of her eyes could be seen. "You belong to nights like this, Jenny," he said softly. "You're so very beautiful." He was surprised to see tears glistening in her eyes.

"Don't be kind to me, Trace. I must tell you how ashamed I am."

"Ashamed?"

"I truly believed you had taken our land. I never believed you would return it to my father. He told me tonight you had. You must hate me for my distrust and my angry words. How stupid you must think I am. Trace, will you forgive me and let me thank you for what you have done for my father . . . for me?"

"I can understand how you must have felt, Jenny. I don't blame you. I blame the ones who made you believe as you did."

"Trace I . . . you don't . . ."

"Don't what?"

"You don't truly believe I shot you?"

"I told you once"—she could see the flash of his white smile—"I'm sure if it had been you, you wouldn't have missed."

"Trace!" she cried desperately. "Don't joke about this!"

"No, Jenny, I don't believe it was you who shot me."

He heard her ragged sigh of relief. Then he reached out to lay his hand gently against her cheek. With his thumb he lightly brushed away a wayward tear.

"I don't ever want to give you a reason to cry again, Jenny. Can't we begin something new; can't we forget all the wrong reasons and create new ones?"

"Trace," she whispered softly. Then she was in his arms, his hungry mouth claiming hers in a hot and passionate kiss that forged them together as if they had been melded into one.

His arm about her waist held her so tightly against him that she could hardly breathe, but she didn't care. She didn't want to breathe; she wanted to devour him; and her open, seeking mouth inflamed his desire to a white-hot peak.

His other hand caught her head and held it so that they were fused in mutual conquest. A soft, muffled groan escaped him as his senses soared. His hand slipped down to capture a soft breast. Their mouths hungered to prolong this sweet, heady assault. They tasted, sapping the strength from each other's limbs, and they clung to each other as a wild, tempestuous river of passion swept them away.

His fingers were gentle now as he reached to release the buttons that confined the sensitive flesh he desired to taste. He bent to capture one hardened nipple, sending a storm of torturous longing through her body. She closed her eyes as the sheer pleasure of his touch filled her with trembling joy. His hands gently cupped her jutting breasts and stroked her smooth skin, savoring the warmth of her flesh.

In the light of the pale moon she was aglow with a luster, shadowed and highlighted and more beautiful

322

than he had ever seen her. He set aside his own sparse clothing, then gathered her body close in his arms. She was a dream, a release of longing that swept every nerve with intense excitement.

She felt the bold urgency of him searing her flesh and heard his heart beating wildly against her naked breast. Beneath her hands his hard muscles felt tense with broiling vigor. Clinging together, caught in surging rapture, they sank to the soft ground.

Her thighs were like satin against his heated skin as they parted to accept him. His kiss touched her, fierce with love and passion, and missed no inch of her quivering flesh. Then he was a hard flame within her. She moaned with the almost unbearable pleasure and they were both caught up in a swelling, surging tide of ecstasy.

They lay together, hushed by the magic they had shared. Trace pulled her tumbled hair across his body and stroked it, inhaling the sweet scent of it. Jenny sighed and snuggled more closely into the curve of his arm.

"So," she whispered as her slender fingers very gently caressed his lean ribs and broad chest, "we have nothing more to fight over."

"Only one thing," he responded with a soft laugh.

"One thing?" she questioned.

"As I said before, we have to decide how large a family we will have."

She smiled tenderly at the remembered question.

"Trace, seriously, what will happen next?"

"We have to get this battle decided. We have to get the ranchers and the railroad to talk. That's the most important thing, to get them to sit down together and work this out."

"There is so much I really don't understand. I just cannot believe Taylor has any motive for wanting to gain our land."

"I don't know what the motive is either," Trace replied. "But I intend to find out."

"How can you do that? If there is a motive, and I still don't believe it, then Taylor will certainly not tell you. Trace, can it be that you suspect Taylor . . . well . . . because . . ."

"Because he wants you?" Trace grumbled. "That's reason enough for me. But if there is something going on that involves the railroad, Maxwell has a right to know."

"Trace . . . the tracks . . . they can go around our ranch, can't they?"

"I won't lie to you, Jenny. It's impossible."

"But . . ."

"Jenny, let's not stir this up tonight. Your father and Maxwell are men who can talk. We don't want to take as much from you as you seem to believe. It's just more lies you've been fed. Let's give it some time, at least time enough to check out someone I think might have answers."

"Who?"

"A friend of Taylor Jessup's. In fact, a very close friend."

"Maybe this friend is responsible for all the problems."

"You mean using Jessup?"

"Yes. He doesn't strike me as a man to be used."

"You're sure of that?"

"I believe," she replied softly, "that he knows how much this place means to us. Why would he have ridden out to tell me he would lend Pa money if he needed it?"

"Does your father owe him money?"

"I . . . I think so. Taylor said he'd be glad to give Pa . . . another loan."

This was a piece of information Trace stored away, but he decided he was not going to let a beautiful night like this one turn into a discussion about the battle between the ranchers and the railroad. He knew it would become a battle between him and Jenny, and he had no intention of letting that happen. He tightened his arms about her, drawing her half across him. Her hair tumbled about him, enclosing them in a cascade of moonlit gold. Their mouths played gently upon each other's while his hands explored a slim, graceful back, then slid down to soft, round hips. He pressed her body against him and she could feel the warmth of his manhood rising hard and firm.

Their pulses quickened and they dwelt in a private world of all-consuming passion. Time stood still, captured by the lovers who knew only each other in their flame-engulfed world.

"I love you, Jenny," Trace whispered against her parted lips. "Believe that, no matter what else you believe. I love you."

Each touch of his hands fanned the fire that grew into passion she could not control. Every part of her yearned to draw him within her and hold him there until the raging desire that tore her was sated and she could rest in his arms. It was a peace only he could give her.

She bent her head and again placed a searing kiss across his mouth, a kiss that could have reduced to cinders all the forest about them. It sapped his strength until his head swam with the intoxicating nectar of her sweet lips.

She meant to be the aggressor, but her intention was short-lived. Trace made her as much a victim of her scalding kiss as he was.

Nature moved about them in soft breezes neither felt, for there was a storm within that would have put the strongest wind to shame.

In the aftermath, they held each other, calm and completely satisfied. Her cheek rested against his shoulder and his strong hands gently soothed her quivering flesh as they lay in languid contentment.

Too soon the moon climbed high. They rose and dressed to the accompaniment of soft whispers, gentle touches, and deep, delicious kisses. Then they walked back toward the house, where Trace bid her a lengthy and very passionate good night.

# Chapter 23

Eileen had waited patiently for night to come. She had dressed carefully to convey a most sensual impression and now she opened the door and looked up and down the hall before leaving her room and walking quickly to the end of the corridor. She stopped before number seventeen.

Very gently she rapped on the door. She heard no sound from within, but she noticed that the light glowing from beneath the door was quickly extinguised.

The door was jerked open so abruptly that she was startled. The room was dark behind him, but she could make him out well enough to see two things: one, he was only half dressed, and two, he had a gun in his hand.

"I really don't think you'll need that," she purred softly. "May I come in?"

For an instant he was surprised, then a smile played about his lips and he stepped aside and motioned her in. He moved to light the kerosene lamps and Eileen took the time to examine him carefully.

He wore only grey breeches, his feet were bare, and he was shirtless. His body was hard with rigid muscles and his chest was broad, though several scars marred the smooth surface.

His hair was ebony and the short, matching beard gave him a piratical look. The black patch was in place over one eye, but the other deep blue orb missed nothing about her.

He limped toward her and stood close enough to inhale the soft scent of her perfume.

"Is there . . . something I can help you with . . . boss?"

"You could begin by telling me your name."

"I thought we'd decided on a name. One name's as good as another. Why is it important?"

"It's funny that I get the feeling I know you. Have we met somewhere?"

"I think," he said in a deep voice, "if we had met before, neither of us would have forgotten it."

Her breath caught at the open suggestion. She had not met many men as exciting as this extremely handsome and so very mysterious man. She was intrigued. Above all else, he exuded an aura of danger and this was always an attracation for Eileen.

"No," she breathed softly, "I doubt very much that we would have." She walked closer to him and ran soft, tentative fingers across the scars on his chest. "You're a very mysterious man, Lucifer," she whispered. "Where do you come from? What caused all this? What do you want?" Her voice grew sultry and her eyes wide with invitation.

He gripped the hand that drifted across his chest. His other arm snaked about her waist and drew her against him. His voice was even more dangerous than his appearance. She shivered as some inexplicable feeling close to fear coursed through her.

"My past is my own. What you buy for your money is my gun. Anything else"—he smiled—"will have to be paid for some other way."

"I'm sure," she breathed softly, "we can find some terms to agree on."

There was a soft chuckle from him as he kicked the door shut. In another few minutes the lamps were again extinguished.

The early morning sun found Trace seated at the breakfast table with Howard and Buck. Jenny placed a hot cup of coffee before him, then sat down.

The large wood table had two six-foot benches on each side. Buck and Howard sat on one side and Jenny slid close to Trace and was pleased to feel a light caress on her slim waist and see the glow in his eyes as he looked down at her.

"Good morning. Did you sleep well?"

"With just a few surprising dreams. Yes, I did." She smiled up at him, her cheeks pink and her turquoise eyes aglow with a light that pleased all three men.

Reluctantly Trace drew his eyes from hers.

"I'm going to be on my way as soon as I can. I think my appearance in town is going to surprise someone. Mr. Graham, can I tell Maxwell that you'll be in soon to talk to him?"

"I'll come in first thing tomorrow. Buck and I have a few things to finish up first."

"I'm sure Maxwell will be pleased to see you."

"I'll go out and saddle your horse for you," Buck said as he pushed his empty plate aside and rose. "You better nurse that side a little more," he suggested, his eyes twinkling mischievously. "Too much activity might create a problem. Besides, just moving around in those tight clothes is problem enough."

Trace chuckled, Jenny blushed, and Howard ordered Buck to hurry and get going while his lips twitched in silent amusement.

The three sat together talking until Buck returned. "All saddled and ready. Say, Trace?"

"What?"

"Did Jenny tell you there's a dance in town day after tomorrow? If you and some of your people come, it might be a good opportunity for everyone from both sides to talk. A few drinks of old Hank Miller's punch and some fun could make people more receptive to new ideas."

Trace again turned to Jenny. "Would you like to go?"

"Pa was going to bring me, I'm sure."

"Well now, I'd like to come for you."

"Why don't you just meet us there? It would take less time."

"All three of you?"

"I'm sure Buck has some other plans." Jenny laughed to be able to turn the tables so quickly on her devilish brother. But her ploy did not work too well.

Buck grinned. "You bet. I'm bringing Emily, the prettiest girl in the territory."

"I'm afraid I'll have to argue with you on that point," Trace returned with a laugh.

"I'll bring Jenny," Howard offered.

"And I'll be there. I have a feeling this is all going to work out fine," Trace declared.

Howard and Buck watched in satisfaction as Trace slid his arm about Jenny's waist and she walked out to his horse with him. When they stood by his horse Trace bent his head to gently taste her willing lips.

"Lord, I'm glad this whole problem has been settled," he said softly. "If I had known what would come of it, I would have forced you to use that rifle the first day I met you down by the river."

"Don't joke about being shot," Jenny demanded.

"Don't you realize, you oaf, that you could have died?"

"I'm not that easy to get rid of, as someone is about to find out." Trace laughed. "I'll see you in town day after tomorrow."

Before she could speak again he caught her mouth in a kiss that completely forced whatever thoughts she might have had from her mind. Then he mounted quickly, smiling at the thought that despite the tight breeches his body had responded quite violently to Jenny's reaction.

Jenny watched Trace ride away. The smile on her face faded into the nagging worry of half-remembered dreams. All the problems were over, her rational mind decided. But then why was she suddenly chilled, and frightened?

When Trace arrived at the railroad camp he became the object of some amusement.

"Hey, Trace," one man called, "told ya ya was gettin' too big for your breeches."

"Yeah!" another shouted. "What happened, you fall in the river and your clothes shrink?"

"Okay, boys," Trace announced with a laugh, "you've had your fun. Now get back to work. Max wants this track into town in time for the dance to help celebrate."

Whistles, laughter, and some rather shady suggestions followed him as he rode to his car. He was surprised to find Allison gone, but he changed clothes quickly and walked to Maxwell's car. Max was more than pleased to see him.

"Where the hell you been, boy? Last time I saw you you was chasin' after that Graham girl. I see she didn't shoot you."

"No." Trace chuckled. "Someone else did."

331

"What?"

"I said—"

"I heard what you said. Now sit down and tell me what happened."

"First, tell me where Allison is."

"She went into town to do some shopping with Eileen."

Trace was surprised that Allison would choose to travel anywhere with Eileen, but he kept his thoughts to himself.

"Now come on, Trace, tell me what happened."

Trace sat down and began to explain all that had happened during the few days he had been gone.

"By damn, Trace," Maxwell declared with a grin, "I knew I was wise to hire you. I'm sorry about your getting shot, but since you're all right, I'd say it was a providential thing. So, Howard Graham is going to sit down and talk to me."

"He agreed to that. The night of the party we could take a big step in the right direction. If we can get the tracks into town by then, it would mean a grand celebration. Then, after you talk, we could head on out into the valley."

"This is wonderful . . . Trace?"

"What?"

"You have any idea who shot you?"

"I don't know who pulled the trigger, but I'm damn sure who was behind it. I hope he goes on thinking I'm dead. He'll be at the party and I'd like to see his face when he sees me."

"He? . . . Who?"

"I think you have a handle on my suspicions."

"Taylor Jessup?"

"Right."

"Jessup told us once he was planning to marry Jenny

Graham. Does that have anything to do with this? You wouldn't just be a mite jealous, would you?"

"No . . . not now. You see, the young lady is question is not going to marry Taylor Jessup."

"You sound certain about that."

"I am. She just promised me today she'd marry me."

"The hell she did! You do things up right, don't you? Are you sure she won't believe you're just leading her on to get the land?"

"Nope. You see, I had the deed to her ranch and I gave it back."

Maxwell blinked, then shook his head and smiled. "I know I'm going to enjoy this story.".

Now Trace laughed as he continued to explain the card game and his winning the land.

"So you gave it back."

"I'd given him my word."

Maxwell's eyes glinted with humor. "You could have given me that land and half our problems would have been over."

"I couldn't do that, Maxwell."

"I know," Maxwell said softly. "That is the reason I asked you to help me build my railroad."

"Thanks, Max."

"For what?"

"For understanding and not kicking my butt out of here."

"Can't." Maxwell grinned. "I've got to get these tracks into town, so suppose you pick up your butt and get it out there and start laying rail. I want to be in town with this engine the night of the party."

"We'll be there."

"I have your word on that?" Maxwell's eyes twinkled with laughter.

"You have."

"Good. I'll start brushing up on my dancing."

Together they walked to the door.


The hotel was quiet, but Allison, who was used to rising early, was already up. She dressed to go down to breakfast, after which she planned to take an early morning walk. She went to her door and had only opened it a fraction when she heard a familiar voice. It was Eileen's.

Allison would never know why she instinctively closed the door just enough to allow her to view the people speaking without being seen herself.

Eileen stood in the hall outside the door of room seventeen and in the dim light Allison could not make out the form that stood just within the door frame.

"I'll see you later?"

"Why not?" came the low male voice.

Eileen laughed softly and reached up to draw his head to hers for a vibrant kiss.

Something about the man set off a familiar chord in Allison's mind. She knew this man somehow. She wanted to observe him more closely and opened the door a little too far. Eileen sensed her presence at the same moment Lucifer did. He gave a muffled curse, drew back within the room, and closed the door.

Eileen walked to Allison.

"Good morning, Allison. Going out?"

"Yes," Allison replied just as sweetly. "Coming in?"

"You little . . . your brother should teach you some manners."

"He did. I wonder why your uncle never taught you any. I thought sleeping with every man in pants was not in good taste for ladies."

"You say one word of this and I'll . . ."

"You'll what? Don't worry, Eileen. I don't spread such dirty laundry . . . unless . . ."

"Unless what?"

"Unless you refuse to take my brother off your list."

"Little bitch," Eileen snarled.

"I've been taking lessons from you."

Eileen, her face pale from rage, spun about, entered her room, and slammed the door.

Allison gazed at the closed door of number seventeen. Slowly she walked toward it. She raised her hand to knock, but her courage left her. Would he think her another Eileen, knocking on a stranger's door? Could she have seen him somewhere before? She sighed and turned away.

Within the room Lucifer stood with his ear against the door. He heard the sigh, then her receding footsteps. He too breathed a deep sigh of relief. He turned and leaned against the door as if his legs had gone weak. "That," he said under his breath, "was a close one."

He limped to the basin to wash, then he dressed and strapped his gun belt about him. Taking out his gun, he checked to see that it was loaded. He walked to the door, opened it a crack, and looked at the empty hall. Once satisfied no one was about, he left, going down the back stairs of the hotel to the alley behind. In a few more minutes he was at the livery stable, where he gave the boy a coin, mounted his well-cared-for horse, and rode out of town.

Taylor sat at his desk with three men sitting opposite him. He had let them in the back door a quarter of an hour before. Since then, they had been in deep and very serious conversation. "You understand what I want done. Everything has to happen at the proper time."

"Yeah, Poe and Stace and the rest are ready. By the time that party is over, the ranchers and railroaders will be doin' more than havin' a standoff. They'll be shooting at each other."

"That's precisely what I want," Taylor said. "Now, during the time between now and the celebration I want you to keep close watch. I don't want any of the parties in question making any . . . close contacts before then."

"We'll keep our eyes open."

"Okay, then get out of town right now. I don't want anyone to see you coming and going."

"We'll be careful."

They rose, and, after taking the precautions to see that no one was in the alley, they left.

Taylor prepared to spend the next few days before the party obviously and very casually going about his business.

Lucifer rode slowly and easily. To anyone who might have seen him, he looked like another misplaced roamer. But he knew not only where he was roaming but what he was looking for.

It took several hours of slow and very methodical searching for him to spot what he wanted.

The man was old and whiskered. His body seemed to bend forward as he slowly walked holding the reins of his burro's bridle and pulling him along.

As the two grew closer together the old man slowed and squinted through faded eyes at the man who rode toward him.

When they stopped within feet of each other, the old man was the first to speak. His voice was cracked from lack of use, and he was overly aggressive.

"What ya doin' blockin' my way, sonny? Get yo behind outta the road afore I gets my shootin' iron and puts a hole through ya."

"Now old man," Lucifer said with a chuckle, "is that a way to talk to a friend?"

"Friend, huh! I ain't got no friends."

"Well, old man, I got the fixins for a good meal and a full bottle for some nippin' if you're interested."

The old man squinted at him in silence for a minute, then he grinned a toothless grin.

"Now why dint ya say that in the first place? I could use a few nips to warm the old bones. Step down from that horse and I'll build us a fire."

They set about in silence making camp. Lucifer cooked while the old man muttered about his lack of speed. After the meal his muttering was replaced by smiles as the full bottle was handed ot him. The old man grabbed the bottle and took a deep gulp of the fiery liquor. He held it for a few minutes, then he gave a grating laugh.

"Now, sonny, why don't ya tell me just what it is ya's after? I never got a free gift from anyone they wasn't a hook in it."

"Now why can't I just be offering you a friendly drink?"

The old man bent forward. His eyes were probing and shrewd.

"Don't give me any lies, boy. I'm too old for that."

"All right." Lucifer laughed. "There's a lot of questions I'd like to ask you. Before I do, I'll tell you that a great deal depends on the answers I get."

"So shoot, boy."

Lucifer leaned forward and his voice was deep and intent. First he explained as much as he thought he knew, then he asked one question after another and the old man answered them as rapidly as they were asked.

Satisfied, Lucifer enjoyed part of the bottle, then gave the balance to the old man. He stood, and the old man looked up at a tall, muscular man, strong of feature and of will.

"So you'll be ridin' back tonight?"

"I have to."

"It's a long pull."

"I know, but there's something very important I have to do."

"Good luck to ya, boy."

"Thanks. Enjoy the rest of the bottle."

"I'll do just that."

He saddled and mounted his horse and with a quick wave he was gone. The old man watched his receding form until the night swallowed him up.


Allison had made friends in the town. She was a bright and giving girl and her offer to volunteer to work for the benefit of the celebration had been readily accepted.

After some decorating of a common hall had been accomplished, Allison joined several others for a late supper. It was a gay affair. Allison was young and vital and she attracted the other young people to her. Of course some of them were young men near her age and several vied with each other for the privilege of walking her back to the hotel.

After selecting one, she and the delighted suitor walked back to the hotel slowly and talked of everything but each other the entire way. In the hotel lobby she bid him good night.

She stepped into her dark room and turned around to close the door. A hard hand closed over her mouth and an even harder arm came about her waist, lifting her from the floor.

Allison had never been more terrified in her life. She was completely immobile and unable to utter a sound.

She could hear his harsh breathing in her ear and felt the tremendous strength of the hard body pressed against her back.

"Shhh," the deep voice cautioned quietly, too quietly for her to recognize the voice. "I don't intend to hurt you. If I let you go, will you promise to be quiet? I only want to talk to you . . . will you promise?"

She thought quickly. If he let go she might be able to escape. She heard a soft chuckle as his voice whispered in her ear.

"I'm bigger and stronger than you and I can prevent you from running. I can hear your thoughts. Do you want me to let go of you?"

She nodded violently.

"I know who you are and I trust your word. Will you promise not to cry out? If you promise I will let you go."

She was totally surprised at this, for now her own pride was at stake. A Cord always kept his word. She had had this drummed into her from childhood. Now she must decide. Slowly she nodded her head.

She felt his hand slowly move from her mouth and his arm from about her waist.

They stood for a moment in utter silence and total darkness. Her heart thudded painfully and she had to swallow forcefully to keep the scream that hovered in her throat from leaping to her lips.

"If you will stand still, I will light the lamp."

She nodded. Then, realizing he could not see her, she gasped out, "Yes."

She heard him moving about, heard the tinkle as the glass chimney was removed from the lamp. She heard the striking of the match and saw the sudden bright glow of mellow light touch the room.

He looked at her across the glow of the lamp and he smiled as her eyes grew wider and wider.

"Oh my God," she whispered.

*Chapter 24*

There simply was no further excuse for Will to stay with Joanne and Georgina other than his growing desire to do so. He had trudged slowly through the stand of trees with a chattering Georgina behind him and had marked the trees to be cut. When this job was finished he had not told Joanne but instead continued to rise every morning and set about doing repair work around the ranch. He enjoyed this kind of work he had always done and for which he felt he was destined.

His experienced eye told him the land was good, and his experienced hand had already begun to make some improvements. Hinges on barn doors swung easily, fences stood without fallen sections, and the horses glowed under careful attention.

Will felt another kind of satisfaction in the return of Joanne's smile and the look of peace in her eyes that had replaced insecurity. He also was aware that Georgina's feelings about him had increased from respect and admiration to deep affection.

Georgina and Will were walking from the barn to the house just before supper on the night before the party.

"Mama made me the prettiest dress, Will," Georgina gushed. "It's blue . . . Mama says I look good in blue.

Do you think I'll look pretty in blue, Will?"

"Little one, you'd look pretty in anything. But don't you go flirtin' with any boys. You're my girl, aren't you, Georgie?"

"Oh yes, Will," she agreed, giggling happily. Georgina did not really remember the last time she had been so happy. Will's coming had changed everything in her life. For the first time in a long time she had seen her mother laugh freely. The thought of Will having to go away one day had been pushed completely from her mind. She simply would not let it happen. Besides, hadn't she prayed every night?

Inside, the house was fragrant with the smell of fresh bread and good cooking. Will inhaled contentedly and smiled across the room at Joanne. "I swear I ain't had so much good food since I was a youngster."

"Will, sit down and eat," Joanne replied. "Georgina, it's going to be a big day tomorrow so you'd best get to bed early tonight."

Joanne was amused to find no resistance in Georgina, who agreed to go to bed as soon as the last of the evening chores had been done. Obediently she bade them both good night and soon found sleep filled with fanciful dreams.

Will and Joanne sat before the fire and talked for awhile.

"Georgina has been a real nuisance since you've arrived, Will. You will have to forgive her. She misses her father very much."

"I know. Besides, she's no bother. I told you once, I've got a way with kids."

"Yes, I remember. The way you get along with Georgina, one would think you had children of your own."

Will was silent long enough for Joanne to realize she had struck a very sensitive subject. "I . . . I'm sorry,

Will. I never meant to pry."

"It's all right," Will said gently. "I've been a long time facing the fact that I have to put memories behind me and start a new life."

"That's not easy to do. I know when Jim died I thought my life was over. If it hadn't been for Georgina, I don't know how I would have managed."

"You're lucky," Will said, his eyes intent on the glow of the fire. "When I lost, it was everything. My farm . . . my wife . . . my child."

"Oh Will," Joanne breathed. "I'm sorry. I didn't mean to hurt you. You've been so kind and so helpful. If Georgina and I—"

"Joanne," Will said firmly, "you and Georgina have been nothing but a blessing to me. It was time that I stopped looking back."

"Are you happy with the railroad, Will?"

"Passably. Why?"

"You don't look like you belong there."

He laughed shortly. "And where do I look like I belong?"

"On the land," Joanne said softly. "You look like a man who needs solid roots in which to plant himself." Will didn't answer but continued to look meditatively at the slowly dying fire. "Do you know what first gave me that impression?" she questioned.

"What?"

"Your hands. They're strong and hard. They look like the hands of a man who fought battles with the earth and won."

"I guess you've got me pegged. I'll tell you the truth. I was looking forward to staying here a few days. I do love the land, and I've been enjoying working here."

"How . . . how much longer will you stay?"

"Not long, I suppose. If the rails are in town by the party tomorrow night, we'll most likely be movin' along the next day."

"Oh . . . I see." Joanne rose. "Well, again I'm grateful for what you've done . . . Will?"

"Yes?"

". . . I . . . nothing. I guess I'll go to bed. Good night."

Will rose to stand close to her. He wanted to say so many things to her, but he could not be sure she felt anything except gratitude for his help.

Both were momentarily wordless as they stood balanced precariously on the brink of something neither could name or begin. Then the moment passed.

"Good night, Joanne . . . sleep well."

She started to say something but decided against it and turned to walk to her bedroom door. She cast one last look at Will, who stood by the fire still watching her. Then she stepped inside and closed the door behind her.

Will stood gazing at the closed door for some time before he took firm control of himself. He turned and again sat before the glowing embers of the fire.

If she were to ask him, he speculated silently, he would stay. He would give no thought to the railroad moving on—if she were to ask him. But he could not bring it up. She was grateful that he had given her this time and had done the work, and she was grateful that he had brightened Georgina's days for awhile. But gratitude was not an emotion on which to build a lifetime. It would have to be something much fuller and stronger than that. But if she were to ask him . . .

It was early morning and Lucifer had ridden out on another quest, this time to waylay the Marshall family before they arrived in town for the celebration.

Earlier he had stood at his hotel window and had

watched the flurry of activity as the crews of men, under the constant guidance of Trace Cord, brought the tracks closer to town. They were to pass just half a mile beyond the city's limits and the excitement seemed to fill the town with an unfamiliar buoyancy.

Bunting had been hung from windows and red, white, and blue streamers had appeared on every pole. Banners had been stretched across the one main street to welcome the railroad to a town that anticipated the advantages its close proximity would bring.

It was like a Fourth of July celebration. People had milled about and children had made the music of laughter ring out up and down the street.

Again, as he had several times in the past few days, Lucifer had watched Taylor Jessup walk across the street from the bank to the side alley near the hotel. He had known quite well who he was going to see and now he had most of the answers as to why.

He had sent a telegraph message two days before and now awaited the answer that would be the final piece to the puzzle he was putting together.

He had also known that Jacob Marshall would be on his way into town to make some kind of deal that included Taylor. He meant to do something about it.

Now he rode along the dusty road toward the Marshall ranch, quite sure he would meet them on their way into town.

He was pleased when he saw the buggy approaching. He stopped and waited until it was nearly abreast of him, then he raised his arm and hailed Jacob Marshall.

Jacob rode with his wife, Beatrice, his two daughters, Emily and Hannah, and his son, Terrance. As they approached the lone rider, both Terrance and Jacob lifted their rifles from the buggy floor.

"You won't need those, Mr. Marshall," Lucifer said. "I only need to talk to you for a few minutes; then you can go on your way."

"Who are you, stranger?" Jacob questioned.

"A good friend who wants to keep you from making a very big mistake."

"Mistake? What are you talking about?"

"Tell me, were you going to see Taylor Jessup before the celebration to have him handle your business with the railroad?"

"That's no business of yours."

"It is if you don't want to be taken advantage of. You have a lot more to lose than you think."

"Why don't you explain just what you have to do with all this? Tell me what you want and I'll decide if I want to listen or not."

"All right," Lucifer said softly. "I'm the man Taylor Jessup has just hired to kill you."

The women gasped, and both men reflexively raised their guns.

Lucifer laughed. "If I wanted you dead, you'd be dead by now."

"Then what do you want?"

"I want you to listen."

"All right," Jacob said grimly as he laid his rifle on the floor of the buggy again and instructed his son to do the same. "I'm listening."

Lucifer began to speak in a clear, crisp voice. The two men listened and soon their expressions changed from mild surprise to total amazement.

Emily watched with interest, as did her mother, but Hannah's eyes remained riveted on the man who was speaking.

Hannah's features were a near duplicate of Emily's tawny beauty. She was a delicate and very sensitive girl who at first looked upon Lucifer with pity.

She had never, she thought, seen a face that combined so much of life. It was young, yet it was old.

It was handsome, yet filled with lines of pain and bitterness. It was lonely, and her young heart reached out in sympathy.

And Lucifer was very much aware of her scrutiny. He was also aware of her beauty and the wide, deep pools of her too innocent yet too knowledgeable eyes. They stung him deeply.

"Go and enjoy the celebration," he concluded, "but don't sign any papers. Keep quiet until I get all of this together. Without proof we can do nothing. But it won't be long until I have all the proof we need."

"I don't know what interest you have in this, stranger, but I'll give you the benefit of the doubt. I won't do anything about making a deal until you show me this . . . proof you're talking about."

"Fair enough. I just want to spare you and some others a lot of grief."

"What's in it for you?"

"That's another thing you'll find out later. It's a personal thing."

"So just when do you plan on informing me about what's going on?"

"I'm just tying up a loose end. By the time the celebration is over, you'll have all the answers you and the railroad need. I have a feeling you'll get together just fine after you know all the answers."

Lucifer smiled, gave a half salute, wheeled his horse, and rode away.

"Damn," Jacob grunted. "Why the hell do I believe what some unnamed gunfighter tells me?"

"Because," Emily said quickly, "we all feel it's the truth. We all feel there's something going on we don't understand. Buck said—" She abruptly closed her mouth on her hasty mistake.

"Buck Graham! Is he mixed up in this?"

"Pa . . . why don't you talk to Buck? He's the same

347

kind of man you are. He's a good rancher and he'll be even bigger."

"Good rancher. His drunken old man is just about to yank that ranch out from under his kids' feet."

"Pa . . . things are changing there now. Mr. Graham hasn't been in town for awhile and he and Buck have been working together. Pa . . . can't you just talk to Buck? . . . Can't you just listen?"

Jacob bit down firmly on his cigar and grunted. The sound was neither negative or positive. Emily remained silent as Jacob slapped the reins against the horses to move them along.

Emily and Hannah sat in the buggy in silence, although both their minds were running in remarkably similar directions.

Emily was hopeful she could bring Buck and her father together at the celebration. She was sure once they stood on common ground they could establish a relationship. She wanted that desperately, but she was determined she would marry Buck Graham no matter what happened.

Hannah was quiet and meditative also. She was envisioning the stranger's face in her mind and wondering why he had denied her gaze as if he had been afraid of what it might see. She was all too aware of the tingle of excitement in her veins and fervently hoped she would see him again.

Taking a route parallel to theirs but far enough away so he would not be seen, Lucifer rode back to town. He went straight to the telegraph office and was given the telegram he had been expecting. Tearing it open immediately, he read it quickly. His lips parted in a broad grin of satisfaction.

"Well, well, Mr. Jessup, seems you have big plans,

my friend. Too bad you picked the wrong people to hoodwink. I guess it's time to shed some light on the subject."

He stuffed the message into his breast pocket and returned to his hotel room. Tonight would be the celebration. He would wait patiently until dark; then he would set some wheels in motion.


The town was ablaze with light. Torches were attached to posts and everything seemed aglow.

The huge meeting hall, decorated as it had never been before, waited only for the arrival of the first train and the gathering of the people who wanted to celebrate this unique occasion. To the merchants of the town the railroad would mean growth, and a way to get merchandise from the eastern market.

The tracks had been laid to a point just a mile outside the town, and most of the workers, including Trace, had gone back to ride the first train in.

People milled around the tracks in delicious anticipation. Will and Joanne did their best to control Georgina's enthusiasm, but it was extremely difficult. She had ridden the train and could not refrain from telling everyone, especially the excited children, that she had been the first to do so.

The Marshalls arrived and it was not long before Buck found Emily. Quickly she managed to separate herself from her family for a few minutes.

"Buck," she said rapidly, "I want you to talk to Papa tonight at the celebration."

"Is he going to let me get close enough?"

"You afraid of him, Buck?" she taunted in an amused tone.

"You bet," he quipped. "But if you think there's even a remote chance that he'll let me get within talking distance, then I'll try. It sure would be wonderful to stop all this slippin' around. I feel like a cheat."

"He's excited about seeing the first train and after he's joined the gentlemen at the punch bowl he'll be in a reasonably good mood. It's the best time, Buck."

"Okay Emily, if you say so," he agreed. His hand gripped hers firmly and she could see the desire to kiss her written plainly in his eyes.

"Oh, Buck," she whispered, "I'll simply die if we don't do something soon."

"You think it's any easier on me? It kills me every time I have to let you go home alone. Don't worry Em, honey, I'll talk to him tonight. One way or another, I'll know for sure . . . Em?"

"What?"

"Would you consider running away with me if he said no?" he questioned urgently.

"Buck, I'd go to the end of the world with you."

"That's what I needed to know." He smiled. "Now go back to your family before they miss you and start lookin'. I'll see you at the dance."

She nodded, then disappeared quickly into the crowd.

Only Hannah knew she had slipped awy, and she also knew the reason why. The picture her sister's rendezvous conjured up in Hannah's mind was not one of Emily and Buck, but an image of herself and the mysterious man on the trail. She wondered how it would be to walk beside him and talk with him. Again she could envision the play of controlled emotion on his face as she watched him. He had sensed her interest; she knew it. She was pretty; she knew that too. Men were always drawn quickly to her. That's why it intrigued her so to see him mentally push her away and withhold all expression from her, as if he were somehow afraid to feel. She ardently wished that

350

somewhere, in all the confusion, she would see him again.

Eileen and Allison, with Taylor to escort them, joined the milling crowd. All three watched with surprisingly different thoughts.

Taylor was experiencing smug satisfaction in knowing that his plan for the evening had already been put into motion. It was a scheme to take advantage of the excitement to cause an incident that would broaden the distrust between the railroad and the ranchers. This time it would be the ranchers who would take the blame for what he planned.

Eileen was gloating. She was certain that all she wanted would soon be in her grasp.

Allison had found new happiness and she could barely wait for Trace to arrive.

The entire town gave a rousing cheer as a puff of grey-white smoke was seen in the distance and the rhythmic chuga-chug of the train could be heard. Whistles tooted, bells rang, and people shouted as the shrill sound of the train whistle echoed down the valley.

The train was greeted with some awe as it chugged to a rattling halt. All the workers had climbed aboard and taken any spot they could find, including the tops of the cars and the iron frame of the cowcatcher, which extended several feet before the engine to clear the tracks of obstacles such as buffalo on the plains or wandering sheep or cows.

Trace and Maxwell rode in the engine with Mackie. They had tried to make a grand entrance into town, hoping that the impressed merchants would help in their negotiations to cross the land in the valley.

Trace was confident that most of the battles were over. He searched the crowd for Jenny and smiled broadly and waved when he saw her.

He leapt down from the engine as soon as it came to a halt. Fighting his way through the crowd, he stopped breathlessly at Jenny's side. Jenny had obviously dressed very carefully for the occasion. Her dress was the same turquoise as her eyes. He could see himself reflected in those deep pools and his heart leapt. "Lord, Jenny," he said just loud enough for her to hear, "you're so beautiful. I've been thinking of nothing but you since I left you."

"And I've been thinking of you."

Trace felt the crowd around him fade into insignificance and lost touch with everything but the glow in Jenny's eyes.

"I wish we were somewhere else—anywhere else but here," he said quietly. "I want to hold you, Jenny."

Jenny could feel his touch even though he stood immobile. She could feel his eyes linger over her until her cheeks grew warm and an uncontrollable trembling made her knees weak.

"Trace," she whispered. They stood unmoving, but mentally they reached for each other.

"Come on, Trace." Maxwell's voice came from near his shoulder. "We've a party to go to."

Trace turned to find Maxwell, Allison, and Eileen standing before them.

"Yes, Trace," Eileen said sweetly. "Do come along. We are late for the celebration now, and Uncle Maxwell is going to be honored."

"I'm ready," Trace said. He reached to take Jenny's arm and drew her close to him.

"Jenny, I want you to meet some friends of mine, and my sister. This is Maxwell Starett, his niece, Eileen, and my sister, Allison."

"How do you do?" Jenny said with a smile.

"Better than the last time I saw you." Maxwell laughed.

"The last time?" Jenny questioned.

"Well, the last time I saw you, you were planting bullets around this fella's feet. I was pretty sure you were trying to do him in. I guess I was wrong . . . wasn't I?"

Jenny was flustered and Trace began to laugh. To Eileen's disgust, he slid his arm about Jenny's waist and drew her even closer.

"Don't let him rattle you, Jenny. I think he was more afraid for his own life than for mine."

Everyone laughed. Jenny greeted Eileen, who nodded her greeting, but Allison extended her hand to Jenny.

"I'm really delighted to meet you." Allison turned her eyes from Jenny's to Trace's and he saw they were filled with bright mischief. She was about to speak again when Trace's firm voice brought her to a halt.

"Don't say anything you're going to regret, Allison," he threatened with a smile. "It's been a long time since I turned you over my knee."

The tables had been neatly turned on Allison, who flushed but remained silent.

"Do come along, Trace," Eileen said peevishly.

Her absolute fury at Jenny's close proximity to Trace was held in check only by an enormous effort.

"Yes," Trace said as he looked down into Jenny's eyes, "I think it's time to dance and have some fun. I, for one," he said quietly, "can't wait."

Allison was beside herself with delight at Trace's more than obvious attraction to Jenny. But more than that it was the look of rage in Eileen's eyes that made her positively gleeful.

All the townspeople and all the new arrivals from the

railroad moved toward the large meeting hall, from which the sound of music drifted. In all their minds this night was both an end and a beginning. All thought the battle with the railroad was over. All were looking forward to a new and progressive time. Tables laden with food and several large punch bowls liberally spiked with strong enough spirits to level all barriers welcomed the arrivals.

Once inside the doors to the meeting hall, Trace again turned to look down into Jenny's eyes. He held out his hand and Jenny slid her hand into his. They walked to the center of the floor where other dancers moved about. He put his hand on her slim waist.

"For now, holding you like this will have to do. But"—his voice grew deep and intense—"it's not enough, Jenny. I want you."

"Come to me later," she whispered.

"I will," he replied as they began to dance.

## Chapter 25

Trace had kept one eye on the door as he waited for Taylor to enter. He wanted to see Taylor's face when he realized Trace was not dead.

Taylor arrived later than he had planned, for he had wanted to make sure his last minute instructions were being carried out. He walked through the doorway with a smile on his face, as if the celebration had been all his own idea. He gazed about the room and suddenly his eyes fell on Trace and Jenny dancing.

Trace missed nothing as Taylor's smile faded and his face grew pale. At that moment Trace had no doubt about who had shot him or why.

At the first opportunity Trace maneuvered himself and Jenny close enough to Taylor and Eileen to stop for conversation.

"Good evening," he said pleasantly to Taylor, noting that it took a great deal of effort for Taylor to continue smiling.

"Well, Mr. Cord, it seems your railroad is moving along quite effectively. When do you think you'll be taking over the valley?"

Trace could feel Jenny quiver with resentment at the obvious blow and suspected that Taylor had fully anticipated her reaction. He wondered if Jenny's faith in him would be strong enough to allow her to ignore such an attack.

"No one in the valley has negotiated with the railroad yet," Trace replied.

"No . . . but you obviously expect them to."

"Maxwell wants to, but he wants to offer them a fair price for a fair amount of land—not all of it."

"Well"—Taylor smiled—"that remains to be seen."

Taylor realized his barbs had struck Jenny, and he was pleased to see that she was still insecure and vulnerable. She did not quite believe in the railroad yet, nor did she feel secure in her trust for Trace Cord yet, and he intended to make sure that by the time the night was over, no trust whatsoever would remain.

"You haven't danced with me, Trace," Eileen admonished.

"My pleasure, Eileen," Trace smiled, but the gesture did not reach his eyes. As they moved away, Jenny's gaze followed Trace.

"Nice to see those two together again," Taylor said. He kept his eyes on Trace and Eileen, but he was aware of Jenny's every movement.

"Again?" Jenny questioned softly.

"Didn't you know? Trace and Eileen have an understanding. As soon as the railroad gets to California they are to be married."

"Really?"

"That's what I've been told. You know how it is." Taylor chuckled. "Marry the boss's niece and the railroad will one day be yours."

"Trace isn't like that."

"Oh . . . you know him that well?"

"Taylor, what are you trying to say?"

"I'm trying to tell you to be careful. He's someone you don't know well. It would be a great mistake to let him walk away with your land."

"I," she said firmly, "don't plan to let anybody walk away with my land."

At that moment they were interrupted as one of the celebrating townsmen asked Jenny to dance.

Trying to keep herself under control was very difficult for Jenny, especially since Trace and Eileen were constantly within view.

The party continued and it seemed that the opposing forces were beginning to move toward each other. There were many smiling, carefree faces in the crowd. Will had not had so much fun in years and neither had an exuberant Georgina. Emily and Buck were most thoroughly enjoying themselves.

Jenny had taken a quiet moment to walk on the porch and let the evening breeze help control her slowly rising jealousy. Eileen had managed to interfere with every moment Jenny had tried to spend with Trace.

Now she stood and regained her composure, or thought she had.

"Out here alone, my dear?" came the sweet, sugared voice that set her teeth on edge. She turned to see Eileen framed in the doorway.

"Just getting a breath of fresh air. I was about to go in."

"I've really never had a chance to talk to you. It would be nice if we could be friends. We seem to have at least one thing in common."

"We do? What is that?"

"Trace Cord."

"Trace . . . what does Trace have to do with us?"

"I . . . well, I had the feeling you were interested in him. It seems he's been drawn out to your ranch quite often."

Now Jenny's temper had reached its breaking point. "Because your friend happened to get himself shot and I was kind enough to keep him from dying doesn't put any chains on him. I'm sure he will do just as he pleases."

"Shot!" Eileen was truly shocked.

"Yes, shot. Waylaid by some skunk who wanted to see him dead."

"Sh . . . shot," Eileen said slowly, as if she couldn't quite believe it. She knew who was responsible, and she meant to vent her anger on him for doing something that could have jeopardized all her plans.

"I do hope you aren't thinking it was one of us ranchers. We don't play that way. We fight our battles out in the open."

"From what I see tonight, it looks as if the battles are all over. I'm sure things will go smoothly now," Eileen soothed.

Jenny was not sure why she felt that Eileen's words lacked sincerity, but she did. Was it jealousy? Did she hate this sugar-voiced woman because she felt Trace had once been involved with her? The answer was a reluctant yes, she was jealous, but there was more to it than that. She was about to question Eileen a little more closely when a young man who was enamored of Eileen's voluptuous charms came to ask her to dance.

Jenny would have returned to the dance then, but Trace's large frame filled the doorway.

"I've been looking for you," he said. "You disappeared."

"I'm coming."

"No . . . let's not go in yet," he said quickly as he stepped out on the porch and pulled the door shut behind him. He walked to Jenny and reached for her, but Jenny backed up a step.

"Are you sure you've been looking for the right woman?"

"Jenny, what's the matter?"

"Nothing . . . I . . . I've just been told you and Eileen Starett. . . ."

"I see." Trace chuckled. Despite Jenny's feeble resistance, he drew her into his arms. "Are you jealous, love?"

"Yes." She laughed. "I wanted to scratch her eyes out. Trace," she began, but his mouth stopped her words effectively with a kiss that set her senses reeling. It was a long, sensuous kiss that left her weak and clinging to him. He held her breathlessly close and heated the soft flesh of her cheeks and throat with kisses that seared her skin and ignited a flame within her.

"I've missed you . . . Lord, how I've missed you."

"Mmmm . . . I've missed you too," she murmured as his lips slowly taunted hers. She looked up at him and their eyes locked together as their pulses raced to the beat of passion. Again Trace lowered his head to capture her soft lips. Her arms came up around his neck and they molded their bodies together. Time seemed to stop as the beauty of the moment held them suspended.

"Jenny?"

"Hmmm?"

"You're not going back to the ranch tonight, are you?"

"No . . ."

"We'll stay in town?" Her eyes rose to his and answered his question without words.

"Yes," she whispered, "I'll meet you."

"Sweet Jenny," he whispered as he kissed her again. "This is the most damnable torture. To have you here and have to let you go."

"Just for a short while."

Their lips blended again and they savored the stolen delights.


Buck stood with Emily and mused uncomfortably that Jacob's eyes had been on him all evening. Dancing in a crowded room had been the only way he could stay close to Emily without Jacob's interference.

"With all this good will going on," he remarked with a laugh, "you'd think it would be easy to speak to him, but damn, I'm scared as a kid caught with his hand in the cookie jar."

"Buck, Father's a gentle man."

"Sure . . . but how gentle is he going to be with the man who wants to take you away from him? Besides, he's not as gentle as you think."

"Buck you've got to talk to him," Emily pleaded.

"I know, I know," Buck agreed, then took a deep breath. "Okay, here goes."

Buck left Emily's side and walked toward Jacob, whose stern countenance never changed. Buck swallowed the huge constriction in his throat and smiled.

"Evenin', Mr. Marshall. Fine party, isn't it?"

"Evenin', Buck," came the terse reply.

To Buck, Jacob's eyes seemed impassible. "Looks like that railroad is goin' to work out all right for the merchants here."

"Looks that way." His reply was just as noncommittal as his first. Buck felt a touch of despair.

"Mr. Marshall, about the railroad . . . you goin' to give them a right-of-way?"

"'Pears to me it might be a good thing for the ranchers too. Maybe I will. Kinda have to wait until we talk it over. Your Pa going to work with them?"

"Pa and I have been talking about it."

"You and your Pa been catching up on a lot

of . . . back work, have you?"

At that moment Buck was certain of the main obstacle that stood in his path. He had to stand his ground now or he would never have Emily.

"Mr. Marshall," he said firmly, "I know Pa had a rough time after my mother died. Seems he had a hard time pulling himself together. But things have changed. Me and Pa are pulling the ranch together. It's got a good future. We're working hard—both of us." His eyes held Jacob's. "Pa's finished with drinking. He's started all over. He's a fine man, Mr. Marshall, and I'm proud of him, no matter what you and the others might be thinking. One day we're going to have the best horse ranch in the Colorado Territory. But whatever happens, I'll stand with my Pa and you and the rest of the valley can think what you want."

He had momentarily allowed his anger to control him and now, as it eased, he wondered if he had destroyed any chance he might ever have.

Jacob's face softened slightly and his eyes crinkled at the corners. He spoke mildly. "You don't have to get so fired up, boy. I wasn't insulting your Pa. But I respect your fighting for him." He motioned to Emily, who came quickly to his side.

"Pa?" she questioned in a frightened voice.

"Emily, this young man is getting kinda out of hand. Why don't you dance with him and cool him off." He started to move away from the surprised pair. "Oh," he said as an afterthought, "why don't you come out to the ranch for Sunday dinner? We can talk about those horses you seem so all-fired proud of."

He moved away now and it was several seconds before the force of what he had said reached the two.

Buck turned to Emily with the glow of happiness lighting his eyes. Abruptly he bent his head and kissed her quickly. His joy filled him to the point that he

361

wanted to shout.

"This is just too good to believe," he told her, laughing aloud.

"I'll be at your house for Sunday dinner, all right, and I'm going to ask him about marrying you too."

"You've got everything planned, do you?" She was grinning.

"You bet! I want you married to me before you decide to go looking around at any of these railroad fellas that are going to be swarming all over the area. Let's dance," he said, his voice softening. "I've got to put my arms around you before I bust."

Unbeknown to Emily and Buck, Eileen and Taylor stood off to the side and watched the happy couple.

"Now is the right time," Taylor said. "You know what you have to do?"

"I know. There will be no problem. The girl is trusting."

"Then get ready. In half an hour I want that boy outside."

"Don't worry, he'll be there," she said confidently as she moved away.


The party was nearing a close. Most of the men were in a comfortable state of semi-intoxication, and the women were relaxed and beginning to gather sleepy-eyed children.

Eileen chose this moment to go to Emily, who was standing with several young friends while Buck and her mother were having a last drink.

"Emily," Eileen said with a smile, "could you come out on the back porch?"

Emily nodded and the two women worked their way through the crowd toward the rear of the hall and out onto the large back porch. From the corner of his eye

Buck watched them go. A mild prickle of something bordering on fear told him he should follow her, but the thought was interrupted, then lost as Jacob asked him a question and he turned back to the conversation. It was several minutes before his gaze began to wander and he realized Emily was not in the hall. She had not returned. He was about to go after her when he saw Eileen return alone. He began to move toward Eileen when a young boy tugged on his sleeve.

"Mr. Graham?"

"What is it, Jimmy? I'm in a hurry."

"I was supposed to give you this note."

Buck accepted the folded piece of paper.

"Note? . . . Who sent it?"

"Miss Emily said you was to get it."

Buck accepted the note and Jimmy quickly scampered away.


Eileen and Emily had just stepped onto the porch and Eileen turned to her.

"What's wrong?"

"I've loosened all the buttons on my gown. I can't reach behind to button them and I'm too embarrassed to ask anyone else. Would you be so kind?"

"Of course . . . turn around." Emily rebuttoned the buttons Taylor had unbuttoned just minutes before."

"Emily, your Buck seems like a very nice man."

"He's wonderful."

"You really haven't had much time to spend alone with him tonight."

"I know." Emily sighed. "But there's really nothing I can do about that."

"I could help you." Eileen laughed. "Say a favor in exchange for a favor?"

"Help me? . . . How?"

"I could go in and tell the young man some beautiful young lady is waiting for him on the back porch."

Emily was delighted with this idea and very shortly Eileen returned to the party alone while Emily waited for Buck.

The note was very short and since Buck had never seen Emily's handwriting, he assumed the feminine-looking script was hers.

Buck:
    I want to see you alone. Please come across the street to the stable. I'll be waiting for you.

Emily

Buck was more than delighted with this idea. He had not had a moment to share with Emily alone. He made his way to the front door of the hall. Once outside, he moved swiftly across the front porch and down the steps to the street, which he crossed at a half run.

He came to the stable door and looked up and down the street to make sure no one was observing him. Then he slipped inside the dark stable.

What little light there was from the moonlight streaming through the windows was not enough to make anything clear. He took a step forward.

"Emily?" he questioned softly. He heard a rustle of movement and started toward it.

The blow on his head was swift and so quick that he had no time to react in defense. Bright stars sparkled before his eyes, then dimmed, and everything went black as he sagged to the hay-covered floor.

The vague forms of two men bent near. One reached to touch him.

"He's out," came a rough whisper.

"Good. Now let's get him out of here." They lifted Buck's inert form and carried him out the back door of the stable into the night.

Emily grew impatient and slightly angry. That he had asked her to stand outside alone while he talked and drank with her father was irritating.

She walked inside and looked about for Buck, who was nowhere in sight. Her father stood across the room and with a puzzled frown on her face she made her way toward him.

"Papa, where's Buck?"

"I don't know, honey. I haven't seen him for the past twenty minutes. Come to think of it, I haven't seen your brother for awhile either."

Emily was puzzled and she continued to gaze about the room. Then she began to move from person to person, asking if anyone had seen Buck. None of them had nor had they seen her brother.

Eileen and Taylor stood watching in satisfaction. Their timing had been precise. Now they waited for the next step to occur.

Before too long, Jacob, Maxwell, Trace, and Jenny were standing together as the slowly thinning crowd moved about them.

Allison joined them and stood near Trace. She had been trying to get Trace alone all evening without making it obvious. But it was just as impossible now, since Jenny was upset and Trace's attention was all on her. She would wait until the dance was over. Once everyone was settled for the night, Trace would return to their car. She smiled to herself, knowing they had a great deal to talk about.

"You don't suppose he's out sparkin' another girl, do you?" Jacob jested, but Emily's angry look brought his teasing to an abrupt halt.

"Well, come on now," Jacob said. "I'm sure he'll be here in a few minutes and have a very good reason for having disappeared."

"Well, Jacob, now that the evening is almost over, suppose we set a time to meet tomorrow. We can get on to business," Maxwell suggested.

"Sounds like a good idea," Trace inserted.

"Fine." Jacob agreed. "Do you all want to come out to the ranch?"

"Well, in my car I have all the maps showing the land the railroad will need. Suppose I have Lee Chu cook us up a good lunch and ȳou people be my guests."

"Good enough. We'll be there at high noon."

"Wonderful."

"I wonder where that son of mine has taken himself off to. I wanted him to drive the buggy home," Jacob remarked.

Allison supplied him with the answer.

"I saw some young boy bring him a note. When he read it, he left the hall. I haven't seen him since."

"I expect he's slipped off to some poker game somewhere, or some other . . . Anyway, I think I shall take my wife and daughters home." He held out his hand to Maxwell, who extended his in pleasure, overjoyed that he had finally breached the wall of defense the ranchers had constructed.

"Pa . . . I can't go," Emily cried. "Not yet. Not until I find out where Buck went. He wouldn't just go off like that without telling someone where he was going."

"Well, maybe him and your brother are together."

"Pa!" Emily said, anger staining her cheeks pink. "Buck just wouldn't go off like that!"

"Now honey . . ."

"Well, it is a little odd, Jacob," Beatrice told him softly. "I'm sure you would never do such a thing."

"Maybe not," Jacob replied, "but I sure as hell don't know how to set about looking for him, and I wouldn't want to run into something that's none of my business."

"Trace," Jenny said worriedly, "it really isn't like Buck just to go off and not say anything. Do you think something could have happened to him?"

"What could have happened?" Trace answered.

"He might have had something important to do and thought he'd be back before the party was over and anyone missed him," Hannah offered casually.

Before the others could comment, the quiet night was shattered by a thunderous explosion. It rent the air with a violent crash that startled everyone into temporary immobility; then they all ran for the front door at once.

Outside the air seemed filled by a large white cloud of smoke laced with orange fingers of flame. Debris was still tumbling from where it had been thrown skyward.

All stood amazed; then the realization struck them all at the same time. The explosion had come from where the tracks edged the town.

"Good God!" Maxwell exclaimed, then he began to run toward the brilliant glow of flame that lit the night sky.

They all began to run now, each one knowing in his mind what he might see, yet afraid to think of the consequences.

When they arrived, a crowd had already gathered. Destruction lay about them. The tracks behind the train were twisted and gnarled. Someone had tried to blow the train apart but had succeeded only in destroying some areas of track and the cars that belonged to Maxwell and Trace. They were still burning.

Maxwell's first thought was of the condition of the

engine and his engineer. Trace was involved in a search for something else, a clue to who had blown up the train. It was then he ran across the two men lying face down in the dirt, facing away from the cars as if they had tried to run and had misjudged the time they had had in which to do it.

He knew them, and he dreaded turning them over to confirm their identities.

The others gathered around him as he knelt to turn both men over.

"Buck!" Jenny exclaimed. Her eyes grew wide with a new kind of fear as Trace turned angry, unforgiving eyes toward her.

"I'll have to agree, Buck must have thought he'd be back to the party before the explosion hit. I guess he and Terrance just misjudged the time they would have to get away."

"Trace, no!" Jenny cried. "You don't believe Buck would do this?"

"It was a good setup Jenny," Trace said angrily, his anger more from his own hurt than from the destruction around him. "Too bad it didn't work. I guess you ranchers really have a way of making a point." He stood up to face Jenny, whose eyes were filled with tears.

"Trace . . . you don't really think he—"

"I think it was more than *he*," Trace said in a dangerously soft voice. "I think he needed someone to set me up, get me to rush here, get me into position to destroy me and the railroad I was bringing. You must have had a lot of fun planning your revenge, Jenny, but don't think this is over. You'd better be prepared to finish what you started, because the war has just begun."

# Chapter 26

The atmosphere around the destroyed train cars began to take on a more antagonistic nature. Railroad men began to eye the townspeople and the ranchers with deep suspicion. And Trace was not the only one who became nervous as the tension grew.

Buck groaned and began to stir, and a few minutes later Terrance did the same. They sat up in a daze. Jenny ran to her brother and knelt beside him, while Emily knelt on his other side.

"Buck, are you all right?" Jenny asked worriedly.

"Uhhh," Buck groaned. He reached to touch his head tentatively and found his fingers sticky with blood. "What the hell happened?"

"That's what we want to ask you," Trace said coldly. "Seems you and your friend's little plans to destroy the train and its tracks kind of backfired."

"Huh? What are you talking about? How did I get here?"

"Suppose you tell us," Trace insisted angrily.

Jenny glared up at him with defiance written on her features.

"He had nothing to do with this!" she cried. "Can't you see he's been hurt? I have to get them both to the

369

doctor's office."

The bright glow of the still-burning cars lit the entire area, and reflected off many emotion-filled faces. Slowly a tension was beginning to grow in the crowd that was frightening.

"We need some answers now!" Trace demanded.

"He can't answer you now!" Jenny nearly screamed. She leapt to her feet and ran to Trace.

"He's been hurt. Leave him alone."

"Damnit, Jenny, he's just about destroyed the line. What do you think I'm going to do, just forget it? We have to talk to him now, so get out of the way. You've done enough for now."

"I? I've done enough? Trace, I had no part of this and neither did Buck."

"After tonight," he said firmly, "Do you really expect me to believe that? I've been fooled once, Jenny. I'm not stupid enough to be taken twice."

"You arrogant bastard!" Jenny cried as she struck him across the face; it was a stinging slap that echoed between them like a slamming door. Trace's face grew hard and he reached out to grip her shoulders. He shook her roughly.

"Don't ever be stupid enough to do that again," he snarled, "or I might not be so forgiving next time."

"Forgiving? Who needs your forgiveness? All we need is for you and your trouble-making railroad to get out of our valley!"

There was a rumble of anger from the railroad workers that shook Trace into more awareness. The situation was fast becoming dangerous. Despite his anger at her and his belief that she and her brother had deceived him, he wanted them out of there before the crowd began to get ugly and out of hand.

"Take him to the doctor, Jenny," he said coldly. "But give him my warning before you do. I won't tolerate

370

any more incidents like this. We'll fight back and you might be biting off more than you can chew."

Jenny helped Buck to his feet. He was shaky and he leaned on her for support. She glared at Trace with a fury in her eyes that rivaled the flames about them. Before she could retort, a grim-faced Maxwell approached them.

"Trace."

"What now?" Trace asked miserably.

"The two men left to take care of the train . . . they're both dead."

The grumbling around them increased in intensity. Even Jenny was aware now that the situation could develop into a fullfledged battle.

"Let me by," she said coldly. She wanted her brother and Terrance away from this threatening crowd as quickly as possible.

"Remember what I said, Jenny," Trace snapped.

"And you remember this, Trace Cord. We're not afraid of you or your railroad, and we're not afraid of a fight either. Keep your distance from the valley and from me, for I swear no train will cross my land and you'll never leave it alive if you set foot on it again. That's not a threat, Trace. That's a promise."

She pushed past him with a weak and staggering Buck and was followed by most of the ranchers, who were attempting to help Terrance.

Trace stood and watched her leave. He was torn by conflicting emotions. He had to believe what his eyes and his common sense told him was so. But his heart refused to be controlled by logic. Despite all that had happened, he still wanted her, and now the gulf between them had widened to create a distance they would never be able to span.

Trace divided the men into groups and set them to

extinguishing the fires and finding the extent of the damage. His mind was on the problem at hand, but his heart followed Jenny.

The doctor examined Buck and Terrance carefully. He shook his head and smiled. "Well, both have got real nasty wallops on the head, but there's been no permanent damage done. I'd say take 'em both home and put 'em to bed. For tomorrow and maybe the day after you both will have rip-roaring headaches, but that's about it."

Jenny sighed with relief. Most of the townspeople had gone on to their homes, and the ranchers' buggies had departed, leaving the town quiet except for the men working on the train.

Buck was helped into the buggy, then sat back with closed eyes, wincing at every rut the buggy's wheels hit.

"Buck?" Jenny spoke quietly.

"What?"

"You . . . you and Terrance didn't . . ."

"Hell no, Jenny. Everything was going fine tonight. I thought all of our problems were solved. I even had Em's father smiling at me."

"Well, what happened?"

"I don't know." He began to relate all that had happened. "Then I got this note from Em," he explained. He grinned then winced in pain again. "She wanted to meet me in the stables. I went in. It was dark and I only took a few steps, then *bam!* Something hit me from behind. I swear, Jenny, I don't know or remember a thing that happened after that until I woke up and all hell was bustin' loose around me."

They rode quietly for some time, then Buck spoke softly.

"Jenny?"

372

"What?"

"You believe me, don't you? You don't think I would have done something like that?"

"Of course I believe you, Buck. I don't remember a time you ever lied to me about anything important."

"I'd never see to killing a man, Jenny," he said softly.

"I know that too, Buck. But . . . someone wanted to kill . . . or someone wanted to make it look like . . ." She sat in deep thought for awhile, trying to put together pieces of a puzzle, the answers to which seemed vitally important yet elusive.

They arrived at the Graham home and Buck very gratefully went to bed. Howard too found his bed, but, for Jenny, sleep refused to come. She lay struggling futilely to keep Trace's angry eyes from tearing at her. She fought desperately, but he invaded every sense. Anger warred with desire. She groaned and turned in her uncomfortable bed, fighting nightmarish battles, all of which seemed to end with the taste of Trace's lips on hers. She was overcome with despair, for she was certain the beauty they had shared was gone forever. After awhile she could no longer fight her tears and she buried her head in her pillow to muffle the sound of her weeping.


Trace was dirty, covered with sweat, and very nearly exhausted. But, with the help of his men, he had extinguished the fire and attempted to clean up as much of the debris as possible. They had buried two of Trace's men and he still raged inwardly at those responsible.

"Trace," Maxwell interrupted his thoughts, "you look like hell, man, and you're exhausted. I think it's time we get a little sleep."

"And with both cars destroyed, just where do you

suggest we do that?" Trace snapped, then caught himself. "I'm sorry, Maxwell. I'm just tired and I'm angry."

"You're not the only one who's angry."

"You mean the whole town?"

"The town is mad at the ranchers, the ranchers are mad at the railroad, the railroad is mad at the ranchers and the town. Outside of that, the situation is under control." Maxwell laughed raggedly.

"Yes . . ." Trace said thoughtfully, "it seems as if everything has been stirred up."

"We still have the engine intact. I've been told it will only take a day or two to repair the rails that were torn up. I don't see what anyone had to gain by this."

"Same old thing, I guess," Trace said speculatively. "I've always felt things were being muddied up to hide someone's real motives."

"Which are?"

Trace laughed. "Damned if I know, but I'm so tired I couldn't put one and one together to make two. I've got to get some sleep. Allison has a room at the hotel. I think I'll go over and get a couple hours of sleep. Maybe I'll be able to do some adding tomorrow."

"Good idea. I'll tell the boys to bed down, then I'll go to the hotel and get some sleep too. I'll talk to you in the morning."

"It's pretty near that now," Trace said as he stretched his sore muscles. "I'll see you in a few hours, Maxwell."

Maxwell watched him slowly walk away. He had witnessed the confrontation between Trace and Jenny and he had read Trace's eyes accurately. The anger was gone now and only the hurt lingered in his eyes. But he knew Trace too well by now. He was tenacious to a fault. Maxwell smiled. Even if Trace wasn't aware of it, Maxwell knew he would go head-on at the problem until he found his answers. He also believed that Trace loved Jenny and was not about to let anything or anyone deliberately destroy that love for reasons yet unknown.


The streets of town were deserted, as was the lobby of the hotel. Trace had no idea which room was Allison's, so he went to the desk and turned the book around to read the names written there. He noted her room number and climbed the steps slowly. His weary legs seemed to want to refuse him any more movement.

Trace found Allison's room and rapped gently. He waited several minutes then knocked again. He heard the rustle of movement within, then saw the ridge of light as the lamp was lit.

"Who is it?" came Allison's soft voice.

"It's me, Allison, Trace. Open the door."

The lock clicked and the door swung open.

"Trace," Allison said in alarm, "you look so terrible. Come in, hurry. I'll get you some water and you can wash all of that dirt off."

Trace walked to the bed and sat on the edge.

"Don't bother with the water," he rasped. She turned to look at him. He slowly lay back against the pillow and in minutes he was asleep.

Allison walked toward him with sympathy in her eyes. She bent to grasp his boots and pull them off. Then she lifted his legs onto the bed and drew a blanket over him.

She stood looking at him for a minute, then she grabbed up her robe and put it on. She moved swiftly to the door and left the room.

She very nearly ran down the hall to the room at the end. She knocked and in minutes the door was opened to her. Allison entered the room and closed the door behind her and leaned against it.

375

"He's hurt and tired and he has more trouble than he needs," she said. "It's time to tell him you are here and what you know. He needs us now."


Will and Joanne had ridden in silence all the way to the ranch. Joanne held an exhausted, sleeping Georgina in her arms.

Both had been frightened by the events that had just occurred, frightened and concerned over the effect it would have on their situation.

Once at the ranch, Will lifted Georgina down and carried her inside. Joanne followed to undress her and put her in bed while Will saw to the horses.

When he returned to the house, Joanne had already built a fire and had made a pot of fresh coffee.

They knew they had to talk, but both were unsure of where to start. As Joanne bent forward to pour the coffee into his cup, he could see tears glistening in her eyes. She handed him the cup, then sat on a small bench near the fire.

"Will . . . maybe you should have stayed to help Trace clear the wreckage."

"He didn't need me. The whole crew was there. Besides . . . I was needed here."

"Yes," she said quietly.

"Joanne . . . I have to ask you something and I need the truth."

"I'll try." She smiled, but his eyes were too serious for the smile to remain.

"What is it, Will?"

"I . . . I didn't think it would happen like this, but . . . I need answers."

"What are the questions?"

His eyes locked on hers and she could not look away.

"I never told you much about me," he began.

"There's no need to, Will."

"I see a need," he corrected. "I want to tell you, Joanne." She remained silent. "I'm a good man, Joanne, a good farmer. I was raised on a farm and I could make the land give me a good crop every year. I had a good farm," he continued, "and . . . I had a wife and a child." He paused to see the effect his words were having on her, but she remained silent. "I loved them," he whispered. "When the war was over, I came home with all kinds of plans to make the farm grow and have more kids. I found my farm burned and the land taxed beyond what I could pay. I found my wife and child dead at the hands of renegades—men of my own land. I was lost and filled with grief. I wanted to die. Then me and two friends, well, we took to roamin' west and we run across the railroad. We were hungry and we needed to work, and Trace, he offered me that, and a little of my pride back. I owe him a debt that's going to be hard to repay, but . . ."

"But?" she encouraged.

"But . . . I want you to tell me . . . now . . . here, if you want me to stay here. I have a feel for this land and I know I can make it good. I also have a feeling for Georgina. I could be a good father, but . . . I want you to tell me if you want me to stay."

"Is this a proposal, Will?"

"I guess you might call it that. I don't want you to think I'm betraying friends."

"I don't think you would know how to betray anyone or anything."

"I want to stay, but only if you want it."

He stopped talking and waited for Joanne to speak. Joanne rose and walked to him and knelt before him.

"I know how hard this must be for you, Will, to choose between me and Georgina and your duty to Trace. Would it make it any easier if I said that it would make me very happy if you decided to stay? I have seen you care for the land and I have seen your affection for my daughter. But"—she smiled again—"I have not seen, nor have I heard, anything about how you feel about me."

Will cupped her face between huge, callused hands. He held her eyes with his and spoke in a tone filled with determined assurance. "I want you to marry me, Joanne. I want us to build a life and a family together. I'll do everything in my power to make you happy."

"Then," she whispered, "I want you to stay, Will . . . I do want you to stay."

She watched his eyes light with pleasure and she recognized a warmth spreading through her that she had never thought to experience again. Slowly he bent his head to touch her lips with his.

Eileen's room was dark, and she lay contentedly in Taylor's arms. Their lovemaking had been a fury of emotional triumph, wild and almost brutal.

"We seem to have stirred things up pretty well," Eileen declared smugly.

"They are so confused now that no one is really thinking about who is to blame for what. By the time they begin to think again, we'll have a few more surprises ready for them."

"Did you see the Graham girl's face when Trace accused her and her brother of doing all that damage?" Eileen laughed.

"It was nothing compared to the faces of those railroad men when they saw the damage those few sticks of dynamite did. The railroaders are convinced the ranchers planned all this."

"And you want them to go on thinking that."

"Right."

"What is our next step?"

"I think it's about time I rode out and had a long talk with Howard Graham."

"Just what is that going to bring us?"

"Well, my dear"—Taylor chuckled as he nipped her ear gently with his teeth—"it seems Mr. Graham owes me a great deal of money, much more money than his ranch is worth. I might just . . ."

"Just what?"

"I might just convince him that negotiating with the railroad would be a very foolish thing to do. In fact, I think I will convince him that it would be unwise even to talk to the railroad."

"You think he will listen?"

"Does he have a choice?"

"What about the Carter place? We need that too."

"I've sent a couple of ambitious men out there to convince Joanne Carter that it would be wise to rid herself of that place and move out. When they are through, she'll be more than delighted to sell the land for very little."

"That leaves the Marshall place."

"Yes, well, that has posed somewhat of a problem."

"But a problem you have solutions for."

Taylor chuckled and pulled her into his arms to ravage her mouth with his and run his hands over the silken curves of her body.

"Oh yes, I have ideas."

"Well, tell me," she urged.

"All right. Marshall's two young daughters, Emily and Hannah. For Emily, Buck Graham would give his life, and for Hannah, I think Jacob Marshall would make any agreement. All we're asking is that he not deal with the railroad. Instead, he will deed to someone else a very large strip of land. After that, we don't have to do much except wait. Of course, you will contact your friends and tell them the land for their train route is open. Then we will be prepared for the final and biggest step."

"Yes," Eileen said softly. "Can you imagine what will happen in this territory when they find out the truth?"

"To say the least, they will be surprised."

"We'll be fabulously rich and in control of—"

Taylor crushed her to him and kissed the words away.


Buck lay in the room next to Jenny's and heard her muffled weeping. His head throbbed so severely that intense thought was almost impossible. He tried to put together the pieces of what had happened, but he came up blank. There was no logical reason for someone to have set him up as the one responsible for the explosion.

He was certain of one thing: what had happened tonight had ruined what fragile connection there had been between Trace and Jenny. No matter how confused he was on other things, he was thoroughly convinced that their quarrel had been deliberately planned and was a terrible misunderstanding.

However sore he felt, he promised himself he would go to speak to Trace the next day. He knew someone was going to have to take the first step, and he was certain Jenny's pride wouldn't let her; for that matter, neither would Trace's.

He began to think, step by step, of all that had occurred since the first rumor of the railroad had been carried to them by Taylor Jessup. He thought of each occasion of confrontation and the same name kept recurring, time after time—Taylor Jessup. He promised himself he would try to look into the circumstances that subtly connected all of them to Taylor.

He wanted to sleep, but his head refused to let him, so he occupied his mind more pleasantly with thoughts of Emily.

Many others were in similar contemplative moods that night. Maxwell spent the entire night trying to sort out how he could rebuild both the destroyed tracks and his relationship with the ranchers, who, he felt, were quite ready to hang both him and Trace.

Emily was not able to rest, for she was still worried about Buck. She had been comforted when the doctor's words had been relayed to her, but she knew very well that she would not be happy until she could feel his arms about her and taste his love again.

Hannah, whom everyone considered the shy rose of the valley, concentrated her thoughts most thoroughly on a man whose name she did not even know, and one whom she might possibly never see again. She envisioned his quick smile that somehow had seemed to change his severe expression to one of youthful handsomeness. She could almost feel the strength of his lean, hard body and what she instinctively knew would be the gentle touch of his hands. She drifted off to sleep at last with a smile on her face and a promise in her heart that if she ever met him again she would make sure he became very much aware of the existence of Hannah Marshall.

Night rushed to meet the dawn and was accompanied by the low rumble of thunder and the sound of softly falling rain. The people of the valley slept, as did the inhabitants of the town, unaware that dawn would bring new conflicts, for while they slumbered, webs of evil were being carefully set to enmesh the unwary.

# Chapter 27

The next day dawned to lead grey skies and the drumming sounds of rain on rooftops and mud-filled streets.

Despite his meager hours of rest, Trace was awake early. Worry furrowed his brow as he heard the steady rainfall. Mud! he thought in disgust. What repair work he had planned to do today would have to wait, for he knew that the beds on which the rails were placed had to be solid and working in mud would make that nearly impossible.

He rose from the bed feeling stiff and sore. The first thing that caught his eye was Allison, who was curled up in a chair asleep. He smiled as he went to her side. She was sleeping soundly, so he bent and gently lifted her from the chair and carried her to the bed. He laid her down and covered her with a blanket. Then he filled a basin with water, stripped off his soiled clothes, and washed his hair and body thoroughly. He hated to put the dirty clothes back on, but he was forced to do so because they were all he had. He decided to go directly to the store and purchase some clothes immediately. He smiled wryly. This visit to the Colorado territory had been extremely hard on his wardrobe.

He left the room quietly, moved down the stairs, and left the hotel. As he entered the store, he was surprised to find Maxwell already there.

"Can't say 'good morning,' Trace," Maxwell grumbled. "As if we haven't got enough of a mess, it had to rain. I'll bet we're knee-deep in mud out there."

"Streets are, so I imagine the track site must be . . . but good morning anyway."

Maxwell laughed. "You buying clothes too?"

"All my clothes were in that car and so were Allison's. I expect what isn't burnt will be scattered across the territory."

"I'll give you an advance on some of your pay so you and Allison can replenish your wardrobe."

"Good. I'm sure Allison will be needing a lot of things."

"What are you going to do today since we can't get the men out to work in the mud?"

"It's time to grab the bull by the horns. No matter what the feelings are, we have to get out an talk to those ranchers. Maxwell," Trace said firmly, "this train is going through that valley and on to California no matter what. We have a right-of-way we can take, and, if I'm forced to it, I will take it. I'd just like to do it an easier way. I'll try talking to them again."

"After last night, they're more likely to greet us with guns than handshakes. But it's sure worth another try. Trace?"

"Yeah?"

"Last night's little episode . . . do you think Buck Graham and the Marshall boy really did all that?"

"Looks like it," Trace answered and Maxwell was alarmed at the bitter tone in his voice. Against his will, Trace's mind had been drawn to Jenny. He had tried in vain to keep her from his dreams and chafed again at the thought that Jenny and Buck had had this all planned and that she had allowed him to believe in what he had thought was real between them.

He was angry, yet he would have given anything to have had the opportunity to be alone with her so that he could drag the truth from her—a much different truth than Maxwell would have imagined.

"Now that I feel a little more presentable," Trace said as he shrugged into a jacket he had just bought and put on a wide-brimmed hat to protect himself from the rain, "I think I will ride out to see what work needs to be done and if the men are all right. I don't want them stirring up a pot of anger and have it go spilling over. I need to keep them and the townspeople and the ranchers apart until I get some of this mess cleaned up."

"I think I'll check on Eileen, then get some breakfast. Then I'll go over to the bank and withdraw some money. The men are going to need their pay so they can blow off a little steam in the saloon tonight. It might ease the tension."

"Maybe, but we've got to keep them under control. They're pretty mad about last night. I thought we were going to have a riot."

"It was close, but I think we can keep them out of trouble."

"Anyone who starts something could be building a situation the railroad will have to pay for."

"I'll caution them to be careful."

Trace laughed. "You'd better make that a threat, not just a caution."

"I'll do that."

"Well, let's get going. The sooner we get around to putting things back together, the sooner we can get through this valley and get out of this Colorado territory."

Maxwell nodded and Trace left the store. Maxwell watched as he left, and the older man was certain Trace had no real desire to leave Colorado territory, in fact, not even the valley, and especially a turquoise-eyed girl who had fought him so angrily the night before.

Trace returned to Allison's room and placed a note and some money on the dresser. Then he left the hotel and walked the long wood sidewalk to the site of the past evening's explosion.

Taylor Jessup stood in front of the bank and watched Trace walk toward the site. He smiled. "Too bad, my friend. That's only the first battle you have lost in this war." He walked to his horse and mounted, then turned the horse toward the valley. He had his own move to make in the game he was playing.

He rode slowly and was several miles from town when he saw another lone rider coming toward him. He drew his horse to a halt and waited for the rider to approach him.

They came abreast of each other and the second rider stopped.

"Morning, Taylor."

"Morning, Howard."

"Pretty bad day," Howard said. "I don't suppose the railroad crew will be doing much."

"No, I suppose not. But then, nobody wants them to be doing much. After last night, I believe all the ranchers are mad enough to see that the Starett line doesn't go a mile further."

"Well, Taylor, I'm not too sure that's what's in everybody's mind."

"Oh . . . you been thinking it over, have you?"

"Yes, I have."

"That's too bad, Howard," Taylor said softly. Howard looked at him through narrowed and much wiser eyes.

"I take it you don't approve of the railroad being stopped here?" Taylor said.

"Maybe I don't approve of some of the methods being used. Two men died last night, and my son and the son of my best friend are being blamed for it."

"No one can prove who blew up that train."

"No, but Trace Cord and Maxwell Starett are not the kinds of men to let this thing go. I don't want my son blamed for something he had no part of."

"You're on your way to town?"

"I am."

"To talk to Maxwell Starett or Trace Cord, by any chance?"

"Yes. I think some of this anger has to be eased. The best way is for at least one of the ranchers to try to talk to them."

"I don't think so," Taylor said coldly.

"Taylor, this has to be stopped!"

"Not yet."

Howard's shoulders straightened and Taylor understood what kind of force he would have to use to prevent Howard from ruining all his plans.

"You'd best not do anything stupid, Howard."

"Stupid," Howard said angrily, "or smart for the first time in a long time?"

"Is your urge to talk to them strong enough that your ranch doesn't matter?"

"My ranch has nothing to do with this. It's only a right-of-way they want, not all my land. I won't be losing anything."

"I'm afraid you have the wrong idea. I mean you might lose your ranch to me."

"You can't touch it."

"You lost it in a game of chance."

"Trace Cord returned the deed to me."

"I see . . . but Howard"—Taylor smiled—"what

about the signed notes in my bank on which you've put up your ranch as collateral. The sum, I believe, is well over thirty-five thousand dollars, a great deal of money. Not as much as your ranch is worth, but"—he shrugged—"when it's sold to repay me, that really won't matter, will it?"

"You . . . you wouldn't recall them now. Taylor, I'm on my feet. I can repay you with the money the railroad gives me, and if that doesn't cover it, I'll make payments. I—"

"Don't go on, Howard. It's no use. I'm going to put it to you straight. I plan on tearing up those notes."

"Taylor."

"In return for your assurance that you will not negotiate with the railroad, nor will you sell them any land. In fact"—he smiled pleasantly—"I don't want you to talk to them at all."

"I can't do that."

"Then I'm afraid I will have to recall your notes tomorrow morning. There are only two alternatives, Howard. Agree to what I want . . . or pay your notes tomorrow."

"You black-hearted bastard! That's blackmail!"

"Call it what you choose," Taylor said angrily. "I don't want the Starett line to move through that valley. You decide now, Howard. Do you want your family to inherit your land . . . or do you want to leave them destitute? Decide now, because I won't make this offer again."

Howard was shaken and Taylor knew it. He had almost lost everything once before and he was afraid to let such a disaster befall his children again. There was only one way out. All he had to do to keep his ranch and start his life over was to refuse to negotiate with the railroad. If he didn't, he knew from the look in Taylor's eyes the banker would destroy him and his children. He could not let that happen.

"What are you doing to this valley, Taylor?" he raged.

"That, my friend, is none of your business. Your business is to save your ranch. Now, what are you going to do?"

"What choice do I have?" Howard asked bitterly.

"None that I can see. Don't take it so hard, Howard. What do you have to lose? In the end you will have your family intact, and your ranch will again be all yours. When the Starett track fails and they are gone, I will personally give you back your notes to destroy. What is wrong with a bargain like that?"

"I don't know what your game is, Taylor, but I love my family too much to hurt them again. Buck and Jenny have worked hard too, and they don't deserve to lose it now." Howard's shoulders slumped. "I'll do what you say."

"You won't negotiate?"

"No."

"You won't even talk to them?"

"No."

"Good."

"Are you finished with me?" Howard snapped.

"No, I want you to ride over to the Marshall's now and talk to them. Do your best to convince them that the railroad is a big mistake for the valley."

"You want me to do the dirty work."

"It will sound so much more convincing coming from you. Besides"—Taylor laughed—"I have no hold over Jacob, and he has no reason to listen to me. But he might just listen to you."

"I feel like a traitor."

"Whatever you feel like, just remember, you are the one who has a lifetime of hard work to lose."

"I'll remember. Damn you, Taylor. I hope you get

exactly what's coming to you—what you deserve!"

Howard jerked his horse's reins and spurred him so that the horse broke into a run. Taylor watched him go with a smile of satisfaction on his face. Then he turned to look toward Howard's ranch. He had another step to his plan and he was going to see to it right away.

Buck and Jenny sat together at the kitchen table. True to the doctor's words, Buck had the worst headache he had ever experienced.

"Why don't you stay in bed?" Jenny demanded.

"Doesn't do much good." Buck grimaced. "It hurts just as bad there. Sure wish someone would invent something to ease a headache."

"Well, rest is a good thing."

"Maybe, but I can't be there anymore. I've got to figure out why someone wanted to blame me and Terrance for that blowup last night."

"Maybe the railroad thought it would put some sympathy on their side."

"Blow up their own train, kill two of their own men? I doubt it."

"Well, how do you explain it?"

"I can't. Not yet. But I'm going to do my best to find out."

Buck rose slowly from his chair.

"What are you doing? Where are you going?"

"Well, first I'm going to ride over to see Emily." Buck grinned. "While her father is talking to me, I might as well take advantage of it. Then I intend to ride into town and talk to Trace."

"No!"

"Yes, Jenny. I don't want him thinking I'm responsible. I have to convince him I'm not. Lord, you think I want them thinking I would kill two men like that?" He saw the resistance in Jenny's eyes. "I know you and he are . . . well, that he was a little rough last night. But maybe he was upset, Jenny. Maybe he didn't mean some of the things he said."

"He meant them," Jenny said fiercely, "and I meant them. I don't want him on our land again. In fact, I don't ever want to see him again."

"Jenny—"

"Buck," Jenny interrupted softly, "let it alone. What was between Trace and me was some kind of game. He's in love with the Starett Line. Well, I'm not going to sacrifice everything for the sake of his precious railroad. If he wants to think I was part of what happened, then let him. I don't care anymore."

Buck, who knew his sister better than anyone else, instinctively felt she was lying as much to herself as she was to him. He did not say the words to her, but when he talked to Trace he intended to make the point very clear that Jenny was not capable of such an act, nor of murder.

"Okay, Jenny. I'm going over to see Emily. Will you be all right alone for awhile?"

"I've been alone before," she snapped, then looked up at him miserably. "I'm sorry. I don't mean to take it out on you. I'll be fine. Don't worry. Tell Emily hello for me and tell her I'm looking forward to welcoming her to the family."

"I'll tell her . . . after I get her alone. I don't think her father is ready for that yet."

Buck rode off and Jenny sat for some time in silence. She had cried out her hatred of Trace to Buck and her mind confirmed that she was right. But why did her deceitful body remember his touch so well? Why did she recall the warm, male scent of him, and why could she not convince her senses that she never wanted to feel his rapturous possession again? She folded her arms on the table and bent her head over them.

She must have been listening to the sound of the approaching horse for some time before she actually reacted to it. Was it Trace? her mind silently cried. She leapt to her feet and ran to the door. The sounds of footsteps crossing the porch grew louder as she snapped open the door and looked into the smiling face of Taylor Jessup.

"Good morning, Jenny. May I come in? I have something very important to discuss with you."

"Yes, of course. Come in." She stepped back to let him pass her, then closed the door.

"What is it, Taylor?"

"Do you know you are very beautiful?" he said softly.

She laughed uncomfortably, for she had been made slightly nervous by the intensity of his gaze. "You didn't ride all the way out here to tell me that, now did you?"

"That and a lot of other things."

"What other things?"

"Suppose we sit down and talk. This is too important to be casual."

"Taylor, what do you want to say to me?"

"Jenny, I want you to marry me."

She stood immobile. The last thing she expected or wanted was a proposal.

"Jenny?"

"I . . . I heard you." She spoke through stiff lips. Taylor moved close to her and took one of her ice-cold hands in his.

"Jenny, I'm going to be a very important man in this territory. I'm already quite wealthy. I can offer you more than you can imagine now. I've wanted you for a long, long time."

He drew her close to him and at that moment she

realized he meant to take her in his arms. She pressed both hands against his chest to keep some distance between them.

"Taylor . . . I . . ."

"Jenny." He was impassioned now, filled with the desire to taste the soft lips so near his own and to feel her body pressed against his in willing surrender. "We'll be rich, Jenny, rich. Once I rid the valley of the railroad—"

"Rid the valley?"

"I mean, once they decide to go, we'll build this area. The ranchers and the town can work together to build. It is a great chance for us, Jenny. We can have the whole territory in our hands!" He was drawing her to him as he spoke. Then he bound her against him while his hot, seeking mouth ravaged hers.

She fought wildly, finally pushing herself out of his arms. She was panting and stared at him in absolute disbelief.

"I don't want to marry anyone, Taylor. I'm sorry, but I'm not in love with you. Please go."

"Not in love with me?" he snarled. "I suppose that Trace Cord is more to your taste."

"That's none of your affair," she cried. Her temper was now threatening to surface.

"It is my affair. Can't you see he and his railroad cronies are liars and cheats? Can't you see they're trying to steal from you?"

"They cannot steal what we are determined to protect."

"Jenny, I can protect you."

"Protect me from what?"

"You don't think they will stop now? They will fight back."

"My father, my brother, and I will protect our own land."

"I want you," he said, and again she was shaken by his firm voice, as if he expected his will to be enough.

"I will not marry you, Taylor," she said with as much control as she could muster.

"But you will, Jenny."

"You cannot order me!"

"But I am," he stated. "And you will marry me."

"Taylor, please get out of here."

"When I walk out that door, Jenny, everything you want to protect and all that you love will go with me."

"I don't understand you."

"Then let me explain, Jenny, my dear," he replied. "Your father is very deeply in debt to me. The notes he signed put up this ranch as collateral. I want my money . . . tomorrow."

"How much are the notes for?" she questioned, trying to keep the shock from her face and the quivering from her voice.

"Thirty-five thousand dollars," he gloated.

Her face went white. "So much," she gasped.

"He was very careless in his drinking and gambling."

"But he can never raise that much money."

"Then"—he shrugged—"this land . . . is mine."

"No," she moaned.

"Of course," he said smoothly, "you can keep it if you decide to use your common sense."

"And marry you," she said.

"Do not sound so defeated, Jenny. I intend to give you a good life."

"I won't do it!"

He shrugged eloquently. He already knew Jenny would do what she felt would be best for her father.

"Then your father had better be prepared to be evicted tomorrow."

"You can't mean this! You can't be so cold and unfeeling!"

He went to her and roughly pulled her into his arms. "Cold and unfeeling?" he said. "No, Jenny love. I am not cold and unfeeling where you are concerned. I have dreamed of you in my bed for a long, long time and, when you are, I promise you I will not be cold and unfeeling."

"Doesn't it matter to you that I don't love you?"

"I will teach you all I want you to know about love, Jenny." He laughed. "I will show you how it is to be loved."

He kissed her again and it gave him a great deal of pleasure to feel her tremble in his arms.

"Jenny . . . you must make a decision."

"I need to think," she pleaded.

"I want your decision and I want it now. You will agree to marry me now . . . or tomorrow I will see to it that this house is burned to the ground."

She felt the tears sting her eyes. They blurred her vision but not her senses. He held her in an iron grip, and to save her home and her father and brother she would have to surrender.

He waited breathlessly. Would she be willing to buy her home with her body? The thought of possessing her filled him with an intoxicating fire.

"Jenny?" he demanded.

"Yes," she sobbed. "I will."

"Then we will be married when the battle with the railroad is over. I don't believe it will be much longer. They lost a lot last night and I don't think the rest of the ranchers will let them pass through the valley."

"All right," she replied.

"If you speak to your father of this, he will do what he thinks necessary to keep you from it. He might even decide that losing everything doesn't matter. He may give up all of this for you. In trying to be noble he will sacrifice everything."

"I . . . I will tell him that I chose to marry you because . . . because I wanted to," she choked out in a despair-filled voice.

"Very good. I must get back to town," he said as he held her. His hands roamed down her slender back to rest on her hips. "I hate to go, but there will be time later to enjoy our new-found pleasure. Jenny?"

"What?" she replied numbly.

"Kiss me."

"Taylor . . . please . . . I . . ."

"Kiss me!" he demanded.

Jenny raised her lips to his, but that was not enough for Taylor. "I want you to give your promise to me, Jenny. If you don't, I will feel our bargain is void. You will belong to me for a long time. I want to be sure."

Jenny closed her eyes and put her arms about his neck. He brought her body tight against his. Her parted lips were sweet and he took his time tasting them to the fullest. When he released her, she remained still and quiet.

"Very good," he said, his voice hoarse with desire. "When we are married, Jenny," he whispered, "I will teach you to love me, to please me. I shall find it very difficult to wait." He moved away from her and went to the door. "Remember, Jenny, my sweet, who will pay the price if you should decide to change your mind."

He left and Jenny stood in deadening silence. Tears she could no longer contain ran unheeded down her cheeks. If Trace's name passed her lips in her anguish, there was no one to hear it.

## Chapter 28

Buck rode with much lighter thoughts than he had had in many months. For the first time in a long time he felt there might be a ray of hope for him and Emily. Jacob had not exactly been enthusiastic toward him, but he had not been hostile either, and Buck intended to press any advantage he might have gained.

When he rode up to the Marshall house, he was as tense as a bow string. What if Jacob decided to toss him off the ranch? He stepped down from his horse and walked up the steps to the door.

Before he could knock, the door was opened by a smiling Emily.

"I saw you coming," she said breathlessly. Her eyes devoured him and melted every sense he had into a pool of delicious need.

"I had to, Em," he whispered. "I can't stand this sneaking around any longer. I need to let your pa know I intend to marry you—and soon," he added with a soft laugh. "It's driving me crazy, all this waiting and wanting. We need to get our lives started, Em."

"I'm glad you came, Buck."

"Is your pa here?"

"He's in the barn. One of the horses got hurt. He's

been nursing it all night."

"Maybe I ought to give him a hand."

"He's awfully tired, Buck. I . . . I don't know about the mood he might be in."

"It's about time I stopped tiptoeing around your father. I'm not in the greatest mood either, and I've got one heck of a headache. But if we're ever going to reach an understanding, now is the time." He smiled into her worried countenance. "Of course you wouldn't send me into battle without a kiss, now would you?"

Emily knew Buck was deliberately putting her in a position where she would have to commit herself. She did not hesitate for long but stepped out on the porch and into his open arms. She raised her lips for his kiss, not caring who saw her now.

"Emily," Buck said huskily as their lips parted, "I love you."

"I know," she replied with a satisfied look.

"Now, I suppose I have to go and tell that to your father."

"Yes." She giggled. "I suppose you do."

"Well," he said resignedly, "I'd better get on with it."

He kissed her quickly, then turned, marched down the steps determinedly and headed toward the barn.

Inside the barn he found Jacob and one of his hands in a stall where a horse lay on clean straw. The horse had a badly damaged hind leg, and Buck's experienced eye determined that the horse was in extreme pain and very near death.

Jacob looked up at him with a worried frown creasing his brows. He was very tired and also angry that he was about to lose one of the best horses he had.

Lantern light that brightend the stalls flickered dully in Jacob's eyes as he looked up at Buck.

"Good morning, Mr. Marshall."

"Sure as hell isn't a good morning for me," Jacob

said angrily. "I'm about to lose one of my best mares. I just don't have time for visiting today."

"I didn't come to visit," Buck said softly. "I have to talk to you."

"Some other time, Buck. Right now I've got trouble, and there's no time for—"

"Mr. Marshall," Buck replied in a voice that Jacob had not heard him use before, "I am the best hand with horses in this valley. You give me room and I'll tend your mare. If I make her well, you give me an hour of your time."

Jacob gazed up at a stiff-faced Buck, whose eyes held his.

Jacob smiled. "Stubborn cuss, aren't you?"

"Yessir, about some things. This is the most important thing in my life."

Jacob contemplated him silently for long enough to make Buck's nerves stretch to the breaking point. But this time Buck was determined he would not back away.

"All right," Jacob agreed quietly. "You look at her. If you're as good as you say you are, we'll talk."

"Agreed." Buck knelt in the hay beside the mare. Gently he ran his hand over her quivering flesh. "There, girl, there," he soothed, "be easy, girl . . . easy."

The mare reared her head and Buck continued to soothe her. It took him some time before he even looked at the wound.

"Nasty," he grunted. Then he turned to the hand who stood by Jacob. "What's your name?"

"Ben."

"Well, Ben, I'd be grateful if you'd go and heat me up some water. I want it boiling. Then there's some plants I want. I'll describe 'em to you. You'll find 'em growing wild out along the edge of the trees. Get some help and get me as much as you can."

Buck went on to describe the plants he wanted and Ben cast an inquisitive look at Jacob.

"Go get what he wants," Jacob said.

"Yessir."

Jacob and Ben watched in fascination after the material Buck wanted had been brought. He quickly soaked the plant leaves in the water, crushing them until they formed a thick paste. Then he grabbed a handful and placed it on the mare's wound. Her legs thrashed wildly and she whinnied sharply.

Both Jacob and Ben gasped as Buck neatly avoided the thrashing, deadly hooves and methodically continued to plaster the hot, sticky substance against the wound.

When he had used it all, he again began to soothe the quivering muscles of the horse with a gentle touch and an even gentler voice. This continued for over an hour. Then Buck took off the old paste and replaced it. In the next two hours this process was repeated again and again. By that time Jacob and Ben could seen an obvious improvement. The mare seemed to be resting free of pain, and the wound has lost its festering look and had begun to look clean and red.

Now Buck placed the last of the paste on a now docile mare. He bound it with pads and strips of cloth. Then he stood up. His head was pounding furiously and he was stiff from being in a crouched position for over three hours. But when Buck turned to look at Jacob, he saw the older man's smile and the slow look of dawning respect.

"Don't keep her down too long. In a day or so she'll be fine," Buck told him. "Now, Mr. Marshall," he said firmly, "you owe me an hour."

"Don't need an hour." Jacob smiled. "Reckon you're coming here asking if you can call on Emily."

"No sir," Buck said, grimly prepared to do battle.

"Emily and I want to get married. We want your blessing."

"My God!" Jacob laughed. "You're sure a damn fast mover, aren't you?"

"Well sir"—Buck grinned—"when you've found something as beautiful and good as Emily, if you move slow you're liable to lose her. I don't want to take that chance."

"You two been meeting each other?" Jacob asked, his face unreadable. Buck took a deep breath.

"I'm not going to start a relationship by lying to you, Mr. Marshall. Yes, we've been meeting. Em and I have been in love for a long time—even before you sent her off to school. But we don't want to sneak around behind your back. We want to get married, have a place of our own . . . have a family."

He waited in breathless expectation for the explosion, but it never came. Instead Jacob smiled and held out his hand to Buck, who took it with a deep sigh of gratitude.

"Now," Jacob suggested with a grin, "suppose you come up to the house. I'll bet there's a couple of women up there who have been holding their breath all this time."

They laughed together, then left the barn and walked toward the house. Emily, who was beside herself by now, had been watching out the window and saw the two men she loved the most leave the barn and begin walking toward the house. She could bear the strain no longer. She ran out on the porch and down the steps to meet them several feet from the house. When they stopped to face each other, she could read neither face.

"Well girl?" Jacob said gruffly.

"Buck . . . Pa . . . if one of you doesn't say something pretty soon, I swear I'll commit murder."

Both men laughed.

"You should have told me a long time ago that this boy was so good with horses. You wouldn't have had to meet him. I reckon we better get him into the family. That way I get a good horse breeder along with a son."

"Oh, Pa!" Emily cried. She threw herself into his arms and he hugged her to him.

"I think I'd like one of those too," Buck said with a chuckle. For the first time they could reach out and touch each other without being afraid. It was a heady experience and Buck found it hard to let go of her. Their eyes met and a silent promise to meet later was mutually understood.

Before any of the three could speak again they heard an approaching rider. They turned to watch him.

"It's Pa," Buck said. "Wonder if something's wrong?" He was puzzled.

Howard rode up to them and dismounted. "Mornin', Howard," Jacob said. "You're just in time to hear some news. Seems our kids are planning to get married."

"That's news that sure makes me happy," Howard replied. "Jacob . . . I'd like to talk to you about something that's a shadow over us all."

"The railroad," Jacob said quickly.

"Yes. How do you stand on them coming out through our valley?"

"Come in the house, Howard. We'll talk about it."

The four entered the house and settled at the kitchen table. Beatrice placed cups of hot coffee before the three men. She was more than delighted at her husband's acceptance of Buck. She had been her daughter's confidante for a long time and had known the objections in Jacob's mind.

Hannah stood unobtrusively in the background, sharing her sister's happiness yet strangely disassociated. At eighteen, Hannah was a year younger than Emily. She was considered the baby of the family,

402

which she often found irritating, for everyone tended to think of her as a child.

She was a woman who kept most of her thoughts to herself. Unlike Emily, who was effervescent, Hannah was often silent. But like Emily, she had developed into a very beautiful woman. Their hair was very nearly the same shade of russet and their eyes a shade of green that fluctuated between the color of fresh grass and the shade of the foliage in the deep forest.

She listened now as the conversation turned to the topic of the railroad's presence.

She could see the looks exchanged between Buck and Emily and knew everything between them was perfect. Yet this only made her feelings of distress more apparent.

What was wrong with her, she wondered. She could not have been happier for her sister, yet she longed for some intangible thing that lingered constantly on the periphery of her thoughts. She tried to deny her visions of the mysterious man and the intoxicating effect he had had on her sensibilities.

"The railroad will have a bad effect on the valley," Howard was saying.

Buck stared at Howard with a very puzzled look on his face. He had the strangest feeling that something was very wrong.

"How do you come to believe that?" Jacob questioned. "I've been thinkin' of sellin' them that strip of land down along the river."

"Then what are you going to do if they block the water? Where is your stock going to drink."

"Well, I don't expect 'em to do that. They know we need water."

"Can you trust them?" Howard questioned. He hated planting such doubts in Jacob's mind, but he no longer had a choice.

Buck sensed there was something behind his father's strange remarks, but he could not determine what it was. His father had never been one to do what he was doing now. He had always made his own firm decisions and had never interfered with the decisions of others. He decided he would talk to his father alone and not bring up the point in front of the others. He'd hear his father's reasons first.

"Howard," Jacob said, "it won't do any harm to just listen to what this Maxwell Starett has to say. Suppose we go into town and talk to him, see what he has to say. Then we can call on Joanne Carter on the way home and talk about it. Better we all make a decision and stand together."

"That's a good idea." Howard rose. "Now seems to be as good a time as any."

"Yep." Jacob grinned. "Now that I know my mare is going to be all right, I guess I can go. You coming, Buck?"

"Uh . . . no . . . I . . . I . . . have some work that's got to be done."

"All right, son," Howard said. "I'll see you at home later tonight."

"All right, Pa."

Jacob again held out his hand to Buck and there was a twinkle in his eyes and a smile on his lips.

"Expect I'll be seeing a lot of you, boy."

"Yes sir." Buck laughed. "A whole lot."

When Howard and Jacob had gone, Buck made a quick excuse to leave. His destination was his and Emily's meeting place. He had been there less than an hour when Emily rode up. She dismounted and he laughed exuberantly as he caught her up in his arms.

\*     \*     \*

Hannah was restless and she did not know why. She was angry at herself, for, despite all her efforts, a form continued to linger before her, unnamed and unattainable, yet she could not seem to shake the magnetic pull that had interrupted her life.

She had to do something, so she made a quick decision.

"Mama, I'm going to ride over to Joanne's. We haven't talked in a long time."

"Take care," Beatrice cautioned. "Will you be riding back tonight or staying the night?"

"I'll stay the night if Joanne will have me, so don't make any supper for me."

"Be very careful, child."

"I will, Mama," Hannah retorted, annoyed again at the childish admonition.

After she had changed into riding clothes, she went to the barn to saddle her horse. Then she mounted and rode away from the ranch, quite unaware of the man on horseback who had hidden himself beneath the trees on a nearby ridge. He watched for a few minutes, then kicked his horse into motion and followed Hannah.


After some time Lucifer rose to his feet and poured a drink from the bottle that sat on his dresser. He found that the enforced inactivity was a thing with which he was finding it difficult to cope. That and a hotel room that seemed to get smaller by the moment were stretching his nerves.

He would have gone out, but the time was not yet right for what he wanted to accomplish, and the last thing he desired was to run across Trace Cord before he was ready.

Again he sat on the edge of the bed. Old memories

crowded his thoughts, old and very painful memories. He absently rubbed the old wound on his hip that had created the limp he would carry forever.

He began to sweat as the pictures returned to his mind. A field hospital . . . pain . . . pain so bad he had begged to die; long days and nights not living or dead but drawn on a rack of pain that had left him a shell; awakening to find it would take months to be able to walk again . . . and even longer to adjust to the consequences of the wound that had eliminated his use of his eye and had necessitated the black patch.

He had other memories that plagued him, memories that had set him roaming, unable to find a spot to stop for much-needed comfort. He remembered too the three men he had killed in defense of his honor and his life. He had used his gun to kill, and the guilt of it had never allowed him to stop running.

He swore and stood up again, unable to bear his confines any longer. His memories drove him from the room.

He made his way down the back stairs. He would have to leave the town for awhile and quickly decided to ride out and keep a watch on Joanne Carter. He had heard Taylor's plans and knew that one day soon Joanne and her daughter would be in a great deal of danger. He would check on her and see that she remained safe until the time was right to bring everything to a conclusion.

He rode slowly, making sure that no one followed him and that nobody saw him who would carry the fact to Taylor or to Trace.

The skies were still grey and heavy with dark rain clouds, but the rain itself had temporarily stopped. He let his horse make its own sure-footed way and sat contemplatively in the saddle, rolling with the horse's easy, swinging motion. He was so relaxed that he was totally unprepared for the sight that met his eyes as he broke from the trees into a small, flat meadow.

Hannah loved to ride and, despite the fact that the air was misty with moisture and the clouds hung dark and heavy, she enjoyed the scenic ride to Joanne's.

A crisp breeze rustled the trees and with it came the scent of newly bloomed flowers mingling with the aroma of pines from the high, snow-covered ridges.

Still unaware of the man who followed behind her, Hannah chose to dismount and walk for a few minutes when she came across a flat meadow. There were wildflowers scattered in profusion and she bent to pick one or two.

It was then that she became aware of a rider nearing her. She looked up quickly, did not recognize him, and prepared to mount and leave.

He saw her action and kicked his horse into a run. Hannah had barely found her seat when a strong arm came about her and lifted her from the saddle. Her frightened horse bolted and Hannah was unceremoniously dropped to the ground.

She was frightened but felt an equal amount of anger. She leapt to her feet as the man dismounted and walked toward her.

"How dare you!" she sputtered. "What do you think you're doing?"

He smiled a smile that sent a chill through her and kept on walking toward her. She slowly attempted to back away, then with a muffled cry she turned and began to run.

He was faster and much stronger. She screamed as he caught her again. He wrestled her to the ground and in moments was astride her and holding her hands over her head.

"What do you want?" she sobbed. "Let me go. Please let me go."

"Now, pretty thing," he said with a laugh, "the boss says I'm to keep you out of circulation for a few days. You're going to have to get used to me because"—he bent toward her—"you and me are going to have some fun together."

She could smell his unwashed body and the rancid odor of his whiskey-laden breath. Helplessly she sobbed as he held both of her hands over her head with one of his and began to unbutton her blouse with the other. The weight of his body upon hers kept her nearly immobile.

Frustrated with the buttons, he grew impatient and angry. He grabbed the front of her blouse and easily tore it away, revealing the soft curves of her creamy body.

"Don't . . . please . . . let me go."

"Now, pretty thing . . . sweet little virgin, you don't know what that sweet body of yours is for, do ya? Well, I'm a good teacher. In a week or two I'll have ya beggin' for more. C'mon now, don't fight so hard," his voice rasped as he began to fondle her flesh and cover her cheeks and lips with rough kisses. "You're gonna like it, pretty thing," he grunted as his mouth took in a bruising kiss and he forced her lips apart. His tongue thrust deeply and she choked and fought, heaving her slim body ineffectually under his. He laughed as his mouth moved lower to the soft skin of her throat and his hand roughly caught one small breast and kneaded it painfully. Her eyes filled with tears and she moaned softly at his brutal touch.

"Like it already, don't ya?" he grated as his hands grew more insistent. "Wait until I really show ya how good it feels. You'll be moanin' for more."

She cried out and fought desperately, but it was a

battle she knew she couldn't win.

So intent was he on the intended rape of the helpless young girl beneath him that the man never heard the approach of another horse. Nor was he aware of the man who dismounted and strode toward him.

He was conscious of nothing but the innocent beauty beneath him when a rough hand suddenly jerked him upright.

He was tossed aside like a child and his face was filled first with shock, then with fear, as he looked up at his death.

He grabbed for his gun, but the gun in Lucifer's holster seemed to leap into his hand. It barked once, and the man fell backward with a bullet in his heart.

Lucifer ran to Hannah, who was just sitting up. She was crying helplessly and trying to cover herself with the remains of her clothing.

He knew she needed comfort, but he was so angry at the thought of her near rape that he dragged her to her feet.

"What the hell is a stupid kid like you doing out here alone? Why aren't you home playing with dolls where you belong?"

Hannah had reached the end of her endurance. She sagged forward and an astonished Lucifer caught her in his arms.


Trace moved about the camp of tents that surrounded the damaged tracks. His men seemed to be under control. Grumbling at the rain and mud. Their ability to go into town helped to temporarily stem the flow of their antagonism.

Trace tried to stay active, but there was very little for him to do and his thoughts continually returned to Jenny.

He fought a battle, pulling himself in all directions. Had Jenny been part of the attempt to destroy the train? Had she really deceived him? Had her words of love meant nothing to her? His memory found those things hard to accept. He could still feel the warmth of her body in his arms and hear the whisper of her voice in his mind. It forced him into a turmoil that he tried to relieve in activity.

It was no use. He had to see her. He had to know.

He saddled his horse and rode toward Jenny's home.

When he arrived, he knocked. When the door had opened and Jenny stood before him, he could only say softly, "Hello, Jenny . . . can I come in?"

## Chapter 29

Jenny caught her breath. He stood before her, tall, handsome, as if in answer to her thoughts. *Too late!* her mind screamed. *For us it is too late.*

She could not allow him to breach her defenses now and stir her senses. She had to control her emotions and the magnetic power he seemed to exert each time he was near her. She understood what she would have to do. She only prayed she had the courage to do it.

He had come for answers and she knew it, but answers were what she could not give.

"What do you want, Trace?" she asked bitterly. "I've heard enough recriminations. Don't you have anyone else to blame for your problems? Why come here?"

"I didn't come here to place blame, Jenny," he said. "I came to see if . . . can I come in, Jenny?"

"I can't see any reason why you should. What you said in town was enough to make your feelings clear."

"Can I come in and talk to you, Jenny?" he repeated. "I have to—"

"No . . . no, Trace . . . go away. We have nothing more to say to each other." She closed the door between them, then pressed her head against the door and tried to choke back the bitter tears.

"Jenny"—his voice was slowly rising in anger—"open the door. I'm not going to ride away from here until you talk to me. This is ridiculous."

"Go away, Trace. Go back to your railroad. Find some other gullible fool to swallow your sweet lies."

By this time Trace's anger was beginning to control his judgment.

"Open this damn door!"

She backed away from the door, alarmed at the sound of his growing anger.

"We're going to have this out, Jenny. I want some answers from you and I'm not going until I get them."

"Answers!" she shouted. "I have no intention of answering any of your questions. You have no right to come here with questions."

There was an abrupt silence outside that stretched on and on until her nerves were screaming. She was about to go to the door and open it to see if he had gone when it flew open with a resounding crash. Trace had used one well-placed kick to force it.

They looked at each other, both overcome with anger. She knew she had to fight him, for just the sight of him framed in the doorway was enough to stir her. He walked toward her and she stubbornly refused to back away. She glared back into his angry eyes.

"Just tell me why, Jenny. If you and your brother wanted to fight, why not do it fairly?"

"You really believe that I . . . that we . . . you fool! We had nothing to do with it—neither of us. Buck would never kill anyone!"

"What the hell am I supposed to believe?"

"The truth."

"Whose truth—yours, mine—whose?"

"There is only one!"

"So simple now, isn't it, when the shoe is on the other foot? When I asked you to believe the truth, you

412

refused. Now you and your people are guilty. Now you want me to believe."

"Then believe what you want. I don't care! You can go to hell, both you and your damn, intefering railroad. Oh, I wish you had never come into my life."

His eyes held hers. He was trying to believe her; he wanted desperately to believe her. It was then that she began to realize that once he accepted the truth he would forget his anger and assume they could begin again.

He moved closer, and her pulses beat wildly. "Jenny," he said gently.

"No," she moaned raggedly. "Go away, Trace. I don't care any longer what you think or feel. If you want to condemn us, do so. If you want to believe we are responsible for what happened, then do so. I don't care. Just go away!"

His anger and his doubts were slowly dying in the face of what was obviously her fear. But what was she afraid of? he wondered. "I'm sorry, Jenny. I've been pushed beyond rational thought. I didn't mean to break down the door. Can't we forget how this happened and just talk. I thought—"

She turned her back to him and tried to summon her strength.

"I . . . I don't care, Trace. It really doesn't matter anymore."

She sucked in her breath raggedly as he came up behind her and took hold of her shoulders, drawing her back against him.

"It matters, Jenny. Don't you see . . . it matters."

"Don't, Trace," she cried.

"I've misunderstood and I'm sorry. For God's sake, Jenny, understand. It was a mistake. I was under a lot of strain and I said a lot of unforgivable things. I should have known you and Taylor Jessup weren't together in this."

"Taylor . . ." she whispered.

He turned her around and studied her face.

"Forget him, Jenny. We can work this all out."

"We can't, Trace," she said miserably. "No matter what you have to say . . . I'm . . . I'm going to marry Taylor Jessup."

"You're what?" he demanded.

"I'm going to marry Taylor Jessup."

"You can't!" His voice rose.

"I can . . . and I will."

"You don't love him, Jenny. Damnit, look at me!" he commanded as he tipped her chin so he could see her eyes. "You don't love him!"

"That's none of your business."

"The hell it isn't my business."

"I am going to marry Taylor."

"Look at me and tell me you love him. Tell me you want to marry him. Tell me what was between us was a lie."

She was crying now and she pushed him from her and turned away.

"Trace, leave me alone."

He grabbed her again and spun her around. Before she could fight back or protest, he was holding her tight against him.

"What can I say to you to let you know how sorry I am for what I said? Jenny, you can't do this."

"I can," she whispered. "I can and I will."

"Is it because you were angry with me? For God's sake, that's a long way to go just for spite, Jenny."

"Will you please go, Trace—please? This is the way it's going to be."

"We'll see," he said softly. He bent his head to kiss her gently, tenderly, and she uttered a sound of sheer panic and tried to escape, but his arms refused to release her. His lips played lovingly over hers, drifting across her cheeks and back to her lips to taste and taste again until she felt faint from the sheer pleasure that began to warm her.

"You belong to me, Jenny. You belong to me, and I will prove to you what I already know—that we love each other and there is no room for anyone else."

Painfully aware that her body was throbbing with a growing passion as he pressed her close to him, Jenny desperately tried to control her responses, but her strength was rapidly slipping away.

Slowly his kiss warmed her. He refused to release her lips once he had captured them. Their mouths lingered together, first gently, then slowly the kiss became more savage, fierce, drowning all her thoughts. Tongues met as their mouths slanted across each other's in hungry impatience.

She closed her eyes and clung weakly to him as his hands roughly pulled apart her dress and his hot mouth seared her flesh. Something wild splintered inside of her and began to grow into indescribable pleasure. She cried out, wondering if she could bear more of this ravaging rapture.

It was magic, beautiful and rare, and she no longer fought. Now she clasped him to her and when their bodies blended she arched to meet his hard, driving thrusts. His sensual assault created an expanding, spiraling flame that burst inside her and carried her beyond the realm of reality. She wanted to draw him within her, hold him and never let him go. Yet a new agony tore at her soul, for, despite the joy they shared now, she would have to let him go.

"God, Jenny," he rasped harshly, "I thought I was going to lose you."

"Trace . . . I . . ."

He stood up from the rug on which they had tumbled

and reached down to help her rise. She took his hand and stood beside him, rearranging her clothes and trying to redeem the torn dress as best she could. She could not bear to meet his eyes.

"Listen to me, Trace."

He chuckled and drew her into his arms to kiss her leisurely again. But his smile faded as he saw her eyes.

"I once said I never wanted to give you anything to cry about again," he told her. "I'm sorry I was so brutal, Jenny. But I'll make it up to you. We have so much—"

"No, Trace," she whispered. Their eyes held as she said the next words quietly. "I will marry Taylor Jessup and no matter what there was between us, it is past. It must die here."

"Jenny, you can't mean this. You love me. This could never have been a lie. Do you think I can let you go now?"

"You have no choice, Trace. Oh, you can force my body to respond to you. I cannot stop the desire your touch fills me with, but that cannot stop what I must do."

"*Must.* You're being forced somehow. What hold can he possibly have over you?"

Now she had been backed against a wall. She knew she would have to give a performance he would believe.

"I'm sorry about what you might have thought, but"—she shrugged—"I just feel that in this battle Taylor is going to be the winner. It is smart to be on the winning side. I must do what I can to preserve my ranch."

"Your ranch," he echoed in a stunned voice.

"My ranch is very important to me." She tried to keep her voice cool.

First his eyes narrowed in anger, then his expression slowly began to express disbelief, and finally he shot her a look that shrewdly assessed her.

416

"Your little act might have worked with somebody else, but not me, Jenny. I'm the one who felt your response. I'm the one who tasted your willing kisses. No, Jenny. I don't believe you."

He turned away and started toward the door.

"Where are you going?"

"To put an end to this. I'll prove your Taylor Jessup is a thief and a liar. Then I'll inform him that whatever hold he has over you has been broken. You'll marry him"—he pointed to her—"over my dead body."

"Trace, you don't understand!" she cried.

"Oh yes, I do. That bastard got to you somehow and convinced you to marry him. He wants your land. Tell me, Jenny, what was it—the ranch . . . your brother . . . your father?"

He saw the answer in her eyes before she could utter a denial.

"I thought so. Damn!" he muttered as he started for the door again. She ran to catch up with him.

"Don't, Trace! Don't!"

"Why, Jenny? Why are you afraid of him?"

"I'm not afraid of him. This is my own choice."

He turned to her and smiled. "Your choice?" He gripped her shoulders and kissed her until her body grew weak and she sagged against him.

"Stay here, Jenny. I'm going to find out just exactly what he's going to do. But let me tell you one fact, Jenny. You will never marry Taylor Jessup, because I will see him dead first."

He was gone before she could find a way to stop him. She stood helplessly, her tears staining her face, feeling as if she had just destroyed everything worthwhile in her life.

Trace rode back to town, trying to sort out the

417

pieces. If he only knew what motive Taylor had for all this. He could not accuse the town's most respected banker unless he could prove Taylor had done something wrong.

He sought out Maxwell to convince him to go to the ranchers now, before walls could be built that they could never scale.

"First the Marshalls," Trace told Maxwell when he had found him at the explosion site. "Talk to Jacob Marshall and make him understand. Convince him, Maxwell. Give him the best you've got."

"What about Mrs. Carter?"

"I'll go out and talk to her now."

"What about the Grahams?" Maxwell asked.

"I'll talk to Howard Graham," Trace said quickly.

"And . . . Jenny?"

Trace explained most of what had happened at Jenny's ranch, omitting the detail of their stirring encounter.

"What do you suppose he'll be up to next?" Maxwell queried.

"Doing his best to turn the ranchers against us one way or the other. Right now I don't think there is too much he wouldn't stoop to. There's something really big he wants to gain and right now I'm so damn mad I will move heaven and earth to find out what it is."

"I'd better get going," Maxwell said. "It takes times to sell a railroad to a rancher."

"Do a good job, Maxwell, or we won't have a railroad left to sell."

"Yes . . . I know," Maxwell agreed with a nod.

Maxwell mounted his horse and rode off. Trace had planned to go back to the hotel to talk to Allison, but the more he thought about it, the more urgent it seemed to see Joanne Carter first. He left town without talking to his sister, who had been waiting impatiently to tell him a secret she now realized she had kept too long. But it appeared she would be forced to wait still longer.

Hannah blinked open her eyes. She lay very still, trying to remember where she was and why she was there.

She lay on a blanket and had been covered by another. Slowly her mind cleared and she recalled the near rape she had survived, and the man who had rescued her.

She turned her head to see him kneeling by a fire. She watched him for a long while, enjoying the opportunity to do so without his awareness.

He prodded the fire with a stick, and it leapt and crackled to light his face with its glow. She studied his features silently for a long while. Then a gentle chuckle broke the stillness.

"What are you staring at, child?"

"I'm not staring," she quickly replied, surprised that he could know what she was doing without turning his head. "And I'm not a child!"

Now he laughed outright and rose to walk to her side. He squatted down near her.

"What were you doing out here alone?"

"I was on my way to see Mrs. Carter."

"And your father, after all the trouble that's been going on, let you go alone? You shoudn't have been allowed to go this time."

"I'm *allowed* to do as I wish," she said sharply.

"Don't get upset, little one," he requested with a grin.

"Stop treating me like I'm six!" she said, her anger surfacing.

"Would you rather I treated you the way your friend was planning on doing?"

Being reminded of the man who had assaulted her

caused her to sit up quickly and search about her. Fear was rampant on her face. She even forgot the fact that her dress had been torn and she was now revealing much of her body. Lucifer's smile faded and he reached to get the blanket and wrap it about her.

"Don't worry," he said gruffly. "He's dead."

She shivered at the deadly cold tone of his voice and the matter-of-fact way he spoke of death.

"Oh," she said weakly.

"Do you know who he was?"

"No . . . but he said . . . something."

"What?"

"Something about . . . the boss said to hold me for a few days . . . and to . . ." She shuddered.

"So," Lucifer said softly, "you were bait."

"Bait? I don't understand you. Please, take me home."

Lucifer contemplated this. If Taylor thought he had succeeded, he might play his hand. If Taylor thought he could, he might use Hannah as a club to make Jacob submit. As usual, he made his decision quickly.

"Sorry, little one, but I'm afraid you aren't going home. Not for a couple of days."

Her face grew pale and she raised her hands defensively before her. "You . . . you aren't . . ."

He laughed again and she found she liked the sound of it. Somehow she received the impression that he had not laughed much in a long time. Her tender thoughts faded at his next words.

"Don't worry. I don't molest children."

"I am not a child!"

"What are you, eighteen, nineteen?"

"Twenty!"

He looked at her and grinned.

"Well . . . nearly twenty," she added lamely.

"How near?"

"Almost."

"Near nineteen?"

"Almost."

He chuckled. "You're eighteen."

"Well," she cried defensively, "you're not much older."

Now it was his smile that faded as he reached out to touch her hair. "I'm a hundred years older than you, little one," he said gently. "A hundred long, hard years."

She looked up at him and what fears she had had suddenly vanished. She was certain he would not hurt her.

"Why don't you tell me why I can't go home?" She spoke the words with quiet assurance.

He looked at her for a long time, then his smile reappeared. Slowly he lowered himself to sit beside her.

"Yes, I think you have the right to know." He went on to explain who he thought was behind her attempted kidnapping and why he was going to let him think for a few days that his plan had been a success.

"Can you prove everything?"

"Pretty much. I just have to let him play out his hand. Are you afraid?"

"No," she said honestly, "I'm not. I'm just curious about what is going to happen."

"What I hope is going to happen is that we're going to join forces, the railroad and I; we're going to prove to Taylor Jessup that he can't run the world by using people."

He turned to look at her again. "I can bet he has already sent a ransom note to your family. I know they'll be scared, but it will only be for a little while."

"I understand."

"Do you?"

"Yes, I do. I want my father and the other ranchers to

see the truth. If I have to stay here with you for awhile, I'll do it. What about telling Trace Cord and Mr. Starett?"

"It's about time for that too." His thoughts began to wander then, and she was content to sit in silence and observe his changing countenance. Finally he returned his attention to her.

"I have a camp not far from here. If you're feeling up to it, we'll go there. Then I'll find some way to get you some clothes. Will you be afraid if I leave you alone for awhile?"

"Not if you promise to come back for me."

"You're trusting, little one. Sometimes that's dangerous."

"But not this time," she said mischievously. "You will come back for me?"

"Yes." He chuckled as he stood up. "I'll come back for you. Now come on, let's get moving."

It took them only a short time to travel to his camp. It was a well-chosen spot, one that would be easily defensible if necessary. He helped her dismount, then set about building a small fire.

"Now," he stated, "keep the fire going, but use these to feed it. I don't want smoke giving us away. Settle down and be comfortable."

"How long will you be gone?"

"A day, maybe a day and a half. There's some food here." He stood near her and reached to touch her hair as he studied her carefully. "You're not afraid?"

"No."

"Good girl. I'll be sure to get you something to wear. You look kind of innocent and pretty wrapped in a blanket, but I'd bet you'd prefer a dress."

"I would . . . but," she had suddenly become shy, "thank you for the compliment."

He smiled, then walked to his horse. In a few minutes

he was gone and she sat by the fire, content to think of her mysterious captor.

Lucifer returned to town, this time very stealthily, for he was quite certain Trace was somewhere near and he did not want to risk a three-way confrontation with Taylor and Trace.

"That would certainly upset the applecart," he mused softly as he closed his hotel-room door behind him. He was certain it would only be a matter of a short time until everything came to a head, and he did not want anyone to spoil what he had planned. We'll just let Taylor Jessup walk into his own trap, he told himself confidently.

He lay across his bed and folded his hands behind his head. It would be some time until it was dark enough for him to move about. Until then he would have to wait.

His satisfied expression faded to a more thoughtful look, and Hannah leapt uninvited into his mind.

She was a defiant child with a lot of courage, he reflected, and very pretty too.

Take it easy, he cautioned himself. She's not for you. You've got too damn many troubles to go sharing them with a girl who's little more than a baby. Besides, when all this is over, you'll have to be moving along before the law decides to look into your past. You have too many debts to pay and there's no room for a woman in your life. Besides—he chuckled aloud—she's not even a woman yet and you like your women a little more . . . knowledgeable.

He tried to eliminate her from his thoughts, but, despite his efforts, he found himself worrying about her.

*       *       *

Hannah too was caught up in thoughts of her mysterious savior. Who was he really? What connection did he have to all of this? He did not belong to the town, or the valley, or the railroad. He just seemed to be a black shadow on the periphery of the battle, yet he was having an effect on all the people involved. He was a puzzle, but a very intriguing puzzle.

She composed a picture of him in her mind and studied it. He was very tall, broad shouldered, and slim hipped. Even his limp added to his magnetic presence. His one blue eye was startling against his tanned skin and against the contrast of his ebony hair and beard. The patch over his other eye drew her as well, and she found herself wondering how he had been injured.

She found she was quite surprised by her reaction to him. He had very effectively kidnapped her and now she obediently sat out in the wilderness alone, waiting for the return of a man who was a complete stranger to her. She wondered at her trust in him, yet she knew not only that she trusted him completely, but that she sensed some tragedy, some very terrible hurt he seemed desperate to hide. Her instinctive urge was to comfort him, to ease what she saw in his face and felt in his presence, yet she knew that he thought of her as a child who needed protection herself.

She closed her eyes and created her own fantasy. In it her stranger smiled and his gaze warmed with the knowledge of her sensitive womanhood. After awhile she slept in the arms of her creation, wishing fervently for the real man to return.

## Chapter 30

Jacob and Howard had ridden slowly, for they had become engrossed in serious conversation. Howard was still doing his best to dissuade Jacob from even listening to the railroad people. Jacob, who had known Howard from the time they had set down roots in the valley together, sensed some strange compulsion in Howard but could not understand its cause.

"I can't see where the railroad can do us anything but harm," Howard maintained.

"I'll admit I've been thinking about all the problems they could cause," Jacob confided, "but it appears to me that even if I were horse trading I'd have to give the other man a chance to speak his piece."

"It's going to open this place up wide," Howard offered. It was a poor reason and he knew it.

"What do we have to lose? The land has been surveyed and filed. It's ours. So if other settlers come on, it will just build the town. I reckon as how that might be a good thing for us all."

"I'm against it, Jacob."

"Howard, you and I been friends a long time. Your word carries a lot of weight with me now that . . ."

"Now that I've taken hold of my life again," Howard

completed. "I had a hard time for awhile. My kids are what held me together." Howard could not mention Trace's influence and help, no matter how much he wanted to, for in Jacob's eyes that would only be a point in the railroad's favor.

"You got a good pair there." Jacob smiled. "Seems you and I are going to be having a wedding one day soon. It appears Buck and Emily have been making some plans without our knowing."

"Your daughter couldn't be getting herself a better man than Buck," Howard stated. "He's a good, honest man and one hell of a horse breeder."

"Yeah. I saw that first hand." Jacob went on to explain what Buck had done for his mare and Buck's subsequent request to marry Emily.

"You agreeable to it?"

"Sure am." Jacob laughed. "Seems Emily's in love with him, but"—his eyes twinkled with humor—"I think I'll be getting some help with my horses too."

Howard chuckled in response. "I wouldn't be surprised if Buck ended up with one of the best horse ranches in the territory."

"My girl will make him a good wife. I guess we could say we did all right for ourselves since we came out here in '47."

"It's been a long, hard fight, but I guess we did. I guess maybe that's why I'm so all-fired set against this railroad. The valley didn't need them before and we don't need them now. Let them go around Roaring Fork Valley and let us live in peace."

Jacob had no desire to argue with Howard, for though he saw that on the surface Howard protested, he believed that somewhere deep inside his friend was not as set against the railroad as he had claimed.

Upon their arrival in town they sought out Maxwell and Trace, only to learn they had both left the area a short time before. When they questioned one of the workers further, they discovered that somehow they had crossed Maxwell's trail and that he was on his way to see Jacob. "Trace," the man explained, "is on his way out to the Carter place. I expect they'll be back in two, three hours."

"Let's go over to the saloon and have a drink, Howard, and wait for them."

Howard agreed and they walked up the plank sidewalk to the saloon.


Maxwell was disappointed that he had missed Jacob, but he hoped he would find him in town when he returned. He was most anxious to try to soothe ruffled feathers. He had been nearly brought to a halt by one small group of ranchers in a valley, or worse, by someone who was using them, and he wanted to do something constructive about it.

After chatting politely with Beatrice Marshall for a short time, he left the Marshall ranch and headed back to town. He had only just ridden up to the track site when one of his men approached them.

"Jake," Maxwell called. "Any way of getting some work done today?"

"Well, I set the boys to clearin' off the twisted track. My God, that dynamite curled up that track like balin' wire. Anyway, once it's clear and if we get a little sun, maybe tomorrow we can get some new track laid. Those two cars is gone beyond help. There ain't nothin' left but a pile of junk."

"Well, keep on it. I think Trace is determined to start toward the valley within the next two or three days."

"I'll do that. Oh, by the way, there was a couple of gents around lookin' for you."

"Who?"

"Said their names was Jacob Marshall and Howard Graham."

"Lord!" Maxwell grinned. "I missed them again."

"Not exactly. They're over at the saloon, waitin' for you to get back."

This was the best news Maxwell had heard in the past few days. He thanked Jake and went to the saloon.

Once inside, he walked to the two men who sat together with a bottle between them.

"Gentlemen, I'm sure glad you decided to wait and talk to me. I've been looking forward to this for some time."

"Then sit down, Maxwell," Jacob invited, "and have a drink."

Howard was quiet. He liked Maxwell and wanted to discuss their mutual problem with honesty, but he could not. There was too much at stake.

Maxwell sat across the table from them. His experienced eye quickly told him that though Jacob might be interested in what he said, some kind of barrier stood between him and Howard. Maxwell was determined to break through it.

"You know without my telling you that I need to cross your valley," Maxwell began.

"I don't see the need," Howard argued. "If you can't go through it, then go around it."

"I can't do that, Howard. A railroad runs on a schedule. If I go around, it's going to cost me in both time and money. The money I can spare, but the time I can't. If I'm late to California, I lose everything."

"This valley means a lot to us," Jacob explained. "We don't want you doing harm, then going off and leaving us to face it."

"What harm can I do except buy a little land from you? If we can, I'd like to negotiate a good trail across your land, which," he explained, bending forward for emphasis, "you can choose. I'll be more than happy to show you the proposed route. We can talk about it. Nothing's fixed so that we can't change it. I want to work with you, not fight you."

"What about our water?" Howard said. "The river means a lot to all of us."

"We need water too, but we're more than willing to share, and to pay for our share. We only want to do good for this valley. The railroad is not here to take anything from you. This town can grow, and we'd like to help it grow."

"Seems to me you plan on going through whether we agree or not," Howard countered.

"Howard, I'll be honest with you. According to law, I can. But I don't want it to be that way. I want to leave friends in this valley."

Howard was trying to find a way to fight, but there was no solid ground on which he could stand.

"Howard," Jacob said, "suppose we look at these proposed routes, then go home and think it over."

"Sounds fair to me, Howard," Maxwell said. "All I want is that you understand my position and give it serious thought. We can work out a bargain where everyone benefits."

"Fair enough," Jacob said. "Let's look at those proposals, then Howard and I will talk about it. We'll think it over carefully."

"That's all I want," Howard asserted.

Maxwell took them to the hotel room and they painstakingly went over his maps. Later, as Maxwell stood at his window and watched them ride away, he was certain of two things. He had reached Jacob, but Howard had not been convinced. He also had a feeling there was more to his objection than the reasons Howard had provided. He only hoped Trace was having better luck with Joanne Carter.

\* \* \*

429

Jacob and Howard stopped when they reached the edge of the valley and each man turned toward his own home. Both were thoughtful.

"Howard, I'll ride over tomorrow night after we've both had a chance to think about this. We'll talk about it then," Jacob promised.

"All right, Jacob," Howard replied. He waved and started for home. Jacob watched him, wondering why Howard had pushed so strongly. Then he shrugged. His thoughts swung toward the railroad. He would do what he thought was best.

When Jacob arrived him, he walked into his house to find a situation that surprised him. His wife sat at the table in tears, and she ran to him when he came in and threw herself into his arms.

"Beatrice . . . honey . . . what's wrong?"

"Oh Jacob . . . my baby . . . Hannah . . ."

"Hannah!" Jacob cried in alarm. "What's happened to Hannah?" He gripped Beatrice's shoulders. "Is she . . . is she all right?"

"Someone"—Beatrice gulped—"someone has taken her."

"Taken! What the hell do you mean taken?"

"She . . . she's been kidnapped."

"How . . . ?"

"Someone threw a rock through the window a little while ago. It had a note attached. Oh Jacob, my little girl . . ."

Jacob almost tore the note from Beatrice's hand and read it quickly:

Stay away from the railroad. Make no deals if you want to see your daughter alive again.

He cursed violently and ran out of the house to gather some of his hands and begin a thorough search.

He had forgotten the railroad now, and everything else but the child he loved.

Howard dismounted wearily. He walked up the steps, across the porch and reached for the door. It was then he noticed it was torn from the hinges. In alarm he pushed it aside and went in.

"Jenny!" he called.

Jenny came from the bedroom, alarmed by the sound of anguish in her father's voice. Buck, who had been at the back of the house, heard the same sound of fear and ran in.

"Pa, what's the matter?" Jenny questioned.

"Sorry, girl. I saw the door and I was afraid. . . ."

"I'm all right, Pa," Jenny said. "It . . . it was an accident."

"Accident! What kind of accident could do that?"

Jenny couldn't think, but a quick-witted Buck came to her rescue.

"It was me, Pa. I was carrying in a load of wood and I tripped and fell up against the door and it gave. I'm sorry. I'll fix it later."

Howard was weak with relief to see that Jenny and Buck were all right.

"See you get it fixed before night, son. We don't want any night varmints roaming into the house."

"I was just about to fix it now, Pa."

Jenny cast Buck a look of gratitude that went unnoticed by Howard.

Buck had come home to find the door in its present condition and Jenny so quiet and reserved that he could not pry the story from her. She had simply asked him to fix the door and not ask questions. She had promised to tell him about it some other time. He had seen things in her eyes that he did not dare question at

431

that moment, and besides, he had his suspicions as to who had broken the door and why.

Buck set about fixing the door and Jenny occupied herself preparing the meal. When they all sat down to eat, they were an unusually quiet threesome. All three sensed the tension, yet none of them knew how to alleviate it.

At the end of the meal Jenny spoke. "Pa . . . Buck . . . I have some news for you."

"What kind of news?" Buck smiled. "I could use some good news."

"Well . . . I . . . I'm going to get married."

Both men were stunned into temporary silence. Then both made the same mistake at the same time.

"So," Howard concluded, "you and Trace have patched up your differences." He was grateful, for with Trace protecting Jenny, he could defy Taylor.

"That's the best news you could have given us," Buck said happily.

"Buck," Jenny began. "Pa . . . it isn't Trace."

Both men were again surprised and completely puzzled. They could not imagine any other man who had interested Jenny enough for her to agree to marriage.

"Just who is it then?" Howard questioned.

"It . . . it's Taylor Jessup," she said quietly.

Now both men were truly shocked. Howard rose abruptly to his feet. He slammed his hand down on the table so hard that both Jenny and Buck jumped. Their father's anger was something neither had seen very often.

"No, by damn!" he shouted. "You will not marry that man!"

"Pa!"

"I won't have it!"

"You don't understand, Pa," Jenny began. But she

could not tell her father the true reason she had agreed to marry Taylor. Jenny had never deceived or deliberately disobeyed her father before and she knew Howard was not going to understand when she did so now, though their security for the rest of their lives depended upon it.

Buck, who still watched in amazement, suddenly felt he was witnessing some sort of sacrifice, by his father as well as by Jenny.

"No, Jenny girl, you don't understand. I can't give you reasons now. I'm just telling you that you can't marry that man. It's wrong. You and I both know," he added in a much gentler voice, "that you are in love with Trace Cord."

Buck watched his sister's face grow pale and saw the white-knuckled hand that gripped the chair. But her voice was steady. She rose slowly to her feet and, containing her despair only by supreme effort, she spoke in a voice devoid of all emotion.

"Pa . . . whatever you think about me and Trace Cord just can never be. I am going to marry Taylor . . . and"—she inhaled deeply, fighting the tears that hovered close—"there is nothing you can do about it, Pa. I never defied you before, and I love you, but . . . I will do this. I only pray you try to understand. Don't hate me, Pa," she concluded in a whisper. "Don't hate me."

She turned and ran to her room and the door closed with a finality that shattered Howard.

Buck turned toward his father and saw a new kind of anguish distort his features. Howard was fighting the hardest battle of his life. He knew Taylor too well now, knew how twisted he was and how heartless. There was no way, ranch or no, that he would let Jenny go to Taylor. He made his decision. Now he would have to tell his son that to save Jenny from making a mistake for which she would pay the balance of her life they were going to have to take a step that would be painful. They would have to give up their home and their land and start their lives over.

He did not want to try to explain everything to Buck there, where Jenny could walk in at any time, so he said softly, "Son, let's go out to the barn. It's time I talked to you."

"Sure," Buck replied. He was still in a state of shock from what had just occurred. They walked to the barn in silence. Once inside, Howard lit a lantern and in the mellow glow of its light he tried to face his son's piercing gaze as he began to explain.

"Good God, Pa," Buck exclaimed when Howard had finished his exhausting revelation. "There's nothing worth Jenny's happiness. We can start over, move out of the valley, and find another place. But we can't let her give herself to him. Pa, if he blackmailed you, he sure as hell must be holding a club over Jenny's head. I'd bet it's the same one, and Jenny is ready to do this just to protect us."

"I know you're right. How are we going to convince Jenny not to do this?"

"Go to Trace," Buck said firmly.

"Maybe," Howard suggested, "she has already told Trace. Despite your attempt to take the blame for it, I have a feeling the door was broken by a visit from Trace. If she sent him away, then she's already told him."

"I don't think Trace would just walk away and take it that easily."

"From the looks of the door, I don't think he took anything easily."

"That was coming in." Buck grinned. "I got the feeling Jenny tried to close him out and he isn't a man to take kindly to slammed doors."

"I'm not worried about how he came in. I'm worried about how he left."

"If I know Jenny, she made a bargain and she'll do her damnedest to stick by it. I'm sure Trace was bucking up against a stone wall and left a little more than mad."

"Well, we've got to do something."

"What do you have in mind, Pa?"

"We're going into town and tell Trace the facts. Then we are going to tell Taylor Jessup to do what he pleases about our ranch because we intend to stand as a family. And as a family we are telling him to go to hell and do his damnedest. We'll stand together."

Buck smiled. He had never loved his father more than at this moment.

"All right, Pa. We'll do that."

Suddenly a voice came from the darkness beyond them. "I'd rather that you two didn't do anything for a little while longer."

Both men spun around, but neither could make out the features of the dark form that stood a few feet away. And they could not be sure he did not have a gun.

"Who are you and what are you doing trespassing on my property?" Howard demanded.

"I'm a friend, Mr. Graham, and if you two will stay calm, I'll tell you a much better plan to see to it that Mr. Jessup pays for what he's tried to do."

"I don't talk to shadows."

Lucifer chuckled and stepped into the light.

"I have a lot to tell you if you've a mind to listen. In another day or so all of this is going to blow. I think y'all had best know a little more."

"Suppose you sit down and tell us."

"If you promise to hear me out, then do what I tell you to do."

"That depends," Howard replied.

"On what?"

"On whether what you want us to do will help both my daughter and the rest of the ranchers in the valley."

"What I plan to do will help everybody involved, excluding Taylor Jessup, who has long deserved just what he's going to get."

Howard smiled for the first time. "Come on in then. I really think we do have a lot to talk about."

Lucifer moved closer. Buck had said nothing, but he had studied Lucifer closely. He knew he didn't know the man, but he was puzzled by the fact that something about him seemed so familiar.

Lucifer was aware that Buck's eyes had never left him and was not surprised by his question.

"Do I know you? Have we met somewhere before?" Buck queried.

"No . . . we've never met."

"You sure as hell look familiar."

"Well, that's not important now. I have a lot of things left to do to tie this all up, so let's get to it."

"We're listening."

In a few, well-chosen words Lucifer explained as much as he thought Howard and Buck should know.

"Now if you two will just keep quiet for another day or so, you might find that everything affecting your valley is going to work out fine."

"That's going to be hard to do if that man comes sniffing around my daughter. It would give me great pleasure to kill him, and if he tries to lay a hand on her I might do that."

"That's one place where I agree with my father," Buck added.

"Well, I'll tell you," Lucifer said with a smile, "Trace Cord is in love with your daughter and from all I've gathered I'm pretty sure she feels the same about him.

436

Taylor's no match for a man like Trace Cord. I have a hunch your daughter is more than safe, and that Trace has no intention of letting her go and, least of all, letting someone like Taylor take her away from him."

"You know Trace pretty well do you?" Buck asked. For some reason he still could not shake the idea that he should know this man.

"I know him well enough," came the noncommittal reply. Lucifer moved to leave.

"Wait a minute," Howard said. "We agreed to wait before we say anything about Taylor and Jenny. But you haven't told us just how he's going to be stopped and what your role is in all of this."

"I'm afraid I'm going to have to ask you to trust me for awhile."

"Trust a man who doesn't have a name?"

"Some call me Lucifer."

"Lucifer," Howard said softly. "One of the devil's sweeter names."

Lucifer shrugged. "It's just a name. You can see now that who I am doesn't matter. The welfare of Trace Cord and his sister Allison, comes first with me, and that means getting this whole nasty situation straightened out. If you'll let me, I'll help you. If you don't, I intend to help Trace anyway. He's a damn good man and he deserves whatever help he gets."

The soft tone Lucifer used when speaking Trace's name convinced Buck that whatever else this man said, he truly had Trace's welfare at heart.

"I agree," Buck said.

Howard looked at Buck and saw his son's conviction; then he returned his gaze to Lucifer. "All right. I agree too. We'll stay here until you send word. Then we come into town, right?"

"Right. You won't regret your confidence."

"I hope not."

"Good night, gentlemen," Lucifer said softly.

In a few minutes he had blended into the night.

Lucifer had tied his horse in the shadows beneath the trees not far from the barn. He moved swiftly to it, mounted, and headed for town.

It was a very surprised Allison who answered the light rap on her door and an even more startled one who listened to his request.

"One of my dresses? Whatever for?"

"Don't ask so many questions, Allison," he replied with an amused smile. "I need it. I'd like that pretty green one you wore a couple of days ago."

"Why the green?"

"Allison!" He laughed.

"All right, all right, the green one."

She went to the closet, removed the dress, and handed it to him.

"Thanks," he said sincerely.

"Are you going to see Trace soon?" she asked softly. Again he smiled at her.

"In another day or so this will all be over. What I'm doing, I'm doing for his good. You trust me in this, don't you?"

"Of course I do."

"Then go to sleep . . . and don't worry."

She watched him go, and for the first time in a long time she went to bed and slept without nightmares.

Lucifer rode through the night. He was anxious to see if he was right—if the color of the dress matched the deep green of eyes he remembered well . . . much too well.

*Chapter 31*

The evening meal was over and while Joanne put an overly excited Georgina to bed Will went to the barn to see to the last of the evening chores.

Finding out that Will was going to stay with them had sent Georgina into a realm of happiness. Joanne sat on the edge of her bed and prepared to tell her that Will was going to be much more than a friend.

She and Will had talked about it some hours before.

"Do you want me to tell her?" Will had asked.

"No, Will, no. This is not for you to do," she had laughed then and chided, "Oh Will, don't look so nervous. Georgina has come to love you."

"As a friend, sure," he had said worriedly. Then he had drawn her into his arms. "But what is she going to say about a man takin' her pa's place . . . sleepin' in her ma's bed."

"Oh Will," she had declared as she had slid her arms about his neck, "Georgina will feel as if she's acquired a new father. Neither of us," she had said in quiet seriousness, "will ever forget Jim, and Georgina will hold that love she had for her father always. But Will . . . she's so full of love, has so much capacity to give, that she'll have plenty of room in her heart for you to have a special place."

"I hope so," he had replied. Then he had concentrated on making sure Joanne's heart was filled with the love he had held at bay for so long.

Now Joanne sat by Georgina, who was quietly finishing her prayers. Then she looked up at her mother.

"Mama?"

"What, honey?"

"Will isn't going away, is he?"

"What makes you ask that, honey?"

"Well . . . you two have been whisperin' and . . ."

"Georgina, that's what I want to talk to you about."

"About whispering?"

"No." Joanne laughed. "About Will. You really like him, Georgina?"

"Oh yes."

"Maybe you love him a little?"

Georgina gulped. "Mama . . . do you think Daddy would care? I mean . . . I love him, Mama, but he's not here. Do you think Daddy would care if I loved someone else too?"

"No baby, he wouldn't care. Daddy would want you to be able to love someone."

"But I'll never forget Daddy."

"Of course you won't. Georgina, Will is worried."

"Will is worried?" Georgina couldn't quite believe this, for she believed that nothing could possibly shake Will. "About what?" she asked seriously.

"Well . . . you see . . . Will would like to marry me. He would like to be a father to you."

Georgina's eyes grew wide as did the smile on her lips. "For always?" she cried excitedly. "He won't go away?"

"No," Joanne assured her, "he won't go away."

"Oh, Mama, I would love that!"

"Good. Then when Will gets done with the chores, suppose we both tell him that we would love him to be part of our family."

"Oh yes, Mama! Yes!" Georgina cried as she sat up and threw her arms about Joanne's neck. They hugged each other and laughed with the pleasure of new-found happiness and hope for a future that held more than the fear and loneliness they had known for a long time.

Joanne told Georgina to be patient and when Will came back inside they would both come in to see her. Satisfied with this, Georgina curled up beneath the blankets and Joanne bent to kiss her.

When Joanne closed the bedroom door behind her she was humming softly to herself. She went to stir up the fire so the room would stay warm. She wanted to sit before it with Will tonight and make plans for their future.

The sound of a footfall outside the door caused Joanne to spin about with a smile on her face. She ran to open the door for Will. But when she flung open the door, she stood face to face with a total stranger.

She was so startled that for a moment she was speechless. She had started to ask who he was and what he wanted when he reached out and gave her a rough shove backward. Then he stepped inside and closed the door behind him.

"What . . . who are you?" she cried in alarm. "What do you want?" She wanted to scream for Will, but she was afraid the call would bring Georgina instead.

"I've come to give you a message."

"Message from whom?"

"From someone who doesn't want to see you and your little girl havin' more trouble than you do now."

Joanne was frightened, but she held herself in control for Georgina's sake.

"What is the message?" she demanded.

"You're to stay away from dealing with the railroad. You're to give the railroad no rights across your land."

Now Joanne was angry, for she had more than a suspicion of who might be behind this threat.

"You get out of my house," she said furiously, "and take a message back to your boss. Tell him I will do with my land whatever I choose."

The man grinned evilly. He had no idea that Will was anywhere near, for he had been told by Taylor that Joanne and Georgina lived alone.

"I was told you might be stubborn, so I'm supposed to teach you a little lesson."

He took several steps toward her and Joanne read the intent on his face. Again fear for Georgina overcame her urge to scream.

He moved closer, ever closer, and Joanne could not contain the absolute terror she felt. His hands reached for her and she fought wildly as he grabbed her. She could contain her fear no longer and, as his arms closed about her and roughly lifted her from the floor, she screamed as loud as she could.

Will opened the barn door and set about doing the chores as quickly as he could. Half his mind was on the work and the other half was on Joanne and the bright, loving future she offered him.

He began to build the ranch in his mind and to think of all the things he wanted to create. He thought of the loving life he would share with Joanne; just the idea of having Georgina for a daughter was more happiness than he ever expected to know again.

He whistled lightly through his teeth as he fed the horses and rubbed them down. When he had finished, he blew out the lantern and stepped outside the barn, preparing to close the door.

The sharp scream that cut the night jolted him and it took him a moment to realize it had come from the house. It was then that he saw the lone horse standing near the corner of the porch.

He dashed toward the house, running so fast he tripped up the steps, but that didn't reduce his speed. He slammed into the door and flung it wide. The sight that met his eyes brought a growl of animal ferocity from deep within him.

The last thing the intruder expected was to have Will storm into the house. He had Joanne bound with one arm and was preparing to strike her with his free hand. His head snapped around when Will entered and he just had time to drop Joanne before Will leapt upon him.

They tumbled to the floor together at the same moment Georgina's door opened and she came out of her room wide eyed at the sight before her.

Joanne ran to her and held her close while they watched the violent confrontation.

Will's fury was that of a wild animal and the man who battled him was suddenly made aware of it as Will's huge fists began to reduce him to blood-covered pulp. The intruder tried to defend himself and landed quite a few blows that drew blood, but Will was beyond reason now. He continued to pound on the assailant until he was the only force holding the man erect.

Will was beyond hearing and ignored Joanne's voice as she pleaded for him to stop. Someone had again tried to hurt what was Will's and he took out all his old frustrations on the now limp and defenseless form in his hands.

This was the scene that met Trace's eyes as he stepped into the open doorway.

"Trace," Joanne cried. "Stop him! Will's going to kill him!"

It took every ounce of Trace's strength to pull Will off his victim. He shrugged Trace off with his massive shoulders several times before Trace could get a good hold on him. Once he did, Will finally let the man drop into a crumpled heap on the floor.

Joanne ran to Will, who grabbed her close and rocked her against him. Blood ran from his nose and the corner of his mouth. One eye would soon be closed and black and his breath was coming in ragged gasps as Joanne tried to explain to Trace what had happened.

"Calm down, Joanne," Trace demanded gently. "Get some water and take care of Will."

She obeyed while Trace went to Georgina and lifted her trembling form in his arms to comfort her.

Soon all of them had regained their composure and could speak more clearly. Trace tied the intruder's hands behind him, intending to take him into town the next day. He planned to return the bloody man to Taylor and tell him such a threat would never work again.

"Will," Trace said in a tone that indicated he would not tolerate disobedience, "I want you to take Joanne and Georgina into town. Use the buggy and get a room at the hotel just for tonight. Maxwell will pay for it."

"What are you going to do, Trace?" Will questioned.

"I'm damn sick of all this," Trace said angrily. "It's time I called Taylor Jessup out. I don't know how many of the ranchers will be behind me, but—"

"This one will, I assure you." Joanne declared vehemently.

Will smiled at her through cracked lips. "You ready to fight, my love?"

"You bet I am!" Joanne stormed. "That man was ordered to do what he did. If you hadn't been here, Will, he would have beaten me and God knows what he would have done to Georgina. Besides"—she laughed

444

now at the warmth in Will's eyes—"he's spoiled a night I was hoping would be very special and I don't think I can let anyone get away with that."

Will smiled and pulled her close to him. He looked at Trace. "I believe the lady is quite angry."

"I believe she is." Trace concurred, grinning in return. He looked at Joanne. "Does this mean you'll consider giving us that right of way?"

"It does . . . if Will agrees. You see," she said as she gazed up into Will's adoring eyes, "the ranch will soon be Will's too."

"Will?" Trace asked.

"Right of way is yours," Will said in quick response.

"Good. Tomorrow Taylor Jessup is going to have a battle on his hands. I have to settle one thing with him that's more important than anything else."

"Jenny?" Joanne inquired with a bright smile.

"Jenny," Trace replied. "For some reason he has her convinced she's going to marry him."

"Marry him?" Joanne was aghast.

"Don't worry." Trace chuckled. "Jenny may be a little stubborn, but I am too. She'll never marry Taylor Jessup, and, if I have to, I'll kidnap her and tie her up for a week to convince her."

Joanne helped Georgina dress while Trace and Will hitched the buggy. Then Trace rode alongside the buggy into town. They left the intruder tied on the floor where he had fallen.


It was very near dawn and Lucifer rode through the pale moonlight with a smile of sheer wickedness on his face and a green dress tied in a bundle under one arm.

Before he had ridden out to redeem Hannah, he had sent several messages. By the time he got her back to town in the morning—possibly late morning, for he was extremely tired and intended to get an hour or two of sleep—there would be a confrontation that would surprise a whole lot of people.

Hannah had obediently kept the fire burning and was now sitting near it. She was not one who enjoyed enforced inactivity, but she truly had had no choice. She could have tried to make her way home, but she had not for she had believed what her captor had told her.

She wondered at herself and what all the young friends she knew would think if they were to discover that quiet little Hannah Marshall had tumbled head over heels for a man who had no name and might not even be around the next day. In fact, she mused silently, he had never given one single hint that he even found her attractive. Instead he called her "child" or "little one," as if she were a baby.

He can't be more than . . . twenty-seven or twenty-eight, she speculated. How can he call me a baby? She asked herself the question merely in self-defense, for she had understood quite well what he had meant when he had said he was a hundred long, hard years older than she.

She had sensed pain; she had sensed an unsettled despair and a deep loneliness, and she would have given years of her life to have touched him somehow, forced him to surrender that part of him that was damaged and allow someone else to rebuild it and help heal the pain.

She sighed and stood up to throw more twigs on the fire. For awhile she remained standing to stretch muscles that were stiff from sitting. Her eyes studied the night about her. The black velvet sky seemed an ocean on which floated a million tiny bursts of light and a warm breeze rustled the trees about her.

"What a beautiful night," she murmured aloud.

"It's almost as pretty as you, little one." The warm voice from behind her caused her to spin about in surprise.

"You scared me," she said. "I didn't hear you come."

He stood just within the circle of light with a bundle under his arm.

"You would be quite a target, little one. Anyone who wanted to sneak up on you could have."

"Well, I'm sorry," she retorted. "I'm not used to being careful. And I'm not afraid. . . ." She stopped talking immediately when she saw his smile fade. Again she was sorry for her foolish words. No wonder, she thought miserably, that he considered her a little girl. She could not control her own words.

He tossed the bundle to her and she caught it, loosening the blanket that was wrapped about her.

In the glow of the firelight he could not miss the creaminess of her exposed flesh.

"Change your clothes," he said gruffly. She bit back words of regret and stepped out of the ring of light to obediently change into the dress he had brought.

He knelt by the fire and stirred it to a new brightness. He could hear the rustle of the dress and he envisioned what he would have seen if there had been daylight. He let his senses hold her image for a moment, then he pushed the picture away. He could not afford an entanglement—not with a sweet innocent like this. There was too much that would always stand between them.

When she stepped back into the firelight he smiled in satisfaction.

"I knew I was right, little one," he said. "You do look very pretty in green . . . and it does match your big green eyes."

"Are you laughing at me?" she asked suspiciously.

"Whatever gave you that idea?" he retorted, unable to quell his chuckle.

She went to him and he had to stand in the face of sincere anger. He also had to admit that she made a picture he would not soon forget, and she faced him with words for which he was completely unprepared.

"I don't know why I irritate you like I do, but I didn't ask to be put in this position and I think I'm being very much a lady to be rational after I've been grabbed, almost molested, and forced to stay by this fire for hours with no answers. Just what is it you expect it will take for me to grow up?"

His eyes lost their wary coldness and reflected sympathetic respect.

"I'm sorry. I didn't mean to upset you."

"You didn't upset me." Her voice softened. "I'm not a foolish child . . . please don't treat me like one."

She stood too close. She was too vulnerable and sweet, and he was tired and his control was at its lowest ebb. He knew it was wrong, but he reached to draw her forbidden softness into his arms.

Their lips met gently and Hannah had never experienced anything so sweet. His arms felt like iron bands about her and his lean, hard body pressing close to hers gave her the feeling that her bones and sinew were melting to fold about him. Slowly her lips parted and his tongue explored the moist inner flesh of her mouth.

He had been lonely too long and had been hurt too deeply, and suddenly the realization of what he was doing exploded in his mind. He was actually trying to seduce a child whose experience amounted to nothing in comparison to his.

He gripped her slim waist in both hands and moved her away from him. They gazed at each other helplessly, for both were still within the grip of an amazing force—a force he could not allow to overcome him.

"Little girls shouldn't play with fire," he cautioned with an amusement in his voice he certainly did not feel. "You might just get burned."

He watched anger leap into her eyes and it pleased him. It was an emotion he could handle much better than the meltingly sweet longing he had seen before. But she verbalized anger in a way he had not expected.

"My dear man of mystery," she said, "I don't know which of us is afraid of fire, me . . . or you."

It was a challenge given by a woman who had never tasted love and he knew it. To save Hannah from future hurt, he was prepared to frighten her now, frighten her enough to help him keep his own control.

He reached to grip her shoulders and jerked her against the breadth of his hard, muscular chest. His arms closed about her, crushing the breath from her, and his mouth, deliberately cruel and nearly brutal, ravaged hers so thoroughly that she nearly fainted. She held him only to support her body, which grew weak beneath his attack. Slowly he dragged her to the ground. She grew panicky and began to fight. But he had not fightened her enough. His hands, searching beneath her skirt, found her body and caressed it roughly. He was thorough, very thorough, for he could hear her begin to cry and felt her body tremble in fear beneath his.

It was only then that he sat up and drew her into a sitting position. Her face was tear stained and she stared at him with eyes so full of sadness that he could hardly bear to look.

He gripped her face in one hand and forced her to meet his gaze.

"This is not the game you should be playing," he said roughly. "Don't pretend to play unless you know the rules. Don't get into something you're too young and sweet to handle. You're a sweet young girl." His voice became more gentle. "Find a nice boy and settle down. Don't look for adventure." He laughed harshly. "It's not too much fun when you find it."

He rose and went to his horse to retrieve some food he had brought. He did this so that she would not see the longing in his own eyes.

She wept softly, for both of them. She had wanted to but had not been able to reach past the barriers he had set. She felt she had to know why.

"Come over here by the fire," he said. "You have to eat. We are going for a short ride pretty soon."

"Where?"

"Into town. I want you safe in a room before daylight. Tomorrow is going to be a busy day."

"I don't understand what is going on."

"It's all right, little one. Trust me."

"Trust you?" She laughed a bubbling, almost wicked, laugh and he found himself laughing with her. They laughed because neither could cry.

They sat across the fire from each other, and ate. He refused to meet her eyes, for he knew it would be too easy to get lost there.

After they had finished, he tossed dirt on the fire to extinguish it. He mounted his horse and with very little effort he lifted Hannah up before him and settled her comfortably. Then he kicked the horse into motion.

She leaned back against him and enjoyed the strength of the arm that curved about her waist. Tired, she let her head rest against his chest and could hear the solid, steady beat of his heart.

They rode without talking, each enjoying the fact that they were close.

Too soon, Lucifer was drawing his horse to a halt behind the hotel. He cautioned Hannah to be careful and to be silent. Then he tied his horse, took her hand, and led her up the darkened back steps.

They made their way to his room and, once inside, he closed and locked the door behind him.

"Now what?" she questioned.

"Now you make yourself comfortable. I have already sent a message to your father that you are safe and will be returned to him tomorrow night. Believe me, I told him where I would bring you tomorrow night, and he will be here."

"Will . . . will you stay with me?" she asked timidly.

"I had planned on it, but I think, under the circumstances, that it would be better if I slept elsewhere."

"Where will you go?"

He went to her and stood very close.

"Kitten, I'm sorry to have put you through all of this. I suppose I should have taken you home the day I found you. I was being selfish. I needed you to help someone who needs help. But I'm sorry if you've been been hurt by all of this." He took both of her hands in his and held them close to his chest. "Hannah, look at me."

She lifted her eyes to meet his and he saw her heart in them. He fought the desire to hold her. Instead he spoke softly, using very gentle words meant to ease her.

"Hannah, you are one of the most beautiful women I have ever known. You have a loving heart. I don't want you to waste it. You deserve so much better than that. I want you to forget me, for my life is something you could not live with. One day someone will come along who is right for you. When it happens, he'll be a very lucky man. For now, you are safe and no harm has been done. Hannah, forget me, for we could never have a life together . . . not like you know it, and I won't drag you into mine."

He bent to brush a light kiss across her lips, then he turned, unlocked the door, and left. She heard the key click in the lock again and she gazed at it for a long time. Then she touched her fingers to her lips.

"No," she whispered, "no . . . I will never forget you."

## Chapter 32

Less than an hour before Lucifer arrived at the rear of the hotel, Trace and Will arrived at the front with Joanne and a sleeping Georgina.

Trace dismounted and lifted Georgina in his arms while Will helped Joanne down.

"I'll take her in if you'll see to the horses, Will," Trace whispered.

"I'll go and help him," Joanne said. "Will you be all right?"

"With one little girl?" Trace laughed. "I think I can manage."

His own devilish sense of humor took control of him at that moment and he went in to tell the desk man that he needed one more room. The wide-eyed man handed him a key. When he carried Georgina upstairs, he took her directly to Allison's room. He kicked at the door and Allison opened it.

"Trace . . . what . . . ?" She found she was no longer surprised by anything that happened in this town.

"This child needs a place for the night. You have a big bed. Can she share it?"

Allison laughed. "Would it make much difference if I said no? Bring her in."

453

Trace did. Gently he laid Georgina on the bed. "Can you get her undressed and tucked in?"

"I'll do my best," Allison said dryly.

"Thanks." Trace grinned and kissed her cheek. Then he was gone as quickly as he had come.

"I'd like to know what's going on around here," Allison said in mild frustration. Then she set about getting Georgina ready for bed.

Trace met Will and Joanne on their way up the steps.

"Is Georgina all right?" Joanne questioned.

"She's fine. Sleeping like a baby . . . in my sister's bed."

"Your sister . . . ?" Joanne began. "But . . ."

Trace reached out and took Joanne's hand. He placed the key in it and grinned.

"Good night, Joanne . . . pleasant dreams. We'll talk about a right-of-way in the morning."

He passed them and was gone. Joanne looked at the key for several moments, then her eyes rose to Will's questioning ones and she smiled.


The streets were dark and completely deserted, but from where Trace stood he could see the glow of tent fires made by the workers who camped near the tracks. He was quite certain Maxwell would be there so he walked toward the brightness.

He was right. Maxwell was getting a report on the day's accomplishments, which had been minimal.

They had tried to clear away some of the twisted tracks, but slippery footing had made it very nearly impossible.

Maxwell had finally given orders that everyone was to bed down for the night so they could get a fresh start in the morning.

He was about to return to the hotel and get some

sleep when he saw Trace approaching.

"Damn," he growled at Trace. "This soft ground has slowed things down."

"I know," Trace replied, "but it's clear tonight and tomorrow will most likely be dry."

"And a damn lot of good it's going to do. The only rancher that I even half suspect might be with me is Jacob. Howard Graham was as stubborn as a mule."

"I think it's likely that Jacob will let us through; in fact, I don't think he was so dead set against it at the beginning. I can tell you something else, though, that might make you feel better. Joanne and Will are going to get married . . . and they're going to give us the right-of-way across their land, so that makes two out of three."

"And what can we do about the Grahams?"

"There's a problem there that I intend to have solved tomorrow."

"Oh? And how do we intend to do that?"

"I'm going to put a stop to Taylor Jessup, one way or the other."

"I don't like the sound of that, Trace. I want to know what you've got in mind."

"He's blackmailing Jenny," Trace grated, "and I have a suspicion, after what you just told me, that he's got some sort of a club over Howard's or Buck's head as well."

"It's certain we can't get through this valley without all three in agreement. What sort of hold could he have over any of them?"

"For Jenny," Trace said thoughtfully, "it's some concern about protecting her family or her home. No, the real problem is either Howard or Buck, but I have no idea which one, or why. You can bet I'm going to find out."

"Trace, how do you know he's blackmailing Jenny?"

"I asked Jenny to marry me. She refused."

"That hardly means she's being blackmailed."

"I'll tell you why she refused."

"She doesn't want to get married?" Maxwell asked with a touch of humor.

"No, she intends to marry." He turned his head so his eyes met Maxwell's. "She intends to marry Taylor Jessup."

"For God's sake!" Maxwell groaned. "If he holds the Graham land, we might just as well forget it, and our railroad as well."

"He'll never hold the Graham land," Trace said coldly. "I intend to see to that."

"Don't do anything foolish. He might be pushing you into something so he can get rid of you. He knows how much I need you."

"He's doing just that. But in this case he has underestimated his enemy. Jenny belongs to me. He could have fought me by any other means and I would have respected it. But not by using Jenny . . . not by trying to hurt Jenny."

"Trace, I know you love her. I just wish there were some way we could find out what hold he had."

"I'll find it . . . and I'll break it."

Maxwell gazed at Trace's immobile face and experienced an inner fury that left him shaken. He was torn between the welfare of his railroad and the welfare of a man he had begun to think of as a son.

"Trace, tomorrow we'll talk to them all."

"Joanne and Will are here in town."

"They are?"

Trace went on to explain the confrontation between Joanne and the man who had been sent to force her to comply with Taylor's wishes.

"Oh, he never mentioned Taylor's name, even after Will almost beat him to death. But we all knew who was responsible. Anyway, I thought it would be best to have them stay in town until we've brought an end to this mess."

"Wise idea."

"We have Will and Joanne's support, especially after tonight. Will is in a murderous mood and, if Taylor pushes him, I'm afraid he's going to get pushed back."

"So," Maxwell said in a relieved voice, "let's go back to the hotel and get some sleep. Maybe we can take care of everything tomorrow. There must be a way, and we'll find it."

"You're right there, Maxwell . . . I'll find it."

They walked back toward the hotel. Their rooms were on the same floor so they walked up the steps together. At his door, Maxwell stopped, then looked at Trace.

"Son . . . be careful. Taylor will do whatever he thinks he has to. He has motives we don't understand. Whatever they are, I don't want you to be hurt. We can sacrifice everything, except lives. Neither my railroad nor anything else is worth your life."

"Thanks, Maxwell. I'll be fine. I have to stop him, anyway I can, with whatever means I have to use."

Maxwell clapped him on the shoulder. "Just be careful, will you?"

"I'll do that."

Maxwell entered his room and shut the door and Trace continued down the hall to his own room.

He stood outside his room for several seconds, not quite sure if he were simply tired, or whether he had really heard the rustle of movement just before he had reached the door.

If Taylor had sent someone to get rid of him, Trace was now in the proper mood to handle it.

He drew his gun, reached slowly for the doorknob, then in one swift movement he was inside the room. He found himself standing nearly face to face with Jenny.

Jenny had been as much surprised by her defiance of her father as he had been. She stood behind her closed door, numb for a moment at the avalanche of uncontrollable events that had so drastically changed her life.

She clasped her hands before her to halt their trembling. She had never been weak, or prone to tears at the least thing, but she fought tears now.

She thought of Taylor and his threat and knew she had to comply with his wishes. But such thoughts were combined with visions of Trace, Trace with his sensitive kisses and the magic touch of his hands that could send her into a brilliant world of ecstasy.

Soon she would be Taylor's wife. But now her heart belonged to someone else and she despaired to think of facing all the empty tomorrows without touching once again the love that would be forever forbidden to her.

She wanted to be in his arms just once more. She wanted to love him just once more. Then and only then would she have the strength to go on with what she must do.

She heard her father and brother leave the house. From her bedroom window she saw them walking to the barn. She believed they were simply finishing their evening chores.

She settled herself as best she could to wait out the interminable time until they would retire for the night.

To her it seemed like hours that she paced the floor and watched from her window for their return.

Finally she was rewarded when the barn door opened and they came out. They were talking together

458

as they walked across the wide area between the house and the barn.

She heard them enter, then move about. Please, she thought wildly, go to bed . . . *please.*

Her taut nerves were nearing the breaking point when she heard their individual doors close and the house grow quiet.

She forced herself to wait one more hour, which took all the patience she possessed. Then she opened her door and looked out into the darkened house.

Very slowly she made her way across the bare wood floor. To her every creak of every board on which she stepped seemed to echo through the house.

Finally she was outside, and she made her way quietly down the steps, then broke into a run toward the barn.

She saddled her horse and led him far enough away from the house so the hoofbeats would not be heard. Then she mounted and rode toward town.

On the edge of town she found a shadowed place and hobbled her horse so it would not stray far before she returned.

She made her way along the dark plank sidewalk until she came to the hotel. Now she was faced with the problem of finding Trace's room and getting to it without being seen.

She peered around the front window of the hotel and searched for the man who worked at the desk. For several minutes she did not see him, then she spotted him sitting behind the desk with his feet propped up. He was asleep, or at least she hoped he was asleep.

She opened the door quietly, stepped inside, and closed it just as quietly behind her. Slowly, one quiet step after another, she made her way across the room toward the large book that lay on the desk and held the names of the guests and their room numbers.

The desk clerk stirred and mumbled something in his sleep, and Jenny froze until he again slipped back into deeper slumber. Then she continued her progress across the room. She was shaking by the time she reached the book and turned it to face her. She read Trace's name and the room number.

With one eye on the clerk, she backed toward the steps. When she reached them she turned and began to climb.

His door was locked tightly, and she wanted to scream and smash it. Then she saw the open window at the end of the hall. She went to it and looked out. The first floor of the hotel had a wide front porch and the roof of that porch was just below her. To her extreme relief she saw that it led all the way across the hotel.

She raised the window higher and stepped out on the porch roof. Quickly she made her way to Trace's window. She breathed another sigh of relief when she found the window slightly open. She lifted the sash and climbed over the window sill, then closed the window behind her. Now she would wait.

In the pale moonlight she could see forms about her and slowly her eyes adjusted to the semi-dark.

The room held the scent of him, a masculine scent of tobacco and leather, the fresh breeze and the pines. She could almost close her eyes and feel his presence beside her.

What she was doing was deadly dangerous and she knew it, but she had to have one last sweet memory to carry with her through the difficult years she knew were ahead. She had to feel his touch once more so she could recall it with another's touch defiled her.

The minutes seemed to drag by. No sound came from the street or from the hotel. To Jenny it seemed as if the world slept, and she wanted it to remain so. She did not want the world and its confusion to spoil this one last night of passion and love.

Then the sound of men's voices in low conversation came to her. Was someone coming back to his room with him? she wondered in panic. No, she decided, for the voices had ceased and only one set of footsteps approached the door.

She stood still, scarcely daring even to breathe. Was he still angry? Would he reject her now that she had vowed to marry his enemy?

Her heart pounded as she heard him pause. She had an instinctive feeling that he sensed someone was waiting for him.

Suddenly the door swung open and he stood before her in the doorway with a gun in his hand that he pointed at her.

She stood in the darkness between him and the window, and she was nothing more to him than a shadowed form, but . . . did he know the sweet scent of her? Yes. Did he recognize the slim form without knowing why? Yes again.

"Jenny?" he whispered in ragged disbelief. He stepped inside quickly and closed the door behind him. Now they stood in silence in a room lit only by one beam of pale gold moonlight.

He could not believe his eyes, nor could he believe his senses, which told him that the dream he carried with him always stood just within his reach.

"Jenny," he whispered again, this time in a tone laced with emotion he was trying his best to contain. He did not move, for he was still unsure she was not a figment of his imagination.

He saw the shadowed form move toward him. Then suddenly she was in his arms and he was crushing her to him. His mouth sought and found the soft, giving one

461

she raised to him. She gave a low, wordless moan as his mouth tested the softness of her lips, warming her until she was mindless under the persistence of his caress.

He was completely engrossed in the pleasure of having her in his arms and exuberant that she had chosen to come to him. Trace gave no thought to the reasons she might have had. He was content for this moment to hold her and to savor her lips. Only when he had regained some control over his wayward emotions did he begin to wonder why.

He held on to her hand and drew her with him to the table where the lamp sat. He removed the glass chimney and turned up the wick. Then he struck a match and lit it, and its light cast a mellow glow through the room. As he replaced the chimney, he lifted his eyes to hers.

A puzzled frown formed on his face, for her eyes told him nothing. A faint touch of alarm rippled through him, but he smiled despite it.

"I'm glad you came, Jenny. I'm glad you've finally seen the truth, that we belong together."

"Trace . . . I . . . I haven't changed my mind."

His smile faded as he slowly digested her words, but the callused fingers that circled her wrist tightened.

"I don't understand."

Her eyes pleaded with him to try to understand this need she could not deny, this hunger he had awakened in her that only he could feed, and she prayed he would accept the condition that they could only have this one last night.

Trace understood all too well her burning urgency to consummate the gnawing desire that had drawn her here, but he could not read the rest of her thoughts.

"Please, Trace . . . don't make it so difficult."

"Difficult?" he repeated slowly, then his eyes brightened with his comprehension of her intention and the anger that followed. "So it's more games you're playing?"

"No," she gasped raggedly, "this is no game."

Slowly he was pulling her toward him. "Good God, Jenny, are you foolish enough to believe that this could ever be the end? Do you believe I would let you go back to him?" He pulled her against him now and she closed her eyes as his breath touched her cheek and his voice lowered to a rough whisper. "Do you believe after what we have shared that you can come here and touch my life again and I will let you go? No, Jenny, I don't think I could do that."

"Trace. . . ."

He lifted her chin so that her eyes met his. His mouth was grim and his eyes pierced her like a sword. "Am I to spend the rest of my life thinking of you in his arms? Am I to awaken in the night and know that you're with him, that he is holding you, kissing you, loving you. No Jenny, this time you ask what is beyond me to give."

Her eyes filled with tears and she tried to move from his arms. "Then my coming here was a mistake."

"Why did you come?"

"I. . . ."

"Why did you come, Jenny?"

"Don't," she sobbed.

"I'll tell you why. Because neither of us can be whole without the other. You're lying to yourself if you think it can be so. You came"—his voice lowered as his arms came about her to bind her more tightly to him— "because you know it is right. You know that when we are together we're close to heaven. And you are asking me to consider hell as a good trade? I won't do that, Jenny. You told me before that I wanted all. Well, I do. And you have come here because you cannot accept less either. You're here, Jenny . . . and you'll stay."

"No, I can't. Oh, Trace, you are right about so many

463

things. I cannot lie about what I feel for you, but isn't there room in your heart for you to understand that there are some things you cannot control?" His arms held her close and she lifted her arms to place her hands against his beard-roughened cheeks. "Love me now, tonight, and let's forget all the tomorrows. Love me now," she whispered as she drew his head down to hers.

He made an inarticulate sound that was half anger and half uncontrolled passion as his mouth took hers with a fierce passion that stormed her senses. His lips were insistent, relentless, demanding. She could not breathe, nor could she fight reason any longer. She was devoured by a searing flame that left her weak and defenseless against its onslaught.

Her hands slipped beneath the rough fabric of his jacket to caress his sides; then she ran her hands up over the breadth of his chest, forcing the jacket off.

In an urgency well beyond control, they fumbled to unbutton buttons, to cast aside unwanted clothing that restricted the touch of flesh against flesh each desired.

The feel of her velvet skin beneath his hands and the way her body arched to meet him was heady wine to his already drunken senses. He lifted her from the floor with one swift motion and in moments she found herself pinned beneath a hard body that to her was a most welcome weight.

His mouth explored her body, the shadowed curves and taut peaks, until a fire was stirred that raged out of control. Now tomorrows did not matter; words and games did not matter; this all-consuming fire swept such thoughts away.

The sweetness of complete surrender, the aching bliss of discovery, overwhelmed them both. She took him within her to merge and mingle their separate needs and made them one. With rhythmic movements he blended them together into a soaring oneness and the night dissolved before a tempest that tossed them heavenward and sent them floating gently downward into a sea of contentment.

Their breathing slowly quieted, their bodies, sweat slicked and trembling, grew still, yet they held each other in a silence neither wanted to break. To rupture it now meant to face reality, and reality held no answers.

"Trace . . ." Jenny finally began.

"Shh, love," he whispered against her hair. "There will be time tomorrow to talk. For now let's not question this. Let's keep this night."

"Tomorrow," she said in a shattered voice.

"Need never come if we don't let it," he finished with gentle assurance.

"You will not listen to me," she replied in a despairing voice.

"About your leaving me, belonging to someone else? No, I will not listen."

He rose on one elbow and while his free hand gently and possessively caressed her skin, he smiled into her eyes.

"You can try to lie to yourself all you want, Jenny, but this"—he bent to brush her lips with his—"is not a thing you can simply choose to give. It is a rare and very special thing that happens between Fate-chosen lovers. You are as much a part of me as the air I breathe or the beat of my own heart. To lose you would be to lose a part of myself that is irreplaceable. I won't let that happen . . . no matter what you do."

"Do you think I can deny what exists between us?" she demanded brokenly. "Do you think I would have come here if I thought I could banish you from my life easily. I thought—"

"You made the same mistake once before. You thought one more night, one more taste, would make it easier. Don't you know that one night, a million nights,

465

will never set you free?" He added gently as he drew her against him, "Don't you know yet that I will never set you free?"

She gave a soft moan as their lips blended in a gentle yet sensuous kiss. In her mind she made promises that tomorrow she would face reality. But for tonight there was Trace . . . and love—love to hold forever against whatever the future might bring.

## Chapter 33

Lucifer propped a pillow behind him and rested back against the headboard of the bed. He watched Eileen as she brushed out her hair. Then she rose with a smile and slowly dropped the robe she wore to the floor.

For a moment Lucifer's smile wavered as he saw the wide green eyes and slim form of another, then he deliberately blocked Hannah from his mind.

Eileen was the kind of woman he knew best, one who enjoyed pleasure without rules, one he could leave without the fine threads of emotion entangling him. He would have no sleepless nights or forbidden thoughts about Eileen, as he would have had with— Again he pushed her away as he reached for the woman who bent near.

He had deliberately chosen to go to Eileen so that she would wipe away the gentle touch of Hannah's lips. He knew Hannah could never be a part of his life and the sooner he erased the tender threads of memory she had woven in his mind the better it would be for both of them.

What could he ever offer Hannah—a life of running and hiding, of being afraid? A life filled with the torture of memories he was still trying to exorcise?

No, he would not put her through that. She deserved far more than he would ever be able to offer her, and he would not sacrifice her happiness, although, for one moment he had allowed himself the pleasure of knowing she would have gone with him if he had asked it of her. It had been a balm to soothe his frayed spirit and he had held it for a moment then had let it go, placing it with other beautiful memories that could never be relived again.

Eileen and Lucifer met in a storm of wild lust, and Eileen never knew that, despite his attempts to the contrary, the man she called Lucifer envisioned someone else within his arms and yearned for the taste of sweeter lips.

Afterward they lay together. Lucifer was tired, but both he and the woman in his arms had motives behind their meeting that went beyond the physical attraction.

"Lucifer?"

"What?"

"Has Taylor approached you about Trace Cord and Maxwell Starett?"

"What do you mean 'approached'?" he questioned with irritating amusement in his voice.

"You know very well what I mean," she said half angrily. She could not be too firm with Lucifer, for she had quickly realized that he would turn and walk away. She had found him too hard to handle, and yet he could ignite her passion to a degree that no one else had ever achieved. She had to admit he was an expert lover.

Moreover, she wanted to use him to rid herself of Taylor. Her anger at Taylor had simmered for a long time and she knew now that she could accomplish what she wanted as well with Lucifer at her side as with Taylor.

She traced her fingers seductively across his chest and down his lean body until she touched him and felt him stir beneath her hand. "He wants you to rid us of the problems of Trace Cord and Maxwell Starett," she said softly.

His chuckle was a low rumble in his chest.

"Does he? Maybe it is time to bring an end to these problems."

"Lucifer, there are other problems we can discuss."

"Such as?"

"Such as what you can do for yourself. Why do you continue to take orders from Taylor when you could do more?"

"What is this 'more' that you're talking about?"

"Listen to me," she said smoothly. "No matter what you claim about yourself, I can see good breeding and brains for myself."

He stiffened in expectant silence. Did she know more about him than he wanted her to know?

"You can have more," she continued enthusiastically, "than you have ever dreamed of having. There is wealth here beyond what you can imagine and a chance to snatch incredible power, power so great one can barely dream of it."

"What makes you think I can handle that?"

"I can help you handle it. The name Starett carries a great deal of prestige. Within that prestige you could discard the ragged disguise you carry. We can work together. We can have it all. And all"—she laughed softly—"is more than even your wildest fantasies can imagine."

"It sounds intriguing," he said casually, trying to urge her to a more detailed confession.

She was caught up in convincing him and with the intoxicating aura of his strength as his hands continued to assault her senses in a slow, deliberate exploration. His lips played upon her and teased her as he continued to entice her to reveal more.

"Just what is this we are going to share?" he whispered huskily.

She laughed exultantly, feeling that he was hers, completely unaware that he would never belong to anyone but himself. She spoke to him of causes and reasons, told him of plots that drew his interest, and he listened very, very closely.

"We must get rid of Trace Cord and Maxwell Starett," she explained, "but, more important, we must get rid of Taylor Jessup."

So, he thought to himself, the rats turn on each other when the cheese is to be shared. I wonder how long it will be until she turns on me?

These thoughts were covered well by the smile he wore. "You have plans you'd like to tell me about?"

"I do." She laughed softly. "If you'd care to listen."

"Oh, I'd care to listen." He answered her laugh with one of his own. "You have no idea how interested I am."

"I can arrange a private meeting between you and Taylor . . . someplace quiet, out of the way."

"Then?"

"Then you kill him," she said.

"And after that?" His casual tone matched hers, but he was disgusted by her brutal attitude and by the suspicion that she would use him as easily as she had used Taylor—for as long as he remained useful to her.

"After that, you will see to the demise of Trace Cord and Maxwell Starett . . . and I will see to everything from then on."

"That will bring an end to the railroad here. I thought the railroad would be important to you and your uncle."

"My uncle," she spat angrily, "the greedy old miser. He won't have any control over my money when he is gone. As for the railroad," she added, "there is another line ready to take over—a line I will own much of. And, as my uncle's heir, I will sell the Starett line. You can share all this and more."

"And all I have to do is take care of these three men."

"That's all."

"Seems like a good arrangement. I'll see to it that Taylor gets what he richly deserves, and I'll personally take care of Trace Cord and Maxwell Starett and their railroad expansion into the valley."

"Good! Now"—she curved one slim, bare leg over his body and reached to draw her head to his—"we can get on to better things."

With slow deliberation Lucifer brought Hannah to his mind. He made love to her because if at that moment he had had to make love to Eileen, it would have sickened him.


Jacob Marshall stared in shock at the message he held in his hand. He had read it over, but he had had to read it again to force himself to believe it:

Your daughter is safe. I will care for her until you can meet us tomorrow at dawn. Meet us at the schoolhouse on the edge of town.

Trace


Jacob was totally exhausted from his search for Hannah. He could not imagine how Hannah could be with Trace Cord, but he was relieved that he had some tangible evidence that she was safe.

"This is damned amazing," he muttered.

"Pa, is Hannah all right?"

Emily too was beside herself with fear and wished for morning so she could see Buck.

"Seems she is," Jacob said with a puzzled frown.

"Seems she's with Trace Cord, and he says we can pick her up tomorrow at dawn. Just like that. No reason for her kidnapping, no word about her, just . . . meet us at the schoolhouse at dawn."

"Then we'll meet him at dawn," Emily said. "If Trace has found her, I'm sure she's all right, or he would have told us so."

"This still strikes me as damn funny," Jacob muttered. "But don't fret, girl. We'll be at that schoolhouse at dawn."

If Jacob was puzzled by the message he received, he was no more confused than Howard and Buck were over the message they received at nearly the same time.

Buck was the one who opened the door at the insistent knock. He did not know who the young man was who delivered the message and he disappeared into the night the moment he handed it to Buck.

"What is it, Buck?" Howard questioned.

"Somebody delivering a message," Buck said as he unfolded the note.

"Who's it from?"

"From Trace."

"Trace? What's it say?"

"Says he wants us to meet him at the old school at dawn tomorrow. Says he has a lot of solutions to all our problems."

Howard found himself wondering just what Trace might know about his problems. For some reason he felt depressed about that. Trace had done so much to help him find himself and he had returned the favor by trying to halt the railroad's progress. But he pushed aside his guilt for now, for he was more worried over Taylor and Jenny.

"Suppose we ought to wake Jenny up and tell her?"

Buck questioned.

"Be a good idea. It would be good for her to realize Trace is working on our side more or less."

"You hate the idea of her thinking about marrying Taylor."

"Don't you?"

"I'd hate to see it, but I've got a strong feeling Trace isn't about to let that happen."

"Well, you go wake her anyhow."

"All right," Buck said. He handed the note to his father as he passed him and walked on toward Jenny's room. He rapped on the door, waited, then rapped again and called out Jenny's name. When he received no answer, he opened the door and walked in. In seconds he reappeared.

"Pa, Jenny's gone."

"Gone . . . where?"

Buck offered no answer but went to the door and left. He ran to the barn, but again only a short time passed before he returned.

"Her horse is gone. She must have left right after we went to bed. Pa . . . you don't think she went to Jessup?"

"Jesus," Howard said through stiff lips. "She can't have done that."

"She was upset . . . she might have."

Howard's face was grey. "I'll kill that man if he so much as lays a hand on her. He can damn well do what he wants with me or the land, but if he hurts Jenny . . ."

"Pa, Trace wants us to meet him at dawn tomorrow at the school. In the meantime, suppose I ride into town to see what I can find out about where Jenny's gone."

"Good idea, son. I'll ride with you. I don't think I could stand just sitting here and worrying."

"We'll have to be careful. Taylor's pretty crafty. He might have Jenny meeting him somewhere. Let's just go in easy like, so no one sees us. We can find out a few things and be at the school long before dawn tomorrow."

"Let's go."

In a very short time they had their horses saddled and were on their way.


Allison was restless. She had shopped earlier in the afternoon, had shared a late supper with one of the young foremen from the railroad crew, and he had escorted her back to the hotel afterward.

Now she sat by the window and let the night air cool her. As she looked across the room at the little girl who slept contentedly in her bed, she smiled. Leave it to Trace, she thought, to present her with problems and questions and dash off without thinking of giving her the answers.

She sighed as she began to recall all that had happened since they had left Georgia, and how their lives had changed after that fateful meeting with Maxwell and his railroad. She thought of Trace and Jenny and wondered if they would ever be able to break the barriers that stood between them.

She wished fervently they could all return to Fallen Oaks. She wondered how Reid was faring with the plantation. She was lonesome for home and for things of the past she could never retrieve. She wondered where her life was going, for she seemed to be midway between nothing and nothing.

The streets of town were deserted and she could hear the soft song of the cicadas filling the night. Again she looked at Georgina. She knew her only as Joanne Carter's daughter. She remembered Joanne from the dance and wondered why her child needed to be cared for here and where Joanne was. It was then she thought of Will, then of Will and Joanne. She smiled to herself. "Darn you, Trace," she said aloud. "If there's been something exciting going on here and you haven't told me, I'm going to skin you! Just you wait, Trace Cord. You're going to get a lesson in keeping surprises. You've sure got one in store for you."

Taylor Jessup had gone to his home after a day in the bank, which had held his attention less than the thoughts of all he was going to have when this confrontation with the railroad was over.

He mentally laid out his plans in his mind and studied them. He was quite pleased with everything. There was only one flaw that annoyed him, one error that he would have to correct—Eileen Starett.

He knew without doubt that he could not trust her, but he had needed all the contacts and information she had been providing since they had first met.

He did not doubt her attraction to Lucifer, nor to Trace Cord, nor, he thought, to any handsome male who happened along. But he most certainly did not want to make Eileen a permanent part of his life. He wanted what he could take from her, and he intended to take it all. But it would be Jenny, beautiful Jenny, who would share the fortune he soon would have.

He thought of Lucifer, that dark shadow of a man who would rid him of Eileen when the time was right. He certainly knew how to handle any situation, he thought smugly. He knew how to use people to his own advantage. He had used Eileen, he would use Lucifer, and, in the end, he would win.

He thought of the mystery surrounding Lucifer and he finally placed him in one category he understood. The man was a predator who would use his gun to kill for the right amount of money, and the right amount of money would pay him off and make him disappear when the time was right.

He turned in his bed and drew the woman close to him. She was kept for the purposes of caring for his house and cooking his food. But he found her a reliable source of sexual release when the mood struck him. She was docile and complied with his wishes without complaint.

He woke her from sleep to fondle her roughly. As he mounted her, he was deciding how he would manage to keep her around after he and Jenny were married.

Lucifer lay awake while Eileen slept in total contentment. He folded his hands behind his head, and the pale moonlight reflected his smile. He had set a cauldron boiling, and it would take only another step or two to see that the ingredients blended effectively.

He thought of each of the participants in the scheme that was being orchestrated by Taylor Jessup and Eileen Starett. In their greed, they would have caused many people to be hurt, among them people he cared about.

With his anger came a feeling of *déjà vu,* as if he had participated in this game before. He knew that this was so and that only the players had changed.

Now he had entered the darkest part of the night, just before the dawn broke, the period that was always the most difficult for him. It was the hour when shadows from the past that were usually locked in his memory were given the freedom to roam. It was a time he hated the most.

With a deep sigh, he eased from the bed so he would not awaken Eileen and he dressed without light. But before he left the room like a silent shadow, he wrote a note telling Eileen that if she wanted him to dispose of

Taylor for her, she must see to it that Taylor was with her at the old schoolhouse at nine the next morning. He laughed as he added his own bit of humor by telling her he would see to it that everything was cleared up then.

When he neared the door he knew was Maxwell's, he took a folded piece of paper from his pocket. Then he bent to slide the paper under the door.

When he stood up, he rapped lightly, then pressed his ear against the door to listen. There was no sound from within. He rapped a little harder and when he listened he was rewarded by a mumbled curse and the creaking of the bed.

Swiftly he moved down the hall to the steps. He was gone by the time Maxwell had lit the lamp and opened the door.

Maxwell muttered another curse when he found no one in the hall.

"What the hell's going on around here? Disturbing people this time of night," he muttered. He was about to close the door when he saw the piece of paper on the floor.

He bent to pick it up, then closed and locked the door.

"What the . . ." he began as he unfolded the note and read:

There are events taking place that will clear up all of the problems. If you want answers, come to the old schoolhouse at dawn.

A friend

"A friend," Maxwell muttered. "Most likely someone who wants to take a potshot at me." He stood thinking. "Well," he said aloud, "I've faced bushwhackers before. There's only one way to find out."

He couldn't go back to bed now, for his mind was

caught up in the mystery of the note. Besides, it was too near dawn already. He dressed and blew out the lamp, then he left the hotel and began to walk toward the meeting place and whatever danger it might present.

The old schoolhouse had been built along with the original building of the town. As the population grew, it became too small. A new wooden building had been built closer to the center of town and to the church. The old schoolhouse had been left deserted until the people of the town could decide what to do with it.

It was surrounded on three sides by large trees that protected it from heavy rains and even heavier snows.

Maxwell was unsure of what he would find, so he approached the door very cautiously. He gave it a gentle push and it swung open slowly. The inside was as dark as pitch. He was deciding whether he should go in or not when an amused voice spoke from inside.

"If I had wanted you dead, you would have been by now. Come in, Mr. Starett."

Maxwell moved inside.

"Close the door behind you."

Maxwell did as the voice instructed. "Who the hell are you?"

"A friend."

"So I see by your note," Maxwell replied. "What answers do you have for me?"

"If you have a little patience, Mr. Starett, there are others coming. I'll answer all your questions at the same time."

Certain at least that the shadowed voice did not mean to ambush him, Maxwell waited in silence.

Grey dawn was beginning to brush the shadows from the room and Maxwell could begin to make out the large, broad-shouldered man who sat upon what had once been the teacher's desk.

The longer Maxwell looked and the clearer the features became, the more Maxwell felt he had seen him somewhere before.

"Do I know you . . . friend?"

"You've never seen me before," came the matter-of-fact reply.

Before Maxwell could speak again, the sound of approaching footsteps came to them.

In a few minutes Buck and Howard came in. They were both surprised to see the two who were there.

"Where's Trace? He sent us a note to meet him here."

"I'm afraid I was the one who sent the note." Lucifer said. "It was important that you be here."

"What's going on?" Buck questioned.

Again Lucifer repeated his admonition for them to be patient. And soon they were rewarded by the door being pushed open and Jacob and Emily coming in.

"Why did you bring her?" Lucifer asked quickly.

"She's worried about her sister. I felt she had a right to be here. Now, where is my daughter? Where's Hannah?"

"Right now I hope she's asleep in a hotel room down the street."

"She's all right?" Jacob asked quickly.

"She's fine. Now, if you will all find a comfortable seat, there are some things you ought to know." They obediently sat.

In a deep, sure tone, Lucifer began to explain all that had transpired in the valley since the arrival of the railroad and who was to blame for the trouble. Jacob's anger grew as he listened to the story of Hannah's thwarted abduction. Buck and Howard were just as upset when they heard how they were being manipulated.

"Once the railroad was driven out, the railroad owned by Jessup and Eileen Starett—"

At the name, Maxwell's face reddened.

"Oh yes, she was selling you out." He continued to explain Eileen's part in it all.

"But, there seems to be . . ." Maxwell said.

"More," Lucifer offered. "Yes, there's more. I'll tell you what they had to gain. Their own railroad first, and second, there is a load of silver here that would have made them as wealthy as kings. But most important of all, there's a movement in Washington to make Colorado a state."

They all exchanged looks of utter astonishment.

"You see gentlemen . . . and lady, they were reaching for more power and wealth than most of us have ever dreamed of."

"And now it's over," Maxwell said angrily.

"No . . . but I think Trace Cord plans to put an end to it today . . . and we're all going to help him."

All five listeners nodded their approval.

"If we can all keep quiet," Lucifer continued, "I think before too long Taylor Jessup and Eileen will be paying us a visit."

"How do you know?" Maxwell asked through his anger.

"Because"—Lucifer grinned—"I arranged it that way."

"And"—Buck chuckled—"just about everything has been working out the way you planned. I still get the feeling I ought to know you. Just what do you have to gain from all this?"

"A little bit of belated justice. Besides I'm"—he shrugged—"just interested."

There was not one person there who did not believe he could have said much more.

"Did you all leave your horses under the trees? I

wouldn't want our visitors to see them."

"I walked," Maxwell said.

"Me and Buck left our horses at the stable and walked too."

"I didn't see any horses out front, so I put our horses around back," Jacob responded.

"Good. Then no one knows we're here. All we have to do is keep quiet . . . and wait."

## Chapter 34

Taylor was quite pleased with himself. He had found a way to rid himself of Eileen. All he had to do was get her where he wanted her.

Eileen was feeling the same kind of satisfaction. She entered the bank with a warm smile on her face, and when Taylor admitted her to his office, she kissed him as if no special changes were going to occur in their plans.

"Taylor," she said in a velvet voice, "Lucifer would like us to meet him at the old schoolhouse. There is something important he has to tell us."

"When?" Taylor asked hopefully. What a good time to get Lucifer to handle Eileen for him.

"We should go now. He said around nine."

"Then let's go."

They left the bank together, and Taylor made it clear to the bank clerks that he was leaving on a matter of business. He explained that Miss Starett hoped to buy some property and he was taking her to see it.

They walked toward the old schoolhouse.

Lucifer's plan might have worked well had Allison

not been looking out her window. She had returned Georgina to a serene Will and Joanne and had made the decision to walk down to the railroad site to see how Trace and Maxwell were progressing with the repairs. She had returned to her room for a wrap and had glanced out the window to see Taylor and Eileen walking along hurriedly.

Allison would never know why she decided to follow them, but some instinct told her they were conspirators who needed to be watched. Besides, she was still determined to discover something about Eileen that would turn Trace's head from her permanently.

Allison turned quickly from the window and stepped out into the hall. Several feet away she encountered Trace, who seemed to be leaving his room as well.


Trace had awakened very early. He had had no intention of going back to sleep while he had the opportunity to close the world away and pretend that the Jenny he held warm and safe in his arms would remain there always.

He buried his face against her soft, tangled hair and inhaled the scent of it. She curled against him, her head against his shoulder and one arm flung possessively across his chest. One slender leg lay across his body, enabling her to nestle close to his side.

No matter what happened, he intended to lock horns with Taylor today. The railroad was going to go through, and Jenny would never belong to Taylor as long as he was alive to stop it.

His biggest worry was, how was he going to keep Jenny from going to Taylor? He knew Jenny would stubbornly defend what she thought was right. To protect her family, she was actually going to sacrifice herself, only Trace had no intention of letting her do that.

His brow, which had been furrowed in thought, suddenly became smooth. He smiled to himself as he thought of how angry Jenny was going to be when he carried the plan he had in mind.

He bent his head and kissed her, felt her awaken, and gloried in her arms curling reflexively about him. In her half-awake, half-asleep state, Jenny enjoyed the pleasure his hard, stroking hands gave her.

His lips were gentle against hers and she never wanted this warm pleasure of waking in his arms to cease. Then the realization of what the day held for her came to her fully.

He sensed it, sensed the moment she came fully awake.

"I'm not letting you go, Jenny," he whispered against her hair. "I can't."

"Trace—" she began, but he interrupted.

"What is it he holds over you, Jenny? Tell me what it is."

"What difference does it make, Trace? It won't change anything. We are both going to do what we must. I am going to marry Taylor, and you must leave and go on with your railroad. Forget about me."

He laughed harshly. "Why don't you just ask me to forget to breathe, forget to think or to feel. That would be much easier."

"You're not making this easy for me."

"I don't want it to be easy for you. I want you to forget everything but what we share. The rest of the world can be damned."

She wanted to cry out that it was much easier for him to say since Allison—the only member of his family— would be safe with him, while she still would be forced to protect her father and brother. She could not utter such recriminations, for she knew he would not want to hear them.

Trace had made a decision and now he began to carry it out. He rose from the bed and Jenny sat up, prepared to rise also. Her hours of running were over, and she would only have memories to cling to.

She watched Trace move about gathering their clothes. She feasted her eyes on him, certain that he would be gone soon.

As he bent to retrieve the clothes, hard, corded muscles rippled under his taut skin. The early morning sun painted his form a burnished gold. His dark hair made his grey eyes seem even lighter and the slow, easy smile he wore when he turned to meet her gaze made a now-familiar warmth blossom within her. If only she could always share his mornings like this, she thought. Then her puzzled eyes became aware of what he was doing.

Slowly and methodically he was tearing one of her petticoats into strips. She could not understand this. If it was anger, it was the most controlled anger she had ever seen, for still he smiled at her.

"Trace, what in Heaven's name are you doing?"

"Just taking a precaution."

"What precaution?" she questioned, completely baffled over what he was about.

He had a small pile of the cloth strips now, and he gathered them up and moved toward her. It was then that comprehension of his motives struck her.

"No!" she cried and tried to escape from the blankets. But he was already upon her, fighting her flailing hands and legs. She battled wildly, but in moments he was seated astride her where her kicking legs were ineffectual and he was holding both arms over her head.

"What are you doing?" She raged. "This is crazy. What are you trying to prove?"

"That you, my sweet," he told her with a laugh, "are not going to leave this hotel room until I have done what I have to do. After that, there will be no chance of your marrying Taylor."

He drew her hands down and began to bind her wrists together. She tried to fight, but he held her easily until her wrists were bound firmly, then he raised them again to tie them to the bedpost over her head.

"Let me go, Trace. Let me go!"

"Not on your life, love. When I come back for you, any thoughts of Taylor Jessup might have had concerning you will have been totally destroyed."

He was alert to the fact that Jenny's eyes blazed and she was about to scream. He gently stuffed a folded piece of cloth into her mouth.

"No screaming, Jenny." He chuckled. "You wouldn't want half the town to find you like this, would you?"

She realized that she had kicked the blankets away and was now totally naked. Her eyes were like twin flames of turquoise fire as she glared at him.

"Although I must say," he said gently as he slid his hand down over smooth curves, "I've never seen anything quite so exciting. I can't wait to get back." He bent to kiss her cheek, then rose.

She jerked at the bonds, but they held. All she succeeded in doing was giving Trace second thoughts about leaving her so soon. Her slim body, golden against the blankets, was enough to entice a saint, he mused. He had to force himself to concentrate on other things. He took up a blanket and covered her, ignoring her muffled words, the meanings of which he was certain he didn't want to hear. He finished dressing, walked to the door, and turned to blow her a kiss, which further incited her rage.

"I'll be back for you, love, as soon as I settle a matter or two, such as where my railroad is going and just whom you are going to marry."

He left the room and was just drawing the door closed when he turned to see Allison.

Neither knew the other's motives and neither wanted the other to know. Allison was sure Trace would be angry if he knew she was planning to follow Eileen about, and Trace did not want her to know that he was about to do battle, or that Jenny was a prisoner in his room.

"Going out, Allison?" he questioned.

"Yes . . . ah . . . shopping," she stammered. She wanted to get away from his piercing gaze quickly. "See you later, Trace."

She walked rapidly down the steps and out into the street just in time to see Taylor and Eileen walking toward the old school. She moved rapidly in the same direction, hoping to find they were having a clandestine meeting about which she could inform Trace.

Taylor and Eileen strode into the schoolhouse together and both froze at the sight before them. Maxwell's eyes never left Eileen's white face. Buck, Howard, and Jacob turned cold, unrelenting eyes on Taylor. And Lucifer, who sat relaxed with a smile on his face, held his gun in his hand.

"Come in," he said softly, "and get comfortable. Some of your . . . friends would like to talk to you."

"You double-crossing son of a bitch," Taylor snarled.

"Tsk, tsk," Lucifer admonished. "Such language from a pillar of the community, and in front of a lady too."

"Did you sell out to the highest bidder," Taylor demanded coldly, "or did you collect from both sides?"

"To tell you the truth"—Lucifer laughed—"I haven't collected from either side yet. Oh, I guess I have to choose between the price Eileen offered to get rid of you or the one you offered to get rid of her."

"Stupid bitch!" Taylor shouted at an even angrier Eileen as the truth struck them both at the same time.

"It's all over, Taylor," Lucifer said, his voice growing colder now. "Everyone in this room knows all about the other rail line . . . the silver . . . the coming statehood. Why don't you give it up before it turns ugly?"

Taylor looked from one face to another, seeing his total defeat in each one. Again Lucifer interrupted his thoughts.

"There's a little matter of a blown-up train and two dead men. Isn't that right, Maxwell?"

"Yes," Maxwell replied in a deadened voice, "but I believe one is as much to blame as the other." He looked at Eileen with an expression of near hatred, adding, "And both should pay the same price."

Eileen's face grew paler, and she took a step toward Maxwell. "Uncle Max—"

"Don't call me uncle," he snapped. "I regret the day I ever saw you. As far as I am concerned, you never existed." His voice died as he deliberately turned his back on Eileen. "I don't want to look at your face again. There will be a ticket for the next stage out of town. You had better take it while I'm still in a generous mood."

Eileen tried to go to him, but Maxwell stepped back as if she were some contemptible thing he could not touch.

"Uncle Max, you can't do this. I'm—"

"You're nothing! You're a deceitful bitch. I'm glad my brother died before he could see what you've become."

"I have a right to—"

"To his money?" Maxwell said bitterly. "Of course you do. But don't forget, I'm his executor and I intend to live a long time. While I'm alive, you will only get enough money to exist on. There will be no more luxuries. You are about to taste the destitution you would have subjected these people to. I hope you suffer a long time and remember your deceit and lies while you do."

Eileen had finally realized that all her plans, all the hopes she had had, were crumbling about her. She looked from face to face and saw each return her pleading gaze with cold, uncaring looks. Slowly she sank to a seat, her eyes wide and filled with tears of self-pity. She had no doubt that Maxwell meant what he said. He did not look at Eileen again.

As far as everyone was concerned, everything had been settled. Taylor, who stood less than a foot or two from the door, was contemplating the options of trying for Lucifer's gun or making for the door. At the moment he felt the door was his best choice, for the deadly look in Lucifer's eyes told him that to try a move against him would bring quick death. He was prepared to do something, and suddenly the opportunity presented itself.

Allison had arrived at the schoolhouse door, which was unusually thick. She stood outside for several minutes but could hear nothing. Sure of the situation in which she would find Taylor and Eileen, she swung open the door.

She was caught totally by surprise as Taylor quickly reacted to her entrance. He grasped her roughly and drew her in front of him, taking his derringer from his pocket at the same time. With Taylor's arm tight about her and his gun barrel pressed to her temple, Allison gazed into the startled eyes of Lucifer.

"Put the gun down," Taylor commanded. "If you don't want her dead, put the gun down."

Lucifer obediently laid the gun aside. His eyes were locked on Allison, who was wide eyed and shaking with fear.

"Don't be afraid," he said to Allison. "He's not going to hurt you."

"You think not? I'll kill her right here if you so much as blink an eye," Taylor threatened, moving to retrieve Lucifer's gun.

"You do," Lucifer said coldly, "and I'll hunt you down if I have to go to the ends of the earth to do it."

Taylor backed up to the door, dragging Allison with him.

"Taylor!" Eileen shouted. "Take me with you."

"You?" he growled. "I should kill you now."

There was no sympathy on the faces of anyone present as Eileen sank white faced into a chair.

"Now," Taylor said, "all of you, back into that corner."

They had no choice other than to do as he ordered.

"Where are your horses?" he demanded.

"Under the trees at the side of the building," Lucifer said, "but you don't stand a chance in hell of getting away."

"If one of you shows his face before you hear that horse leaving, I'll blow her head off." After issuing several more orders, he backed out the door he had just opened, then pulled Allison out and elbowed the door shut. The padlock that had been on the door hung open. He took it in one hand, slid it through the loops of the lock, and snapped it shut. Then he prodded Allison ahead of him to the horses.

He made her mount, then mounted behind her and jerked the horse into motion. He went around behind the school and through the trees to make a circle around the town.

He returned to the bank, which he entered through the back door. Once there, he forced Allison to a seat and set about emptying the contents of the safe into a small black satchel.

Lucifer had slammed against the door as soon as he had heard the click of the lock, but it was too late. Since the school had at a later date served as a temporary jail as well, the only two windows were quite effectively barred.

Lucifer cursed and began to search for a way to get out.

All the men had been forced to toss their guns out through the bars and Lucifer's had been confiscated by Taylor. It seemed they were helpless.

Within the bank Taylor forced Allison to remain motionless while he bound her hands behind her and then tied her to the chair with a cord from the draperies that hung at his window. Then he stood before her.

"Where is your brother, Trace?"

"What are you going to do?"

"Do?" He smiled a smile that told her exactly what

492

he intended. She had seen Trace leave the hotel and knew she could buy some time.

"He's still in his hotel room. He came in very late last night and he was tired and did not feel well." She hoped he would believe her at least long enough to go see. Time was what she felt was needed. If Lucifer could get free, Taylor's hours would be numbered.

"Well," Taylor said coldly, "I will see about that. Maybe I can arrange for him to have undisturbed sleep permanently."

He tore off a small piece of her dress and pushed it roughly into her mouth; then he picked up the satchel and left through the same back door.

She wriggled and tugged until she felt the cords burn her arms, but she finally managed to get free. It came as a total shock to the clerks in the front room when she tore open Taylor's office door and ran through the bank to the street.


Trace had gone to the bank and had been informed that Taylor had gone to look at some property with Eileen Starett. He was more than sure this was not true so he started toward Taylor's house, where he thought they might have gone for privacy. Once there, he was informed by a sullen housekeeper that Taylor was not there.

He went to the railroad site but could not even find a trace of Maxwell. He wondered if Maxwell had slept late.

It had taken him a little over an hour to accomplish these fool's errands, and he decided to return to the bank.

He approached the bank and was less than five feet from it when Allison burst through the doors and into his arms.

"Oh Trace," she sobbed, "I'm so glad to see you. Hurry! Hurry! We've got to get them out. We've got to catch Taylor!"

"Allison, stop chattering. Slow down and tell me what happened."

As quickly as she could, Allison explained about the school and her capture and that the others were still locked up.

"Come on," he said. They ran as rapidly as they could across the plank sidewalks that were slowly filling with townspeople. Soon they were standing before the school and Trace was ordering those inside to stand back.

Within the building everyone backed away from the door, including Lucifer, who had a mysterious smile on his face as he stepped into a shadowed corner.

Trace withdrew his gun from its holster and aimed one shot at the lock. The bullet struck it squarely and the bent wad of metal flew from the door.

When the door was pushed open, Trace and Allison rushed in.

"What in God's name are you all doing in here?" Trace demanded.

"I sent for them," came a soft voice from behind him. Trace spun around and he and Lucifer looked at each other for several long, silent moments. It was Trace who spoke first in a choked voice filled with emotion.

"Michael," he whispered. "Michael, is it . . . ?"

"It's me," Lucifer replied. "Alive . . . back from the dead."

Allison smiled smugly as the brothers threw themselves into each other's arms and held each other for several moments. She was only too happy to introduce the others to her long-lost brother, Michael Cord.

"I should have known," Buck said. "He sure as hell

looks like you, Trace."

"Your brother," Maxwell marveled. "Why didn't you tell someone, Michael? Why didn't you tell Trace?"

"Because Taylor and Eileen thought I was a gunfighter. They confided in me. I felt if I talked to anyone or someone recognized me, they might get wind of it. Once they were wise to me, I would have been of no use to you."

Trace had been looking at Michael in silence, absorbing the black patch and the limp as he moved. Michael realized that Trace, the brother with whom he had shared so much, was thinking of the pain he must have suffered, and thinking of the disaster that had caused it. He noted that Trace's eyes were suspiciously moist.

"Well, it's all over now," Allison said as she reached with a happy smile to take the hand of each brother. "We can begin to rebuild our lives. We can all go on with the railroad and when that job is finished, we can go home, together."

"Yes," Michael said softly, trying with his assured attitude and quick smile to make Trace believe that the past had been buried. "It's all over. We're a family again. Somehow we can start over. I . . . I think going with the railroad will be good for me. I have to keep moving."

Trace did not want to commit himself to anything in front of Maxwell, for now that Jenny was safely his, his plans were taking a whole new turn. He promised himself to talk over the future with Michael at the first opportunity. He was extremely pleased with the turn of events, until Allison spoke.

"You would have been proud of me, Trace," she said with a giggle.

"I am, kitten. I can imagine you were frightened to death."

"I was, but I was so afraid he was going to come after you. I remembered you were in the hall when I was leaving. You were going out too, so when he asked me where you were, I said in your hotel room."

Her smile faded as Trace's face drained of all color. His eyes held a fear Allison had never seen there before. He grabbed her roughly by the shoulders and shook her.

"Trace!" Michael cried. "What's wrong with you?"

"You sent him to the hotel after me?" Trace snapped quickly at a now-frightened Allison.

"Yes . . . I . . . I knew you weren't there."

"Oh God," Trace groaned as he started for the door.

"Trace wait! What's wrong?" Michael called after him.

"Jenny! For God's sake, Jenny is in my room at the hotel." He could not bear to tell them that he had left her tied and helpless. The pain of that was almost too much for him.

Trace bolted out the door and the others followed as fast as they could.

Once inside the hotel, Trace climbed the steps two at a time, praying silently that Taylor had not decided to come after him but had chosen to run instead.

When he reached the door, he threw himself against it. It gave easily, much too easily. He stood in the center of the room and an overwhelming agony ripped through him as he gazed at the empty bed.

Pieces of cloth with which he had bound her were still tied to the iron posts of the bed. They had been neatly sliced. There was an indentation in the bed where Jenny had lain.

He was frozen in the face of the evidence of what he had done. He could not bear the anguish that washed through him as he imagined what had been in Jenny's mind as she had lain there and watched Taylor come closer.

Michael appeared beside him and soon Allison joined them.

"Get some fresh horses, Michael," Trace said coldly. "I'll trail that black-hearted bastard to Hell and back if I have to. And when I find him, he had better not have hurt her, or I swear to God I'll kill him!"

## Chapter 35

If Trace had seen Taylor's face as he entered Trace's room, he would have felt an even stronger desire to kill.

Jenny lay, wide eyed with terror and watched Taylor approach. He could scarcely believe his eyes. She was totally helpless to resist as he sat down beside her.

"What a stroke of luck," he said. "I'm afraid this time Trace has made a very drastic mistake. I shall have a hostage he will gladly give his life for."

Jenny's eyes filled with tears as Taylor made no effort to untie her but slowly drew the blankets aside.

"Lovely," he murmured. "I am afraid your lover has left you in a rather compromising position."

He stood up and took a small knife from his pocket. He reached down and retrieved Jenny's dress from the floor. Then he cut the cloth bindings that held her.

"Don't scream," he cautioned, "or your lover will find your body." He threw her the dress as she took the cloth from her mouth, and he ordered, "Put it on . . . and hurry."

She obeyed, grateful for the dress and the chance to shield herself from his hot gaze.

"You're going with me."

"Where are we going?"

"To a safe place."

"Taylor . . . let me go."

"No, I want your lover to come after you."

"He won't come after me," she lied. "I already told him I had decided to marry you. He is going away."

"It's too late for that lie," he said. "All I want before I go is to kill him, and you are the bait that will enable me to do it."

"But he won't come!"

"Tell me"—Taylor grinned—"why did he leave you like this? Why were you naked and tied? I'll tell you. Because you came to him last night and he decided to keep you."

"No."

"Yes. Come over here," he ordered. She walked closer to him and he reached out and grabbed her arm, drawing her close.

"We are leaving here. One false move from you and I will not hesitate to kill you, understand?"

She nodded and he moved to the door, dragging her along. They made their way down the back steps and to the back door of the stables. He checked inside, saw that no one was about, then pushed her inside.

"Saddle two horses," he told her and again she obeyed. A short time later they had left the town behind. Jenny was surprised to find them heading in the direction of her ranch.

Once there, she was ordered to put the horses in the barn. When this was done, he pushed her ahead of him into the house.

"Now we wait. Soon your father and brother will be back."

"What are you going to do?"

"I told you. I'm going to pay Trace Cord back for ruining my plans for a fortune."

"And then," she said quietly, "you are going to

500

kill us?"

"Maybe."

She looked at him intently, then she smiled bitterly. "Don't play games with me, Taylor. I know you for what you are. I was foolish to have ever believed you. I never should have denied Trace what he wanted. We could have ended all this."

"Did you deny him anything?" Taylor laughed.

"My love. I denied him that. When he comes for me, I will never deny him again."

She could see that her words angered him, but she no longer cared.

"When he comes—and he will come—I will kill him."

"What good will that do you?"

"I have plenty of places to go, Jenny," he said, amused at her fear. "Before I go, I want to make sure the man who caused my failure is dead. I don't fail at anything without repayment. So settle yourself down to wait, because as soon as he begins to think, he's going to head out here."

Jenny sat in silence, trying to find a way to warn Trace, for she was just as certain as Taylor that he would come.

With the aid of Buck, Trace and Michael began a search to determine the route Taylor and Jenny had taken. Quite sure Taylor would not travel by the main road, they began to look for double tracks that led away from town.

It took several long hours, hours that frayed Trace's nerves until he became silent and grim faced.

When they did find the tracks, they slowly began to follow the trail. But before they had gone too far Trace knew, or thought he knew, where Jenny was. It was a chance. If he left the trail they followed now to pursue his idea, the trail might be lost, and so he was forced to make a decision.

"Michael, you and Buck follow the tracks. Leave a trail for me. If I'm wrong, I'll come back and pick it up."

"And if you're right, you face him alone," Michael protested quickly.

Trace smiled. "But my brother and my brother-to-be won't be too far away."

"Far enough for you to get killed before we get there," Michael again argued.

"I'll be careful."

"Sure you will," Michael said. "I was raised with you, remember, big brother? You'll go in after him, Trace," he said seriously. "Let me go with you."

"Michael, I need to find that trail. Jenny can't be lost to me. I couldn't stand that. I'm taking one hell of a chance and if she isn't there . . . then I want you to be the one on his trail."

"All right, Trace, but promise me one thing. If he's there, you'll wait for us."

"I can't promise you that."

"Why?"

"Because I think it's me he's waiting for."

"I didn't find you to lose you again," Michael said softly.

"We've got a lot of time to make up for," Trace agreed, "but it wouldn't mean as much to me without Jenny. I love her, Michael. I've got to get her back."

"All right, Trace," Michael replied. He had surrendered because he understood how Trace felt about Jenny. He knew because he had drawn on a vision carefully stored away, and permanently forbidden.

They separated and, with grim determination, Trace headed for the Graham ranch. It was nearing sunset when he arrived, and he watched the house for quite some time for any sign of life.

Just as dusk colored the area with its grey shadows, a thin wisp of white smoke announced to Trace that the house was occupied. Now he would have to get Jenny safely out of there, and there seemed to be only one way. He rode straight toward the front door.

Jenny had prepared some food at Taylor's order, but she had refused to eat with him. She sat at the table, praying that Trace would not be foolish enough to come for her.

Her prayers were not to be answered. She closed her eyes and Taylor laughed softly as they heard the lone horse approaching.

Trace dismounted. He sensed he was being watched but knew he had to find Jenny. With one precise step after another he walked across the porch to the door. He swung open the door and looked across the room. Taylor stood with Jenny before him, a smile on his face and a gun in his hand.

"Jenny, love," Trace said gently, "are you all right?"

"I'm fine, Trace."

"He didn't hurt you?"

"No . . . I . . . oh, Trace, why did you come?" she cried.

"Jenny, I'm sorry to have left you like that . . . I'm so sorry."

"How very sweet," Taylor said. "Now she will have to watch you die."

"Taylor, let her go," Trace urged. "I'll stay here and you can do what you want, but let her go."

"I can't do that. I'm going to kill you, but before I do,

I want you to know that I'm taking Jenny away with me."

"I will die first."

"No, you won't, though what I plan for you will make you wish you had. Do you know about the brothels of San Francisco, Trace?" Taylor laughed because the answer registered on Trace's face. "She'll be lost in there and no one will ever find her. I might just shoot you and let you live to think about that."

"You are insane," Trace snarled. "A piece of filth. You had better kill me, for if you don't, I guarantee you you're a dead man."

"You spoiled a lot of plans for me. I think it's poetic justice that Jenny pay the price. After all, if it hadn't been for her, you might have been gone by now."

It was an impossible situation, for Trace could see that Taylor was rapidly tiring of these verbal exchanges. He knew the moment Taylor decided to shoot. He could read it in his eyes.

Several things happened at the same time. The back door slammed open, and Taylor spun around, Jenny fell to the floor, and Trace leapt.

He struck Taylor with all the force he possessed and they tumbled to the floor. Michael and Buck, who had come from the back, raced to Jenny and drew her out of the way.

Michael and Buck watched as Trace vented all his rage on Taylor, watched and made amused comments as the fight went on.

"Has a wicked fist, doesn't he?" Buck quipped.

"Has a nasty temper too. I never could put one over on him when we were boys."

"Looks like Taylor bit off more than he could chew."

"I had thought of telling him that somewhere along the line, but I guess Trace is doing it well enough."

The battle ended when Trace struck a last, punishing

504

blow and Taylor fell back, unconscious. Jenny had been paralyzed by fear, but now she cried out his name and threw herself into Trace's welcoming arms.

"I thought," Trace gasped out, "that you two were following another trail."

"Don't blame me," Buck said. "Your brother is the one who changed the plan."

"Now you know, Trace," Michael reminded him with a laugh, "that I always resented taking orders from my big brother. Besides . . . I didn't want you shot."

Trace laughed heartily, then Michael joined him. Buck and Jenny could only stare in fascination as the brothers embraced again. Then Trace turned to Jenny.

"Suppose we put an end to all this and start something really special together? What do you say, love? How about marrying an ex-railroad man?"

Jenny put her arms about him and raised her lips for his kiss.

"I love you, Trace Cord," she murmured as their lips met.

# Epilogue

The celebration for Will and Joanne's wedding was one of the biggest the town had ever seen. Trace finally announced his plans to everyone just before the ceremony.

"I'm taking Allison and Jenny back to Fallen Oaks," Trace told Buck and Howard. "Maxwell has agreed to let Michael take my place and go on to California."

"Michael has problems," Howard said quietly.

"Yes," Trace agreed. "He has to find his own way. We talked of the hell he's been through. I would like to see him come home with us, but he has ghosts to fight and he wants to fight them his own way. So he is going to California with Maxwell."

"Well, maybe he just needs time," Howard said.

"Yes," Trace replied. But he had seen Hannah Marshall's face when Michael had announced his plans. She was in love with Michael and Trace believed his brother knew it. He wondered just how far Michael would have to go before he realized he could not outrun bad memories but would have to stand and fight them. He had tried to talk Michael out of going.

"I have to Trace," Michael had said quietly. "There's been too much hurt. I've killed . . . well, too much. I have to find out if it was worth the price I'm paying. I have to go on. But I'll be home one day. Reid's got the plantation running and you and Jenny need time alone."

"Michael . . . what about Hannah?" Trace had asked. "She's in love with you."

"She's a baby, Trace, a sweet little girl. I won't ruin her life with running. Let it go, Trace . . . let it go."

"Can Hannah?"

"She'll have to."

Trace doubted it. Trace knew his brother too well and was certain he would return one day, when he finally realized Hannah held the peace for which he was searching. He only hoped it would not take Michael too long to see the truth.

Several days after the wedding celebration, Trace and Jenny stood with the rest of the crowd and watched the railroad move out into the valley. Three months later it was past the valley and gone.

Trace and Jenny walked the tree-shaded paths of Fallen Oaks. They had been married just two weeks earlier. The moon was high and Trace looked into her eyes as he kissed her glowing face.

"I'm so happy, Trace. I never dreamed I could be so happy. Buck and Emily wrote me. The ranch is doing well and Pa is fine."

Trace pulled her tightly against him and kissed her most thoroughly.

"You're happy. That's what matters. I want to keep you that way forever."

"Forever is a long time."

"Then," he murmured, "let's start forever right now."

She agreed as her lips parted under his possessive assault and she felt the warmth and security that only Trace could provide. She was home, she had Trace, and together they would share the promise of forever.